S0-BOF-816

Regiment of Women

NOVELS BY THOMAS BERGER

Regiment of Women

A NOVEL BY

Thomas Berger

Little, Brown and Company

BOSTON   TORONTO   LONDON

Copyright © 1973 by Thomas Berger

All rights reserved. No part of this book may be reproduced in any form or by any electronic or mechanical means, including information storage and retrieval systems, without permission in writing from the publisher, except by a reviewer who may quote brief passages in a review.

The characters and events in this book are fictitious. Any similarity to real persons, living or dead, is coincidental and not intended by the author.

LIBRARY OF CONGRESS CATALOGING-IN-PUBLICATION DATA

Berger, Thomas, 1924–
  Regiment of women : a novel / by Thomas Berger.
    p.   cm.
  ISBN 0-316-09242-8
  I. Title.
  PS3552.E719R36   1991
  813'.54 — dc20   90-23513

10 9 8 7 6 5 4 3 2 1

BP

Published simultaneously in Canada
by Little, Brown & Company (Canada) Limited

PRINTED IN THE UNITED STATES OF AMERICA

TO ZULFIKAR GHOSE

To promote a woman to bear rule, superiority, dominion, or empire above any realm, nation, or city, is repugnant to nature; contumely to God, a thing most contrarious to His revealed will and approved ordinances; and finally, it is the subversion of good order, of all equity and justice.

JOHN KNOX, *The First Blast of the Trumpet Against the Monstrous Regiment of Women*, 1558

1

THE DENTIST'S DRILL of the alarm probed viciously into the diseased pulp of his dream, and Georgie Cornell awakened. His baby-doll nightgown was up to his sternum, exposing both his pudenda—he never wore the ruffled panties, which chafed—and his thrusting breasts. His member would remain tumid until he tinkled. He staggered to the bathroom in his bunny slippers and did his business.

The bathroom mirror had too harsh a light. He returned to the bedroom for first look at himself, lighting the flanking pink lamps on the vanity table and sinking to a seat on the pink-skirted bench. Blah. It was getting harder every morning to make a joke of what he saw. He was *twenty-nine* years old. He put a finger at each temple and pulled the pouches and birdtracks taut, made himself a temporary geisha boy.

His eyes were trying to do something behind the restraint. He released them, and they wept, foolishly: he felt no worse this morning than on any of the others in the past—he began to count the weeks, months, years. Suddenly a cavity of absolute dread opened from his navel to his backbone.

He seized the pink Princess phone and called his shrink.

"I'm going up the wall," he said. "I can't make it through the day."

"See you at ten," she replied, after keeping him forever on Hold. "Meanwhile, try to be a man."

"Isn't that the trouble?" But he said it to dead air. Dr. Prine's impatient manner was part of the therapy. He understood that

9

intellectually, but emotionally it often rankled. Were there more favored patients with whom she dawdled? That stripling with the marvelous ankles who was often leaving the office as Cornell arrived. Cornell's legs were only so-so; they looked best in black or blue-gray pantyhose. They were almost repulsive when left bare, tanning unevenly in summer and in winter turning livid behind clear nylon.

Now that he had made the appointment, a certain tranquility came over him. A leisurely foam bath and an electric shave of face, chest, and calves also helped. He was almost composed as he returned to the bedroom, rosy from the towel and fragrant, and though his search for a decent pair of pantyhose was unsuccessful and he would have to put on a set of which the right ankle was laddered, he put a fingertip in his mouth and stayed together.

In bra and bikini briefs he did his eyes. When they were finished the mirror told him he would get by. When he had brushed his auburn hair, which was straight and gleaming and turned up softly just above his shoulders, he was actually pretty, or anyway formerly pretty: after a certain age a retroussé nose seemed no longer stylish. He was something of an old boy. But he was far from finished. It was amazing how his spirit had risen. At this moment he could yet believe that one day the right woman would come along and carry him off.

Still in his underwear he drank a cup of instant coffee and ate an unbuttered oblong of melba toast. Then he slipped into a little white tailored blouse and a pleated skirt in Kelly green. Beige pumps and matching purse completed his outfit. Having clipped on a pair of silver circlet earrings and run three slender bracelets, thin as silver wires, over an elongated left hand, he closed the door behind him and secured all three locks.

The elevators in Cornell's building had been out of order for a week, and the stairways were dog toilets. You also never knew when you might meet a sex criminal or, perhaps worse, a junkie desperate for funds with which to maintain her habit. Three men had been robbed at knifepoint in the corridors or the lobby, and a freckle-faced manicurist, a tall, gentle fellow with whom Cornell had often exchanged idle chatter at the mailboxes, had been maimed for life by a savage beating at the hands of a degenerate after she had emptied his purse.

Still, the building was safer than most in the jungle of the East 70's, and the rent for Cornell's one-and-a-half was still fairly reasonable as those things went, being temporarily arrested by law at fifteen hundred a month. How long the current controls would be operative was in doubt, but meanwhile he enjoyed the classic but rare rent-to-wage ratio, working one week to earn the rent for a month, though the actual take-home from $1500, after deductions and levies, was currently $947.63.

The burly doorwoman, her face a purple bag of muscatel-swollen veins, shifted her shotgun to the other arm and winked at Cornell as he emerged from the fire door into the lobby.

"P.A.," she said.

Pollution alert, as usual. Cornell fished his gas mask from the purse and put it on. The doorwoman waited until he had blown the mouthpiece clear before depressing the switch that opened the inner door of the airlock in the vestibule. He breathed in and out the requisite five times and then signaled her to admit him to the sidewalk. Not unexpectedly, the outer door jammed after having gone only a third of its travel, and he had to squeeze out sidewise into the morning. At such a time he was pleased he had been modest about the silicone injections: with larger breasts he would never have escaped.

The usual throng of derelicts, some of them quite young women, had formed their gauntlet on the sidewalk, and Cornell steeled his soul to run it. His purse was of course equipped with a snatch-resistant shoulder strap, and he clutched the bag itself.

He closed his ears against the more loathsome obscenities and kept his gas-mask windows on the concrete passing under his pumps—a prudent technique, anyway, owing to the high incidence of dog droppings. But the coffee bubbled in his tummy. What an outrage that a sizable portion of his hard-earned salary went to maintain these hyenas on welfare! He supported them so they could abuse him. He did not find this irony amusing. He was a compassionate man and acknowledged his obligation to the less fortunate, victims of a society in which he could function, at least with the help of Dr. Prine. But at the moment, if he had had a flamethrower he would have incinerated these scum, one of whom, a brunette with a skin condition and sucking a stained cigarette, followed him for half a block hooting filthy imprecations, and before dropping away, goosed him painfully with the neck of a wine bottle. How these people could survive outdoors all day without a gas mask was beyond him.

However, once clear of the menace, Cornell's spirits lifted. The sun was out, infusing the murk with a lovely lemon-yellow light, and random zephyrs would occasionally swirl away the smog for a good thirty feet ahead of him, revealing other persons hurrying along to work, lady executives in their homburgs and pin-striped suits, and little office workers like himself, some in colorful frocks which made him feel drab, but even more with whom he could hold his own. Cornell usually avoided the faddish and stuck to the basic classics in which you really could go almost anywhere. He saw a few boys with great legs, but his own were better than the average, a bit thin in the calf, maybe, but how awful it must be to have thick ankles!

Ah, there was a little stocking shop: PANTYHOSE SPECIAL, $31.50. He popped in and took advantage of the sale, purchasing three pairs, then, his derriere towards the door, exchanged the ones he was wearing for a new set. He worked discreetly under his skirt, but when he left the shop, a truck driver, stalled in traffic, tipped her cap to him: she had seen his behind, no doubt. He blushed and turned his head.

No buses ran during the high-pollution hours, so he walked

north to the frontier of the Republic of Harlem at 110th Street, turned west and followed the turreted wall across town. At the Lenox Gate, a strapping coffee-colored sentry cradling a submachine gun waved flirtatiously at him with her free gauntlet. He supposed he should have resented that—black women wanted white men for only one purpose—yet he was flattered and let a faint smile ripple his vermilion lips, walking a bit more loosely both to maintain and to parody the white reputation for voluptuousness, though as he had so often read, and also experienced, it had no basis in fact.

"I am a simple person," he said to Dr. Prine, as he lay on the carpet of her office floor, looking at the cuffs of her navy-blue trousers. "All I want is peace of mind."

Her black oxfords strode away.

"You see," he said to their diminishing heels, "I don't envy women. I fear them. I fear you. I feel so defenseless. I'm afraid right now that you will beat me savagely. This alternates with a fear that you will ignore me completely. I want desperately to be desired. On the other hand, I am terrified at the thought of being raped."

The shoes marched back and a large leather sole descended onto his face, but arrested itself before his nose was actually crushed.

From above came Dr. Prine's harsh voice, which never failed to thrill him with its edge of brutality. "You must keep no secrets from me. Puke it all out. You can't expect to get better if you retain that sort of poison." She kicked him in the ribs then.

He cried out in pain, and shouted up: "I hate you! I hate women! I've never had a successful sexual relationship. There's no hope for me. Admit it!"

She bestrode him, and commanded: "Look at me."

His eyes rose along the knife-edge crease of her right trouserleg and verged over onto the flat fly when at the appropriate eleva-tion. On up across the vest, with the heavy gold chain and Phi Beta Kappa key, to the striped tie, the stiff white collar fringed by the lower margin of the self-adhesive nylon beard, pepper-and-salt, neat. The mustache, he thought, was her own, black and sparse. She had a full head of vigorous gray hair, which she wore a bit longer than the current fashion. Massive spectacles in black horn-rims were supported by a nose the jutting imperiousness of which made it seem larger than it was.

She could be called a handsome woman, but it was difficult for him to imagine his assessment of her had she not been his thera-pist: only a pervert could look at his psychiatrist impersonally—which in itself was a revelatory thought. At the core, Cornell did not believe he was ill: perversely, he did not accept the reality of his perversion. Which may have meant he was even sicker than he didn't think he was.

"Irony, Georgie, is weakness."

He hastened to assure her: "Oh, I'm not being ironic, Doctor."

"Don't interrupt!" she ordered, and continued. "It is the loser's means of coping. It is a way of assenting without really agreeing, and turns back on the man who practices it. A grudging, nig-gardly acquiescence is useless. No cure is possible unless you sur-render in the heart." Suddenly she turned rather tender, and caressed his cheek with the side of her shoe.

He was touched, and apologized for his earlier outburst. "I didn't really mean I *hated* you, Doctor."

"Oh, you didn't, did you?" She was grinning cruelly.

He struggled up to his knees.

"I want you to like me."

"You're not my only patient," she said, and strode away.

Now came the moment that he dreaded. From a cabinet she took out her dildo and strapped it over the navy-blue trousers.

He rose. "Is that necessary again?"

"Afraid so, Georgie. Until you voluntarily, freely, accept reality, this treatment will continue, distasteful as you can be sure it is to me."

He pulled up his skirt, lowered his new pantyhose and the bikini briefs beneath them, and bent over the treatment table, forearms on the white-paper cover.

The moment of entry was always worst, after which all else, though scarcely pleasant, was downhill. He looked back along his ribs, head under his left arm.

"Is it lubricated?" he asked, his eyes watering in anticipation.

"You should bring along a cork to bite on," said the good doctor, skewering him. He closed his eyes and saw a crimson vista, which gradually darkened to deep purple.

"What do you feel?" Dr. Prine asked after several thrusts.

He could have lied, of course, but she was terribly keen.

"Maybe something's happening," he said through his clench of jaw.

"Don't fake it, Georgie, and don't force it." She rammed him again. "Unless it happens of its own accord, it's worthless."

But all he felt, in soul and sphincter, was pain. He had been frigid all his life.

The soothing suppository in place, pants up, skirt down, he paid her in cash.

She counted the bills. "You are fifty short," she said. "I told you I was increasing the fee to three hundred when you got your raise. I don't want you to run around with extra money in your purse. That's very degenerative. This therapy must mean more to you than a new wardrobe. Unless it represents a certain sacrifice, it will not be efficacious."

"But I didn't get a raise," said Cornell. "That must have been someone else."

"The point is, I've already made up my mind," the good doctor told him severely.

He gave her another fifty-dollar bill; he would eat no lunches until payday.

"Doctor," he asked, "do you really see any hope for my recovery?"

"That's not at all easy to say." She turned to the safe behind her desk, concealing the dial with a shoulder as she twirled it. "A *recovery* is not what we are seeking. You haven't backslid. You've never *been* there. Recidivists are simple to treat. They know what they've lost. You, on the other hand, may quite genuinely not have the capacity to be a man. There are such persons."

"And what happens to them?"

"Come, Georgie, don't play games with me. You know as well as I. Let's hope it doesn't come to that." She opened the layered iron door and placed the money on one of the stacks of bills which clogged the interior. She ran a cash-and-carry business, of which the Internal Revenue Service probably did not know the half. Cornell admired her for that: the government flushed tax money down the twin toilets of welfare and military expenditure, supporting degenerates and producing billion-dollar rockets which regularly exploded on liftoff. Yet when a girl friend once gave him a gold brooch, he phoned the IRS to ask whether he should have it assessed and list the value on his next return. "Are you a full- or part-time prostitute?" he was asked. Anyway, the brooch soon turned green.

Dr. Prine closed the safe and tested the handle. She then took a cigar from a desktop humidor and with an onyx-inlaid cutter clipped a wedge from the tip. She proceeded to char the other end with a kitchen match. At last she placed the cigar between her teeth, ignited it with another match, and puffed. Cornell always got pleasure from observing this ritual. He had once been dated by a girl who occasionally permitted him a drag on her cheroot, and he had liked it, even if it wasn't masculine.

"Don't worry," Dr. Prine said finally, flooding him with rich blue smoke, "you're still some distance from castration. *I* haven't given up, so don't you." Her eyes crossed as, without taking the cigar from her mouth, she inspected the burgeoning ash. She levered the intercom and told the receptionist to send in the next patient.

The newcomer approached the door as Cornell emerged. They avoided each other's eyes. Cornell saw a pair of exquisite legs in textured stockings, and smelled sandalwood as they passed. He couldn't help it: he flamed with jealousy.

Dr. Prine's receptionist was an ex-convict.

"Goodbye, Paul," Cornell said to him.

Paul had many years before been a patient of Dr. Prine's, but his illness had proved to be beyond the reach of psychiatry. He had persisted in dressing as a woman, in sweatshirt, baggy pants, and cowgirl boots, refused to shave for days at a time, chewed tobacco and spat into potted flowers. Finally he had lost all semblance of control, appeared at the apartment of a female acquaintance, forced her at knifepoint to strip and don lacy male panties and frothy brassiere and perform an obscene dance while he smoked one of her brier pipes. He was soon thereafter apprehended by the police and subsequently received the maximum sentence. After the emasculation he of course went quickly to fat.

Paul now returned Cornell's congé with a dull, eunuch's smile which hardly creased his bovine face. He must have weighed 250 pounds. His memory was also enervate.

"Goodbye, Mr. Corning."

Cornell had been coming here for three years.

Cornell's office was only a sixty-block walk from Dr. Prine's high-rent district on the Upper West Side. He went south via Central Park West and its continuous façades of plate glass on both sides, with bumper-to-bumper truck traffic between. At Columba Circle he met Broadway and followed it to the glass monolith on the corner of 53rd Street, the home of the giant publishing firm for which he labored: Philby, Osgood & Huff.

Above the inside elevator doors were listed the various subsidiaries and the floors relevant to each: The Osphil Press, Huff-books, Huff House. Of the three original partners, Philby was dead, Constance Osgood was now in senile seclusion, and only Eloise Huff survived.

Cornell deboarded on the eighteenth floor and greeted the brunette receptionist.

"Morning, Willie."

"It's almost noon, Georgie," said this snotty creature. "How some people get away with it is beyond me." Willie flipped his lacquered bouffant away, and Cornell did something similar with his own swanlike neck, though not without protruding his tongue. Rumor had it that Eloise Huff, the big boss, was getting into Willie's pants.

Speak of the devil. No sooner had Cornell pushed through the glass doors of Huff House than who appeared but old Eloise herself, baggy tweeds, eternal pipe, and brushy mustache: her own lip-hair, and not the paste-on device currently in fashion; she was inordinately vain about it.

On her way to the toilet, her impatient hand already at the top of the zipper. Her kidney condition was well known.

Cornell had not been able to phone in that he would be late. No one would yet have been at work when he left home, and he was closeted with Dr. Prine thereafter. To call en route would have been pointless even could he have found a public telephone that functioned. The last time he tried, he left the booth after depositing three zinc dollars for as many replays of the synthetic monologue of the robot operator.

Luckily, old Eloise was as usual in a state of egocentric oblivion.

"Hello, Johnny," she said. "Back from lunch already? These mornings get away from me when I'm reading manuscripts. I'll just send out for a malted today, I think." She burped. "Off my feed these days. Fifteen-twenty years ago I was a three-martini luncher. Could drink most authors under the table." Her gray mustache was stained yellow from the pipe, and dandruff flecked the shoulders of her old blazer. If she was laying Willie, he was to be pitied. Cornell's stomach rolled at the thought of being touched by such a dirty old woman.

He smiled and murmured something—Eloise never listened to anybody but herself, anyway—and trotted down the corridor. Before he cleared the range of Eloise's reach, however, he felt her sharp pinch of his left buttock. He seethed all the way to his desk, but that was the sort of thing you had to put up with if you were a working boy.

"Kid," said Charlie, as Cornell reached the cubicle they shared, "Ida's gonna chew your rump."

Charlie as usual was ill-shaven, and there were grease stains on the front of his dress.

Screw her, Cornell mouthed silently, with reference to Ida Hind, senior editor and his immediate superior.

"Maybe you ought to," Charlie cried. "You can use all the help you can get." Charlie's wig was a fright; he was balding under it. His beefy face wore no makeup. His stomach extended farther than his falsies, and the latter were out of balance, the left one having strayed almost into his armpit.

"I was at my doctor's," Cornell cried indignantly.

"I told her that you probably were." Charlie's fat cheeks bulged in humor. "Why you pay that quack to ream you is beyond me. Ida would do it for nothing."

Cornell put his purse in the lower desk drawer. To gain room for it he had first to push clatteringly back the collection of cosmetic bottles, jars, and tubes there. He saw a spare pair of pantyhose, new in cellophane, which he had forgotten he owned. He sat down and gasped at the sight of the overflowing In-box.

Charlie kept it up. "She's got the hots for you, son. Old Ida is the house stud. Her office door has been closed for an hour. She's probably putting the blocks to that little first novelist who came in from the Midwest. He was unaware that a paragraph in his contract obliges him to lay for his editor. Prone on the desktop, his creamy white hams being violated by her brutal claws searching for the mossy crevice of delight."

"Come on, Charlie. I've got to get to work."

"I'm quoting from his book," Charlie protested. "I did the first reading, you know." Some of the unsolicited manuscripts were given to the secretaries to read. Cornell generally tried to evade that chore; you got no extra pay for it, and the books were usually hopeless. Not that he thought that much about the books that Huff House published, which lately had been running heavily to memoirs from retired stateswomen, with an exposé or two thrown in of professional wrestling, roller derbies, and the like. Cornell's own taste was for romantic novels, but you hardly ever came across one any more.

"Recommended it unreservedly," Charlie went on, "as a sensitive, passionate account of a young man's deflowering."

Cornell ignored him and began to type from a letter that had been dictated by Ida the afternoon before. He had never finished his Speedwriting course, and improvised a good deal, then often forgot what certain *ad hoc* abbreviations signified. The missive at hand was addressed to a has-been named Wallace Walton Walsh, whose first novel had been a super-seller about twenty years before, but whose subsequent volumes had grown ever less successful throughout the years since. The message which Cornell now tried to unlock from his runic scribble was Ida's rejection of WWW's latest manuscript—diplomatically couched, naturally, but in essence an unequivocal No.

Cornell felt sorry for the poor old hack, who, as was well known, had served his term as Ida's paramour.

DEAR WINSOME WALLIE,
Well, love, what can I say about FRIENDS OR FIENDS? Here and there are unmistakable reminders of the old [what was that word, *mgc*?], but frankly, Wall, most of it you have done before and, if you'll pardon my saying so, better. Remember the characters from UPSHOT

[the original blockbuster]—Clara and Harvey and Simone, such rich, rounded ctrzn [*characterization, of course!*].

Now before you start hollering, my darling Three W's, let me assure you I realize you are trying something new, to break out of the [oh, pee! look at this:] stjkt f tdtnl tknk n açv nu mgs, and I admire you for making that effort, Wall, believe me, when you have long since earned the right to sit back and—

Cornell handed his stenographer's notebook to Charlie, glazed fingernail pointing to the cryptic passage.

"Would you have any idea what I wrote there?" The earlier *mgc,* he suddenly understood, meant "magic."

Charlie was himself typing, sporadically following some copy to the left of his machine while reading an opened book on the right. He took the notebook and provided an instant translation.

" 'Unmistakable reminders of the old magic.' "

"No, this one."

" 'To break out of the old straitjacket of traditional technique and achieve new meanings.' What doo-doo."

"How can you read my shorthand?"

Charlie laughed. "I started out here working for Ida. She says the same thing in most of her letters." He passed the notebook back to Cornell. "Not only is Wally getting the boot, but he also has to read that crap. But, as usual, sympathy is misplaced. That's precisely the kind of prose for which WWW is himself noted. She probably picked up his style years ago when she was banging him." Without transition he said: "When are you going to learn real shorthand? Or the Stenotype—then you could become a court reporter and get out of here."

"What about you?" asked Cornell.

"I never get around to anything," said Charlie. "Including suicide."

"What banned book are you reading today? Certainly nothing published by Huff House."

"A classic criminal text." Charlie turned back to it without further identification. He actually did openly read proscribed works, obtained through some underground source of pornography, but always in pocket-sized editions that could be quickly concealed. In the case of some really raw title he might cut off the cover and glue on another from a harmless volume—*The Gentle Man's Guide to Needlepoint,* say, disguising the text of *Men Without Women,* a collection of stories notorious for their shameless perversity, by—

"Hey, Charlie, who was the author of *Men Without Women?*"

Charlie shushed him and deftly covered the book with a sheaf of correspondence.

"I don't know, Charlie, you take all kinds of chances, but when it comes to me, I can't even ask—"

The motive for Charlie's furtiveness was soon apparent. Cornell should have known better. A stern voice spoke to the back of his head.

"Georgie, I want a word with you."

He rose and, on weak ankles, followed Ida Hind into her office, across and down the corridor.

Ida was cleanshaven, skull as well as face, and the latter was naked even of eyebrows. Sometimes while dictating, Ida gave Cornell the treat of watching her apply the electric razor. If he had had to localize his hatred for Ida, he might have done it in her ears, which projected obscenely from her head at 85-degree angles.

Ida now reached down inside the collar of her turtleneck sweater and relieved an itch in the area of the clavicle.

"Georgie," she said, staring with her lashless eyes, "what am I going to do with you?" After she shaved, Ida washed her entire head with alcohol. She glistened.

"Call my analyst," he answered indignantly. "Go ahead. That's where I was."

"I've done that already, Georgie. And do you know what Dr.

Prine told me?" Ida paused to let the foreboding establish itself. Cornell could happily have lighted her with a match when she was wet with alcohol. "I'll tell you. 'Georgie Cornell is hopeless, I'm afraid.' That's a direct quote. 'He's beyond the reach of effective therapy.' " Ida did something with her throat. "That's what Dr. Prine told me, and I am telling it to you now, not to be cruel—please believe me when I say that, Georgie—but because I think the time has come to face facts and not to sweep them under the carpet any more."

Cornell crossed his legs the other way, and Ida did not fail to mark the movement. She was a notoriously horny devil, but too much of a pro to bed any secretary of hers. However, Cornell had no other defense except weeping, and it was too early to use that.

"Georgie," said Ida. She came around in front and leaned her behind against the rim of the desk. She clutched the right lapel of her tweed jacket. Cornell sat below her, peeping up under his false eyelashes.

"What I have to suggest," Ida said, "is nothing terribly drastic. But I think a little transfer might be the answer to both our problems—I mean, the problem we share. Namely, that the present job doesn't seem to jibe with what either of us needs. As it happens, an opening has fortuitously, uh, opened up. Now don't scream before you hear me out. Stanley—you know old Stanley."

Cornell could not long endure Ida's browless stare. He was alternating between the colored book jackets on the shelves to left and right and the window behind the desk with its yellow smogscape.

"Stanley?"

"Stanley, our old Stanley," Ida said impatiently.

"Stanley the janitor?"

"Stanley the custodian," said Ida. "He is leaving us for a well-deserved retirement."

That was good news. Perhaps now the roller-towel in the men's lounge would be changed more frequently. Stanley was supposed to be an old boy friend of Eloise Huff's. He had got the sinecure when she was done with him. That must have been years ago. Now Stanley was an ancient harridan, slumped over his mop.

But suddenly the pitiful image was flushed from Cornell's mind.

"Oh, no," he moaned. "Oh, no."

Ida's voice, hitherto drifting, at once came into sharp focus.

"Georgie, it takes you two days to type a letter, all week to find a contract in the files. You are habitually late in the morning, and you leave as early as you can in the afternoon. About the only good thing that can be said is that you aren't insolent. In fact, you are rather sweet. That's why I haven't even considered firing you. I want you to understand that, Georgie, though I have been under considerable pressure to do so. I realize that your fecklessness is due to your personal problems. You are distracted. You stare into space when you are being addressed. In fact, you're doing it now."

Ida leaned forward and put a hand on each of Cornell's shoulders, looking into his face. He was forced to stare back. Her head was like a bowling ball.

"I have been more than patient," Ida said solemnly. "So much so, in fact, that there has been some talk." She laughed with a certain brutal sound. "If you get what I mean." She pushed him back and herself away, with a great shove.

Cornell made a tactical simper, mainly to relieve his own embarrassment. He loathed being talked to confidentially about himself, unless he was paying for it, as with Dr. Prine, and thus retaining his self-respect.

"Well," Ida went on, "you *are* an attractive boy, dear, and I'm a normal woman." She smirked vainly. "And then some."

"I *am?*" Cornell was trying to hide his repugnance, but his gorge rose. Now was the time to sob, and he did so.

"I don't want to be a janitor and clean toilets!"

"Now, now, none of that," said Ida. "You promised to let me explain. I'm not asking you to take a cut in pay. Not all the job is in the rest rooms by any means. The offices are mopped and dusted, and you can choose your own time for that: either before working hours, in the morning, or just after everybody leaves at the end of the day. It amounts to only an extra hour or so. As to the lounges, they are quickly managed: only three basins and three stalls in each." Ida winked horribly. "You will do the women's john too. When it's empty, of course! Throughout most of the body of the day your time will be your own. You'll be on call for paper or soap, but otherwise you can occupy yourself as you see fit. Stanley has made an entire fleet of model ships from toothpicks in his spare moments over the past twenty years. He has a little work-nook in the corner of the custodian's closet— have you ever seen it?"

Ida turned to a shelf. "Here's a Roman trireme that I think is rather cunning." She picked it up gingerly and handed it to Cornell. "Easy, now. The glue is probably brittle."

Even as she spoke, one of the tiny oars came loose and fluttered to the floor. Cornell bent over to fetch it, and as he came up he saw Ida trying to see his breasts through the neck of his blouse. This event, combined with her earlier reference to the gossip which linked them, suggested he might through sexual means cause the whole matter to be drastically reconsidered.

He returned the oar and the model galley, allowing his hand to linger against hers. He could feel his tears drying on his cheeks. It was time to squeeze out more. He put his face into his lap. He was certain that Ida had enough of the brute in her to be made lustful by a man's weeping. He was right.

"Come on, now." She put her hands onto his shoulders again, then soon slid them down his arms.

But the door was flung open at that point, admitting some old, whory-looking type with teased hair, heavy orange pancake makeup, and green satin over soccer-ball breasts.

Ida pushed Cornell away so vigorously that he and his chair almost toppled over.

"Wallie!" she cried.

The newcomer glared redly at Cornell.

Ida said guiltily: "I've got one sick secretary on my hands, Wallie."

Cornell realized this was Wallace Walton Walsh, the has-been novelist. And was he old! The troweled-on pancake was badly eroded. Vultures had left tracks at the corners of his eyes, porters had abandoned steamer trunks underneath. Heavy, flabby arms like whole liverwursts in the foolishly sleeveless dress, varicose veins below the skirt. Imagine a man of his age wearing satin. It was almost too disgusting to be pathetic.

Walsh clopped to the desk on his platform shoes and rooted furiously through the papers there.

"Where's my book?" he demanded, big breasts swinging, old chins wobbling, crimson mouth like a burst pomegranate, the teeth behind it a false blue-white.

Ida rummaged in a drawer and found a thick, tattered manuscript secured by a rubber band. The title page showed an enormous coffee stain. Walsh ripped his property from Ida's clutch, at which shock the rubber band broke and he was left holding front and back sheets as the inner pages fell into a heaped mess on the floor.

Walsh squatted and gathered them up, a grotesque spectacle. He rose and screamed.

"Six months! You've kept this six months."

Ida remained cool. "A letter is on its way to you right now. I'm afraid the situation has changed in the past few years, Wallie. We can't give most of our fiction away, and you know, we have to face the fact that publishing is after all a business." Her voice trailed off.

Walsh slapped her face.

Even with a reddened cheek Ida retained her composure.

"That wasn't necessary, Wallie."

"Oh," Walsh screamed, "go to hell, go to hell!" He broke down for an instant and smeared his makeup with distraught fingers. Recovering, pointing the handful of loose manuscript at Cornell, he said: "And take that little tart with you." He marched out on heels which, Cornell noticed, were badly run over. Also, his slip was showing about an inch and a half. What an old horror he was.

Ida lowered her shaved head. "Once we were lovers, you know. That's the tough aspect to this." She breathed dramatically. Her face, where it had been struck, was now in full flush. Walsh had a spongy-looking but large hand. "What can you say to someone like that?" said Ida.

She plunged her arm into a lower drawer and withdrew a flat bottle of either gin or vodka, most likely the latter because it was odorless. Ida had a boozer's reputation but you never smelled anything on her. She tipped the bottle up and swallowed mournfully.

"Georgie, this would never have happened if you had got that letter out." She tossed the exhausted pint into a rosewood wastebasket. "Nuff said. Get your In-box cleaned up today. Tomorrow you report to Stanley, who will show you the ropes."

When Cornell returned to the cubicle, Charlie said: "Don't tell me: you got canned. You've been asking for it, old buddy." He dramatically turned his stout back to Cornell. "I can't stand losers." Then he peeped over the shoulder of his infamous cardigan. "I can let you have a few bucks." He swiped back the tangled mess of his fright wig and swung halfway around. "Hell, man, lots of guys have been fired in their time. I have myself, and more than once."

Cornell told him about the transfer. Charlie scratched his fat nose.

"Well, it's not the end of the world." He slapped his knee.

"I got an idea! How about feeding with me tonight?"

Cornell thought about it for a decent interval. He had not had a date with a woman in ages, but he did not want to advertise his loneliness.

At last he said: "I'll have to make a call first."

"Don't cancel anything," Charlie said earnestly. "I meant if you were free. I want to talk over something."

Cornell felt a little rotten. Charlie, he suspected, had not had a date for the past ten years.

"No, no, that's O.K. I just remember she changed it to tomorrow night. She couldn't get tickets for tonight." He tried to think of a show in case Charlie asked him about this hypothetical engagement.

But Charlie did not. He said: "Oh, swell. You'll have to take potluck, though."

Cornell had been to Charlie's place a couple of times before. Charlie's meals were none too delicate.

"Don't go to any special trouble," Cornell said. "This news has taken away my appetite anyhow. I'd quit if I had the guts. But jobs are hard to get nowadays. Before I came here I was out of work for three full months, and the economic situation has got worse since then."

Charlie turned sardonic. "Well," he said, "it's still better than hustling."

Cornell said bitterly: "I don't know if it is."

"Oh, I can assure you of that." Charlie gave Cornell a meaningful look.

Cornell's new pantyhose were sagging. He lifted his fanny off the chair and hiked them up. Charlie was still staring at him when he looked back.

"Are you trying to tell me something?" Cornell asked archly. He knew Charlie was trying to distract him from self-pity.

"Whoring," said Charlie. "Real lowdown and dirty streetwalking. I've done it."

"Sure you have."

But Charlie did not smile. "Ten years back, during the Depression. Talk about being degraded. You tell yourself that your customers are even lower than you, but you don't really believe it down deep. I never had any illusions about my beauty, and when I was younger I had some skin trouble on my face, turned out to be an allergy to hormone creams." Charlie looked at his belly. "My figure was better then, but not much. You wouldn't believe how much business I did, though. Handsome, well-dressed women would pass up the other fellas, who were some of them pretty teenagers, and take me. You explain it. I couldn't."

"Charlie," Cornell chided him, "you're making all this up."

However, the story did succeed in raising Cornell's spirits. Charlie was good at that. He took nothing seriously and had no pride, but his heart, behind the cynical armor, was soft as nylon fleece.

"I wish I was," said Charlie, shrugging dolefully. "That wasn't exactly my high point in life. I was rolled a couple times before I learned how to take care of myself. You know, they stay dressed and fool around while you get your clothes off, then grab your purse and run out of the hotel. What are you gonna do? Go to a cop? Or you'll pick up a cop, some plainclothes bitch from the Vice Squad. With your pants around your ankles, she'll flash a badge. Payoffs are what they're usually after. They're all crooked. And then there's the real mean type who will pocket your evening's take and run you in anyway. Who're you going to appeal to? It's her word against yours in court."

Cornell began to believe this, and was stunned.

"Believe me," Charlie said, "I've seen all sides of a man's life and most of them are shit."

Cornell sighed. "What's the answer then?"

Charlie produced a ghastly sort of grin. "Keep your powder dry. Whimpering won't help." Suddenly, though, he looked vulnerable. "I used to cry a lot. Then one day I saw myself in the mirror." He grinned again, this time in better humor. "Can you imagine how I look crying? Like beads of grease on a ham. I realized at that moment I was not just another pretty face."

"Charlie . . ." Cornell said compassionately. It was all he could think of.

Charlie got out his purse and took from it a wretched-looking compact. The mirror inside was cracked.

"I don't know why I bother doing this," Charlie said, grimacing at his own image. He slapped on some powder from a dirty puff.

"I'm going across the street for a hero sandwich," he said, rising. "You still on your diet?"

"I'll go off it tonight at your house," Cornell told him.

Charlie made his frumpy departure. Before the evening was over, he would probably break out his pornography collection. His sex life was all perverse fantasy: transvestite pictures, women in dresses, lace nighties, panty girdles and bras; men dressed as airplane pilots, boxers, soldiers. Most of this stuff was of little interest to Cornell. He looked at it only to humor Charlie.

But there was one photograph that did stir him strangely. It was the most obscene gem in Charlie's lode. An infant was depicted as sucking a breast—the breast of a *woman*. Oh, it was a shameful thing, outlandish and probably faked. The breast was much too large to be that of a normal woman, who would have bound hers tightly from puberty on. But the adult who was pictured did have the smaller facial features of the average female.

The baby seemed to be sucking his heart out, the tiny voracious mouth covering the entire nipple. The woman, if such she was, wore what Cornell saw as an evil, demonic smile.

The picture was the dirtiest, filthiest, most thrilling thing Cornell had ever seen. He could never resist looking at it, and during his sleep thereafter never went without a nightmare. That was one of the many things he had not told Dr. Prine.

Women are called womanly only when they regard themselves as existing solely for the use of men.

GEORGE BERNARD SHAW, 1908

2

CHARLIE LIVED in the area called East River Park. There had apparently once been a stream flowing through that neighborhood. New York was characterized by names that referred to bygone geographical features: Kips Bay, Morningside Heights, Central Park, etc.; and the vast sewage system separating Manhattan from New Jersey was still known as the Hudson River.

According to Charlie, a repository of negative information, the East River buildings had been erected in the 1990's on a ground of compacted garbage. The weight of the enormous tenements had caused this fill to settle over the years. Charlie's building still survived, almost alone amid the cairns of rubble which commemorated the other houses in the original project, but the exterior walls were badly cracked and the structure stood at an angle. The elevators had been unusable for years, and because of the slant Cornell felt giddy climbing the stairs.

The pollution alert had, unusually enough, been cancelled just after the evening rush hour, owing to a sudden, brisk west wind. Cornell was not wearing his mask, and he could smell liver frying on the fifth floor. On the sixth, the crack in the outside wall was wide enough to look through: Cornell saw a slatternly man in curlers reeling in a washline crowded with panties and bras.

Charlie lived on the seventh floor, behind a dented door which Cornell now, after taking a moment to catch his breath, rapped upon with a fist gloved in beige suede.

Charlie opened up. He wore an ancient, stained peignoir that looked like a souvenir from his days of whoring. It was trimmed in lank feathers, several of which moulted as he stepped aside to let Cornell in. He also wore infamous mules, the toes of which were open to display three yellow, unpainted nails on each large foot.

Cornell identified the foul odor as that of boiled cabbage.

"I hope you didn't go to any trouble," said he, searching for a place to deposit his purse. The doorside table was littered with unopened junk mail: samples of depilatories and mascara, etc., which Cornell recognized, having received them himself and having tried them all—but never having afterwards been able to find those brands in the shops he patronized.

"Here," said Charlie, taking the butter-soft plastic-calfskin handbag—a little birthday remembrance from Cornell to himself—and hanging it on the doorknob.

Cornell had to move a discarded girdle from the sofa cushion he chose to sit on; the others, he remembered, had loose springs that hurt your heinie.

Sooty satin shade on the endtable lamp, and the bulb was too bright. He didn't relish the thought of having his twenty-nine-year-old lines highlighted for Charlie, even old Charlie, scarcely a competitor. Cornell was wearing especially light makeup, after witnessing the scene with Wallace Walton Walsh. He extinguished the lamp.

"You look like a billion dollars, as usual," said Charlie, without a trace of jealousy. He really was a good sort. "But I should have warned you to be casual. You don't want to ruin your good clothes in this dump."

It was true that Cornell had gone to some pains, even though he was going to dine with another man. But he was like that. Even on lonely weekends he shaved and did his eyes, splashed on cologne. He wouldn't think of going to the hallway incinerator in curlers and housecoat. Today, after finishing up the contents of his In-box, as ordered (much of the material therein he filed in the wastebasket: he had already been demoted to janitor; Ida did not understand the principle of incentive), he had slipped out of the office a bit early, gone home, and washed and set his hair. For two days his natural coiffure would outshine any wig, but then soot and humidity would cause it to go dull. But you couldn't wash it too often, else the ends would turn brittle. He was also trying out a new shade of lipstick, pale tangerine, the perfect complement to his jersey sheath in beige, shoes in tobacco brown, matching bag, patterned hose, amber circlet at the wrist, and a little accent of gold at his bosom, a cunning little owl, souvenir of a past affair that had ended badly, as they usually did, but that could not be blamed on the miniature owl.

Cornell assured Charlie that, on the contrary, his place was very—uh, comfortable.

"Well," said Charlie, clapping his thighs, "let's have a beer while the corned beef 'n' cabbage is boiling."

Cornell wasn't much of a drinker. He seldom touched the hard stuff. He didn't hold it well, going rapidly through giddiness to something rather ugly. Women were misguided who sought to ply him with liquor en route to bed. A glass of wine was his speed, but he supposed Charlie would have offered wine if available.

"Oh, nice," he said. Beer would bloat him.

Charlie went to the battered half-refrigerator under the counter of the kitchenette, which was scarcely more than an alcove, took out a quart bottle that had already been opened, and filled a glass mug. Cornell closed his eyes as he drank. He did not want to see whether the glass was clean, for there was nothing he could have done about it if it weren't. Charlie gulped at his own mug. He had probably already had a few.

"Let me top that up," he said after Cornell had had only two sips, extending the slimy bottle.

"I don't want to get tipsy," Cornell said.

"Come on," said Charlie, "unbend. This is Liberty Hall."

By the time Charlie served up the corned beef and cabbage, they had killed the entire quart, and Cornell could feel it. He could sense a certain recklessness in his soul.

Charlie brought the discolored pot to the card table at which they were to eat and forked down a half-head of cabbage on each plastic plate. He had previously hacked from a hunk of corned beef a portion, replete with fibers, for each of them.

"Put some margarine on it while it's hot," Charlie said. "I'll get the mustard and another bottle."

"I don't know if I can handle much more," said Cornell.

"Live a little," Charlie said.

Cornell was feeling no pain as he chewed the last of the twine-like meat. The truth was that alcohol made him feel rather effeminate. He found himself almost enjoying this crude provender. If he confessed that to Dr. Prine, she would probably use the word "vulva-envy." If he got drunk enough, he would think of her as an old quack.

He laughed aloud, and told Charlie: "I'm drunk."

"Good," Charlie said. "Have another." He pointed to the bottle. "I'm going to spring my proposition on you in a little while. But, first, if you don't mind, I'm going to get into something more comfortable."

Cornell laughed again, indicating Charlie's ancient negligee, which had continued to lose feathers. Fresh beer stains had joined the egg yellow, fruit jam, and unidentifiable smears already in place.

"More comfortable? What, a towel?"

Charlie's answering smile made him suddenly queasy. Was Charlie homosexual? Perhaps he had been biding his time for a year and was now about to make the big push.

Charlie lumbered into his little bedroom. Cornell rose unsteadily and shook some crumbs from his skirt. Then he got the compact from his purse and visited the john, an appalling place full of dirty towels and drying lingerie. He cleaned off the toilet seat with paper before sitting down and making water. He plucked at his hair in the spattered mirror and refreshed his makeup, which after dinner was always a little weary, particularly under the eyes.

When he emerged, Charlie was standing in the bedroom doorway. Cornell felt himself going faint, his vision blurring as if he were swimming in murky water. He clutched the jamb of the bathroom door.

Charlie advanced on him.

Cornell shook his head violently.

"I warn you, Charlie. I'll defend myself. I may be somewhat smashed, but I'll fight."

"What the hell are you talking about?" asked Charlie. "You're drunker than I thought."

Almost screaming, Cornell demanded: *"Why are you dressed as a woman?"*

For Charlie wore baggy corduroy slacks, a plaid wool shirt of the lumberjack type, tattered sneakers, and no wig. He was bald in the middle, between two fringes of graying fuzz. He held the beer mug in the left hand, and in the right a big black cigar.

"Charlie," Cornell said. "In the name of friendship, I ask you: are you queer? I have to know. We can even remain friends. But let me say this: I'm not. Whatever problems I have in being a man, deviate sex is not one of them."

Charlie laughed brutally, with a great burst of cigar smoke. Cornell's heart sank.

"I think I'd better leave now," he said. "Thanks for dinner." He clutched his compact to his bosom, and with the other hand offered to shake with Charlie. It was too bad, really. Charlie was currently his only friend of either sex.

Charlie roughly, femininely struck his hand aside. "Don't be ridiculous. I'm no faggot, for Mary's sake. You should know better than that. You've seen my collection of porn. Any man-to-man stuff there?" Charlie was roaring. It occurred to Cornell that perhaps Charlie was drunker than he.

Cornell hesitated. Charlie came towards him, reached for him. Cornell started to slap his face, but a miraculous alteration took place in his flying hand: it became a fist, it struck Charlie's stout chin, and Charlie landed on his behind.

Charlie sat there on the floor, laughing. He did not seem to be hurt.

Cornell felt awful. He helped his friend up.

"I'm sorry, Charlie. I don't know what got into me."

"Forget it!" Charlie said expansively. He went to the refrigerator. "I guess it was a shock for you to see me. I never did it before in front of you. You have to know somebody pretty well."

When Charlie had refilled the mugs and come back, Cornell took a sip of beer and said: "I'm under a strain these days. I don't have much of a love life."

"You're kidding," said Charlie. "With your youth and looks."

"Youth! I'm twenty-nine, Charlie. Each morning I have to work harder at the vanity table."

Charlie was still smiling ironically. He could not relate to another man's problems. This annoyed Cornell, who after all was only held together by Dr. Prine. And then even when he had been younger, the women he seemed naturally to attract were crude libertines, most of them, out to seduce him with as little effort as possible. He seldom had dated anyone who would *talk* to him, treat him like a human being; was that too much to ask? Of course, Dr. Prine's interpretation was that he unconsciously elicited this treatment, putting out vibrations that kept sensitive women away while advertising his availability to brutes.

Charlie's cigar butt had gone out. He lighted it, and now it stank.

"Things are tough all over," said he wryly. "Everybody's been twenty-nine in his day."

"Not everybody," Cornell said with feeling. "They're using teenagers in the fashion ads nowadays. Those smooth faces and fresh eyes. You see them all over the streets. That's what women go for. They get older and older, and their boys get younger every year." Cornell savagely drank some beer. "I'm a has-been, Charlie. I haven't had a date in months, and I haven't had an *interesting* date in years."

"I have *never* had one," said Charlie.

Well, Cornell was not unsympathetic, but he disliked being one-upped, especially in this area. He had earned the right to his own anguish. Surely, everyone had been or would be twenty-nine, but this was *his* twenty-ninth year, the loss of *his* youth forever. And he had also just lost his job, or what amounted to the same thing. And had not Dr. Prine told Ida that he was hopeless? He cried so often as a tactic that he had almost forgotten how to do so genuinely: he felt like it now. His hand still hurt: he had punched Charlie in female style. His world was in ruins, yet Charlie insisted he was to be envied. Such blatant injustice shriveled his soul.

In desperation he came out with the ultimate.

"I'm frigid, Charlie."

Charlie shrugged, unmoved even now.

"I always have been, Charlie."

"So what else is new?" Charlie drank deeply from the mug.

Because it had not worked, Cornell felt as if covered with filth. He shouldn't have confessed that; now Charlie had something on him. You could never really trust another man. Suppose he did meet a fascinating woman. It could happen. There were a few gems around who were not driven dotty by adolescents, superior females who understood the value of mature men. Charlie could bad-mouth him around the office: "Georgie is frigid, you know. Told me himself!"

He gulped some beer, and saw traces of tangerine lipstick on the rim of the mug: it had been sold to him as indelible.

But Charlie suddenly spoke sympathetically.

"Why don't you just turn your back on 'em, kid?"

"Who?"

"Women," said Charlie.

"The choice has been more or less taken out of my hands." Cornell took another bitter swallow from the mug, or intended to: a torrent escaped and wet the bosom of his beautiful dress.

"Oh, shit!" Ordinarily he never talked like that, but now he didn't care. He felt the clamminess reach his breasts, and said the worst: "Mother's milk!"

"Wow!" said Charlie. "You're not the Nice Neil I thought." He was still not taking Cornell seriously. But he did get up and fetch a sponge.

"No," Cornell said. "I know this fabric. I have to soak this out thoroughly and immediately, or the dress has had it."

He went to the bathroom, pulled the dress over his head, and plunged it into the basin under a running faucet.

Charlie appeared in the doorway.

"There's a housecoat on the hook behind the bedroom door," he said, pointing with his cigar butt. "It's not in pristine condition, but a little better than my negligee, anyhow."

In half slip and bra Cornell entered the bedroom. He saw in the dresser-mirror that taking off the dress had disarranged his hair. He found a brush and used it, wincing as it clogged with the thick strands and pulled his scalp. His rolling eye saw the open closet, and therein a pin-striped woman's suit on a hanger. Just like Dr. Prine's. He went there and saw, next to the suit, a herringbone-tweed sports jacket. Gray flannel slacks. Double-breasted gabardine suit. Cordovan brogues on the floor beneath. On the inside surface of the door, a tie rack, filled: stripes, polka dots, solids.

He really hadn't dreamed Charlie went so far.

He dawdled there, looking, touching. He went to the dresser and saw himself in the mirror. He wore the tweed jacket, unbuttoned, his brassiered tits sticking out. How weird. He buttoned up. The jacket was too large; there was room for his bosom. With his bare neck the effect was more that of a loose outer coat. He made a stern, woman's face at himself in the mirror, squaring his jaw. Behind him, Charlie peeked in the doorway.

"There's some shirts in the middle drawer." He withdrew.

The shirt that Cornell chose was white with a candy stripe. He put a striped tie under the collar and tried to make a knot.

"Charlie!" he cried. "How do you tie a tie, for goodness sake?"

Charlie entered. "It's not easy to be a girl, first time out," he said in levity.

He took the silken snake from Cornell, put it around his own neck, tied the slipknot, then took it off and handed it back.

"Just put your head through the noose, old buddy," said he. "Best way to learn is to have the teacher stand behind you, arms around your neck. But I'm still sensitive about your earlier suspicions."

"You'll never let me live that down."

"I might even prove you right! You make an interesting-looking guy." Charlie pointed to Cornell's mirror-image, which was now feminine throughout the trunk, though the slip showed below the jacket and the very virile earrings hung above the shirt collar as did his fall of hair, and between the auburn wealth was his fair face with its cupid's-bow lips and elaborate male eyes.

"Well," Cornell said, moueing, "might as well go all the way now. May I have a pair of trousers?"

Charlie offered him a choice of the flannels or a cavalry twill in tan. He accepted the latter. The waist was too large. The half-slip fell down over the trousers.

"Should have taken that off first," said Charlie, as Cornell expanded the elastic and let the garment fall. He stepped out of the clingy folds. He still wore his highheeled shoes.

"Take your pick," said Charlie, bringing the cordovan shoes from the closet. In his other set of fingers was a pair of thick brogues in pebble-grain brown. Cornell took the latter because they were most outrageous, with soles a half inch thick and a heavy leather heel twice that and further reinforced with metal plates shaped like segments of an orange.

So there he stood, in complete drag.

"The hair is certainly wrong," he said to himself in the glass.

Charlie had an answer for that. He produced a black, woman's wig, the interior of which proved sufficiently capacious to accept Cornell's natural growth when piled up and stuffed in. He sighed as he thought of his long brushwork before leaving home.

"I'll look like a mess when I take this off," he said. He pettishly poked up a sportive strand.

The mirror now showed the most bizarre image of the evening. He looked much more outlandish than when his hair had been down, for now he appeared as a woman who wore male makeup.

Charlie handed him a jar of cold cream and a wad of Kleenex. "And take off the earrings."

The next time Cornell stared at himself he saw a woman. For an instant he was delighted, but then pleasure became fear. He had satisfied his curiosity. Why did he linger in women's clothes? His fingers were at the jacket buttons when Charlie said something that halted them.

"It's hard the first few times not to be a parody."

"But that's just what we are," Cornell said in relief. A burlesque, a harmless little deriding of the sexual condition, both branches. He determined to enjoy the game. Goodness knows, he had not been amused in ever so long.

After they had returned to the living room and more beer, Charlie stared at Cornell, and asked: "How long have you been going to Dr. Prine, Georgie?"

Cornell was offended by this turn, but he didn't want to give Charlie the satisfaction of a sensitive response. He counted on his fingers. His nails were still painted, of course, and looked strange with the shirt cuffs and tweed sleeve behind them. "Almost three years. But before that I went to a couple of others. I've been going to somebody for my entire adult life."

"Have you been helped?"

"Let me put it this way: what I tell myself is that I might be a lot worse if I hadn't had the treatment. I'm surviving. I'm not ecstatically happy, but on the other hand I haven't slashed my wrists lately." How much beer had he drunk by now? He felt it. And his legs were terribly warm in the trousers. He did not find women's clothes enormously comfortable.

Nevertheless, he said: "I guess all of us would rather be girls in the next life." He laughed wildly. He didn't mean that, exactly, but he wanted to get back at Charlie.

"I don't ever want to be a woman!" Charlie cried with heat.

Cornell thought this statement very odd indeed, in view of their current costumes, but he merely took another drink of beer.

Charlie began to rave. "Nothing in Nature, or in the history of the human race before the second half of the twentieth century supports the theory that women are superior to men. Again I'm talking about real history, as opposed to the lies we were force-fed in school."

Cornell shook his head. "I just can't accept that a whole educational system could be completely wrong. I mean, it might be biased somewhat, but how could they lie about everything?"

As suddenly as he had become abstractly belligerent, Charlie deflated. "Ah, hell," he said. "I'm no militant. Too old, too tired, too scared. I begin to burn if I have a few drinks and think about the situation, but I wouldn't have the guts to join the underground and do something about it."

"Is there really an actual underground? I've heard that but never quite believed it."

"Haven't you ever seen any of their literature?" said Charlie. "They leave it around men's rooms and dressing rooms in stores.

You sure never see anybody passing it out. You know the punishment."

"Castration, allegedly," said Cornell. "But you never hear of anybody being arrested. If they really exist, they must be pretty careful."

Charlie shook his head. "The female Establishment suppresses that stuff, Georgie. They don't want to give publicity to such a movement. You might think it would be a deterrent to advertise the capture and emasculation of a rebel, but they don't want the public, especially the male part, to know there's even such a thing in existence." Charlie rose, heavily. "And maybe there isn't, in any organized form. Maybe just some little crank with a mimeograph machine in an attic somewhere. The System's still here, anyway."

Cornell chimed in amiably: "Here before us and it will be here long after we are gone. You can't fight Nature, Charlie: it made us men and we are stuck with it." Yet here they were, wearing unnatural attire. Well, nobody expected logic from a boy.

Charlie unzipped one of the sofa-cushion covers and took out the large manila envelope containing his filthy pictures.

"Here's your favorite, Georgie," he said, handing Cornell the photograph of the woman giving suck to a baby.

It had lost its excitement for Cornell. It seemed routine tonight, not shocking nor disgusting. Perhaps he had looked at it too often. But then it occurred to him for the first time that the picture might well be bogus.

"You know," he said, "this could easily be a fellow. There's nothing feminine about it, after all."

"It's an old picture, Georgie. It's authentic, all right. Breastfeeding really happened in the time when women reproduced."

"Why did you get me over here tonight? You said you had an idea."

"So I have, Georgie." Charlie padded back to the sofa in his sneakers and sat down. "It's your new job. You'll have access to all the guys at work, in the only place where we get any privacy."

He reached into the envelope and came out with another photograph, an eight-by-ten glossy this time, and held it face forward at Cornell. It showed two naked persons, one supine with spread legs between which another, prone, was contained.

Disingenuously Cornell asked, "Wrestlers?"

Charlie ignored this. "I've got a source for all the prints I want." He grinned.

"So?"

"You're being pretty dense, Georgie. You'll have a market for these in the men's room." He misinterpreted Cornell's frown, got up, and came over, his thick forefinger on the picture. "This is a *man* on top. His *penis* is inside this woman's *vagina*."

"But the one on the bottom has long hair, and the one on top has a crewcut," Cornell said. "And you can't see anything between them. It's all theoretical." He had inspected this picture the last time he visited Charlie, but as with the photograph of the alleged mother, only tonight did he question its authenticity. Wearing female attire had changed him somehow; he had a new skepticism.

Charlie was exasperated.

"What's got into you, Georgie? Maybe I should make some coffee to sober you up. Now, be serious. I can get a wholesale price, see. We'll put on a stiff markup. Real raw stuff like this isn't easily come by. We'll split the profit, you and I. Who couldn't use a little extra loot these days?"

Cornell grimaced. He had never been so insulted in his life.

"Is that your proposition? I should peddle filthy pictures in the toilets? To warped secretaries?"

Charlie lowered the photograph. He looked at Cornell for a long moment.

"Do you have to be snotty about it, Georgie? Couldn't you just say yes or no?"

"I didn't mean *you*, Charlie."

Charlie plodded to the couch and returned his pictures to the envelope. From the back he looked even more shapeless in women's clothes than in men's.

Cornell had not intended to be cruel, but *he* was the one who had been insulted first. Still, there had been no malice in Charlie's proposition: the insult arose from his assumption that he and Cornell enjoyed a common taste. And Cornell was not without responsibility for this error: he had on other visits shown interest in the picture of the so-called mother and child. Charlie was quite a sweet old thing; he always complimented Cornell; darn few other men were capable of generosity; Cornell wanted to be fair.

"I shouldn't have said that, Charlie."

Charlie shrugged the bag of his back.

"I hope you won't stay mad," Cornell said winningly. "You're a good friend."

"Forget it." Charlie turned and made a reluctant gesture towards the beer bottle. "Pour you a nightcap?"

"You want me to leave?" .

"I didn't say that." Charlie breathed heavily and poured Cornell's mug half full.

"You're angry, though."

"Georgie, how would you react if I called *you* warped? Do I do any harm with my pictures? Sure, it's against the law imposed on us by women. But whom does it hurt? No woman will look at me, so what chance do I have to be normal?"

"I can understand that," said Cornell.

"Can you? I doubt it. First you suspect me of being homosexual. Now this." Charlie sat down with his own mug.

"I wasn't attacking you, believe me," Cornell said. "It's just this new job. The very thought of it makes me crawl with shame. I don't see how I can face the other boys tomorrow, mop in hand.

Filling the toilet-paper holders. In comes that nasty receptionist, who has always hated my guts. Oh, Charlie!"

Charlie remained preoccupied with himself.

"Georgie, I warned you again and again that you were putting your ass in a sling with Ida. If you're going to goof off, you must do it cleverly. Trouble with you is, you can't help it. Look, in the long run, I don't do any more work than you, if as much, but I don't lose things and I don't forget things. I haven't got a raise in years, but I never get reprimanded. You call attention to yourself—probably because of your good looks. But then you don't use your looks to benefit yourself. For example, if you had any sense now, you would call Ida at home and ask tearfully if you could come to her house and discuss the transfer. Be hysterical—that scares women. Most of them have some guilt about the way they treat men. If you howl and scream enough, she'll see you. Then when you get there, be all soft and unresisting, weeping sadly. Most of them find that sexy. Basically, they're sadists."

"I couldn't possibly do that," Cornell said. "I just couldn't."

Charlie displayed his fat palms. "There you are."

"I've got some pride," said Cornell.

"So use it to push your mop," Charlie said.

"Suppose she made a pass at me."

"That's the idea," said Charlie.

"I couldn't go through with it. The idea of being touched by that loathsome creature . . ."

"O.K., then."

"It's difficult enough even if I like the girl."

"Yeah," Charlie said. "You mentioned that." He was bored and unsympathetic. He scratched his belly inside the shirt and looked at his nails.

Cornell swallowed more beer, though he was indeed badly bloated by now, his abdomen pressing against the belt. He also got that way from Coke and other gaseous soft drinks, and sometimes from sheer nervousness. When he suspected he would be offered effervescent beverages, he took the precaution of wearing his panty girdle, but then, of course, he tended to suffocate. It was always a choice of either vanity or comfort. He decided against mentioning the subject now: Charlie's belly was naturally protuberant.

"Do you suppose," he asked, "that any men really enjoy sex?"

Charlie got interested. "I'll tell you this, Georgie. In my years I've learned one thing: that you never know what's in the other fellow's mind or soul when it comes to that subject. I don't mean just that there are liars around: I mean that I think often enough a man doesn't really know *what* he feels. You know what you are *told* to feel. An anal orgasm is supposed to be a fantastic experience. You can read that in almost any issue of any men's magazine. And wasn't that the point of that sex manual we published last year?"

"I didn't read it."

"That was one of Myra's projects," said Charlie, who was secretary to Myra Turlish, another of the senior editors. "Something like thirty-five thousand letters came in, most of them from men, and most of them confessing they had never had an anal orgasm."

"Frankly, it doesn't surprise me," Cornell said. "I have never understood how it could appeal to anybody. And what do you suppose a woman gets out of it, when it comes to that?"

"Power," Charlie said. "Pure and simple."

"I can understand necking and petting," said Cornell.

Charlie persisted. "What more brutal and obvious assertion of power could you find? There you are, on your stomach, helpless, and they're riding you."

"Maybe if the facts were out, something could be done."

"What?"

"Well, therapy," Cornell said. "There must be lots of poor boys who don't know where to turn for help. That's sad." He went ahead and opened his belt before his swollen stomach burst it. He now had room for more beer or more anxiety, whichever was bloating him worse.

"The way you've been helped," Charlie said. He thrust his mug into the air between them. "Yeah, yeah, I know what you said: you might be worse. But that could be said of anything, right? I developed some back trouble a year ago, and the doctor strapped me in a support which didn't give me any relief but added more discomfort. 'Without it you'd be worse,' she said. After a while I threw the damn thing away, and the trouble eventually stopped by itself. Cost me a week's pay for nothing."

Cornell said solemnly: "I didn't have a choice when I first began my therapy, years ago. Either that or killing myself. And now it's gone on so long that I wouldn't know what to do without it. And Dr. Prine's better than the others I went to." He paused. "I think. She's tougher, but then that's supposed to be good, I think. She insists the whole thing about not being able to experience orgasm is self-indulgence."

"Yeah," said Charlie. "It gives you pain instead of pleasure. It's selfish and lazy to feel that way."

"Wait a minute, Charlie. It makes sense, you know. I mean, it's reality, isn't it? You can't change it, so you have to accept it. There's no other alternative."

"There used to be," said Charlie, tapping the envelope of pictures.

"You mean that deviate stuff."

"It wasn't perverse in those days." Charlie shook his head. "I don't know, Georgie, you've been thoroughly brainwashed. You've swallowed everything you've been told. You think that's the masculine role, to sit and wait and accept passively. You're a nice little boy, there's no getting away from that. But if you really were happy with that role, you wouldn't be spending your time at Dr. Prine's—and you wouldn't be a janitor."

"What would I be? Are you happy?"

"I thought we had already gone over that. Hell, no. But I survive. I accept my position, but I don't accept that it is right. That's the difference between us—or *a* difference anyway." He smiled stoically. "Another one is that I'm ugly and I'm old. And that's the one that really matters in the end, I guess."

Cornell suddenly felt desperate. "Charlie," he said, "what I'm about to tell you I've never told anyone before. Not even Dr. Prine. Maybe that's why I haven't made much progress in the therapy."

Charlie frowned and put his envelope of pictures back into the sofa-cushion cover. Cornell waited him out before resuming.

"I was eighteen at the time and just about to graduate from high school. I had my first big date. Oh, I was interested in girls, but they weren't interested in me. I didn't have the technique to attract them. Anyway, this one was a college girl, a couple years older than I."

Charlie drank elaborately, then honked into a handkerchief, peered into it, folded it another way, and returned it to the pocket of his corduroys.

"I was thrilled: not only my first date, but she was taking me to her Junior Prom, at one of the big hotels.

"So there I was, a skinny thing in my first evening gown, a pale-yellow satin number, strapless, and I had very little to hold it up with, so it was hooked so tight I could hardly breathe. She brought me a gardenia. I was a vision, I tell you, of something or other. My face was somewhat broken out already, and the condition got worse from nervousness, so I was plastered with makeup like a clown. Judith was so handsome in her white dinner jacket and maroon cummerbund. . . .

"We danced till early in the morning. She was a marvy dancer, and dancing was one of my few talents. Every now and again she would pull me off the floor and behind one of those potted palms in the ballroom and whip out a pint of port wine and we'd take a drink. By the end of the evening, we were both pretty tight. The things you'll do as a kid!"

"Yeah," said Charlie. "I used to juice a lot at that age." He thrust his sneakered feet out at angles.

"I had been too excited to eat all day," Cornell went on. "Hadn't had a bite since breakfast. And dancing cheek to cheek that way, well—" He was embarrassed and stared into his beer mug. "I got an—erection."

"Many a one I had in those days," Charlie confessed smugly.

"I began to get this pain," said Cornell. "It felt as if I had been kicked in the belly. I was so naive then I thought maybe I had appendicitis. I held out as long as I could, but finally told her I was sick and asked her to take me home to the high-school dormitory. She was plenty annoyed, and I was scared she would never date me again, but by then I could hardly stand straight. So she got her car—I forgot to mention she had a really neat white convertible—and she headed north onto the Hudson Sewer Highway—in the opposite direction from my dorm.

"I didn't know what she was up to, but I didn't want to be a wet blanket. Sitting down helped my condition, too. I wasn't in such agony any more. Well, you know those big concrete and steel ruins up at 168th Street? Old bridge pilings, or something?"

"Bridge to Jersey," Charlie came in authoritatively. "When there was a river there. It collapsed when I was a little kid. They made toy models of it—of the collapsed bridge. I had one. It fell without warning, I believe, during a windstorm. It was used as an overpass above the sewers. Quite a few people were killed."

He obviously wanted to dwell on this calamity, but Cornell pressed on.

"Judith had had even more wine than I, and she drove at a crazy speed, weaving all over the road. I don't know why she wasn't picked up. But suddenly she put on the brakes and swerved off the highway and in behind a big pile of rubble from that bridge. Mary! She was on me like an animal before the engine stopped turning over. I was a virgin, on my first date. I thought she had gone crazy. It was all so sudden that I didn't even resist at first.

"Then, pinning me down with one arm, she opened the glove compartment and took out this enormous dildo. I had never seen one before except in dirty pictures. I'll never forget the sight of that bludgeon in the light from the dashboard. It was the size of a policeman's nightstick."

Charlie shouted competitively: "That's what I *got* the first time! I was raped by a cop when I was thirteen! She used her club!"

"She began to strap it on over her tuxedo trousers. The hideous realization came over me of what it meant. I opened the door and tried to get away, but she grabbed me and pulled me back onto the seat. I screamed and howled, but she managed to turn me over and ripped my skirt to the waist and tore my panties off—"

"I fainted when I got it," Charlie cried. "I tell you—"

Cornell's voice fell away almost to a whisper.

"I can't remember precisely at what point something clicked in me. I was never an aggressive boy. I certainly don't think I could be called effeminate: I was terrible at sports, totally uncoordinated. In school I was good at sewing and cooking, things like that. I won a prize for my needlework. But when she touched me with that thing, it was like throwing a switch. I lost control of myself. It was as if I turned into another person. I twisted around. I grabbed that loathsome thing and ripped it off her. Now it was me who became animalistic. I tore her trousers off and her undershorts—"

Cornell gulped air. He had gone too far. He should not have begun this. After all, how well did he know Charlie? Charlie stared at him, conquered now, clutching his fat knees, his naked scalp pebbled with sweat.

"Go on," Charlie cried. "What happened, Georgie?"

Cornell covered his teeth with his lips. He kicked one shoe with the other.

"Who knows what would have happened had not a police car come prowling. That area was a well-known lovers' lane in those days, and muggers had been attacking the cars, robbing the women and raping the men."

Charlie rubbed his wet forehead.

"You mean they caught you?"

"I sat back and they went by."

"She didn't scream or anything?"

"No," Cornell said. "She pulled her clothes together and drove me to my dorm in utter silence. And she didn't report me afterwards. But I can tell you I stayed scared for a long time."

"What do you think you would have done?" Charlie asked in awe.

"I hate to think," said Cornell. "I don't want to talk about it further. I have probably said too much already." He squinted at Charlie. "I don't think there's any statute of limitations on attempted rape of a woman by a man."

"The other way around," said Charlie, "is only a misdemeanor, and then it has to be proved in a way that humiliates the guy." He looked at Cornell. Suddenly he showed embarrassment. "I'm sorry," he said. "I shouldn't have kept pouring the brew."

Cornell was annoyed at that. "I'm not drunk." Actually, he was, but he didn't like Charlie's easy assessment, again a form of disparagement. He rose from the chair, and noticed that it felt funnier to stand in women's clothes than to sit.

"I wonder if my dress is dry—dry enough to put on, anyway. I've stayed too long already."

Charlie maintained his queer expression.

"Georgie," he said. "About those pictures—I didn't mean to taunt you. How was I to know?" He pulled at his chin. "You always seemed so goddamned masculine to me. All the women at the office have got the hots for you, including old Eloise. I wondered why you didn't use that to do yourself some good. I just didn't understand."

It was one thing to confess a deviate act, but quite another to see the inference drawn from it—or, rather, not from the event, but from your own account of it.

Cornell scowled. "I was a kid, a virgin, and full of port wine. That's powerful stuff, Charlie. I mean, *you* have a couple of beers and you put on female clothing. I wonder what you'd do if you tried wine?"

Charlie's mouth fell. "Don't be catty, Georgie. You live in a glass house, after all. There's no harm in what I do."

"But it *is* against the law, isn't it?" Cornell asked, honing a hostile edge on his voice. "And so are your dirty pictures, and I'll bet if you ever revealed your fantasies you'd be up for castration."

Charlie was pricked.

"At least I'm no rapist!" he cried.

"And I'm no ex-whore!" said Cornell, tossing his head in the style he had learned from TV and movies for the expressing of indignation. But it felt strange in these clothes. He must get back into his own, and go home, put on his nightie and drink his warm milk and swallow his pill, and wake up tomorrow morning in reality again—in fact, as a janitor.

"Get out of my house!" shouted Charlie. "I don't have to take that sort of thing." He stamped his foot and looked as if he might burst into tears, revealing a petulant side of his nature that Cornell had never suspected. And he, Georgie Cornell, was supposedly the emotional cripple! He raised his eyebrows and flattened his mouth.

"You belong in the toilets!" Charlie added, his red, wet, corpulent face quivering with spite.

Cornell tore his purse from the knob, slammed the door, and

marched furiously down the stairs. Well, that was the end of his friendship with Charlie! He had been a fool to drink so much. Reaching the ground floor and the trash-strewn entrance hall, he felt as though he might throw up, but a man was just coming in from the street, a pretty young fellow hardly more than an adolescent, and Cornell's competitive feelings triumphed over his queasiness. His hand went from his mouth to his hair—*and he felt the female wig, looked down and saw the woman's brogues and the cuffs of the feminine trousers.*

"Excuse me?" asked the young man, fluttering his false eyelashes. "Were you looking for some company?" He was obviously a cheap little streetwalker who took Cornell for a woman.

"No!" Cornell said in a near-screech. He turned his head and left the building, walking rapidly, awkwardly, in the heavy shoes.

His clothes! But he simply could not face returning to Charlie's apartment at this moment. He should not have drunk so much, true; but Charlie had behaved very badly. What a fraud Charlie was. The corduroys and bald head, the cigar and dirty pictures, were but the stage properties for a childish fantasy. Tell him a real story of the worm turning and see him blanch. Charlie was pathetic, but it would take a while to forgive him. Other men were so self-indulgent.

Terror time: two women turned the corner and came his way. He held his breath and attempted a woman's walk: square-shouldered, no undue tension in the calves, a coarse, preoccupied expression, and hands swinging.

They went by without a glance. He had made it! In exultation he looked back. They had stopped. A lighter flared. One sucked on a pipe. The other looked at Cornell, who quickly turned away, too quickly, flipping his hips.

"Hey, don't I know you?" called the one without the pipe.

Cornell began to scurry.

"Hey!"

Easy, easy, Cornell told himself, *don't run. Play it smart.* It was the worst advice. He stopped, swiveled his head, and said: "Oh, hi."

Within a few moments he was arrested as a transvestite by this team of plainclotheswomen. As irony would have it, they were off duty, on their way home from the prizefights.

Sensible and responsible women do not want to vote. The relative positions to be assumed by man and woman in the working out of our civilization were assigned long ago by a higher intelligence than ours.

GROVER CLEVELAND, 1905

3

"IT WAS THE WALK," said Detective Elaine Stedman, as they took him to the precinct station.

"You're awful big for a woman, and then the walk," added Detective Carol Corelli, who was herself a big girl, five-foot six or seven, with the weight to go with it. Cornell was five nine. "If you're going to go in for these kind of things you ought to get the walk down pat."

"It's the first time I've worn this type of shoe," Cornell said ruefully. "They're so heavy." He tried to imitate the officers' long, flatfooted stride; not that it made any difference now.

"And for shit sake," Corelli said, in the same not unfriendly tone, "there was some small chance you might have got away with it if you hadn't been swinging a purse!"

"Oh, Mary!" said Cornell. "I forgot about that."

Corelli guffawed. Her arm was linked with Cornell's, and she jostled him.

Stedman was less jocular. "You pervs!" she said. "Maybe the doctors are right: you want to get caught, deep down."

Corelli agitated his arm again. "This is just a job for us. Don't get the idea we like it."

"You've certainly been decent," said Cornell. "Thank you for not handcuffing me."

Stedman said roughly: "We ain't doing you a favor. That's policy now. The public might think we was collaring a real woman. How would that look?"

Cornell's despair inhibited him from attempting to explain how he had come to this pass. And insofar as he had first put on the clothes voluntarily, he *was* a transvestite. If such practices were against the law, and they were, he deserved to be punished. He would surely do better to keep mute until he was formally charged, and perhaps even then as well, and at the trial throw himself on the court's mercy. He certainly could not implicate Charlie.

But he did not know how much torture he could endure. The police had a fearsome reputation.

At the station he was booked by a fat sergeant; his purse was emptied and the contents inventoried. He was given a receipt. Then he was fingerprinted.

"Here's another mistake," Cornell said, holding up one of Cornell's pink-painted nails. She shook her swarthy, pockmarked face.

Cornell grimaced helplessly.

He was told to wait on a wooden bench against a dirty wall. He sat down between a wino with a purple face and green teeth and a youthful offender who suffered from acne. The latter wore a black-leather jacket studded in chrome; the former, a vomit-stained ex-Army overcoat. Because of the wino's stench, Cornell moved closer to the youth, who promptly spoke to him.

"Hey, girlie, you wouldn't have a butt on you?"

"No, and I don't imagine we are allowed to smoke in here anyway," Cornell said primly, drawing his knees together.

"Mother's milk!" cried the youth, her sneer erecting her pimples. "You're a perv! Get away from me." She shoved him towards the wino and shouted at the desk sergeant: "I don't wanna share no cell with a perv. I got my rights."

The sergeant ignored this protest, but soon a uniformed officer came and took the juvenile through a door to the rear of the station.

"Knifed another kid," said the wino, in quite a reasonable voice despite her infamous appearance. "That type of punk ought to be locked up. Crime against the person. That's bad. What *you* do don't hurt nobody."

Strange where one found sympathy. Cornell smiled at the derelict, who showed some faint evidence of having once been a winsome woman; nor was she all that old. What was her story? But he knew better than to ask. He merely smiled at her.

"Don't get me wrong," the wino said. "You're disgusting. I just say you're harmless." And with that she passed out and fell towards him. He leaped up and gave her the rest of the bench.

"O.K., Georgie," Corelli said, coming to fetch him. "Let's have a little talk." She led him down a corridor and into a little interrogation room furnished with a plain wooden table and several chairs, on one of which Stedman was already seated, her jacket open and her holster showing.

No rubber hoses or thumbscrews were in evidence, and no spotlight to turn into one's eyes. Already Cornell had begun to understand that much of the legend about the police was exaggerated. These two detectives, for example. They were rather pleasant-looking women. Stedman might even be called handsome in a rugged sort of way. There was a glint of hardness in her hazel eye, but not, Cornell thought, anything like potential cruelty. And Corelli had a certain sweetness about her.

She put her hand on his wrist now, and said kindly: "Tell us about yourself, Georgie. Contrary to what you've probably heard, we really want to help people like you." She unbuttoned her rumpled suit jacket and her tight collar, and loosened the tie.

"Make yourself comfortable," she said, with an amiable wink. "It might turn *you* on to wear a tie, but I can't wait to get home at night and take mine off. Whoever invented that style for women ought to be sent up the river for life."

The reference to imprisonment was, however, chilling to Cornell.

"I don't suppose you would believe," he said quietly, "that this is the first time I've ever worn one."

Corelli moved her heavy shoulders. "It's no skin off my ass. Tell us about it."

But Stedman broke in coldly. "Are you a fag, Georgie?"

Cornell vigorously shook his head.

"Let me put it another way," Stedman said, her eyes stern. "Do you have, or have you ever had, intimate sex relations with another man? Now we want you to think about that for a while. There's a pretty wide range, see. What about when you were in school? Think back. Many guys engaged in a little mutual masturbation when they were that age. Nothing really criminal in that, but it's indicative, see."

"Never," said Cornell. "Absolutely never. I never even much liked other boys and men. I've had few friends."

"Never the friendly squeeze of a pecker? Come on, Georgie. It'll show up eventually anyway. Might as well get it over with."

"Nothing whatever," Cornell insisted. "I don't care how far back you look, you'll find I'm clean."

Stedman slammed her open hand on the table. "Well, you're not clean now, are you? You dirty little pervert!"

The loud report caused Cornell to hop in his chair. Corelli touched his wrist again.

"Calm down, honey," she said almost affectionately, and then to Stedman: "Elaine, maybe I should talk to Georgie alone for a while."

Stedman got up and pushed back the chair with her calves. "Don't take any shit, Carol. You're too easy on these slime." She left the room.

"Elaine's a little nervous," Corelli said. "The way I look at it, we hold all the cards. Once we bring somebody in, he don't have a prayer unless he cooperates. Most guys have sense enough to see that sooner or later." She sighed. "Me, I'm the patient type. I got all the time in the world." She chuckled. "You're the one with the problem. Not me."

"I certainly want to cooperate," said Cornell. "You caught me redhanded." He put his hand piously between his breasts. "I will just have to take my punishment like a man."

Corelli's smile broadened. "Bullshit," she said.

Cornell raised his eyebrows. "Excuse me?"

Corelli pulled her left earlobe. She still wore her felt hat, just as detectives did in the movies, and now she put one forefinger up and pushed it off her brow.

"Listen, Georgie," she said. "We know you're a sardine. We're after the big fish. One little secretary in drag ain't worth our pay. Get me? Where'd you pick up these threads?" She reached across the table and fingered the lapel of the sports jacket. "Better material than I can afford, even if I resell the apples I steal!" She guffawed and explained. "You'd go crazy in this job without a sense of humor."

Cornell had had no practice at deception. He extemporized desperately. "From a guy," he said. "A little dark guy in a plaid skirt and cardigan, a clothes-pusher I guess you could call him, hangs out on a corner near where I live."

Corelli had her notebook out and employed a pencil on it, but when Cornell looked he saw only what seemed to be aimless doodles.

Cornell sucked his lip. "I think his name is Artie."

Corelli finally took her hat off and laid it on the table. Her hair was cut to simulate the kind of pattern baldness natural to Charlie's head and revealed when his wig was off. This style had been fashionable three or four years before, during the administration of President Alice Womrath, along with baggy trousers and bow ties. Corelli wore the former, but her solid blue necktie was a four-in-hand.

She stared genially at Cornell.

"Georgie, I'm going to be fair with you. I'm not going to pull the cat-and-mouse act you probably expect if your idea of a police investigation is from TV. I don't care about 'Artie,' if there is such a person. I don't even care about those clothes." She widened her eyes. "No, I don't. That surprise you? Well, it's true. I can foresee a situation in which me and Stedman find we made a little mistake in pulling you in, so we take you to the door, pat your behind, and send you home."

Cornell did not quite believe what he heard, but allowed himself to feel some relief anyway, and in so doing was for the first time conscious of how scared he had been. He clasped his hands and relaxed his diaphragm, and at that moment of utter vulnerability, his face was slapped viciously by Corelli.

He yelped, and Corelli's hand came back the other way and got him again.

The detective leaned across the table, supporting herself on one fist, her fat, ugly face in his, and shouted.

"Or we might snip your balls off, fella!"

The door opened and in came Stedman, saying: "Take it easy, Carol."

Corelli pushed herself up and swaggered from the room.

Stedman told Cornell: "She works too hard."

Cornell realized that the detectives were playing on his emotions, being bad and good guys alternatively. He had heard of such techniques. His face smarted terribly. He refused to cry, but he did not know how long he could continue to protect Charlie.

Stedman was carrying a long sheet of paper, its end ragged as though it had been ripped from a machine. She held it up for Cornell's benefit.

"Just came in off the ticker," she said. "Let me tell you about yourself." She began smugly to read from the paper. "Born 2003 in Birth Facility 1097, Los Angeles, etcetera, etcetera. . . ." She skipped down several inches.

"Wait a minute," cried Cornell.

"Now *here* we are." Stedman punched the paper. "Apprehended shoplifting age 12; diagnosed, puberty problem; psychotherapy." She raised her head. "Actually, that is all in abbreviations, but I can read it as fast as if it was written out."

"I wasn't born in L.A. in 2003," Cornell said.

"You weren't?" Stedman frowned and rechecked the first line of the dossier. "The hell you weren't." She scowled at him. "You can't lie your way past the computer, buster."

"I was born in 2018, in Facility 1182, in Jersey City."

"The hell you were."

"Well, do I look forty-five?"

Stedman squinted at him, and then returned to the paper. "Then you were sent to Nursery 2305 in Birmingham."

"Not at all! It was Number 1111 in White Plains."

Stedman's face turned gross when she was puzzled. Her nose elongated and her lips protruded. Cornell wondered whether it might have been easier on him to confirm the erroneous data. The police were notoriously proud of their central information system, which listed every male person, from infant to dotard, in the country.

Stedman sneered at the paper, balled it, dropped it, and tried to kick it as it fell, but missed. She took a notebook from her pocket. "All right, give me the vital facts yourself, but don't try any funny business or the computer will show you up." She added earnestly: "The computer's O.K. It's the people who run it make the mistakes."

So they were not infallible!

Cornell repeated the information.

Stedman said: "Georgie, when we pick up a guy your age, we know one thing. It's not a simple case of transvest. A young kid, maybe, but not somebody old as you. You say you don't have a record. You say furthermore this is the first time you ever wore a jacket and trousers. O.K., I'll buy that. Surprise you?"

She wrinkled her forehead.

"I'll tell you what it means. It might mean you finally cracked after all these years. But I don't think so. You look pretty cool to me, no tears, no hysterics. Ninety-nine out of a hundred of them will break down when Corelli bats 'em around after her sympathy act. Not you. You make little jokes."

Stedman put her forearms on the table and lowered her head so that he could see along the part in her hair, all the way to the cowlick. She spoke to her hands.

"You want to know what we're going to make you for? Criminal conspiracy. Now if you want to confess to that right here and now, maybe we can talk business."

Cornell had crossed his legs in the wool trousers. His thighs now burned frightfully, and the heavy shoe on the hanging foot felt as though it contained an artificial foot.

He hardly recognized his own voice. "I don't understand that at all," he said.

"Don't ask me to explain," said Stedman. "I don't know what you people want. You got everything now. You get doors opened for you and never have to pick up a check." She grimaced, got a dirty toothpick from her pocket, and began to chew on it.

"Conspiracy?" asked Cornell. "Conspiracy for what?"

"Aw shit, Georgie," Stedman said, pushing back her chair. "You're in Men's Lib up to your titties."

Cornell covered his gaping mouth. Stedman leered, reached over, and grabbed at his groin. Involuntarily he seized her wrist, twisted it, and felt some diabolical pleasure as she howled and went sideways. He leaned across the table; his hand was large and powerful on her slender tube of bones. She cried out for Corelli.

Someone came in behind Cornell and brought a blunt instrument down upon his borrowed wig. His own hair, packed underneath, proved insufficient protection, and an explosion of ink obscured his brain.

When Cornell awoke, he found himself on a cot in a jail cell. His head did not hurt until he turned his neck to look about, and then it felt as if it belonged to someone else: not exactly painful, but unearthly. His probing fingers discovered that Charlie's wig was gone, and that beneath his own hair was a tender protuberance.

Another man lay in another cot to his left. To the right was a wall of concrete blocks; in back (oo! dizzy), a little ventilating grille, high up; ahead, an iron door. He turned his head with his hands and looked again at his cellmate, who wore a gray prison dress and felt slippers.

The man's eyes were open but fixed on the ceiling, in the center of which, flush with its surface, was a source of incandescent light.

Cornell said: "Are you awake?"

The man turned his head on the folded gray blanket that served as pillow and answered: "Hi, welcome aboard. I'm Harry." His hair was red, worn in pageboy style, and cut in bangs.

"Georgie Cornell."

"You don't look too good. You want to throw up or something?"

Cornell nodded. "Maybe."

Harry got up and found a tin bucket in the corner.

"Here," he said. He turned his back and plugged his ears. But Cornell's nausea failed to crest.

"False alarm," Cornell said, but Harry did not hear him. He pulled at the hem of Harry's dress.

"That's the effect of the shot," said Harry, sitting down on his own cot.

"I was hit in the head."

"But it's the shot that makes you sick to your stomach."

"Did I get one while I was unconscious?"

"Probably," Harry said. "They always give you one even if you're willing to talk. They never trust you."

Cornell raised his arms to look for punctures and saw the gray sleeves of his own prison uniform. Then he clutched the bucket and vomited into it.

Harry groaned. "You took me by surprise." He went to the other bucket in the corner below his bed. It was filled with water. He wet a towel in it and returned to Cornell.

"What kind of shot?" Cornell asked, after he had wiped his mouth. Then: "Ow! My head's thumping now. Could you give me another wet towel?"

"That's your only towel all week," said Harry. "And," pointing to the bucket, "that's our only water supply for the day."

Cornell fell back on the cot.

"Truth serum," said Harry. "Whatever you are hiding, they've already got it."

"That's a relief," Cornell said. But then he remembered it would mean poor Charlie's arrest as well. He closed his eyes.

"What's the charge, anyway?" Harry asked.

"I was wearing women's clothing." How embarrassing it was to say that! He forgot poor Charlie momentarily, and his head as well. He sat up and said quickly: "My first offense. It was just a little joke, sort of, and then I got into an argument with my friend and found myself in the street. I'm not a pervert."

Harry's voice was cynical. "That's what we all say, isn't it?"

Dizzy and ill as he was, Cornell felt resentment.

"Speak for yourself."

Harry said quietly, but intensely: "I'm up for the Big One."

Cornell shifted his supporting elbows and squinted to clear his eyes of pain. Harry was a small man, with delicate features. His complexion was pallid in the jailhouse light. Of course no makeup would be permitted here.

"Big one?" Cornell asked, wincing.

"Do you know anything bigger?" said Harry. "I raped a woman."

Cornell fell onto his back.

"But," Harry said, "I'm not going to give you any nonsense about being innocent. I did it all right, and I enjoyed every moment of it, and I would do it again."

Cornell listened to Harry's ugly laugh.

"You little pipsqueak," Harry said nastily. "Big radical you are, with your women's gear! Listen, this is not the first time I did it, either. It's the only time I was caught."

Cornell looked at the recessed light in the ceiling and weakly waved his hand.

"Please," he said. "Don't consider me as a competitor. I'm here as the result of a stupid mistake. I'm not a habitual criminal or a conspirator, radical, or any of those things. I'm a secretary for a publishing firm, and I got into this horrible mess by accident, and I feel like killing myself."

But Harry went smugly on. "It's the knife for me. Well, I can take it. I'll end up as a eunuch, but at least I know what it is to live like a man for a few years."

He was some sort of maniac. Cornell wanted to get him off the subject. He was frightened to be confined with such a person.

"If I got that shot you speak of," he said, "I betrayed my best friend."

This distracted Harry. He jeered. "Another flaming revolutionary, I bet. Parading around with his cane and spats and brier pipe."

"More or less," said Cornell in relief. "He's no more a menace to society than I am. He does that in his own home. He's not hurting anybody." He realized he was quoting poor Charlie. "I understand that what I did can't be tolerated, of course. I was picked up on a public sidewalk."

"You're talking to Harry the Rapist," Harry said cynically. "Don't come on with that holier-than-thou stuff." He lowered his voice but was even more brutal. "You've had your fantasies of fucking a girl."

Cornell recoiled. Talk all you wanted about how every man had a little perversion in his heart, it was appalling to meet a genuine practitioner.

"That is, of course," Harry added, his voice growing sinister, "unless you're a dirty little faggot." He rose and took a step towards Cornell's bunk.

Cornell sat up and balled his fists.

"Don't try it."

Harry grinned sardonically. "Pretty aggressive for a so-called normal boy, aren't you?"

"I'll defend myself," said Cornell.

Harry's grin changed to something less nasty. "You look like Gina Antonelli," he said, referring to the current boxing champion, whose name even Cornell recognized.

Cornell shamefacedly lowered his hands, remembering he had actually struck Charlie earlier that evening—if it was still evening. He began to suspect that Harry was only baiting him.

Harry now smiled and extended his small hand.

"I had to check you out," he said. "We guys have got to stick together." He pumped Cornell's forearm. "I'm not bisex. I go for girls only. I can't control myself when I see a pair of trousers."

He sat down on the cot, seemingly losing his earlier bravado. "I know they call it a crime, a sickness, but I've been that way all my life."

What could Cornell say? His head thumpingly reminded him of its damage.

"You know," Harry said sadly, "I don't know why they don't do it to us at birth."

"Do what?" asked Cornell, feeling his crown.

"Emasculation. Then they could do away with the prisons. It all comes from that, doesn't it?" Harry made two fingers represent a scissors. "Snip them off on the babies. Simple, huh?"

"Didn't they try that at one time in history?" Cornell asked. "It changes the metabolism or something, I think they said in school. They got a bunch of zombies." He was sorry he said that: it was going to happen to Harry, who was nicer now, and they did have to share the cell.

"Naw, that's not it."

"Well, you asked," Cornell said pettishly. He disliked the type of man who did that, a commonplace sort, actually: one of the reasons Cornell could not endure most other males.

"I'll tell you the reason," Harry said.

"Yes, you tell me." Funny how even a rapist would try to score off you in this way. Men!

"It would take the fun out of it for them."

"Fun?"

"They're sadists," said Harry. "All women. Take the balls off a man and he won't want to resist. The whole business of winning, conquering, requires a victim who is not defeated to begin with."

"It's easy to be paranoid," Cornell said helplessly, not unaware of the ludicrous banality of so addressing a violent criminal. But his head was really bothering him now.

"Do you mind," he asked, "if I drop off for a while? This is all very new to me. I guess I've lived a sheltered life."

"Listen, kid," said Harry, "you've got a chance to beat the rap. Why not take it? Do you owe it to those other guys to spend ten-to-twenty in stir?"

Cornell opened his eyes. "Others? There was only that one. Mary, I feel awful about him! But I couldn't help it, could I, if I got that shot?"

"How can you blame yourself? Nobody's responsible for what she says under sodium pentathol."

Harry got up and unfolded the blanket at the bottom of Cornell's cot. He drew it over his cellmate, with astonishing tenderness. "There's no hope for me," he said. "I was in it all by myself. But if I had a gang, I'd turn them in. I'd hate to do it, mind you, but ten-to-twenty's too much to pay for any loyalty. I'd turn state's evidence and make a deal. And any of them would do it too. You've got only one life."

He gently smoothed Cornell's forehead. "Go to sleep now. We'll figure something out."

He had turned into a sympathetic person. Imprisonment brought men together.

Cornell was awakened by a rattling on the iron door. Harry went to the slot and pulled in one gray plastic tray and then another. He brought Cornell's meal to him.

"What is this, dinner or lunch?" Cornell asked in a croaking voice.

"Breakfast."

Cornell gingerly swung himself to a sitting position.

"I slept all night?"

"If you don't believe me, feel your chin," said Harry.

Cornell had a medium-heavy beard, and he had not shaved since before going to Charlie's. His fingers felt quite a growth of emery paper.

"Better get that off right after breakfast," Harry warned him. "Inspection is held soon as they have taken back the trays. I've seen men put in solitary for a growth of whiskers you couldn't see with the naked eye."

"What do I shave with?"

Harry pulled from under his own cot a wooden box and took from it a battered electric razor, an extension cord, and a small mirror. He produced a screwdriver as well.

"We have to take the cover off the light," he said, pointing to the ceiling. "There's an outlet next to the lamp socket—it's illegal, and we have to screw the plug out and hide it before the weekly inspection. But that's the only way you can shave. They won't let you have blades and lather. And you have to be cleanshaven all the time."

Cornell breathed. "But that's unfair! How do they expect—"

"That's the way *they* are," said Harry. "You have no rights in here, and you get no decency. But you better get to work on your breakfast. We have only five minutes. Fortunately, the coffee is always ice-cold anyway."

One of the compartments in the tray held a plastic cup full of black liquid. No milk or sugar was in evidence. The edible portion of breakfast was literally a crust of stale bread, with nothing to spread upon it.

"If they catch you with a beard," said Harry, "it's solitary. There you get water and moldy bread. Whereas here we do get soup for lunch and a bowlful of stewed slop for dinner in which you sometimes find a shred of meat."

Cornell chewed the bread. He thought of something.

"I don't even know where we are, Harry. Is this still the police station?"

"It's the Rink."

"Where is that located?"

"You're kidding."

"I told you I've never been arrested before. I don't known any of the terms."

"The Men's House of Correction," Harry said. "Rockefeller Center, where else? This cellblock's called the Rink, don't ask me why." Harry wasn't eating; he sat there watching Cornell. "Another one of the blocks is called St. Pat's. Cons make up all kinds of names for things. When you first come in, you are put in the Rink to await arraignment. After that, they move you to another one to wait for the trial, St. Pat's or maybe the Rainbow Room—there's a name for you. That's got the worst reputation. It's the oldest part, used to be a subway tunnel. It didn't fall in like most of the others, so they used it for a jail."

"Are we underground here?"

"Oh, sure."

The door rattled again, and Harry seized Cornell's tray and his untouched own and handed them out the slot.

"Do we ever see any of the guards?" Cornell asked.

"Forget what I told you about shaving? Five minutes again."

Harry took the screwdriver and climbed onto his bunk. He was just tall enough to reach the ceiling receptacle. He unfastened two screws and handed them down to Cornell. Then he carefully removed the frosted glass in its metal frame and lowered that to his cellmate.

"Now give me the extension, and plug the razor into the other end."

The cord was still too short to permit Cornell to sit while he shaved. He stood, holding the mirror in one hand and the razor in the other. His hair was a disaster as a result of having been crammed under the wig and then slept on all night.

"Do they give you a hairbrush?" he asked, wincing from the pain of the ineffectual razor as it pulled at his whispers. "Ouch! And what about makeup? I'm going to be all blotchy after this."

"Think they care about your beauty?" Harry asked cruelly.

Cornell felt his chin: still very gritty. "Have you ever thought about the inconsistency, Harry? A man can't have a beard, but he is at the same time forbidden to show any baldness or to cut his hair short. It doesn't make sense, does it?"

It was a rhetorical expression, and by no means original, but Harry's silence struck Cornell as having somehow a positive charge. He turned the little mirror to catch Harry's face.

"You've already shaved?"

"While you were still snoozing," said Harry.

"You must show me the trick. You're not marked at all. I'm being torn up by this darn thing." The less it cut, the harder Cornell rubbed his cheeks and chin, so that he was sore and red and still unshaven.

"I don't have a heavy beard," said Harry, stooping to his box of treasures and finding a comb therein. He held it back over his shoulder.

"Oh, thanks." Despite the warnings, Cornell worried less about his beard than about his crowning glory. He let the razor dangle on its cord and started to work with the comb on the vulture's nest of his hair. The lump on his scalp was still sensitive.

"Well," Harry said, "if you're not worried, I am." He seized the razor and, supporting Cornell's chin in his left hand, began to shave him. He was gentle and deft, and Cornell was touched.

"I don't want to see you get in any more trouble," Harry said. "I'd like to see you beat the rap. I don't see how the cause is served if you stay in prison. If you don't care for yourself, think of the Movement."

"Harry!" Cornell said. "You're as bad as the detectives. Believe me, I wouldn't know how to join a conspiracy if I wanted to. That's against the law. For twenty-nine years I've been the most *legal* little boy imaginable. If I'm not halfway across the street when the RUN light comes on, I dash back where I came from. I don't really know what got into me last night. But I had a rough day. I got fired, you see, or rather demoted to a job that's worse in some ways than having none. And then I let myself be talked into having more beers than I could handle, and then into putting on those wretched clothes. But I guess I will get some consideration for its being my first offense, won't I?"

"They don't take transvest lightly, old boy," said Harry, holding the razor away and feeling Cornell's face. "It depends on how the judge feels that day, whether she had a good night's sleep and isn't dyspeptic, etcetera, etcetera. You could easily be up for the whole twenty unless she recommends mercy. You'll be in your fifties when you get out."

"Forty-nine," Cornell said quickly.

Harry shook his head. "That would be a terrible waste."

He suddenly handed the razor to Cornell. Almost immediately therafter the door clanked and squeaked open, and two uniformed women entered.

Harry stepped to the foot of his cot and stood at attention. Cornell let the razor dangle on its cord and followed Harry's example, standing rigidly between the bunks.

One officer felt Harry's chin. The other dropped a coin on his cot. It bounced off the taut blanket, and the officer caught it in her gauntlet. Then she turned to Cornell.

"Give me your number," she said.

"Number?"

She took off the leather gauntlet and struck him across the face with it.

"We make short work of your kind in here," she said. She ripped the extension cord from the overhead socket and the razor fell to the floor. Behind her, the other guard made an entry in a notebook. "Bed unmade, also." Another scribble in the book.

"I'm sorry," Cornell said, "but it's my first day and—"

She struck him again. He covered his face.

"For every demerit," she said, "your arraignment is delayed another week. You've got four demerits already."

Cornell put down his arms and asked desperately: "Where can I get a list of the rules? I don't want to break any more."

"Five," said the guard. "You just initiated a conversation with an officer, and that's a demerit." She was a large woman, very near his own size, with a crumpled nose full of broken veins. "Anything more to say?"

Now he knew better than to answer, and she said: "Refusing to respond to an officer's direct question," and the other guard wrote that down.

Cornell knew he must not panic. The officer brought her coarse face very close to his. He held his breath so as not to smell what he was sure was her foul exhalation. He tried to concentrate on the visor of her cap.

"We'll break you," she said with venom. "Never doubt that." Then she spat in his face and both officers left the cell.

Harry slumped his shoulders. "I told you they were rough," he said. "Actually, you got off easy. I've seen 'em kick the crotch out of a man for less. That means you still have a chance."

"For what?" asked Cornell, toweling the spit off his face. He had to be careful: it was the same towel with which he had wiped himself after vomiting.

"To turn state's evidence."

Now Cornell let himself panic.

"Maybe I'll just kill myself!" he said. "I've got *nothing* to tell. If they gave me the truth serum, they already know that, don't they?"

"It doesn't work with everybody," said Harry. "Certain systems resist it. That must be true with you, else you wouldn't be rotting away down here."

Cornell screamed: "But what if I have nothing to tell!"

"They'll never believe that, I can assure you."

Cornell sank to the edge of the cot. "Then maybe they didn't get Charlie's name out of me?"

"Charlie," said Harry. "Is he one of them? I knew a Charlie Willis, but he wouldn't be your man. He's already in prison. And I also knew a Charlie Seaton, but he wasn't any activist."

"Neither is Charlie Harrison! He's just another secretary. He keeps a wardrobe of women's clothes and has a collection of pornography." Cornell stamped his foot. "Why don't *you* believe me?"

"Don't get sore," said Harry. "I'm your cellmate. That's a closer relationship than any friendship on the outside. To survive we'll have to get along. I'm sorry I didn't have time to check you out on the rules. They aren't that complicated. You never address a guard unless you're asked a question. You must know your number. Prisoners are never referred to by name. Turn around. Your number is 33 45 93."

"It's on my back?"

"Stenciled," said Harry.

Cornell asked Harry to turn around. "You're 33 15 01." Funny he hadn't noticed that before.

"Have you been here long?" he asked Harry.

"Seven months, two weeks, and three days. I should be arraigned any day now."

"Arraigned?" Cornell cried. "That isn't even the trial, is it?"

"It certainly isn't," said Harry. "That's when you are charged with the crime. Don't even talk about the trial! It doesn't matter much anyway, frankly. The burden of proof is on us, and not the state. We're considered guilty as from the moment of arrest. And of course you *are* guilty, as you admit. The only way you can escape punishment, or at least get a lesser sentence than the one you richly deserve, is to make a deal, give them information —" He reacted to Cornell's threat to become hysterical, broke off, threw up his hands, and said: "But let me clue you in to the resources of this place."

Harry went to a vertical pipe that ran up the corner below Cornell's cot. "See this steampipe. This is our telegraph. The prisoners talk to one another this way, circulate news, even tell jokes. It won't take you long to get the hang of the code." He rapped it with his knuckles.

After a moment an answering tapping was heard.

"That's Gillie. He and Randy are right underneath us. That's the outside wall to your bunk; behind it is solid earth. On my side is a storage room, so the fellows below are our only contact."

"What are they in for?" asked Cornell. But Harry was listening to a message at the moment, the taps naturally meaning nothing to Cornell.

Harry said: "Lunch is potato soup. Their cell is above the kitchen. They can actually hear the talk down there, through their pipe, and they have cells on either side of them. They run a real message center. Last night some guys tried to break out of the Rainbow Room by tunneling through the walls. Lots of rotted concrete there, easy to get through but dangerous. The wall collapsed and dropped a couple tons of concrete on them. They should have known better. Nobody makes it out of here."

"I guess I should put the cover back on the light," Cornell said, not wishing to dwell any longer on the hopelessness of his situation. He stooped and pulled the box from under Harry's bed. He was looking for the screwdriver.

"I'll do that," Harry said sharply. Harry's hands were on his shoulders. Cornell almost went over backwards. Harry bent, plucked up the tool, and pushed the box out of sight.

Harry held the screwdriver like a weapon.

"You probably wonder why they don't take something like this away from me," he said, jabbing the air. "It could be used as a dagger or a lockpick. That just shows how confident they are that this place is escape-proof. And even if you got out, which is impossible, they'd pick you up immediately. Where would you turn for help? Their informers are everywhere."

He climbed onto the cot and replaced the lamp cover.

To have shaved himself Harry would have had to go through this business with the light—cover off and cover replaced—operating the buzzing razor in between, all without awakening Cornell. That was hardly possible.

Harry had not, however, shaved earlier that morning. He had in fact never shaved in his life. A faint growth of pale hair showed on his upper lip and the angles of his jaw were covered with a dusty golden down.

Cornell was embarrassed by these observations. He certainly had no intention of discussing them with Harry at this point. He had no one else to depend on.

So he said: "Seven months! How do you stand it?"

Harry put the screwdriver away. "By *not* thinking of the worst to come," he said. He grinned strangely—at what, the anticipated castration? "By thinking instead of the satisfaction I got when I screwed that woman."

Cornell felt repulsion again.

Harry went on: "I was her maid, see? I cleaned her kitchen and I cleaned her toilet, and I even did her laundry." He had neat little white teeth. Through them he now said: "But I fucked her, man. One day when she was bawling me out as she did all the time: not enough starch in the collars . . ." He punched his hands together, reliving this degradation. "She'd throw her tampons in the john bowl, and I'd have to unclog it. You'd think, wouldn't you, with all the marvels of modern science, they'd do something about menstruation!"

With this complaint it seemed to Cornell that Harry had passed from the personal to the social, but his cellmate's rage now took on a special tone.

"Menstruation makes no sense at all. It should be abolished! But chemically: a pill or powder. Lots of women are afraid of the knife. Why should you—they—have to undergo a hysterectomy? Fucking scientists! You can be sure they take care of themselves, but they won't let the secret out."

Cornell cleared his throat. "Well, that's one advantage we have over women." Harry stared at him briefly in what he could have sworn was hatred. Cornell did not understand him at all.

"Gee," Cornell said. "I wouldn't think their troubles would worry you."

Harry's eyes cleared. "Yeah," he said roughly. "They can all bleed to death." He went to the water bucket and drank from the dipper.

Cornell was reminded that he had not peed in ever so long. Part of the pain in his lower belly, for which he had blamed anxiety and dread exclusively, was no doubt due to this.

"Uh, Harry," he said, "I guess we must do our business in this other bucket?"

"That or in the ventilating duct," Harry said coarsely, pointing to the grille high on the wall. He stood there grinning while Cornell pulled up his skirts.

"Could you turn your head, please?" Cornell requested. Someone had undressed him thoroughly: his blue bikini underpants and his pantyhose were gone, and in their stead he wore ugly bloomers in white cotton, and no stockings.

"You'll have to get over that false modesty," said Harry, but he reluctantly turned away.

The rim of the bucket, especially at the two points where the metal came up in arches to secure each end of the wire handle, was painful to the biscuit—the old childhood name for the bottom, which came back to Cornell, who had not pulled down panties of this sort since he had been in the primary grades.

He really did not feel all that better when he finished.

"What happens here if you get sick?" he asked.

"You die," said Harry, turning back to watch the bloomers rise again.

"You know," Cornell said, letting the shapeless skirt fall into position, "I don't know if it is right to treat people this way, even criminals. I mean, take me. I make one mistake, and here I am. Now, it seems to me that some people who were inclined to crime would think, well, I'm going to be horribly punished for the most minor of things, so I might as well do something really bad. If I'm caught, what difference would it make?"

"You're thinking like a man," said Harry. "What do women care about such distinctions? They've got the power, and they're going to use it as they see fit. Besides, they wouldn't agree that it is a minor crime for a man to pose as a woman. That's theft, isn't it? You're stealing what belongs to them, and what is worth more than sexual identity?"

"*Personal* identity," Cornell said with some vigor. "I like to believe that I'm Georgie Cornell first, and second a man—or second, an American, and third, a man. I think sometimes this sexual matter is carried too far. You have to eat and sleep whether you are man or woman, and if you are cut, you will bleed—"

Harry was shaking his head and slowly waving his hand.

"That's just playing with words, Georgie, and you know it. You've always been a cipher, only now you've been moved into another column. You're a zero in the statistic on how many perverts have been arrested this week, month, year." He was sitting on his cot, and he slapped his knee. "Look, men are bigger on the average than women. Women dominate them by moral, intellectual, and psychological means. That couldn't be done if it were a matter of sheer physical strength. You were a head taller than either of those detectives."

"But one had a blackjack and struck me from behind!" Cornell protested in an impulse of pride, which he regretted an instant later: he was boasting about his effeminate streak of brutality. "I was foolish to resist at all, though," he added. "But I just saw red when I was slapped. I've always been like that. I remember in school when another boy slapped me I'd scratch his face and pull his hair." Something was wrong with this memory. He found it and blushed: actually, he would punch his tormentor, balling his fist like a girl.

"Women," said Harry, perhaps fortunately paying no attention to Cornell's embarrassment, "are more intelligent than men, but less emotional. They have to run the world; they do not have the time to squander on personality. They must deal with things, with issues, and with people as things and issues. How could the President, for example, cope with international problems if she were personally vulnerable to every little slight, real or imagined? You must admit, if you are honest, that the fundamental concern of a man is his own vanity." Harry smiled. "Now, of course, that, or rather what comes from it, can be charming, so charming, in fact, that it can even lure certain women from the stern path of duty—"

Cornell frowned. "I've never managed that," he said. "I've read about it in novels or seen it in pictures, but in life I can't recall distracting a woman for more than fifteen minutes. Or maybe I've always met the wrong ones. Raving egomaniacs, most of them. You listen to them talk about their work and politics and sports and their bank accounts and their fascinating friends —whom, by the way, you never meet, any more than you get access to their bank accounts—and then you try to talk about what interests you or even about your troubles, I mean, you can be in the most distress, and what do they do? Listen? No, they begin to paw you."

He restrained himself. He was getting too bitter.

"Women, Harry," he said, "are by nature very selfish people."

For some reason Harry's genial smile broadened into almost a laugh. Then he quickly straightened his mouth to say: "Well, I'm just acting as devil's advocate here. We should know our enemy—that's my motto."

"Enemy?" asked Cornell. "That's a bit strong, isn't it? They certainly can be painful, but then so can one's fellow men. One thing can't be said of most women: they're not spiteful or back-biting. And then if you think of it, what's the alternative? What kind of world would it be if men ran it? Mary!"

Harry squinted at him. "You're talking treason to the cause, now, aren't you? Isn't that what your bunch wants? 'Power to the men!' " He balled and raised his little fist.

Cornell said quietly: "There you go again, Harry. You're doing it again. I'm just not going to argue any more. If you insist on calling me a male-liberation revolutionary, in spite of my protestations to the contrary, what can I do? It's impossible to prove you're *not* something. I just hope the court is not as stubborn as you."

Harry smiled again. "Sorry," he said. "It's just that you don't seem all that upset by the accusation."

"I try to control my emotions," said Cornell. "I used to get hysterical a lot when I was younger, but that sort of thing ages you rapidly. I'm going to be thirty soon. I have to get some dignity to replace my lost youth."

He stared at Harry. "One of those detectives you mentioned said I was a cool customer. . . . How did you know I was a head taller than either of them?"

"Huh?"

"You mentioned the detectives."

"Oh. Well, they brought you in here last night, didn't they?"

"I was unconscious."

"Yeah, and they took off your clothes and put you in the uniform. They looked like rough customers. I pretended to be asleep."

"Did you see them give me the truth-serum shot?"

"I imagine you got that at the precinct station."

"Was I talking when they brought me in here?"

Harry shrugged. "Well, yeah. I heard the name 'Charlie,' to be honest."

"Oh, Mary."

"You couldn't help it," Harry said sympathetically. "You probably named the others, too."

"Poor Charlie," Cornell groaned. "I wish I could be sure, though. There are lots of Charlies."

"Charlie Harrison. He works at your company," Harry said.

"I just told you that."

"You said it last night, too," Harry replied quickly. "I was just confirming it when I asked you before. I was hoping you gave them the wrong name. My heart really fell when I heard you confirm it now."

"You think he's been picked up?"

"It's simple to find out," said Harry and went to the steam-pipe and tapped at some length. Then he listened to the brief reply. He shook his head in admiration.

"Those fellows know more about this jail than the superintendent, I'll bet."

"Well?"

"Oh, sure," said Harry. "Charlie's in a cell near them."

Cornell lowered his head to his knees. He had not wanted certainty. He had asked for it in that hypocrisy by which one hopes to delude fate.

"Life has been pretty rotten to him," he said to his lap. "He was once a streetwalker."

"That's only a misdemeanor," Harry said in an automatic, official kind of voice.

[The female hyena] is dominant over the male. . . . She is larger, stronger, takes leadership. And as if to emphasise the irregularity she has through natural selection developed false testicles, masses of fat; and her attenuated clitoris hangs down in excellent imitation of a penis.

ROBERT ARDREY, 1972

4

CORNELL COULD NOT get to sleep. The narrow cot, the thin mattress, the sour odor of the blanket, the memory of the greasy mess of the third feeding, were scarcely conducive to rest, nor was his recurrent guilt about Charlie. But he was kept awake by thoughts of Harry.

As Cornell had prepared for bed—a splash of cold water on the face, a wetted finger for a toothbrush—Harry as usual did nothing about himself. Harry did not visibly wash and yet looked clean; had not eaten all day and yet seemed healthy; had been generous, warm, tender—and aggressive, cold, hostile. He was a mercurial type. You never knew where you stood with him.

The cell had got chilly and damp, or perhaps it had always been like that and Cornell took notice only when he was faced with the period of compulsory repose. After the trays from the final serving had been handed out through the slot, Harry informed him that the light would shortly be extinguished and the cell kept dark for seven hours.

Cornell shivered, went to the steampipe and felt it: dead-cold iron.

Harry spoke sharply: "What are you doing?"

"It's cold in here."

"Let that pipe alone," said Harry. "Gillie and Randy will think it's a message."

"I just felt it," Cornell said. "I didn't tap."

"Just get away from there."

Cornell's hand went to his hip. "Listen here—" He did not

intend to take orders from a rapist. But then his basic reason overcame his pride. It made no sense for them to be at each other's throats within this narrow enclosure. He dropped his hand and smiled.

But Harry leaped across the cell and seized the bosom of Cornell's dress.

"Don't you ever talk to me in that tone," Harry cried. "You little punk!" Though he was considerably shorter than Cornell, he pulled Cornell in close, then thrust him away.

Amazingly enough, this attack did not threaten Cornell's control. He astonished himself by going limp. He was operating on some sort of instinct.

"When I tell you something I don't want any lip," Harry said furiously. He pulled Cornell in again, nose below his cellmate's chin. "Get that and get it good, buster."

"Yes, ma'am." Having blurted this unthinkingly, Cornell remembered the source of his instinct: years before, he had had a teacher who handled him similarly.

Harry roared: "You fresh punk." He brought up his knee and drove it at Cornell's groin, but owing to the difference in their heights, he struck too low—a miscalculation the teacher had never made, nor for that matter Dr. Prine, who often employed this technique in her therapy.

Still being politic, however, Cornell pretended he had been damaged, howled, clutched his midsection, fell onto the cot, and wept. The light went out shortly thereafter.

Eventually Cornell straightened out, pulled up the blanket, pulled it down again slightly after he smelled the leading edge, and lay there looking into blackness. Harry remained silent. Cornell considered apologizing. He had had no ulterior purpose in addressing Harry as a woman. Pure accident. *Violent* and *female* were complimentary adjectives, as even Harry would admit. In blunt-instrument and knife murders, *cherchez la femme* was the investigatory principle. Yet as Harry had pointed out, *they* were smaller than we—though not than Harry himself, who was only five-four or five. He must have raped a tiny woman. He was undoubtedly helped by surprise. Perhaps he had been armed. He did not seem terribly strong, could never have pushed Cornell around that way without cooperation. Which was another reason for Cornell's failure to fight back: he had not felt seriously threatened.

Cornell frowned, and was conscious of the lump on his head: diminished, less sore now, but still tender. Corelli had been strong enough to give him that, but a blackjack would be effective in the fist of a child.

Harry was still quiet. You couldn't even hear his breathing. Should Cornell apologize? It would be awfully uncomfortable if they stayed on the outs, with only nine feet square between them. But then it really wasn't fair if Harry considered himself the injured party. He didn't own that steampipe. Pervert! Cornell stuck out his tongue in the dark. The blanket had ridden up again and he got a very unpleasant sensation as he tasted the wool.

Poor Charlie was now in jail too. What must he think of Cornell? Perhaps Harry could send a message through the steampipe explaining the seeming betrayal. Else Charlie might think it the issue of spite. No man could be blamed for what he said under truth serum. However, Cornell was relieved that he had not been tortured into making the revelation. That would have led to the same end, and he would have suffered considerable pain on the way. He abhorred pain. That's what he so hated about sexual intercourse: it hurt.

"Hyperaesthesia is a symptom of your sickness," Dr. Prine had told him.

"But it hurts!"

"You only *think* it hurts,'' the good doctor would say.

"But if I think it does, what's the difference?"

"Georgie, Georgie . . ." Then she would proceed to hurt him.

Cornell had lost his virginity at eighteen. In his last year of secondary school he had majored in art appreciation. His term paper in the senior year dealt with the meaning of that enigmatic simper on the face of Leonarda's Mono Liso. "Leonarda was a Lesbian," wisecracked Jimmie Wilhelm, a smart-alecky classmate. "That made Mono laugh." But Cornell had been very solemn about it, humorless adolescent that he then was. He remembered writing: "Leonarda was undoubtedly madly in love with Signor Liso, but he was promised to another. Mono, however, was touched by the devotion of the great painter, and his smile is one that endeavors to apply the unctuousness of pity." The teacher struck out the misused word and red-penciled "unction" in the margin. She gave him a B-plus for the paper, the highest grade he had ever gained.

For a while thereafter Cornell had worn his hair in the style of Mono Liso's and daydreamed of breaking the heart of some great painter. With this vague project in mind, he had on graduation listed himself with the Employment Facility as seeking "work in art on the administrative side," and as luck would have it, a midtown gallery needed a boy to do clerical work. Cornell applied and was hired. At the end of the first week, he repelled an attempt at rape by the gallery owner, a husky, hairy Greek-American named Basilica Dondis, who had made a fortune in shipping and retired from commerce at fifty to indulge her love of beauty by a tax-deductible means.

She fired Cornell forthwith. Weeping, he adjusted his dress and left the gallery, running, literally and figuratively, into the outstretched arms of Pauline Witkovsky, arriving to hang her current show of epic battle scenes. Witkovsky was at this point in her career toeing the threshold of fame—this was to be the show, indeed, that established hers as one of the essential names on any roster of contemporary pictorial greatness.

To naive Cornell, however, product of an art-appreciation course that had only just reached Thomasina Gainsborough by the end of term, Witkovsky looked a pudgy nonentity in turtle-neck and paint-stained jeans.

"Hey, wait a minoot," she said, thrusting him back for inspection. "You look like a nice piece of cooze. How'd you like to be fucked by a famous artist?"

Cornell made himself rigid. "I'll scream if you don't let me go!"

"Bullshit," she said, breathing garlic at him. "Half my show is sold out before the opening."

He went limp. "You're not Pauline Witkovsky?"

She released him. "Just got the word," she said. "*Time*'s review will be a rave."

Cornell gasped in admiration, hand going to his hair, which he knew must be disheveled from Basilica Dondis' pawing.

"I'm Georgie Cornell," he said. "I consider it a privilege to meet you, Miss Witkovsky."

Witkovsky goosed him. "You call me, kid, when you get hard up. I like your obsequious style. I'm in the book. If I ain't too busy, you come to my studio and I'll throw a fuck at you." She swaggered into the gallery.

Cornell had no success in finding another job in art. Perhaps Dondis had blacklisted him with the other galleries, or perhaps there were merely no openings. Those to which he applied were already staffed with one or more youths of his age but of another order of sophistication, as he could see by their languid bodies and charred eyes. He also went around to the newly organized Municipal Museum, to form which the old Metropolitan, Modern, Guggenheim, Whitney, Frick and eleven other degenerating institutions had been combined, the fat trimmed from the assembled collections (the forgeries discarded, the second-rate daubs, as determined by the new school of multum-in-parvo criticism, destroyed; the stolen works returned to their rightful owners or the heirs thereof), and the remaining twenty-five pictures and six sculptures displayed in the new facility, those tunnels of the old Columba Circle subway station which had not fallen in during the general collapse circa A.D. 2050.

The guard collected the ten-dollar entrance fee and laughed in Cornell's face when asked directions to the personnel office.

"We only hire three people, and the waiting list is two years old."

Cornell turned to leave, and the guard said: "Don't you want to see the stuff? We don't make refunds."

So he went on in, the guard, having bolted the door, following him with her shotgun. When she was satisfied that he was neither thief nor vandal, she took the weapon from his back and used it as a pointer.

"Nobody but nobody understood paint like old Carmen," she said, pressing the twin muzzles against a canvas labeled, with ball pen on a three-by-five index card Scotch-taped to the cracked wall, "Philippa IV—Carmen Velasquez."

"Fabulous," said Cornell. "Too bad it's damaged." There was a rent in the mouth of the depicted face.

"Whatchuh gonna do?" asked the guard. "Hooligans get in somehow, no matter how close you watch. They punched a hole there and put a cigar in it." She shook her capped head. "Young girls with too much time on their hands, poolroom toughs, car-strippers. Hold up candy stores, mug old people, rip paintings. Oughta put 'em in the army. It straightened *me* out years ago, I'll tell you that."

At the end of one corridor that was blocked by debris, Cornell suddenly felt the guard's hand on his buttock. They were alone in the museum. He had to use all his diplomacy, make a date for after closing time, indeed, to get out intact. There seemed to be a surfeit of dirty old women in the art world.

Not that Pauline Witkovsky was clean, mind you, but at least she was under thirty-five. He boldly decided to call her, found the number in the book, but chickened out several times in the phone booth, losing a series of zinc dollars in one of those installations that, like the museum, gave no refunds. Finally, with his last coin, he took the plunge.

Witkovsky answered on the first ring.

"Fuck you," she said. "Whoever you are."

He gave his name.

"Have I fucked you?" Witkovsky asked.

Cornell explained how and where they had met.

"Listen kid," Witkovsky said in her raspy voice, "I wouldn't remember you if I *had* fucked you. So you better get your ass over here."

. . . Cornell's reminiscence, in the darkness of the cell, was disturbed by an odd event. He heard Harry get up and walk across to his cot; he felt him look down, heard him say softly: "Georgie?"

Undoubtedly he wanted to apologize for his earlier performance, but now Cornell saw nothing to be gained from quick forgiveness. Let him wait a little—a spiteful decision, maybe, but Harry must understand that moodiness was no excuse for bad manners. Cornell remained silent in voice, but breathed audibly, regularly, as if in slumber.

Harry did not ask again. After a long moment his slippers were heard gliding away. He was next at the cell door, scratching thereupon. The bolts were soon thrown; the hinges faintly squealed; light entered and was corrupted by Harry's exiting shadow; the door clunked shut.

Harry had left the cell.

This event was so extraordinary that Cornell was immediately discouraged from making any effort at all to explain it. He was stunned in the present, and escaped to the past. . . . The phone book listed Witkovsky's address as Chase Manhattan Plaza, a long walk from the fleabag men's residence where Cornell was then living, at 70th and Fifth.

Harry had left the cell? That made no sense. Cornell called his name, rose, and felt the other bunk. It had been no illusion.

The man was gone. He groped around in the dark, found a pail, and peed in it. Too late he remembered that he had forgotten to ascertain whether it was the slop bucket or the one with the drinking water. In the grip of that horror he was of course desperately thirsty. He crawled about the concrete floor on his knees. No, there was the other bucket, the dipper handle protruding. He gulped some metallic-tasting liquid, which in the chill of the cell was yet tepid. The combination made his teeth chatter.

He returned to bed and cocooned himself in the blanket. He hated suspense. In detective novels he turned to the last chapter just after reading the first. He also disliked analysis, and was embarrassed by anything that could not be translated into instant emotion.

—Chase Manhattan Plaza had turned out to be a huge rubbish heap among the ruins of several buildings that had once been made chiefly of glass, judging from the greenish chunks in the rubble and the gritty powder underfoot. His pumps were covered with it. Witkovsky must have given this address in jest. There was no possible place here for a studio. Nevertheless, Cornell had tramped about, virtually ruining his last pair of shoes and snagging his stockings on the rusty edge of a fallen girder.

At last he reached a concrete parapet, giving onto some sort of dry well which the rubble had filled to within ten feet of the brim. He flapped his hankie to clear the dust from a fanny-spaced portion of the parapet and sat down. Scarcely had this happened when he heard, from behind him, a vile obscenity, though rather cutely pronounced. He turned and saw Witkovsky at the top of a ladder rising from the filled well.

She wore an unspeakable coverall, splashed with paint, torn out at the elbows, unbuttoned at the fly.

"Shithead! You're trespassing." Her face was smudged with filth. She could have been a member of the company of derelicts who had harassed Cornell on the route down when he had strayed into the Skid Row of midtown Park Avenue and been cursed, kicked, and spat upon for his error.

"Miss Witkovsky, I met you outside the Dondis Gallery. . . ." He went through it again.

Witkovsky's indignation became sullenness.

"I don't sell pictures behind my dealer's back," she said. "I never allow the public into my studio. I have contempt for people who think me a genius, and I ignore everyone else."

She went down the ladder. Cornell looked over the parapet and saw what he had not seen on the earlier cursory glance: that the mound of rubble sloped away on one side and that the walls of the well were glass, or apparently once had been such, with some panes remaining and others replaced with plywood sheets. He watched Witkovsky slide one of the latter aside and admit herself to whatever subterranean space lay beyond.

Now, in those days, Cornell still possessed some spirit. Furthermore, he was desperate. He had been terribly lucky to find the job at Dondis' so soon, and terribly stupid to give it up so irresponsibly; he understood that now. At this point he would have surrendered his virginity to anybody who would have taken it.

He thought otherwise a quarter-hour later, after he had shamelessly gone down the ladder and into Witkovsky's studio, explained his plight to the eccentric artist, been thrown onto a foam-rubber mattress and brutally penetrated with a massive dildo.

Once she had had him, however, Witkovsky showed her gentler side, for behind that hard shell she was not the world's worst gal.

"Artists have to be tough," she told him, "to survive in a commercial culture. And if the Philistines ain't bad enough, your so-called admirers will eat you up to feed their own squalid little egos." She put some Vaseline on his bruised parts and then dusted the area with Mexican Heat Powder. She patted his right ham. "Don't take it so hard, kid. You would have lost it sooner or later anyway, and at least I'm a celebrity. A pimp might of grabbed you and sold you to a series of slobbering old women, pocketed most of your earnings, and kicked your ass out when you lost your looks."

She helped him to his feet and pushed him towards a door. "Go in the toilet now and fix your face."

He looked at himself in the bathroom mirror and murmured: "So that's making love." The tears had made his eyeliner run down in two black lines. What a boy must do to survive!

When he came out, Witkovsky asked: "Want a bite? I forget about eating when I work."

Her kitchen had been improvised at one end of the large but low-ceilinged and dark room. At the other end a big canvas was spread upon the concete floor, with tubes of paint and brushes scattered nearby, the area illuminated by floodlights on tripods.

While she went to a little half-refrigerator and took out packages of frozen provender, Cornell looked at the work in progress on the floor. It seemed to him a magnificent beginning, already populated with a host of brawny women assaulting male nudes against a backdrop of classical architecture, columns, arches, and the like. On the horizon, not yet reached by pigment, were charcoal outlines of hills: seven, by his count. He tried to remember from his art-appreciation courses the principles by which one judged a picture. Color. Yes, the flesh tones, always very important, glowed. Perspective. This seemed very accurate, from the prominent figures in the foreground to the much smaller hills in the distance. Moral significance. . . .

He called: "Miss Witkovsky, I'm admiring your new painting. Am I right in thinking it concerns ancient Rome?"

Witkovsky shouted back: "You can call me Pauline, for Mary's sake!" She slammed a pot down on a two-burner electric hotplate. "Shit, food bores me. I wish you could live on pills." She tore open a frozen-food container and dumped the solid rectangle of its contents into the pot.

Cornell went back to the kitchen area.

"Here," said he, "let me." He reached for the spoon she held.

"You?" asked Pauline. "With that face and body, you're also a cook?"

"My minor was home-ec," said Cornell. He looked into the battered vessel and saw a glutinous-looking mess of melting succotash.

Pauline cocked her head and smiled at him with her yellowed teeth. "Hmm." She patted his rump. "I could use somebody like you around here." She patted him again. "How's the old heinie now?"

He smiled back. "Better. I guess one gets used to it in time."

"First is always worst," Pauline said. "You're a cute kid." She kissed his cheek. "What'd you say your name was?"

"Georgie."

"Well, Georgie, so you like the picture? It's *The Rape of the Sabine Men.*"

The next day Cornell got his suitcase from the residence and moved into Pauline's studio. He never got to like sex any better, but fortunately Pauline was not as erotic as she had pretended to be at the outset, especially when working on a major canvas. Her typical day began with a glass of lemon juice and hot water, to open up her bowels, and then she settled down to hour after hour of pigment and brush.

In the midafternoon he would prepare a sandwich on which he took some trouble—perhaps chopped egg mixture with piccalilli, slice of tomato, on wholewheat toast—put the paper plate and the cup of tea beside her on the floor, and steal quietly away to his kitchen corner, where he was already at work on dinner, which he generally made an elaborate affair. Always a first course, often soup as well, homemade, none of your tinned stuff, followed by a good solid roast or hearty casserole—he had persuaded Pauline to buy a little electric oven, and he worked wonders with it. Finally, a real dessert, fresh fruit and thick cream, or chocolate mousse, never the packaged puddings and frozen strudels Pauline had formerly eaten. They were both putting on weight.

Dinner was served on an enameled steel table which he had cleared of the tubes of paints, palette knives, and turpentine rags, which he spread with the lime-green linen mats Pauline had let him buy. There were napkins to match, decent china plates of a simple conservative design, and the cutlery he kept polished. The center bowl of paper flowers, flanked by tall candles, completed the scene, an island of graciousness and serenity amid the stormy chaos of a working artist's studio.

Those were the golden days. They both labored from morn till night. He kept the kitchen and bathroom spotless, and there was always some mending to be done for Pauline, who was typically rough on clothes, or laundry, or checkbooks to balance, bills to be paid. Her accounts had been in quite a mess when he moved in. The true artist, she was indifferent to such matters, and to all else, really. At first he would be hurt when after a hard day's painting she sat down at his lovely table and fed like an animal, spitting onto the floor fragments of foods she did not recognize or like, conversing in grunts, even belching vilely if the need arose.

But as he persisted, she began to change, to notice the dishes with some particularity, even to savor his cuisine. She went so far as to develop an appetite for certain favorites: tarragon chicken, breast of veal stuffed with a forcemeat of sausage, authentic Irish lamb stew.

"I'll still take a broiled steak and baked potato," said she, wiping her mouth with the napkin now and not the tail of her blue work-shirt. "But there's something to be said for this fancy-ass bellyfiller."

Pauline had dropped out of high school in her final year and hit the road. She pumped gas for a while in Juneau, Alaska; was on the bum in Flagstaff, Arizona; joined a work gang resurfacing an asphalt road near Davenport, Iowa; and discovered her pictorial talent only when the other itinerant laborers in the Kansas bunkhouse admired her random sketches on the bunkhouse wall: luscious seminudes, men with one thigh bared or in bulging lace undies.

"A bunch of us used to go into town at night," she reminisced. "Drink and fight in taverns." She put her neck at an angle and asked Cornell to find the scar, a thin white tracing just behind her dirty ear. "That was a Hell's Angel switchblade. I got her in the guts with a broken beer mug. Like butchering a sow, I tell you! I don't know if she made it. I blew town. I bet the sheriff's still lookin' for me."

Cornell loved these stories of a life so far beyond his purview. Until now he had been a sheltered schoolboy.

Later Pauline took a sketch course at the YMCA in Wilkes-Barre, Pa., where daytimes she worked as mechanic in a garage and body shop. . . .

—Again Cornell's recollections were interrupted by the opening of the cell door. Harry had returned. His slippers could be heard moving to the other cot, which then creaked under the weight of a descending body.

Strange, strange it was, but Cornell did not dare to speak. It was none of his business. If explanation there was, Harry would no doubt give it next morning. And Cornell had better get to sleep without further nostalgia for the happy time of old—which anyway had ended unpleasantly: the halcyon days had come to an abrupt end when Pauline finished the Sabine picture. She went out to deliver it to Dondis and returned stinking drunk with a little redhead in tow. When Cornell protested, Pauline showed him the door. He was too proud ever to go back.

He was philosophical now about the affair. Artists were all like that, no doubt. And no doubt they should be permitted their delinquencies. In later years other women had been quite as cruel to him without the justification of creativity: Alice, who beat him more than once, was an accountant; Martha Headway, a used-car salesman.

. . . Perhaps with a good night's sleep he might arise early enough to do a passable job with the razor. Cornell missed his little apartment. He had always been ill at ease in the group residences, full of chattering, spiteful, jealous males. He really was a private sort of person, content with his own little corner of the world, if not precisely happy. Now it was gone.

Harry was still sleeping when Cornell awakened, or at least he was in bed, face turned towards the other wall. The ceiling light was on. Cornell lay there watching him. No way of telling what time it was. Harry was the only gauge of their schedule. Cornell awoke with that understanding. Harry was a very special person.

Cornell at last coughed loudly, turned the other way, and shut his eyes. Harry could be heard getting out of bed. He came over and shook Cornell.

"Come on, lazybones," Harry said. "Hit the deck. They'll be here soon."

Cornell rolled over and with simulated difficulty opened his eyes.

"Good morning," he said. "If it is morning."

"Light's on," said Harry. "That's how you tell."

Harry's brazen smile was infuriating to Cornell, all the more so because it was painted across a beardless face.

Cornell swung himself to a sitting position and probed with his feet for the slippers.

"You go ahead and hook up the razor and take your shave," he told Harry. "I'll wash first."

"I'm all done already," Harry said, with a demonstrative rubbing of the chin. "Nothing seems to wake you."

"I'm a terribly sound sleeper." Cornell said this in his childish, mock self-accusatory style, with eyeballs rolling up into his forehead and little shoulder movements. He had learned this in adolescence, watching the professional cuteness of teenaged actors. Women seemed to like it, or anyway those who doted on boyishness. He had not done it in a long time, though; it was somewhat grotesque at twenty-nine. He was using it now to conceal his surveillance of Harry.

Cornell had awakened with the conviction that Harry was a woman. He knew not whence this idea had come; nor, for that matter, why he had not enjoyed, or suffered, it earlier. The clues had been there. In fact, Harry had not made a very good job of the imposture. There was in that negligence an implied insult to Cornell's powers of eye and mind. Somehow his pride was more badly wounded than it had been even by the demotion to janitor, the arrest and jailing. One thing Cornell could never endure was being deceived. He was by nature extremely gullible. He knew that. But the alternative was cynicism. He would rather be dead than cynical. He never wanted to know how things *really* were, which always ended up as hopeless. Perhaps it was not deception, then, but revelation that he found unacceptable: Harry should have done a better job.

"You're a very quiet person,'" he said. "But why do you always replace the cover of the light, when it only has to be taken off again for me?"

Harry squinted at him, then seemed to make a conscious effort not to stand on this point.

"The guards make spot checks without warning. Better to go to a little extra trouble than to get caught. I was up and shaving an hour ago when the light first came on. No need to wake you, sleeping soundly as you were."

It was just barely possible that he was telling the truth. But *he* was *she,* so therefore all the particulars, even if true, were but aspects of a general lie.

"But," said Harry as Cornell prepared to stand up, "I don't mind going through it again." He fetched the screwdriver from the box.

"But why should you bother?" Cornell asked. "Let me." He reached for the tool.

Harry pulled it away. "You might hurt yourself," he said.

"But I'm taller than you. You can barely reach the socket."

Harry stepped onto his bed and began to unscrew the framed panel of glass. He had very fine ankles and remarkably neat kneecaps. His feet were unusually small for even a man of his modest height. But the width of his pelvis was significantly larger by the same gauge. The jail dress was tight across the hips, then suddenly slack at the waistline. The bosom was indeterminate. The rounded chin was smooth and pale; the nostrils were tiny and divided by the most delicate filament; the red pageboy was a wig; and he had no Adam's apple.

Cornell stood up, pressed his cheek against the gentle swell of Harry's soft abdomen, and, clasping his arms around and under her bottom, which was more ample to the touch than to the eye, he lifted her off the bed, held her for a moment, and threw her down. He had intended to do this more violently; he was strangely inhibited: she felt so light and yet so full. He wanted to hurt her, but in some magic way that would produce no damage. He developed a kind of heartbeat in his groin.

And then an excruciating pain, for no sooner had she hit the bed than she came up again with two claws into his testicles. He recoiled onto the other cot, and she followed him, hooking in again. A spasm lifted his right knee forcefully. It took her in the solar plexus. She became a sphere, rolling between the beds, arms around calves, spine to floor, buttocks high: she wore jockey shorts, and not the standard male jail-underwear.

Cornell seized the electric-razor cord and bound her in that position.

He had never seen quite that combination of hatred and pain

on a face, male or female. She had lost her powers of speech.

"Well, *Harry*," said he. He had difficulty in speaking. He seemed to have a volleyball between his thighs. "Well."

She gathered herself and spat into his face. He was bending over, to favor his sensitivity as well as to address her.

He wiped himself on the sleeve of the dress.

"You're a filthy spy, aren't you?"

The first spit had taken all her available strength. She pursed her lips again but they froze in position. He knelt beside her, spreading his legs as wide as possible, which helped.

"The name's Harriet, isn't it? Well, Harriet . . ." He was in a rut: had he nothing better to do than gloat? Yes—worry about his next move. The guards would arrive soon. He had no plan whatever. He had acted on impulse, out of spite, revenge, bruised vanity. But Harry—Harriet—was one of *them*. He tried to think, chattering meanwhile to distract her from his desperation.

"You should have been more clever. You're arrogant, Harriet, and it has made you lazy. You could at least have pretended to shave. And then slipping out last night before I was asleep— that was just plain stupid, Harriet. But you did get one thing out of me: poor Charlie's name. There wasn't any truth serum, was there? You tricked me. Well, I've got you now!" He felt a growing panic. It was all he could do to keep his fingers from his mouth.

And then the rapping at the door!

But breakfast came first. He clutched his left breast and remembered that. He slid open the panel, standing to the side, and accepted the trays. Spilling the contents to the floor, he got back to Harriet and closed her opening mouth before she could cry out. In the struggle her wig had become askew, and he pulled it off now. Her own blonde hair was in the short, neat cut of a woman.

He tore a strip from the hem of his dress and gagged her.

She pretended her blue eyes were bullets, and executed him repeatedly.

A weapon to use against the guards—that was what he needed. Else they would throw him down and emasculate him on the spot. There were two of them, one as large as he, and both carried truncheons. Besides, they were trained to violence. He was just a little secretary. Suddenly he had an instant of remorse. He examined Harriet to see whether she could breathe.

Could he not surrender, with a plea of insanity?

He loosened Harriet's gag and narrowly evaded the set of white teeth she aimed at his hand.

She could speak quite clearly now.

She said: "I'm personally going to hack off your nuts."

He re-gagged her.

"Listen, Harriet. I wish you would listen . . . Please listen: everything I told you was true. I'm not a militant revolutionary. I don't belong to any underground. I just had a few beers and put on a sport jacket. That's all, I swear. I don't know why I threw you down just now. It was some kind of crazy impulse. I'm sick. I've been under the care of a psychotherapist for years. You can verify that. I'll release you and take my punishment. I'm a very disturbed person. My doctor can tell you that. Look, if I untie you, won't that prove I'm basically harmless? I don't expect to get off scot-free, but maybe there's a place for me in some state-run psychiatric facility—" He loosened the gag again.

Harriet snarled: "I'm going to get me an axe, and I'm going—"

He silenced her once more.

Weapons. He pulled her box from under the cot and searched through it, finding, of all the arrogant things, a carton of Tampax.

He grimaced at Harriet. "Why, you brazen bitch!" She did as much as could be done with a gagged mouth and venomous eyes.

Ah, he found a comb. In the brief self-defense course given at school when his class reached puberty, the teacher had maintained that a mugger or rapist could be rendered ineffective by means of common objects found in any purse, properly manipulated. Comb as dagger, hair spray as poison gas, and so on.

While he was deliberating, the cell door swung open, and the guards entered. In a trice their truncheons were to hand. The nearer guard was the one as large as he. Her porcine nostrils expanding in anticipated pleasure, she raised her club and waded in.

Men have broad and large chests, and small narrow hips, and are more understanding than women, who have but small and narrow chests, and broad hips, to the end they should remain at home, sit still, keep house, and bear and bring up children.

MARTIN LUTHER, 1566

5

AFTER KNOCKING OUT both guards, Cornell stripped the uniform from the larger and got into it: tunic, trousers, and a cap into the crown of which he tucked his hair. A snug fit, particularly in the crotch, but possible. The shoes, however, were a problem. But he could not go down the corridor in his jail slippers. With much stamping and more pain, he finally encased his feet in the heavy brogans, which were stretched so extravagantly that nothing remained of the laces to tie. The excruciating pressure virtually petrified his feet—but the effect might prove useful to remind him to walk effeminately this time. Cornell was now potent, alert, and charged with an energy which enabled him quickly to see the underlying strengths in superficial weaknesses.

Punching the first guard had been his second experience at deliberate violence. By the third occasion he was already an old hand. He grabbed the truncheon from the first woman as she fell and slammed it on the cap of the other. He had been assisted by their astonishment. Obviously they were stunned by his failure to fall whimpering at their approach. When he raised his fists, the beefy guard froze, her club in the air. He hit her right on the chin.

He bound them with the extra belt and shoelaces. Big Bertha lay in her striped drawers and a none too clean T-shirt. Under the latter could be seen the wide canvas bandeau with which she compressed her fat breasts against the barrel chest.

Cornell opened the door and peered cautiously into the corridor. It was empty. Hearing groans behind him, he went back and gagged both guards with their socks. He avoided looking at Harriet. When he returned to the door, the passage was still clear, and he stepped out and locked the cell behind him.

He saw a series of iron doors. Harriet had also lied when she said they were alone in the block. There were five or six cells on either side of theirs, as well as a regular line of doors along the opposite wall.

He had little hope of getting out alone. The answer was a mass escape, a riot. He began to open cells with the master keys he had taken from the guards.

"Freedom!" he shouted in. "Let's go!"

He had opened four cells before he noticed, in dismay, that no one emerged. He plunged into the fifth, shouting exhortations.

Two old men stood at attention.

"Come on, fellows," Cornell cried. "We're busting out!"

The prisoners maintained their military attitudes. Cornell seized the nearer and shook him.

The old man spoke in a quavering voice.

"Thirty-three oh-oh two seven."

His number! Cornell took precious time to react to that.

"How long have you been here?"

"Thirteen years, ma'am."

Cornell seized him again. "I'm a man, man! We're busting out!"

The old fellow's eyes rolled up into his forehead and he crumpled in a faint. Cornell let him fall and turned to the cellmate.

"I knocked out the guards and took this uniform. I'm not a woman."

Like the other, this one gave his number. It was even lower. Cornell stared for an instant into his rheumy, fixed eyes, and dashed out and into the next cell.

There, in a prison dress, stood Charlie Harrison.

"Charlie!"

Charlie gave his number.

"It's me, *Georgie*," Cornell cried. "Come on!"

Charlie stood rigid.

"They tricked me, Charlie," Cornell said. "I didn't betray you knowingly." He waved his hands in front of Charlie's face. "Are you drugged?"

At last Charlie spoke, opening his mouth like a dummy and hardly moving his lips.

"Surrender, Georgie. They'll get you."

"I don't care," Cornell shouted. "Anything's better than this."

He seized Charlie's wrist and tried to pull him out, but the stout man had a formidable inertia.

"Charlie!"

But he could not budge this coward, and time was short. He let Charlie go and raced into the corridor, expecting to be met by a squad of uniformed huskies. But the passage was still empty. He adjusted his tunic and made sure his hair was yet in the cap.

Once more he called to his friend in vain, and then he followed the turn of the corridor. More cells. He would not waste any more effort. These men were mice.

Another turn. Scarcely had he negotiated it when a cell opened and two guards emerged, pulling a limp, weeping prisoner by his hair.

Cornell opted for boldness.

"Need a hand?"

It worked. The guards hardly glanced at him. They were too busy gloating over their miserable captive, a young man with long blond hair of which each had a fistful.

"Get your own!" one of them said to Cornell. "This one's ours."

"Mine!" said the other, and each tried to pull the victim in her own direction.

Cornell marched on, trying to close his ears to the youth's pathetic groans. He might have endangered his own getaway had he tried seriously to intercede. But it was more than that. The captive happened to be a large, robust young man. He was not resisting in the least as two women, of median size for their sex, dragged him along the concrete floor. Indeed, he was too heavy for their combined strengths. They could not have budged him had he not helped by paddling along, dachshund-fashion, on his four paws.

Propelled by disgust, Cornell rounded another corner and found himself before a barred door, beyond which was a kind of vestibule. A slovenly-looking guard, stogie in side of mouth, cap on back of head, sat behind a desk. Her feet were on the desktop, and she seemed either dozing or stupefied.

His nerve diminished slightly. He tried quietly to open the door with his keys, but none would enter the lock. The guard's head suddenly fell onto her chest. He leaned against the bars, observing her, and the door swung open. It had not even been latched.

He paused at the desk and hefted his truncheon, then decided against busting another skull. Revenge was not his game. But how arrogant they were! The jail was hardly guarded.

Across the vestibule was a door with a frosted-glass panel. He opened it and was outside the Men's House of Detention, a fact he confirmed by reading the legend on the obverse of the glass. He was still underground, but free. He took the staircase and mounted to an upper lobby lined with what had apparently been shops in some former time but now were occupied by derelicts, gypsies, and the like. Rockefeller Center had an infamous reputation and was avoided by any boy in his right mind. Cornell had never been there before, and intended now to leave as fast as he could if not obstructed by the ruffians in residence.

Seeing some burly, dreadful creatures just ahead, he instinctively tightened his behind and moved to bring his purse up under his arm—and felt the truncheon instead. He had nothing to fear. He was in uniform and armed. Nor, when he drew closer to the malignant-looking bums, did he see the usual hostility on the features of these degraded women. Indeed, they touched index fingers to their caps and shuffled aside.

He passed through the front of the building, a great jagged hole where the main doors had originally swung, and around a mound of trash made by the bums' litter and the rubble that had fallen from the upper stories into the avenue. More derelicts thronged the street. Cornell marched through them with impunity. He was enjoying this, and steered for one group simply to see them scatter obsequiously.

Had he really overwhelmed Harriet and knocked out two guards? There was no precedent for that sort of thing in his history. And here he was again in women's clothing. Fate had begun to impose upon him an inexorable effeminacy. With this thought he turned west on a crosstown street and suddenly lost his nerve. Of course he must turn himself in. He had no place to go. The apartment would be staked out, and his money was in the purse that had been taken from him in jail. His feet now hurt abominably in the heavy, binding shoes, and his constricted crotch had begun to ache.

In pain and terror he continued to propel himself along, oblivious to his direction. Other people, respectable types, were also abroad now. The brown-mustard sky told him it was morning. He had no gas mask, and would die of asphyxiation—no sooner had he formulated this solution than he saw no one was wearing a mask.

His next observation was that he stood on the corner of Broadway and 50th Street, very near the building in which he worked. It was the morning rush hour. He leaned against a lamppost and took the breath he had been suppressing. He should probably just go on into Huff House, report to the janitor's closet, and claim his mop. He might have time to tidy up the men's room before the police arrived. Surely that would make a good impression. Perhaps his assaults on Harriet and the guards could be interpreted as resulting from a temporary nervous seizure: he had that long history of psychotherapy. Certainly he would not expect to get off scot-free, but—

But, but, but! He took his fingernails from his mouth and saw that he had drawn blood. He saw too that he still wore the nail polish he had applied before going to Charlie's. A uniformed guard from the Men's House of Detention with tangerine nails! His panic now became particular. He was seized by the desperate conviction that the means to safety resided in a bottle of oily polish remover. He kept such among his emergency cosmetic supply in the bottom right drawer of his desk at Huff House. There was a drugstore just across the street from his lamppost, but dressed as he was he could hardly make the needful purchase.

The usual queue had formed at the desk of the security officer in the lobby. A wall clock gave the time as 8:39. Work began at ten for publishing people, but some of the other tenants in the huge structure, insurance companies, mutual funds, and the like, opened their offices at eight-thirty or nine. The officer was examining I.D. cards. Cornell automatically joined the line and sought to fetch up his purse. Again he found the dangling truncheon, and again it was a source of strength. He stepped imperiously from the end of the queue and strode past the desk, saluting the uniformed woman with an insouciant wave of the club.

He left the elevator at the eighteenth floor and entered the offices of Huff House. They were empty of people, silent, strange. He went to his cubicle and found the polish remover and cotton balls. Seeing the neighboring desk, he thought of poor Charlie. When he had finished cleaning his nails, he raised both hands together, palms outward, and inspected the job. His hands were not his most attractive feature, the fingers shorter, thicker than he would have liked. In compensation he grew his nails rather long and trimmed them to pointed arcs.

He set his jaw now, took up a pair of clippers, and cut the nails straight across at the margin of the quick. Going from strength to strength, he found a pair of shears on Charlie's desk and proceeded to cut off his hair just above the ears, guided only by touch and peripheral vision. Until the rough cut was finished he lacked the nerve to lift the mirror of his spare compact. Around he went, blindly, across the nape, the thick auburn strands falling softly to the floor.

He put the shears down and plucked off the hairs that clung to the adhesive serge of the uniform. At last he studied himself in the tiny mirror, recoiling at first, then with comb and brush and more scissorswork making the best of the crude job. But he could not of course see the back of his head.

He walked to the men's room and pushed open the swinging door—He must remember that sort of thing! He spun and, crossing the corridor, plunged into the women's lavatory. The second thing he saw in the glass over the washbowls was that one of the toilet stalls was closed. He made a faucet gush to match the roar of his blood, then shut it off as impulsively.

Whoever sat in there produced an almost palpable silence. His eyes cornered on the mirror, Cornell began to steal towards the door. He had only a few more paces to go when the stall opened slowly and a wretched figure emerged. Cornell was at once amazed and relieved to recognize old Stanley, the janitor whom he had been assigned to replace. From Stanley's stooped shoulders hung a shapeless dress of bombazine, with collar and cuffs of a white which age had yellowed. His ankles were thick in cotton stockings, and his shoes were run over.

Stanley shook his gray-bunned head and spoke in a miserable whine.

"I know I done wrong, ma'am. But I didn't *use* the commode. I was just sitting on the closed top. I finished cleaning up, see, and was taking a rest. I'm retiring after today. I put in many years of faithful service, ma'am. It seems hard I would get a bad report on my last day."

Cornell had never known Stanley well, and besides the old

man was notoriously nearsighted. He might just get away un-recognized. Once again boldness seemed the answer. He returned to the glass and combed his hair as a woman would, with brisk strokes across his temples. He said nothing. The onus was on Stanley. But then he saw, as he had not earlier when preoccupied with his hair, that overnight he had acquired the usual growth of whiskers. He had walked for blocks while wearing a woman's uniform and a man's shadow of beard. Many females of course wore false beards and mustaches, but a stubble was unmistakably male. He gasped, and Stanley came up behind him.

Cornell covered his chin with one hand and gestured for Stanley's benefit with the other.

"I'll overlook it this time," he sternly told the old man.

Stanley's voice had changed. "You're not exactly a police-woman, are you? You're some sort of watchman or guard." His tone altered further. "You're not exactly a woman, are you?" He put an astonishingly forceful hand on Cornell's shoulder and turned him. "In fact," he said, "you're Georgie Cornell."

Without deliberation Cornell threw a punch at him, missed, and was felled by a combination karate blow made by Stanley—or so he assumed: Stanley struck him so quickly and so deftly that he could not see precisely how it was done. He was sitting on the tile floor, looking up at the old man, who was certainly not as old as one had thought and perhaps not even a man.

"Oh, no!" Cornell wailed. "Not you, too."

Stanley put out a hand and raised him.

"Are *you* a woman?"

Stanley's smile was grim.

"Certainly not."

"Who are you, Stanley?"

"I was going to ask you the same question," Stanley said.

"Are you going to turn me in?" Cornell was wondering whether he might get in a sneak punch, anyway, thereby gaining a moment in which to dash for the door.

"Well, I might," said Stanley, his formerly rheumy eyes now quite keen behind the glasses.

Actually, the blow Cornell had tried to strike *had* been a sneak punch and got him nowhere. He decided against further violence.

"They'll castrate me, Stanley," he said. "Don't be a traitor to your own sex."

Now Stanley barked a laugh. He clapped Cornell on the arm.

"Come on, boy," he said, leading the way to the door. He snorted. "Who would have thought it? Georgie Cornell! The most obsequious, submissive little boy in the office. You've got a better act than me." He frowned. "Or you had, anyway. Fill me in on this uniform. Is this an independent adventure? Why didn't you contact the Organization?"

This was all Greek to Cornell. He related his series of catastrophes as they walked along the corridor that led to the mail room. Stanley seemed to have a particular destination.

When he had finished his story, they were standing before a freight elevator. Stanley pushed its button, and it began to hum.

Stanley said: "The lesson is obvious, isn't it? A man cannot get anywhere on his own. These individual rebellions are doomed to failure from the beginning. They are mere sentimental exercises, perhaps ultimately even masochistic. Sometimes they are actually rigged by the Female Establishment."

"I don't understand these things," said Cornell. "I'm just an ordinary sort of boy, and I did a foolish thing, and I'm in terrible trouble." He simpered at Stanley—then caught himself. For an instant he had reacted to Stanley as he would to an authoritative woman, turning on the helplessness, the appeal for sympathy. It occurred to him that he did this irrespective of sex: power was the determining factor.

"Let me explain," Stanley said. "Sometimes a woman in disguise, a *provocateuse*, a secret agent, will foment a meaningless little revolt, one that is easily crushed. The idea being—" The elevator arrived and opened, and they boarded it. Stanley pushed the SB button, and resumed: "A single match is lighted, and quickly blown out. This demonstrates that starting fires is useless." He peered at Cornell. "You need an organization to touch off a holocaust."

Cornell was feeling the back of his hair: strange.

He nodded at Stanley, though he was still in the dark about everything. However, it was good to have an ally at last.

"You're a lucky boy, Georgie. How you got all the way here from the jail without being picked up is amazing. Even in that uniform you're not at all effeminate. Your movements, your gestures are outlandishly virile." Suddenly he patted Cornell's shoulder. "That's no criticism. You're a brave lad. We can use you."

We? But Cornell decided not to ask questions. Obviously Stanley was taking him someplace, and it *had* to be better than wherever he would have gone on his own.

The cab reached the bottom of the shaft, the door slid back, and they stepped into the subbasement, all concrete and naked light bulbs, overhead pipes and ducts, some with valves so low that the men had to crouch. Stanley led the way to an iron door labeled in red: DANGER—HIGH TENSION—DO NOT TOUCH.

Stanley pulled up his skirt. His stockings were rolled and gartered just above the knee, old-man style. From under the garter he took a key and unlocked the iron door. It was dark inside, but he found a flashlight somewhere and plunged ahead.

"Wait for me!" cried Cornell, who did not want to be electrocuted. He could hear something humming ominously to his left.

Stanley's flashlight soon showed a large wooden crate against a wall of solid concrete. He handed the torch to Cornell and moved the crate out from the wall, revealing a jagged hole only large enough to admit a person who was doubled over. He bent and crawled through.

When Cornell had joined him, Stanley reached back in and pulled the crate up snug. They were now in a high-ceilinged tunnel of some sort, and Cornell straightened his back. Ugh, he was stiff and getting no younger. Stanley certainly seemed to be in good shape for a man of his age—whatever that was.

"Stanley," Cornell said, "are you going to tell me where we're going?"

Stanley's light played off the gray walls.

"Why don't you just wait and see for yourself?" he said.

They went along the tunnel for some distance and made a turn which Cornell had expected because light came from beyond it. What he had not anticipated, however, was that two individuals were concealed behind the corner, and when he rounded it, they seized him.

"Take him—or her—into the command car," said Stanley.

Cornell, being propelled by his captors, saw a series of metal cars upon a track. He thought he recognized it from photographs as an old subway train. The system had collapsed years earlier.

He was taken along the platform to the last car on the right. The train could obviously travel nowhere: a pile of rubble rose halfway to the roof of the tube ahead.

He was brought firmly through a wide middle door and into a place of parallel plastic-covered benches, before which, here and there, were little coffee tables that were being used as desks by—well, some of them were dressed as men and some as women.

He really didn't know the difference any more. Would he ever get back to normality, where a man was a man and a woman a woman? And what was Stanley—Stanley who now proceeded to take off his gray wig and then his bombazine dress, to roll down the female chino trousers that he wore underneath and tuck the tail of his T-shirt into the waistband. He had no discernible breasts. His hair was cut short and grew sparsely above his forehead. He seemed to be ten years younger.

Cornell was still being held by both arms.

He said: "Who are you, Stanley? And if you're a woman, why don't you just take me back to jail?"

Stanley ignored these questions and put one of his own to Cornell's guards.

"What do you think?"

They both let Cornell go and stepped away from him and peered. Cornell returned the inspection. If they were women, they were outsized. One was a good six feet tall, husky, swarthy, and wearing a plaid Viyella shirt and flannel trousers. The other was even taller, but slender. He had dark-blond hair and wore the kind of sweatsuit that one of Cornell's girl friends, an athletic type, had donned for workouts in the gym: for a while she had held the local Y record in pushups.

Cornell thought of these persons as "he" for convenience' sake; he didn't know what they were.

The swarthy one told Stanley: "There's only one way to tell for sure."

Stanley said: "Strip, Georgie!"

Blushing violently, Cornell began to carry out the order. Ironically enough, though he was wearing his second outfit of female clothes in three days, this was the first time he had ever *taken off* a pair of pants, having been undressed by the detectives after he was knocked out. He slipped out of the tunic now and stood there in the cheap prison brassière and fiddled with the belt buckle, getting it open only to run into the tricky cross-hook-and-button arrangement of the waistband that had been much easier to put on than it was to unfasten.

At last his trousers fell, and holding his breath, he hooked two thumbs into the elastic of his bloomers and swooped them down.

"Congratulations," said Stanley, putting out his hand. The other two wanted to shake, as well. There stood Cornell, bare from waist to mid-thigh, knock-kneed with shame, lower abdomen crawling.

Stanley was smiling. "Pull 'em up," he said. "You made it. You're a man, all right. Welcome to the Movement."

Cornell was suddenly exasperated. Angrily he reclothed his lower body, making the zipper scream.

All three of them still had their hands out when he was done. He fetched his tunic from the seat and got into it.

Stanley said, in a placating tone: "We had to be sure, you see. Their agents are everywhere. This is the only incontrovertible proof."

The lean blond said: "Welcome, Brother!"

"Put 'er there, Brother," the swarthy man cried, and seized Cornell's limp hand and pumped it.

"Georgie's a hero," Stanley told them. "He just busted out of jail, alone and unassisted."

At this, the several other men seated behind the little desks rose and clustered around Cornell. He had forgotten about them.

"Meet your Brothers," Stanley said, and began a quick round of introductions that Cornell hardly heard. However, he had begun to be mollified.

"Are you by any chance some kind of male-liberation group?" That had finally dawned on him. He was answered by genial faces and chuckling murmurs, backslaps. Someone produced a cigar, someone else a light, and Cornell found himself puffing.

"Fellows," Stanley said to the assemblage, "Georgie's revolt was spontaneous, visceral and not intellectual, and triggered by the repression. It is another proof that their tyranny assists our cause. Any of you who still have lingering doubts, who think we should collaborate with the moderates in working for liberalization, should now know better. Georgie would not be among us were the clothing laws less severe. As you know, there are liberal elements within the Establishment who have tried to introduce laws permitting men to wear slacks, pants suits, and other female-type attire. Our policy is, and will continue to be as long as you wish me to be your Chairman, in adamant opposition to these measures."

Cornell blew out some acrid smoke. He would have liked to drop the ugly cigar down a toilet, but he felt obliged to be comradely.

Stanley said: "The liberals are as much our enemies as the women, and even more sinister. At least you know where a woman stands. But a weak-kneed, flabby, whining reformer is the most disgusting organism on the face of the earth, a traitor to his own sex. I respect a policewoman, for example. She is ruthless, brutal, vicious, but she is after all honestly serving her cause, whereas the treacherous, prating little scum of a moderate turns my stomach."

Now he made his uplifted hand into a fist and shook it. "Georgie will now be wanted for jailbreak. The sentence for that is castration."

Women are not altogether in the wrong when they refuse the rules of life prescribed to the world, for men only have established them and without their consent.

MICHEL EYQUEM DE MONTAIGNE, 1588

6

FRANKIE, the big swarthy man, showed Cornell to his quarters, the last car at the other end of the train from the command post. In between were other cars containing typewriters, mimeograph machines, a tailoring shop, and a kitchen-mess hall facility. They threaded their way through all of this and the men in attendance.

Cornell was still stunned and said little. Frankie introduced him to the others as a "revolutionary hero" and recounted his exploits in jail. He was the recipient of numberless handshakes, backslaps, and even little fake punches in the area of the belt buckle: effeminate expressions, it would seem, especially when offered by male militants; but there was so much he did not understand.

Triple-decker bunks filled the dormitory car, with stall showers and toilets at either end. Between the tiers of bunks were gas-pipe-racks for clothing and wooden footlockers.

"You have quite a choice," said Frankie. "Most of our people have cover roles out in the world, some as men and some as simulated women. They might occasionally spend a night here, but they have apartments or rooms on the outside."

Cornell chose a top bunk somewhere near the middle of the car. It made no difference to him. Frankie showed him the clothes rack and an empty footlocker.

"All I have is this uniform," said Cornell.

"We'll go to the tailor shop and have Murray fit you up," Frankie said.

"Just a little sweater and skirt would do. And a pair of low-heeled sandals. My feet feel like they've been amputated."

Frankie laughed. "It'll take a while to get used to," he said. "But unless your job requires you to go out as a man, you wear what you have always known as *women's* clothing, down here." He laughed again at Cornell's frown. "There's an awful lot to learn, and you've been with us only an hour. Believe me, we've most of us gone through it in our own day, and we're sympathetic. You have to begin all over again with the development of your personality. It's like being reborn. Your head will spin at times. What is important is that your heart is in the right place. You've proved that. It took quite a man to do what you did."

Funny. If Cornell had had to explain what motivated him to attack Harriet, which started all of this, he woud have said: his outrage at being deceived. He was, or had been, a trusting sort of boy. He had grown less naive in the past forty-eight hours; therefore he would not disabuse Frankie. Instead, he looked modest, lifted both wrists and let them fall, and asked Frankie about himself.

"How did you come to join the Movement?"

Frankie twitched his big, crooked nose.

"I almost beat a girl to death," he said. "She made advances to me. I went a little crazy, I guess, but I didn't know what to do. I panicked. I was an innocent kid then. They didn't get me. I hid out, living like a rat, stealing food at night, creeping through these tunnels by day—which is how I found this place, and the Movement."

"When was that?" Frankie was obviously older than Cornell.

"Eight years ago," said Frankie. "I haven't been out of here since. I'm still wanted, and I could hardly use a disguise. I don't look much like a woman, even in women's clothes. Oh, I guess I could get Jerry—he's our plastic surgeon—to give me a new face and I could get new I.D. papers, and go up as another man, but I kind of like it here, among the Brothers, where I never have to even see a rotten woman. If I went up now, I'd probably kill the first one I came across."

Frankie was a fanatic. Cornell wondered whether they were all like that. Despite what he told Dr. Prine in his hysteria, he himself had never hated women, and he did not intend to do so now. He did not even hate Harriet. In fact, he had a strangely tender feeling towards her. Why not? They had grappled, and he had won.

Frankie stood erect and inflated his big chest.

Suddenly he said, with piety: "Of course, brutality is not the answer to brutality. We must never become what *they* are."

"A picture of you appeared on TV last night," Stanley told Cornell next morning.

In the interim Cornell had been provided with a complete female outfit: chino slacks, knitted shirt in navy blue, and fawn-colored desert boots. Beneath this he wore broadcloth shorts, a T-shirt, and the prison bra. A little tailor shop, administered by a little man named Murray, occupied an end of one of the subway cars. Up in the normal world Murray was an alteration seamster at Bergdorf Goodman.

After an enormous breakfast of flapjacks, fried ham and eggs, which Cornell (who until his lunchtime tuna-on-whole-wheat never took much into his stomach but instant coffee) could barely nibble at, Frankie had conducted him to what seemed to be the command car, because Stanley was there. It was otherwise empty.

Stanley wore his janitor's dress, wig, and glasses.

He said: "Actually there were two pictures. One was described as the portrait from your high-school yearbook. You had bobbed hair. The other was a snapshot taken at a beach, more recent than the first, but the face wasn't very clear. You were wearing a white bikini."

Cornell hadn't slept too well, though the bunk in the dormitory car was more comfortable than the prison cot. He kept awakening and trying to remember where he was.

He said: "I never have been photogenic."

Stanley nodded briskly. "What matters to us is that there are very few people who would recognize you on the basis of these shots, if that's all the police have. And it must be, because they have certainly ransacked your apartment by now. What about your friends, lovers, co-workers? Could they provide more recent pictures?"

Cornell smoothed his upper lip with the lower. He missed the taste of lipstick.

"I have this funny way: I look different on every snapshot."

Stanley suddenly stared at Cornell's breasts and put out a hard finger.

"Those may have to go."

Cornell's smile was ill.

"We have our own plastic surgeon," Stanley said. "He's self-trained but quite good. His cover role is as nurse at Beth Israel Hospital. He has assisted at a number of operations and kept his eyes open. He has stolen, one by one, a full set of surgical instruments. Get those tits off and maybe a little work on the nose, and you'll pass anywhere. That should be our first concern—protecting you against discovery. The Movement takes care of its own. Then we shall ask you for something in return."

Cornell frowned. "The facial change I can understand. But the breasts? Why must they go?" Not only had the silicone injections cost him a pretty penny; the operation had been much more painful than promised; surely taking them off would be even less pleasant. "After all, most men have breasts of some kind."

"Now, that's an interesting statement," said Stanley. "In reality it is women who would grow them naturally if they did not bind their chests at puberty. When women produced young, the mammary glands were functional, secreting milk. Is it not degrading, now that tits are useless, that we are the sex who wears them?"

At this moment several other men filed into the car and chose seats on the parallel benches. They were all attired in normal male clothing, i.e., dresses or skirts, no doubt because they would shortly be en route to their respective employments in the normal world. It must have been about seven A.M. Cornell had been awakened by Frankie at six and directed to a little stall shower without a door—also without a showerhead! Frankie had dashed a bucketful of icy water on him. They had no running water supply down there. The toilet was chemical. Ugh. Afterwards, that ghastly breakfast.

"Come along," said Stanley, taking Cornell's arm and leading him up the aisle to the head of the car. "This is our Council." To the men he said: "This is Georgie." He gave a brief account of Cornell's jailbreak.

Frankie had left the car, and Cornell had never seen any of the other men before. They were all obviously older than he and none of them was especially attractive. One wore nurse's whites; another, a waiter's peach-colored, matching dress and cap from one of those chain restaurants, Child's or Schrafft's. The rest were probably typists and receptionists, switchboard boys.

"Brothers," said Stanley, "Georgie's example is instructive in several areas. First, he was by no means a conscious rebel. He was rather a typical male conformist, a serf, a lackey, mindlessly accepting the status quo.

"He even had breast injections." Stanley turned to Cornell. "I'm not trying to embarrass you, Georgie. The Movement has no time for personalities. We here are your Brothers, not individuals. That is our strength. We are one, not many. The self has but one function with us: self-criticism. No Brother ever criticizes, disciplines, or punishes another. One does these things for himself, in the presence of his Brothers. There is no hierarchy of power here. Don't misunderstand my position, for example.

I am an equal among equals. I am addressing the Council because I have something to say. If they disagree, they will let me know in no uncertain terms."

Stanley resumed speaking to the other men.

"Yet it was Georgie, the tame little robot with no history of militancy, who revolted violently and now is a wanted man, a sexual desperado. What this suggests is that there are other Georgies out there who need only sufficient provocation to rise up and proclaim themselves real men.

"It is our responsibility to provide them with that provocation, that stimulation, and the necessary leadership. I think that Georgie has already begun to understand that the simple revolt is not enough. Were it not for the Movement, he would either have already been recaptured or, alone and impotent, he would have been awaiting that terrible moment when the police arrived."

Cornell would have liked to sit down. Perhaps he should not have been so rough with Harriet. He remembered the hatred in her eyes. Maybe he should have tried to explain that it had been merely personal. Perhaps he should now confess as much to Stanley and the Council. His predicament was becoming altogether too institutional, too symbolic. Cornell had a profound abhorrence of misrepresentation, yet he often had found himself helplessly acquiescing in a companion's opinion, assumption, or taste —merely to be nice. At the least this frequently resulted in extreme discomfort: having to dine on Mexican food, say. At the most—well, there were inevitable junctures at which self-denial failed. Friends were disabused, felt betrayed: why had he let them go on thinking . . . ? At worst, there had been that evening with Charlie, the issue of which was that he stood here, misrepresented, misrepresenting by his very presence, and Charlie rotted in jail.

But the Movement was the first fellowship to which he had ever been offered entry. These men admired him, felt his cause was one with theirs. That he *had* no cause was the latest item in the series of ironies that had begun with his leaving Charlie's apartment dressed as a woman. Reality had been reversed ever since.

"To me, the most significant, and encouraging, aspect of Georgie's rebellion is his age," said Stanley, and asked Cornell: "You're still under thirty, aren't you?"

Cornell was flattered by this assumption; also it was again true that he did not want to disappoint his friends.

"Oh, yes." He smiled at the audience. So he would see the end of his twenties in another five months: Stanley had not said "*well* under thirty."

"I don't have to remind you," Stanley went on to the members of the Council, "of our difficulty in attracting young men to the Movement. Our mimeographed manifestoes, distributed surreptitiously near YMCA's, dancing and sewing classes and the like, have, if picked up at all, quickly been discarded on the sidewalks. And while it is true that the average policewoman is a lazy, subliterate timeserver, there are some zealots on the detective force, pathological man-haters, shrewd and deadly."

Cornell wondered whether Harriet was of that company. In his experience of her, she had scarcely proved shrewd and not deadly at all, at least in performance.

"And there are also informers." Stanley shrugged. "We are asking a young man to take quite a risk. He cannot very well stand there openly reading our literature. If he is seen slipping it into his purse for clandestine examination later on, he is putting himself in danger of an even more serious charge."

Stanley coarsely made a fist. He was an odd mixture of elements, with his janitor's dress on the one hand and his feminine gestures on the other.

"I have always maintained that to move men, especially young men, much more than revolutionary rhetoric is needed. We must offer them something more exciting, something satisfying, an opportunity for the exercise of true pride rather than the temporary pleasures of shallow vanity.

"Enslaved as we are and have been for more than a century, men have survived. We are basically more durable than women. Their death rate has been rising every year as ours has fallen. But there is still no substitute for youth. And that we did not have in the Movement"—he smiled at Cornell—"until yesterday. Now the problem is how to use Georgie to the best advantage. He cannot of course return to the world in his former character. He is a wanted sex criminal. Whichever role he is to play, his appearance must be altered. Something done with his face and also with his figure. Jerry, what do you think?"

The man in the nurse's uniform leaped up and briskly approached Cornell.

"Let's take a look at those boobs," he said. He was small, dark, and sharp-featured. "Just lift your shirt."

Cornell lifted the hem of the knitted shirt in his two hands. Before raising it he turned away from the audience.

"Georgie," Stanley said, "we can't afford false modesty in the Movement." Jerry, the nurse, seized his arm and turned him around.

Cornell exposed his bra. Jerry deftly reached around to the groove of his spine and undid the hooks.

Oo, his hands were cold!

The nurse peered under, squeezed, and kneaded both breasts. "These aren't injected," he said. "These are mammary prostheses! Hell, one incision for each and slide it out." He turned to Stanley. "It couldn't be simpler."

Cornell said: "I *always* thought they were injected."

Jerry wrinkled his nose. "You didn't even know what was put into your own body?"

"I guess I didn't look too closely. I can't stand operations."

"These are much more expensive, a better job all around.

They're safer, and they keep their shape. What did they run you, ten thousand?"

"Twelve."

Jerry sneered. "Know what a pair of those inserts go for wholesale? That's why surgeons drive Rolls Royces." He checked the bobby pin that held the winged cap on the back of his head.

Meanwhile Cornell stood there with his dugs hanging out.

The nurse had to make his disparaging point. "Two hundred at the outside. It's just a silicone rubber bag filled with gel." He smirked, shrugged, and, his white nylon skirt swishing, returned to his seat.

"Well, then," said Stanley, "when could you do it, Jerry?"

"Monday's my next day off." Jerry's white-stockinged legs were crossed, one squat-heeled shoe dangling.

Cornell lowered his shirt. He had chosen a general anaesthetic for his breast implant. He supposed he had now fallen in the estimation of these men. Jerry was a mean sort. And the idea of a male doctor was not appealing. There were a few around, specializing in men's intimate problems: prostate disorders and the like. But Jerry wasn't even an M.D.

Cornell realized that Stanley had asked him something.

"Excuse me?"

Stanley frowned through his steel-rimmed glasses and repeated the question.

"How do you stand with your sperm service?"

Stanley obviously thought him at least five years younger than he was! You registered at eighteen. If you hadn't been called up by age twenty-five, you were exempt. For once Fortune smiled on Cornell; his lottery number had been very low, and his years of eligibility were luckily those in which the birth quotas had been receding along with the economy, and also because casualty figures in the Balkan War had dropped away, owing to the long stalemate, etc., etc. All he cared about was that he had missed that loathsome sperm term, six months of living in a barracks, eating a high-protein diet, and being milked every so often.

He found it impossible to admit at this point that he was almost thirty.

"I've been lucky so far. I've got a very low number."

"I've given the matter some thought," Stanley said to the Council. "Willie, in your job at the draft board, do you have access to the records?"

He was answered by a stocky man with a glossy head of too-black dyed hair. Nor could Cornell condone such lavish use of blue eye shadow and the oversized bangle earrings that swung wildly as the man uncrossed his blunt knees.

"Most of the week I'm there by my lonesome," said Willie. "With my typewriter and electric heater—my legs are cold even in summer!" He was one of those vain men who injected little personal data into every statement, the kind who were so tiresome at stocking counters.

"Are the important files under lock and key?"

"Oh, no," said Willie. "Well, that is, they are supposed to be, but the keys are always dangling from the cabinets where anybody—"

Stanley forced him to answer. "Then you do have access to them, and to the lists of call-ups?"

"I certainly do," Willie cried, smiling vainly at his neighbors. "I really manage that office. Miss Wilcox—she's president of the board—says she doesn't know how they'd get along without me!" Suddenly he grimaced. "But I just get a clerk-typist's salary. When I think about it, I get *so* mad."

Another man, a bleached blond with a gray complexion, tapped his platform shoe on the floor and nodded vigorously. Jerry slapped his own knee.

"Hell," he said, "I've assisted at operations where the surgeon was too drunk to hold the knife, and that damned woman has an estate in Greenwich and an oceangoing yacht. Don't tell *me.* I haven't had a raise in five years."

"All right," said Stanley. "The list of injustices is endless, as we all know. We have filled many a manifesto with them, and yet I can't name a single Brother who has joined us for any such simple reason. The average man, I'm afraid, has been so conditioned all his life to think of himself as inferior that his reaction to the misfortune, the persecution, of his fellows is, if he himself has not suffered as much, an ugly feeling of triumph. If he has been victimized—and all men have, so I should rather say, if he is conscious of his victimization—then with his servile mentality he thinks that at least he's not alone.

"Jealousy, Brothers, is the operative emotion of men: of men as they have been debased by women! Not of men as they once were, not of instinctive man, not of historical man until a century ago!"

Cornell was astonished to see that Stanley's teeth closed violently at the appropriate places in his phrasing, that his fists were clenched and shaking.

But Stanley soon got hold of himself. "I've been thinking about the sperm camps," he said abruptly. "Morally as well as physically, they represent one of the most crucial areas of male exploitation. Young men are conscripted for this service, required to live in virtual imprisonment, and receive a niggardly honorarium that is scarcely sufficient for a Coke or two at the post exchange and the weekly movie in the rec hall. It is six months of abuse.

"Whereas women volunteer as egg donors, spend a few days in a luxurious hospital in which every comfort is provided, and receive an extravagant emolument, plus the subsequent mandatory two-month vacation-with-pay from their employers, men often return from their own service to find that their jobs are gone."

Stanley was working himself up again. Cornell knew all these facts, but had never thought much about the injustices which they allegedly represented. Stanley did not mention that it took only one egg for conception, but millions of sperm—well, actually, he believed only one little wiggly sperm thing was necessary, but multitudes had to be provided owing to the possible incompatibilities and inadequacies of many, the male role being lacking in certainty even at the very basis of life.

"Brothers," Stanley said slowly. "I'm going to talk turkey. We haven't made a significant gain in years. We all perform little acts of sabotage in our jobs, but Marty's disconnecting phone calls at his switchboard, Garry's misdirecting his boss's letters, and I include my own operations in the women's washroom at Huff House, shutting off the hot-water supply, altering the ballcock so a toilet won't flush properly—"

So that was what Stanley had been up to in the booth when Cornell encountered him the other day: how childish could you get?

"—these things contribute, we agree, to the general malaise of American society, the pervasive feeling that nothing works, nothing can be counted on, but I think they will hardly result in bringing down the female power structure in the near future.

"Sperm service is hated, dreaded, by American youth. Brothers in the Los Angeles Movement broke into a draft-board office last year, if you recall, and destroyed the records—alas, to no avail, duplicates having been deposited in the state headquarters."

Willie nodded, swinging his earrings. "We do that, too."

"Precisely," said Stanley. "But you could alter someone's status. You could find Georgie's record and make him 1-A and add his name to the next shipment."

Cornell's heart tried to batter an exit through the plastic prosthesis in his left bosom.

"A female bureaucracy is on guard against those who would flee obligations. If we tried to get someone *out* of the sperm service there would surely be trouble. Not so with getting Georgie *in*."

Cornell crossed his arms beneath his bosom and squeezed.

"They'll never look for that. Now, what's the point of this? Here's my thinking: these are healthy young fellows, precisely the sort we would like to reach but have not been able to because we haven't come up with a program that appeals to them.

"My plan is to offer young men something that has obvious and, if managed properly, prompt results. In short, once he's in the service, Georgie foments a strike in the sperm camp."

Cornell shook his head to ward off a faint. He missed the feeling of the long, swinging hair he had possessed an eternity ago.

Willie protested. "That won't work! For goodness' sake." The others gasped and muttered.

A thin ash-blond spoke urgently. He wore a tan wash-and-wear shirtwaist dress. "The sergeants were absolutely vicious when I served. You couldn't ask a decent question without being abused! And the food! It's supposed to be high-protein, but it's just *awful*." His voice broke. "I'm not even talking about being hooked up to those vicious machines."

Willie's continued headshaking resulted in the loss of an earring. He slid from the seat and squatted to retrieve it, looking all knees and bulging calves. Cornell was still shivering. Willie regained the seat and cocked his head to screw the earring back on; his lobes were not pierced.

While his fingers were still at his ears, he said: "It's not going to work, Stanley. It'll just get those boys emasculated."

"I'm not sure what you mean by 'strike,' " said the blond, his neck all cords and bones, matching his legs. "You don't get a chance to refuse anything. I mean, you are hooked up to that horrible milking machine, and it just drains you without you doing anything. When I was in, there were some fellows who would pass out, and then they'd give them what was called a 'finger wave,' reach up through the bottom and massage the prostate—"

Stanley said hastily: "Let's not go into the gory details, Marty."

Which admonition piqued Marty to say: "Well, Stanley, you were 4-F, weren't you? Easy for you to talk."

Stanley looked severe. "Do I detect a spiteful note there, Marty? Let's not compete in injustice-collecting with our Brothers."

Marty colored and looked down between his navy-blue pumps, showing the dark roots of his hair. "I'm sorry, Stanley. I didn't mean to be personal."

Stanley made a moue of acceptance. Then he said levelly: "Let me first deal with Willie's dire prediction. They are not going to be quick about castrating anyone whose purpose it is to furnish semen. Wouldn't you agree?" He looked about. "In fact, the threat of emasculation, while often used, is seldom carried out anywhere these days—in this country, at least. With their understanding of power, women are careful not to waste their ultimate weapon. The mistress-slave relationship is more subtle than it would seem. The exertion of power must be a continuing process, not a fixed state, which is why men are not emasculated at birth. The slave must not be rendered incapable of knowing, feeling poignantly, that he *is* a slave."

Funny. Harriet had said the same thing. Cornell had now begun to prefer Stanley's theoretics. He hoped Marty wouldn't start again with the horror stories. Yet those horrors were what the boys in the camps had literally to endure. Having escaped his own term, he had never really sympathized with the victims. He was willing to feel guilty for such selfishness. *Yet why should he pay?*

"Now," said Stanley, "let me explain what kind of strike I mean. Perhaps I shouldn't use the term 'strike' at all. There will be no show of resistance. In fact, when the effects are felt, the perpetrators will pretend to be as disturbed as the authorities."

He chuckled mirthlessly. "And there will be no reason to doubt their sincerity."

Stanley paused. Cornell knew he was going to say something dreadful.

"This is beautifully simple. The machines will collect no semen! Georgie will get the boys to masturbate just before milking time."

Woman may be said to be an inferior man.

ARISTOTLE, 4th century, B.C.

7

CORNELL, nude, had waited forty-five minutes, along with his fellow conscripts, who were also bare, in a stark corridor of the Selection Center. The wooden bench was very uncomfortable on his fanny, and he was embarrassed by the male genitals that were hanging everywhere he looked: more by them, oddly enough, than by his own. Naked men were so ugly.

Because of his mission, he was supposed to get to know the others. He had tried to strike up a conversation with the boy on his left, a ringleted brunet.

"I wonder how long this will take?" Cornell cordially crinkled his eyes.

"I'm in no hurry, I'll tell you that," said the boy, showing the tip of his tongue.

"I guess we're all praying to be rejected."

The boy's tongue continued to emerge, and when a sufficient length was available, put a fresh sheen on his lip gloss.

"I'll just die if I'm turned down," said he.

"You *want* to go?"

"I just won't feel like a man. I'll just die."

Cornell was not prepared to meet this argument. How do you like that: six weeks of indoctrination and training, and it had occurred to nobody to tell him he might run into a patriot.

He gestured tenderly, almost touching the boy's wrist. "I hope you make it, dear. I really do."

The object of his good wishes fingered a ringlet and turned away.

A wide, brawny man with a head of woolly brown curls sat to Cornell's right. At one point their naked thighs had touched, and the man gave him a dirty look. Which is why he had chosen the other one to talk to. Well, he could hardly have done worse!

The robust fellow was conversing with the man on the other side. To get his attention Cornell found it necessary to lean close. Their shoulders touched.

The man turned slowly, his large nose high and his eyelids lowered.

"Really," he said. "Do try to keep your body to yourself."

Cornell forgot his mission. "I *beg* your pardon," was his frosty response.

He decided it would be politic to wait until they were all dressed again before making further overtures to his fellow recruits. Such feeble aptitude as he had for exhortation was ruinously diminished by the common nudity, men naturally tending towards paranoia when stripped. A good many boys sat with crossed hands in their laps. He sighed and felt a sensitivity in the thin red scar below each nipple. Jerry had excised his boobs six weeks earlier. The stitches had been taken out long since, and the skin had certifiably healed, but any unusual intake of breath was a reminder of that surgery, as was a damp day. Supine on the sheet-covered subway bench which served as operating table, Frankie pressing that mask over his face and dribbling ether on it, wrestling Frankie to the floor of the car, being overpowered by reinforcement Brothers, green-gowned Jerry approaching with the gleaming scalpel. . . . The ether was the worst part: he vomited for the next twelve hours.

Now, as he saw, here and there around him, boys with protuberant mammaries, he wondered again what real need there had been for his alteration. Who from the old days could have identified him from the curve of his breast? And anyway, scarcely a week later—his chest was still sore—Jerry had gone up his nostrils and done something to the cartilage to change the shape of his nose: black eyes for the next fortnight. When the bandages were removed, he and the stranger he saw in the mirror shrieked at each other. Eventually he got over the shock. He had not been actually defaced, just coarsened somewhat, the nose broader and no longer retroussé. Perhaps he was now, in a way, more attractive. He tried to make the best of it; but the loss of his breasts still rankled.

At last the door at the end of the hall was opened by a stout little soldier in the uniform of the Sperm Service staff.

"O.K.," she shouted, pointing her finger like a pistol, "First!" When the man nearest the door rose and went through it, she ordered the others to move their asses along and close ranks. Cornell took the precaution to raise his behind and not slide along as some did, collecting splinters and squealing. He had arrived early; there were only a half-dozen ahead of him.

Even so, it was a good hour before he confronted the young medical officer in the examining room. She wore the chino summer uniform, the twisted-snake insigne on one side of the open collar and a silver bar on the other, top of T-shirt visible in the vee, stethoscope around her neck, and a mirror on her forehead.

"Skin it back and milk it down," she said.

"Excuse me?"

The doctor had been looking at Cornell's groin. Now she lifted her pale eyes to his face.

"Your peter, fellow. Peel the foreskin back as far as it will go, then push it up again, squeezing the shaft right down to the head. . . . Mmm, all right. Let it go now." She looked up with a sneery smile. "You're clean." Then: "Corporal!" Looking around. "Where the fuck is that goldbrick?"

The doctor shook her crewcut head and picked a flashlight off an examination table. "I gotta do everything myself." She bent and directed the torchbeam into Cornell's crotch. "Ruffle up your pubic hair, so we can see whether your crabs are healthy."

She peered, then snapped off the light. "O.K." She made quick, negligent entries on a document attached to a clipboard.

Cornell's resolution to endure this sort of thing stoically was still firm. His weeks with the Movement had then, apparently, worked a change. He had always been notoriously craven in doctors' offices.

The medical officer pointed to his chest and snickered.

"Changed your mind?"

Instinctively, Cornell's hands came up to cover the scars below his deflated breasts.

"You boys!" jeered the doctor. "Skirt lengths are one thing, but cosmetic surgery has a tough time keeping up to date. What did you have, uplifts? And now the style is the low, soft profile, huh? But you got fed up and had 'em taken out altogether. Right? What about the new tattooing? Gonna have that done? And then what, when that goes out?" She shook her head. "And it will, it will."

Actually Cornell had never yet known a boy who had been tattooed. That was one of the extremist things that did not exist outside the pages of the high-fashion magazines: skinny models with butterflies on their shoulders, birds around the navels, etc., and even with them it was probably decals. However, he remembered that when breast implants had first turned up in *Vogue* and *Harpers Bazaar,* he and everybody he knew had said the same. Less than a year later he had had his pair inserted. That was three years back. It was premature to say the style was dead. A sore subject to him, in more ways than one.

The officer seemed in no hurry. She lighted a cigarette and leaned against the table.

"Relax," said she. "Corporal Toomey's probably got one of the conscripts in a broom closet. She's the big asswoman at this station."

But at that moment the corporal entered from a door at the rear, carrying a stack of small glass saucers on a towel. She began guiltily to explain her delay.

"That damn sterilizer takes forever nowadays, Lieutenant. I wonder if it's on the blink?"

"Bullshit, Toomey, bullshit." The officer grinned and winked at Cornell. "Was it a nice piece of cooze?"

Toomey was, or pretended to be, obsequiously indignant.

"Aw, ma'am, come on." She put her burden onto a little white-enameled table. "I burned my hand, I was in such a hurry. Oowah!" She sucked a finger.

The lieutenant tore from a roll a disposable plastic glove, the kind you wore during the night if you went to bed anointed with hand cream, and having covered her right hand, dipped the index finger into an open jar of Vaseline.

"Assume the angle," she said to Cornell.

Once again he wanted elucidation, but the corporal came behind him, pushed him to the examining table, bent him over by a hand between his shoulder blades, and held a glass saucer to his penis; the doctor swooped the lubricated finger up his rectum and massaged a point of unbearable pressure way up inside; something distintegrated in a rush like a breaking boil, and Cornell ejaculated into the vessel.

He was given a tissue for drying. He felt as one was supposed to after castration. He was directed to leave by the rear door and did, walking with his toes spread, as if the floor were surfaced with glare ice.

In the next room was another lineup of naked boys on a bench: those who had preceded him in taking the lieutenant's finger. They were waiting for the next phase of the examination. Cornell's stoicism was absolute, no longer even conscious. The large man who had been his righthand neighbor in the first waiting line was again in that situation. He turned from an impassioned dialogue with the boy on his other side and stared beseechingly at Cornell. His eyes were damp and glistening tear-tracks ran down to his blue jaw. He was no longer waspish.

"Did you ever . . ." he said in a voice gone to sob.

Cornell felt himself shrug, and heard his own callous answer as if from afar. He was actually remote from all this squalor.

"One fingerwave won't kill you."

The big man shivered. His chest was covered with stubble, and he had no artificial breasts. His lipstick was a near-maroon.

"I didn't know it would be like this. I hadn't any idea." He was leaning towards Cornell now. "I was deferred for years. I thought I'd never have to go. I'm just under the line. I'll be twenty-five next week. You kids can take it better than me. I'll die!"

As it happened, Cornell had never found it possible to disabuse the Brothers of the belief that he was still eligible for the sperm draft. He simply could not confess that he was almost thirty to a group of men who thought him five years younger. He was here today because of vanity: it was vanity's finger that had massaged his prostate. Now this hysterical creature to his right also assumed that he was still a young man: this fellow who Cornell would have said was himself a good thirty-five.

"I was jilted," said his neighbor. "I wouldn't have caused any trouble. I've got too much pride. But she wanted to get me out of the way. She's a municipal official. She got me deferred all those years, and now she got me drafted within a month of my twenty-fifth birthday." The man slumped against Cornell's side and made snuffling sounds.

Cornell tolerated the weight for a while; it meant nothing to him. He had been rendered incapable of feeling. Emotions were useless when an utter stranger could penetrate your body and cause a hidden, private gland to perform publicly. He had never known what integrity was until now, after he had lost it.

"You're very kind," the man said, against his arm. "You're an understanding person." The man straightened his trunk. "My name is Jackie."

"Georgie," Cornell said numbly. He was still holding the tissue at his groin. He looked between Jackie's legs and saw that so was he. "I wonder," he said, "where we can dispose of these." All these boys had gone through the same thing: a benchful of ejaculators. That was the idea of the sperm service, after all. But to acknowledge any sense in his situation seemed senseless. He remembered a boy years ago in school who claimed to have masturbated to a climax, but he was a crazy kind of kid, ostracized by most; he could have been lying. It was a shocking thing to boast of, loathsome to hear. Of course it was normal for boys to stroke themselves in early adolescence and feel the warmth and gentle tension, relieved finally by a pee of high pressure. But to provoke the discharge of this alien fluid, this snot, this filth. . . .

Jackie had given him some answer, which he did not hear. Jackie's toenails were pink-polished; his large toes were crooked, probably from wearing pointy shoes. How men painted, adorned, and even mutilated themselves—for women?

A person with three stripes on her sleeve came through a door and began to read from a clipboard.

"Abbott, Bumbaugh, Costin, Laird, McGonigle." She looked over the board at the nudes along the bench. "Get up and sound off when your name is called." She repeated the list, and the appropriate boys rose. "Follow me." She went back through the door with the naked men in tow. They were an unattractive lot for their youth: bowlegs, protuberant behinds, pimpled backs. Cornell could certainly hold his own in this company. He realized he was still thinking in a fashion that the Movement decried: men should not be competitive with one another and so misdirect the energy that should be focused against the female enemy. It was a woman who had given him the fingerwave—but his Brothers had put him in the position to receive it.

Jackie said shyly: "Could we be friends, Georgie? I've heard that's the way to survive the service—have a buddy."

The door from the ejaculation-room opened and Corporal Toomey emerged, half-carrying the young boy who had earlier told Cornell he would die if rejected. He looked as though he were expiring at the moment, chin in chest, rubbery legs, face white as unflavored yoghurt. Toomey dumped him on the bench and smirked cynically at Cornell.

"Takes the stuffing out of some of 'em," she said.

Cornell discovered he was coming back to life through compassion.

He spoke gently to the boy. "Can I get you something, dear? A drink of water?"

The boy shook his head. And just as well, for though Cornell had been sincere in his offer, he had no idea where he would have got water, or for that matter where even to dispose of the Kleenex he still clutched.

From the other side Jackie said, with false sympathy: "The best thing is to let him alone, Georgie." Jackie was jealous. Men!

"He's a good fellow," Cornell said, to Jackie but for the boy's benefit. "He's got a lot of courage—more than I had when his age."

"How old are you, Georgie?" Jackie asked.

Cornell turned back and said to the boy: "It hit me hard, too. You'll get over it. I'm feeling better already."

"I still hurt," Jackie said, jealously. "I can hardly sit." Cornell felt him dramatically shift from one buttock to the other.

The boy looked up, showing his tear-dampened makeup.

"You don't understand," he said in an agonized whisper. "I *liked* it. It actually gave me a thrill. I couldn't help myself. I let go." He sobbed. "It was horrible."

Cornell thought about this for a while.

At last he said: "You mean you—" He coughed. "You mean you *did* something in the saucer?"

The boy's head moved in shameful assent.

Cornell reassured him. "You were *supposed* to. That was the purpose of that phase of the examination. They had to get a specimen to test." Oddly enough, he was also explaining it to himself. Actually, he had been, or should have been, prepared for the fingerwave by his Movement indoctrination. But at the shock of the execution thereof, his memory had blanked.

The boy's eyes dilated. He was ten years younger than Cornell, if not twelve, but he had a skin problem on his forehead, and his ringleted coiffure was not the best choice for such a bony face. His figure was on the skinny, sinewy side, but he probably looked stunning in clothes.

"Are you sure?"

Cornell realized that this innocent, who reminded him of himself at an earlier age, was a perfect subject on whom to begin his assignment.

"Certainly," he answered. "You stick close to me from here on. It'll be easier than if you're all alone."

The boy smiled shyly. On Cornell's other side, Jackie emitted a groan.

"I'm feeling very queasy," he said. "I think I've got a temperature. Feel my head, Georgie."

Cornell now had two followers. Jackie was the kind who could be manipulated by playing on his envy. That might prove useful. He touched Jackie's brow with two light fingertips.

"Maybe a degree or two. An aspirin might be a good idea."

"I wouldn't have nerve to ask," said Jackie, delighted at the attention. "The personnel are so brutal."

Cornell decided on a bold stroke. He went to the door through which the sergeant had taken the candidates. He rapped twice, turned the knob, and entered a room full of cubicles. The sergeant sat at a nearby desk, checking off items on her clipboard. She glared at him.

"Where you been?"

"I wasn't called, Sergeant. There's a sick boy outside, and I wondered if you had an aspirin for him."

"Get your ass out of here until you're called." She pointed to the door and lowered her head.

"Yes, ma'am. But in view of our function, I thought we were

supposed to be maintained in good health." He did not wait for the reaction, but turned on his bare heel and went outside.

He told Jackie: "It's O.K."

Jackie gave him a worshipful look. Only after he sat down did Cornell wonder at himself. Whence came this unprecedented assurance? And even while naked! He grew fearful. He had probably cooked his goose with that sergeant. He turned and stared at the boy.

"My name's Georgie."

"Mine's Howie."

Before he knew what he was doing, he was shaking the boy's hand, feminine style. It was the Movement's regulation greeting. He had got used to it during the weeks in the subway tunnel. Howie stared in amazement as Cornell pumped his limp hand.

Luckily he had finished before the sergeant came through the door. She carried a paper cone of water. When she reached Cornell, she opened her fist and revealed two aspirins.

Gruffly she said: "Here."

Trying to obliterate the smugness from his voice, Cornell pointed at Jackie. "It's this man."

"Don't make a habit of it," the sergeant told Jackie, thrusting the tablets at him. Then she raised her clipboard and called another list of names. Cornell's new pseudonym was first: "Alcorn." Howie proved to be "Andrews." Three other men stood up at the appropriate sound, and the five followed the sergeant into the next room. Jackie gasped disconsolately at being left behind.

Each man was directed to take his own cubicle. Cornell sat on the chair provided. In time a middle-aged officer appeared. She was small, stout, and gray.

She said: "I'm Captain Wilmer. I'm a psychiatrist. You cannot fool me." She peered intensely at him. "Are you emotionally stable?"

Cornell had been instructed to answer all such questions curtly, dispassionately. Stanley had said: "Do not attract attention to yourself."

"Yes, ma'am."

"You look like a dirty little whore."

"Yes, ma'am."

"Are you?"

"No, ma'am."

"Why did you have your breasts removed?"

"They're going out of style, ma'am."

"Would you rather be a woman?"

"No, ma'am."

"Ah, you hate women!"

"No, ma'am."

"Have you ever had anal therapy?"

Stanley had told him never to admit to having received psychiatric treatment. He must not stand out as an oddball.

"No, ma'am."

"You could use it," the little doctor said, her beady eyes boring into his. "Even if you think otherwise. It would help to make you a healthier man. It will be available at the camp. Think about it."

She left, crying loudly: "Alcorn, O.K."

The pseudonym had been chosen by the Council as more or less an anagram of his real name and thus easier for him to accept and remember than one altogether alien. His chest was flat, his nose was blunted, and his hair style was gamine, short, brushed forward, with little feathers at the ears.

"All right, Alcorn," the sergeant called out. "Go through the door, down the hall to the disrobing room, get into your clothes, get your baggage, and report outside to the trucks." She spoke in a weary, contemptuous monotone.

From the PFC in charge, Cornell reclaimed the wire basket in which he had left his clothing, stepped into his bikini underpants and half slip, and put on the wash-and-wear shirtwaist dress for which Murray the tailor had exchanged the chino trousers and female gear he wore in the subway tunnel. It had been strange at first to dress normally again, and disheartening to look down at the flat bosom. He wore no hose, it being midsummer and hot. His shoes were simple penny loafers.

With the change of name it had not been necessary for Willie to look up the records for Georgie Cornell, so his true age was irrelevant. A new file was added for Georgie Alcorn, age 25, with a bogus history. Like most governmental bureaus, the Sperm Service was smothered in reams of paper, incompetently filed, and no official cared as long as the quotas were filled with living bodies.

Cornell's principal difficulty lay in maintaining the distinction asked by the Movement: one must be of one mind, but two styles of demeanor. Mentally, one was a Man. This identification had been simple enough all his life. But according to Stanley, maleness meant being forceful of spirit, not necessarily always downright aggressive, but possessing the capability of so being when the situation demanded. As, in fact, Cornell had been in his escape from jail.

But Cornell had spent almost thirty years in supposing that such a condition of soul was peculiarly feminine; and all the world outside the subway tunnel agreed.

Further to complicate the matter, in his assignment Cornell now had to *act* as a man by the Movement definition, while continuing to appear as a normal, passive male by accepted standards so as not to attract attention to himself.

He now wondered whether he had gone too far in extracting the aspirin from that sergeant. He picked up his clutch purse and the little valise, containing only a change of underwear and a nightie—uniforms would be forthcoming at camp—and, smiling at the sour-looking one-striper who managed the disrobing room, went through the door and into the parking lot, where three large, olive-drab-painted trucks, with white stars on their doors, were drawn up.

A thin, tall-for-a-girl corporal took his name and checked it off on a roster.

"On board, Alcorn," she said, and when he started for the second vehicle—because of some quirk, the same by which he never took the very first stool at a lunch counter—she shouted: "The first truck, jerk!"

He restrained an impulse to make a snotty rejoinder. The bed of the truck was dark under a canvas roof, and very high above the ground, with only one cast-iron step for access. He hitched up his skirt to take the steep climb, and in a quick turn of head saw the corporal ogling his exposed thigh. Cornell stuck out his tongue.

"Here." A boy's face looked out and a hand was extended to him. He clambered up. There were facing benches along the sides of the vehicle. One was filled with conscripts. The other side still had some room, and he sat down, his suitcase at his knees. He had banged someone with it in the awkwardness of boarding, but heard no complaint.

He looked across and said to any of the three young men in that area of the bench: "Sorry."

One of them smiled, one moued, and the other's general expression of melancholia did not change. The smiling one had given him the hand.

"Hi," said he. "I'm Gordie."

"Georgie."

Gordie was a husky lad with long blond hair and quite a bosom. Cornell did not remember having seen him during the examination, and wondered whether the breasts were prosthetic.

"I wonder," said Gordie, "how long we'll have to wait here."

With great assurance Cornell said: "We'll pull out for camp

as soon as the truck is full." Even if he had no way of knowing that; perhaps they must stay until all three vehicles were loaded.

He thought he saw, now that his vision had adjusted to the lack of light, a certain resentment in the face of the boy who sat on Gordie's right, a wan brunet in textured stockings. Cornell realized he must be careful: he himself did not much care for know-it-alls.

He took off the edge: "At least that's what I *think*."

"I wonder where we're going," asked Gordie.

Cornell checked an impulse to answer this, though he was equipped to pronounce the alternatives: Staten Island or New Brunswick, N.J., the two local sperm camps. He wanted to de-alienate the brunet.

"Don't ask me," he said, shaking his head in a clueless, self-deprecatory way.

The brunet turned back and said quickly: "Camp Kilmer, I just know." He recrossed his legs the other way. "I just hate Jersey." He gave Cornell a defiant look.

To which Cornell responded ingratiatingly: "I know what you mean." But the brunet turned away again; he was not to be won so easily.

A new arrival was trying to get aboard. Cornell beat Gordie to the tailgate. It was Jackie.

"Georgie!" he said. "I was afraid I'd never see you again." Cornell pulled him up.

"Where's Howie?"

Jackie callously elevated one shoulder. "Probably rejected. Probably sterile." Lowering the shoulder pettishly, he banged the brunet with the overnight case he was carrying.

The brunet rubbed his textured knee and gave Jackie a resentful look. Jackie was totally indifferent. Cornell understood that Jackie was the feckless, self-concerned type of boy who might bring him more trouble as friend than as enemy. He decided a little discipline might be in order.

"Watch that case, for Mary's sake," he told Jackie. "And sit down. Right here."

Jackie accepted these orders almost gratefully. The brunet, however, had another grudge now, having suffered without being noticed. Cornell could see *he* had got the blame.

He decided to show compassion. "Poor Howie," he said to the truck at large. "He's the boy who was next to me inside. He's very patriotic. He'll probably kill himself if he's 4-F."

The brunet said spitefully: "He's a fool then."

"You and I know that, but he's awfully unsophisticated." He was taking a certain chance: there might be other patriots in the company and, Stanley had warned him, spies as well. "We are all willing to do our duty, of course, but if, through no fault of your own, you can't—"

"I know lots of fellows who haven't been called up," said the brunet. "You make friends in the right places. *I* could have. I probably should have." He was very vain.

"Gee, I wish I could have," Cornell said, giving the fellow an admiring once-over. This proved successful. The brunet came off it and actually smiled.

Cornell moved to exploit his advance. "Hi, I'm Georgie."

"Farley." Farley lowered his eyes in embarrassment at his abdication from hostility. Cornell sensed it was time to let him alone for a while. And anyway, there suddenly was Howie, who climbed into the truck without assistance, canvas bag swinging from a shoulder strap. He wore a tartan miniskirt and scarlet knee-stockings and was a far cry from what he had been when last seen.

He was radiant, bubbling. "I made it, Georgie!" Jackie uttered a doleful sound.

With Howie's arrival, both benches were filled. The corporal slammed the tailgate with an awful noise, and almost immediately the truck moved off, just as Cornell had predicted.

And it turned out that Farley had been right about their going to Camp Kilmer, in New Jersey, another piece of luck for Cornell, because this was the sort of success that might sweeten the temperamental brunet.

The Lincoln Tunnel was foul with seepage from the Hudson Sewer above, and most of the men put on their gas masks. Jackie, wouldn't you know, had forgotten his, and Cornell had to share his own mask with that exasperating acquaintance, holding his breath in between.

The camp, the gates of which they first saw receding from the back of the truck as it bumped along towards the interior, looked unprepossessing, and the façade of the barracks at which they deboarded maintained the same bleak tone. A stout sergeant appeared, cigar in the corner of her mouth and a dark stain on the front of her open-necked chino shirt. She arranged them into a single line and led it into the one-story frame building.

The interior was rather more attractive than one was prepared to find. There were flowered curtains at the windows and matching bedspreads on the cots. Continuing the scheme, little vases filled with plastic blossoms hung from the wooden posts which supported the roof, posts which themselves were painted pink, as were the walls. Each bunk shared a fuzzy turquoise bedside rug with its neighbor. Behind the cots were standing wardrobe closets, also turquoise, closed with shirred draperies, rather than doors, again in the fabric of the bedspreads and curtains.

The sergeant cried a halt when they were all inside. She began to read names from a roster and point to consecutive beds. Jackie, Cornell, Howie, and Gordie, in that order, were along the middle of the east wall. Farley was across the aisle. Unfortunately, Cornell had to share his closet with Jackie.

It is within my knowledge that a man who had weighed many human brains, said that the heaviest he knew of, heavier even than Cuvier's (the heaviest previously recorded), was that of a woman.

JOHN STUART MILL, 1869

8

EARLY ON THE FOLLOWING MORNING they were issued their uniforms: simple one-piece, knee-length dresses in apple green; black shoes with squat one-and-a-half-inch heels; three pairs of opaque pantyhose in a muddy brown; three pairs of white cotton underpants of the kind you wore as a schoolboy; and to those who needed bras, two (for the first time Cornell did not regret having lost his boobs: the brassières looked coarse and excessively stitched). There was also an exercise outfit consisting of pleated, flared-leg shorts in navy, two white pullover blouses, bobby socks, and sneakers which they were warned to keep sparkling.

A light cardigan, a raincoat, a plastic shower cap, and six plain handkerchiefs. A shoulder bag of green plastic, containing a compact and change purse. Also a vanity kit that was far from sufficient: card of hairpins, cheap comb, lipstick in one sickly pink shade for all, and a steel safety razor and a dozen blades. Cornell had been advised by sperm-term veterans in the Movement to bring along his own cosmetics and beauty-tools. All the conscripts had so done. Jackie's suitcase contained little else, being crammed with portable hair drier, electric shaver with manicure attachments, a set of heatable hair rollers, hormone creams in the giant-sized jars, and whatnot. The first thing he did on unpacking was look for a receptacle into which to plug his devices. The one he found was labeled "110 v.," which was good, but also "Direct Current," which was very bad, the hair drier operating only on

A.C. Nothing would stop the silly boy's hysteria but Cornell's promise that Jackie could share his machine.

They had dined the evening before, their first, on steak and eggs, a hearty repast in which few made more than a dent. They were chided about this by the medical officer who strolled, inspecting, about the mess hall: a lean, sallow woman, she was an incongruous advocate for a robust diet, but then, it was their semen that would be drained, not hers.

Dessert was a handful of vitamin capsules for each, washed down with a half pint of whole milk.

The sergeant extinguished the barracks lights at ten o'clock. At ten the next morning, by which hour most of the boys had risen long since and performed their toilets, several being in curlers, she returned with a metal triangle in one hand and a little mallet in the other, and was in the act of striking the latter upon the former when, face full of indignant wonder, she reacted to the passing parade.

"What are you boys doing up?" She pointed with her little mallet. "You just get back in those beds!"

Thirty men began to carry out the order.

"Oh, no, you don't," the sergeant said. "You don't get into bed with your clothes on. You undress and put on your nighties, and you be quick about it."

When this was accomplished and thirty heads touched thirty pillows, the sergeant strode to the center of the room.

"Now hear this," she said, holding the triangle at one hip and the hammer at the other. "You are to sleep twelve hours a night, from ten to ten. Anyone out of bed between those hours, except for a quick trip to the john, will be in trouble with me, personally, and I am rough as a cob." She lifted her instrument and struck it three times, *bing, bing, bing.* "This is the morning call. On hearing it you will rise." She produced the signal again. "Well, all right, get those lazy heinies out of bed!"

Thirty men docilely arose and began to dress.

Jackie was whining about his uniform.

"Don't we get slips? Look how this skirt hangs without a slip underneath!" He flipped through his issue of pantyhose. "Perfectly hideous. Oh, why can't they be sheer!"

"I guess the idea is durability," said Cornell. He had modestly got into the dress first. Now, reaching up under the skirt, he pulled off his civilian black-bikini pants and stepped into the cotton panties of a style he had not worn since small-boyhood. At least they weren't as grotesque as the jailhouse bloomers.

"Well, they aren't durable either," Jackie said. "Here's a run already. Oh damn! Will they give me a replacement, do you think? Or will I just get abused if I ask?"

"I'll speak to the sergeant," Cornell promised.

"She looks like she can be nasty. This is a terrible place, Georgie."

"Now, don't keep telling yourself that. We've got to make the best of it for six months."

It would take more than a slip to make Jackie's uniform presentable. The dress was far too small, the skirt far above his knobby knees, and the style was not intended to be mini. At the bosom the buttons strained the holes, mainly because of Jackie's barrel chest: his boobs were modest today. Their size changed with his outfits.

Howie, on the other side, had got a good fit, but, being only eighteen, he looked good in anything. But Cornell himself did not fare badly. His dress was slack on top, of course, but sleek across the fanny and hips, and the hemline fell properly just below the kneecaps.

"Howie," Cornell asked. "Do you mind telling me about those?" He gestured at the boy's rounded breasts. "Are they injected, or what?"

Howie shrugged. "They're just balled anklets. That's all. I used to use paper towels, but you could hear them rustle." He was a naive sort.

They were seated on folding chairs in the camp theater, along with hundreds of new conscripts from the other barracks. A middle-aged officer walked briskly from the wings to stage center, before an enormous, blank motion-picture screen. She wore a gray crewcut and a well-tailored uniform, above the left breast pocket of which were several rows of multicolored ribbons.

"Welcome to Camp Kilmer," she said into the standing microphone, after tapping it smartly to see if it was live. "I am your commanding officer, Colonel Peckham. You are at the beginning of your sperm term. Some of you may be apprehensive now, but I think I can say you will soon find it more of an adventure than an ordeal. Thousands of young men have passed through this camp in its long history—and before that, thousands of young women, en route to the wars, and many of those brave girls are buried in some foreign land, having sacrificed their lives in the defense of democracy.

"This very camp is named for one of them—Joyce Kilmer, the poetess who authored 'Trees' and subsequently died in combat. That was a century or more ago, and yet she is not forgotten.

"Be assured that while your own contribution may not be so spectacular, it is valuable—uh, very valuable."

The colonel looked into the palm of her hand; she seemed to have a note there.

"Now, the next item on the agenda will be a training film. Watch this closely. Experience has shown that the semen-gathering process can be somewhat frightening to certain conscripts if they come to it without intellectual preparation. This film was created with just such a purpose in mind: it will remove and/or correct the false impressions that many of you may have gotten from sperm veterans of other eras. Techniques have been vastly improved in recent years. Old vets may have told you horror stories about the inefficient, even dangerous, milking machines to which they were strapped, etcetera, etcetera. Most of these tales never held water."

The colonel smiled and shook her close-cropped head. "And insofar as they did, they do so no longer. At this installation we have the latest equipment, and our technicians are graduates of an intensive training course. They are supervised by doctors. You have already had two of our meals. The government spares no expense in maintaining the quality of the high-protein diet. I urge you to eat everything on your trays. It is put there for your own good, to ensure your continued health and provide strength for your efforts.

"I also recommend that you cooperate, with good will, in all phases of the program; that you participate wholeheartedly in the supervised recreation. That way the time will pass like a dream. There are rewards for doing your duty, and there are penalties for failure to do it. This is not a penal colony, and speaking as your commanding officer, may I say that no sight pleases me as much as a new crop of bright young faces and robust young bodies.

"I wish you good ejaculations!" She looked over their heads at the projection booth in the rear of the balcony and snapped her fingers. "Roll the film."

The lights went out. Jackie leaned against Cornell.

"I bet she can be mighty nasty."

There were other mutterings in the auditorium, which seemed more stifling in the dark. It was beginning to be a hot day outside, and the place was neither air-conditioned nor effectively ventilated. Some conscripts were not given to using deodorants. Cornell raised his handkerchief, on which he had fortunately sprinkled some cologne before leaving the barracks.

The lights went on again, and the colonel marched onto the stage.

"Now hear this," she said. "Anyone caught talking during the picture will be dealt with." Cornell saw Sergeant Peters rise at the end of the row and glare at her group.

The lights were extinguished, and the picture came on the

screen in glaring color, accompanied by a lively show-tune played by an invisible string orchestra. A litle group of young men, in the Sperm Service uniform, were seen sitting in a lounge full of chintz-covered furniture. They smiled, chattered, and passed a dish of what looked like foil-covered bonbons.

Over this scene a title began to appear, as if being written by an invisible pen, in flowing pink script: *Introducing the Sperm Service* is what it said when finished.

The benevolent voice of a female narrator was heard.

"You boys are about to embark on an enchanting voyage." At which the men on the screen turned and giggled at the camera. One of them popped a bonbon into his mouth and licked the fingers that had held it.

"This picture is a travelogue of that voyage. Come along!" A roly-poly fat sergeant came into the lounge, smiled at the men, and then took in her pudgy hand the square chin of one husky blond. "You look so sweet today, Maxie." Maxie simpered. "I think I'll put you at the top of the class."

Maxie gasped happily and rose. She took his hand, and the camera followed them through a flower-stenciled door, which opened by an unseen agency.

"The other boys," said the narrator, "are a wee bit jealous, boys being boys. But they know their turns will come. And they also know that dear old Sarge Winters, a twenty-year veteran of the Sperm Service cadre, loves all her lads."

Now Winters and Maxie were in a room with pale-blue wallpaper and a cerise rug. A kind of sitz bath of turquoise plastic occupied one corner. The sergeant proved it was full of water by dipping in one fat finger. Since there were no faucets on it, Cornell wondered how it had been filled. There was a false sort of tone to this whole thing.

When the camera next went to Maxie, he was magically wearing a semitransparent pink peignoir, which parted to the knee as he lifted his large foot and gingerly touched the big toe to the surface of the liquid.

"Oo."

"Too hot?" The sergeant was concerned.

"Oh, no. It's dreamy."

His back to the camera, the sergeant taking off the peignoir and holding it to screen his descent, Maxie lowered himself into the bath.

The violins played, Maxie's blissful face was seen in closeup, eyelids softly lowering. Then Sarge Winters' genial dewlaps were seen, then a bowlful of tea roses, then back to a view of Sarge bundling Maxie in a huge fluffy pink towel.

"Would you believe," asked the narrator, "that this is all there is to it? Well, it is! Maxie will now have a lovely meal in the recently redecorated dining room, take a nap in his comfy bed, and be ready for the usual evening of fun: a new hit musical, a fashion show of the season's collections. On other nights there is discothèque dancing, or a famous name from the world of coiffure will give a demonstration hairstyling, a body-specialist will give figure analyses.

"Your sperm term is so many things. You are doing your duty. You are serving your country. You are making new friends. You are realizing your potential as men. And you are having *fun!*"

The music swelled up once again, and across the broad figure of Maxie, who, swaddled in his pink towel, smiled beatifically, the pink script began to appear: *Produced by the Sperm Service, U.S. Army Medical Corps, Department of Survival.*

Cornell had been summoned to the company commander's office. He arrived there with some trepidation. Had he already been spotted as a troublemaker?

A swarthy first sergeant told him to wait, but hardly had he sat down on the camp chair than a woman in olive-drab trousers and shirt, two silver bars on one side of the collar and a caduceus on the other, emerged from an inner office.

She wore a stern, feminine sort of smile. Cornell tried to keep his chin up and his gaze guiltless.

"Georgie Alcorn?"

He nodded timorously.

"Come in, please."

A stark, military room, containing only a desk, its chair, and a cardboard carton on the floor behind. The captain sat down. Cornell stood rigidly so as to inhibit an impulse to tremble.

"Relax," said the captain. "At rest, as we say in the women's army." She had wavy brown hair in the short Army cut, shaved clean for an inch above the ears. "Alcorn," she said, head down, examining some papers. "Alcorn, I've had some reports on you already."

Cornell covered his mouth.

The captain looked up with a genial grin. "Very good reports, Alcorn. You seem to be a natural leader, with unusual presence for a man. I like that. You're not one of the typical simpering young boys we usually get. I see you're almost twenty-five, just under the wire. But the real stuff doesn't just come automatically with age."

"Yes, ma'am."

The captain frowned abstractly. "Alcorn, I don't have an easy job here. Sometimes I'd rather be back with the shrapnel, mortar bursts, and booby traps in Rumania—I left a hand there." She lifted her left arm and showed the rounded pink stump at the cuff.

"Oh," Cornell began, "I'm terribly—"

She cut him off. "No, no, no! I'm a *soldier*, Alcorn. I knew what I was getting into, and I brought back a DSC." She waved the stump once in a counterclockwise circuit, then put it away.

"I didn't bring you here to boast of my exploits. Alcorn, I've found in handling men that a woman can go only so far. It's finally a matter of biology, I think. Boys have secret places in their characters which only another male can really understand. Now, we could be absolute tyrants here, but we don't want to be except as a last resort. It works out better for all concerned if things run well, if the boys don't just perform their duties as a kind of drudgery into which they've been forced, but willingly, even enthusiastically. It makes my job easier, and time flies for them. Before they know it, their term is up and they all go home —enriched, really."

The captain frowned. "But it's another story if sullenness develops, or hysteria, spitefulness, and so on—the sort of emotional problems that invariably crop up when men are in the company of their own sex for very long."

"Yes, ma'am."

"What I'm getting to, Alcorn, is: I want you to be barracks leader for your, uh, barracks. This post carries no extra money but considerable authority. In fact, you will be just under Sergeant Peters in the chain of command—unofficially, in a technical sense; naturally, the AR's and AW's both specifically forbid the official appointment of any male person to a position of authority—I refer to the Army Regulations and Articles of War." She held her head back and looked up her nose at Cornell.

"But in a meaningful way, you will be part of this line of power, and in Peters' absence will be responsible for executing her orders, which, of course, may in many cases emanate higher up, higher than me, even, from the colonel or the divisional general, and so on, and maybe eventually the Secretary of Survival and even the President."

The captain plunged her only hand into the cardboard box behind the desk. Cornell had assumed it was a container for waste paper. She brought from it a little hat, a cloche, in canary-yellow felt, the crown encircled by a green grosgrain ribbon, its split ends trailing at the rear.

"This is the barracks leader's badge of authority: the B.L. bonnet. We think it's quite attractive, and I've never heard of a boy who disagreed." She handed it across to him. "Try it on."

Cornell found the issue compact in his shoulder bag and, having blown the powder off the mirror, looked at himself. It was actually quite cute.

"Cute," said the captain. "You have a sweet face, Alcorn."

When Cornell glanced at her over the open compact, she cleared her throat and spoke gruffly.

"I've decided you should be B.L. of your barracks, Alcorn. I hope you agree. Now, report to Sergeant Peters." She lowered her head and began to leaf through the papers.

Back at the barracks, the yellow cloche caused the movement of heads, first to look, then to reverse in jealousy. Only Howie and Gordie were generous, both smiling in admiration, the latter saying: "How darling!" Even sycophantic Jackie's nose was out of joint. "*I* didn't get a hat," he said. "*I* never get anything."

Cornell did not dare to ascertain whether Farley, whose bed was across the aisle, was present and looking. He explained his new position to the three friends.

"It's somewhat embarrassing. Imagine *me* giving orders." Yet he already felt a sense of power from merely being in the position in which he could wonder at it.

Young Howie said: "Oh, you'll be marvelous!" And blond Gordie shrugged his big shoulders. "I know the boys would rather have you do it than that awful Sergeant Peters."

"Will they?" asked Cornell, cocking his head. "Will they?"

A brunet on the way back from the lavatory stared at the hat, sniffed, and flipped his face in the other direction.

Jackie was sitting in a depressed attitude on the edge of his bunk. He coughed. "I think I'm coming down with something."

Cornell said: "I'm supposed to report to Peters. The captain didn't spell out my duties."

Gordie patted his shoulder in a sweet way. Jackie sneezed.

The sergeant's quarters were in a little private room at the end of the barracks. She had her own bathroom there, but was given occasionally to appearing in the men's lavatories, presumably on inspection. But of what? She had a randy eye.

Cornell knocked on her door and was answered by a coarse "Yeahhhh?" He gave his name. "Oh, come in!"

She lay in T-shirt and trousers on her bunk, reading a comic book and smoking a cigar the odor of which was so filthy that Cornell feared he might swoon. With his scented handkerchief he fanned a channel through the blue cloud.

"I've been sent here by the cap—" He coughed violently. "She appointed me—"

"B.L.," said Peters, grinning. "On my recommendation." She swung her stockinged feet to the floor, sucked a mouthful of smoke, and expelled it in a blast which mushroomed off the far wall, on which were scotch-taped several magazine photos of boys in frilly black underwear and garterbelted black hose.

Peters patted the cot alongside her thick thigh. "Take the weight off." Cornell sat down near the end. He found her physically repellent, and he could use such air as entered the door, which he had left ajar.

"I picked you out, Alcorn. I like your style." She put the slimy end of the cigar between her lips and spoke around it. "I don't mind your looks, either. Haw, haw!" She held up two fingers. "You and me have to work together." She scissored the fingers to demonstrate. "These kids need a strong hand—me. And a velvet glove—you. This is the first time some of them have been away from a school dormitory, ya know? Now lemme tellya what I wancha to do: you'll be responsible for gettin 'em up in the morning. That's reveille—not the real reveille we got in the women's army, with the bugle and all, and falling out on some cold morning that freezes your ass. Lucky you were born with a dong, Alcorn!"

Peters guffawed again and moved herself nearer Cornell, near enough to reach his knee with her gross paw. Cornell adjusted his bonnet and moved subtly away.

"Then you march 'em two abreast, like you seen me do, to the mess hall for breakfast. Don't count cadence or anything. We used to try a real military march, but men can't keep in step worth a shit—we had everybody stumbling and tripping, so it's a just a nice, easy walk now. After breakfast you lead 'em right to the classes, the interpretive dancing, needlework, and so on—I'll give you the mimeo'd schedule, but in a day or two you'll have it in your head. Same thing, the rest of the day."

Cornell was wondering what duties Peters reserved for herself: at this rate he seemed to be doing everything. Perhaps she sensed this: she moved closer to him and handled his knee again.

"I'll take over on collection days."

"Collection?" He hadn't much more of the bunk to slide to.

"The semen, kiddo! That's why you're here, remember?" She leaned across and kicked the door shut with her left foot, which meant she was already on him. She clasped his neck, whipped the cigar from her yellow teeth, and pressed two tobacco-tarred lips upon his startled mouth. He went backwards and banged his bonneted head against the wall. His legs flew apart, and her hand shot under his buttocks, squeezing them painfully. She was of a formidable weight, the unresistant soggy kind. Nevertheless, with a sudden out-breath he threw her off, and onto the floor.

He was ready to regret that, when she came up grinning.

"Hard to get, huh? I like that, Alcorn. And I can wait. I'm going to plug you, kiddo. Never doubt that." She breathed sterorously from exertion and lust.

Cornell stood up, adjusted his B.L. bonnet, and stepped daintily around the sergeant.

"I'm sure we'll work together very well," he said softly, and left the room in a neat, precise stride, almost colliding with Farley, who was just outside the door.

Farley's eyes were not serene. Had he been spying? Cornell would have liked to slap his ratty little face. Instead, he smiled.

Farley glared at him, and then at the cloche.

"What an awful color," he said. "Pee-yellow."

Cornell put a finger to his own lips. "Shhh!" He pulled Farley a few feet into the main barracks room and whispered: "You'll get in trouble, dear, if she hears you. This is supposed to be an honor."

"Well, I wouldn't want it," Farley said spitefully. He looked as if he might cry at any moment.

Cornell linked arms with him. He was stronger than Farley, and forced him to walk along the aisle.

"Don't think I want it," he said. "But I don't like to make waves. *They* can be terribly brutal, you know. And the rest of the boys are pretty pitiful, not like you and me, dear. We must do what we can for them."

"Why?" Farley looked indignantly through the side of his dark hair.

"They're our fellow men."

"Screw them," said Farley. "No man has ever done anything for me."

"How many *women* have?"

Farley's lower lip came out. They had reached his bed, and Cornell released him. Farley sat down on the cot and put his disconsolate face in his hands.

Cornell said: "Farley, I wish you'd be my friend."

Farley looked up, his eyes disturbed by mixed emotions.

"Well," said Cornell, "think about it, anyway."

He turned and started across the aisle.

"Georgie," said Farley. Cornell turned back. "I'm sorry I was bitchy. The hat is really very cute on you." He colored and averted his face.

Cornell sighed inwardly. He wondered how often he would have to go through this sort of farce. Men!

He crossed the aisle. Jackie was sitting on his, Cornell's, cot: he didn't like that.

"How did it go?" asked Jackie.

"O.K." He decided not to tell of his experience with Sergeant Peters. He wondered whether Peters would think he had. Some women liked to be known as Doña Juanas, on the theory that men, masochistic conformists, were more easily overwhelmed if psyched by a reputation. Peters was very likely just such a brute.

He kept his account to a mere statement of his duties.

"How are you going to wake up on time?" Jackie asked, leaning back on one hand, just as if it were his own bed.

Cornell frowned. "Jackie, would you mind—"

Jackie said: "I've got it!" He went to the wardrobe behind the beds, pulled aside the flowered curtain, and came out with a little yellow alarm clock, the face of which was a clown's; the hands were representations of a clown's gloved fingers, the index outthrust, and one arm shorter than the other. It was a child's timepiece. Jackie was so silly, but he really was goodhearted and impossible to hate.

All in all, Cornell had not made a bad beginning for his mission. He had made several friends. He had the confidence and approval of the authorities. He even had an official function. He felt sure he could continue successfully to resist Peters, and he suspected that the captain also had a gentlewomanly letch for him.

He was supposed to report once a week to the Movement, as well as at any time of emergency. Oddly enough, this was to be done by telephone. There was actually a phone line into the underground headquarters; not a properly sanctioned one, but a tap from the basement connection of offices in the building above, namely those of Huff House. The telephone service was normally so awful that this went unsuspected—as did everything else in the old subway tunnel, so far as he could tell, confirming the Movement theory that the tyranny of women was exceeded only by their inefficiency.

Cornell wondered privately why, then, men remained the underdogs. But he would no more ask that of Stanley or even Frankie than he would ask Sergeant Peters how she expected to conquer him physically when he was a head taller than she and in much better condition.

The next morning he was awakened by his own internal clock thirty minutes before Jackie's alarm was scheduled to sound. Instead of rolling over for another half hour's snooze, which he would certainly have done without the B.L. bonnet, Cornell got up, shaved face, chest, and armpits, and did his face. His eyes were simpler than in the old days: almost no shadow and softer with the liner, a style that seemed better to suit the new nose. He was coming to accept that revision, no longer pinching it gently in wonderment.

Jerry really was a remarkable surgeon, considering the crude conditions under which he performed—considering that he was a man. Cornell had once forgotten himself and said that to Frankie. He couldn't help it. He hadn't changed that much, if at all. Sometimes he just had to be realistic: there must be some reason why women ran the world, because *they did.* Not even the Brothers could deny that.

Frankie had grimaced and said: "Georgie, Georgie, you're just going to have to work harder on your values." Then he went into the familiar historical theory by which the Movement sought to explain everything: that men had once had power but lost it through pity for women. Blah-blah, blah.

Cornell peered into the mirror. Was that a visible vein on his nose? No, merely a loose hair. A *hair?* He feverishly examined his scalp. It looked as if it were thinning, though not specifically; he couldn't find a particular area of loss, but the strands he took between thumb and forefinger felt strange, lacking in substance.

He brushed and shaped his hair with his eyes shut part of the time. He didn't want to see if any more fell out.

At last he got hold of himself, returned to the dormitory and exchanged his nightie and robe for the green uniform and yellow hat, adjusting the latter in his compact mirror, pulling little curls out below his ears. Did the captain mean it when she said he had a sweet face? If so, how many more years would that last? You never think your own face is sweet, yet if someone else says it is, you can see what they mean.

Cornell gave himself one more sweet expression, closed the mirror, and strode along the aisle, crying: "All right, boys, you've had your beauty sleep. Rise and shine!"

The recumbent men began to stir and murmur. Cornell harried them amiably, with that little touch of mockery that boys expect from those in authority. Until she fired him, Ida had usually addressed him in that tone. He missed it in the humorless Movement.

"Come on, children. Time to play!" The men grumbled, and more than once Cornell had to pinch the toe of some persistent sleepyhead. Several of the boys had gone to bed in curlers, many in masks of face cream. Jackie of course had done the works: he had treated his hair with one of the many concoctions from his portable drugstore and had turbaned a towel over it. His face was concealed behind a hardened cover of greenish mud, through which his eyes peeped out defenselessly, without the false lashes.

Sergeant Peters stayed in her room and probably would sleep all morning while he performed her duties. After the boys were dressed and made up, the beds had to be put in shape. He knew that from the morning before, when Peters had marched up and down, commanding. Cornell did it more gently, though some of the men were awfully slovenly when it came to putting away their nightclothes. He had to admonish one big redhead whose shorty pajamas were left where the man had stepped out of them: on the bedside rug.

Finally the job was done, all the coverlets in place, all the wardrobe curtains drawn, and a detail of four boys had zipped around with dry mops and taken up the balled dust, loose hair, and chewing gum wrappers. Cornell then led his group to breakfast, where, supposing he should set an example, he performed a heroic feat with the mountain of scrambled eggs and accompanying logjam of sausages. He ate a good third of it. To compensate he would try to skip lunch. He could not bring himself to chide the boys who picked at their meal. It was obscene to face that much food in the morning.

Peters had not yet furnished him with the mimeographed agenda, but yesterday they had returned to the barracks after breakfast. So they did it again today. He was wondering whether to wake up the sergeant when it came to his attention that he hadn't seen Farley since the night before. He now remembered that Farley's bed was already made when he was waking up the others. In the heat of his responsibility, he had not reacted seriously to that observation, and had assumed Farley was in the bathroom. He had not noticed him at breakfast.

Another thing Cornell did not possess was a roster against which he could check attendance. A man could desert without his being the wiser. Mary! Suppose Farley had run off. Could *he* be blamed? Cornell went through the lavatory, looking into the showers and each open toilet booth. The last one was closed. "Farley?" No answer. Suppose Farley had sat down on the toilet and slashed his wrists. Cornell's limbs turned numb. He rapped on the door. "Farley?"

It was Jackie's voice that wailed: "I'm not feeling well, Georgie!"

Cornell returned to the dormitory. Gordie sat writing a letter on flowered notepaper. He had one of those correspondence kits which when unfolded made a little lap desk.

"Have you seen Farley?"

"Who?"

"The brunet." Cornell pointed at Farley's bed.

"Oh, is that his name? I haven't met him." He hadn't seen him, either. Nor had Howie. Farley was not the kind who attracted notice from anyone but Cornell. He was a loser, like poor old Charlie. Cornell seemed to have an affinity for such people. He tried to help them, and the result was that he got into trouble himself. What would happen to *him* if Farley had deserted? Was that a mean thought? What would happen to poor Farley?

Cornell hurled himself onto his bed. All his new confidence was gone. He raised his head: he was crushing the B.L. bonnet. He would report to the captain and surrender the hat. He was unworthy of it, having lost a man. He sat up and removed it from his head. While he was doing so, his distracted glance happened to travel up the aisle to the door of Sergeant Peters' room. It opened, and out came Farley. Even at that distance one could see he was unshaven and his hair was a disgrace.

Cornell replaced the cloche and marched towards the sergeant's room, passing Farley midway.

"Morning, Farley," he said sweetly.

Farley looked as if he were going to avoid Cornell's eyes, but at the last moment he glanced sideways through his tangled hair.

"Morning, Georgie." His voice was dull. He must have had a hard night. His stride was slightly pigeon-toed.

Peters was a sight in her striped shorts, belly hanging over the waistband, the low lumps of her strapped breasts in the T-shirt. She stood next to her bed, yawning, stretching. Two crescents of yellow sweat-stain showed in her armpits.

Cornell didn't look for her dildo.

"Sergeant," he said. "If I'm to do my job, I need a roster of the men."

She swept some loose socks off the tabletop and found her clipboard underneath.

"Roster's beneath the duty schedule," she said, handing it over.

"Thank you, Sergeant."

Peters yawned again and went into the bathroom, letting down her drawers en route.

Cornell discovered the second privilege of the barracks leader, the first being the bonnet: he was not expected to participate, or at any rate not very ardently, in the activities to which he led his men. These were largely in the home-economics area— cooking, sewing—the beautician field: makeup, hairstyling. Then there were arts & crafts: dancing, fingerpainting, and whatnot. From what he could see, the curriculum was a little less sophisticated than that of the average boys' high school, so it would be redundant for many of the conscripts. But he could understand that the Sperm Service had a problem in keeping the men occupied. They were here, as Peters said, to be milked. The rest was waiting.

As to that milking, he was interested to see that nowhere on the duty schedule did such an entry appear, yet the day-to-day program for the week's events was a fixed one which apparently held good throughout their six-month term. Every Wednesday morning was given over to Knitting & Crocheting; every Saturday evening a film was shown; and so on. Unless the semen-collection was masked behind some innocuous designation such as "Outdoor sports—badminton, field hockey, etc.," Sunday afternoons, there seemed no provision for it in the schedule.

This was strange indeed. Cornell sat on a folding chair in the corner of the room in which his boys were learning the craft of flower arrangement from a dreamy, pudgy man named Hughie Hayworth, like most of the instructors a civilian.

The more Cornell thought about the omission, the more puzzling it seemed. He could of course question Peters about it, or the captain. He was after all a kind of official, appointed by them. But he remembered that Peters would take over from him when a collection was due: the one job retained by the lazy sergeant. If he, Cornell, had no authority in this area, a question might be considered impertinent.

Cornell bit his underlip and looked around the room. The flowers they used were paper, of course. Hayworth was very deftly manipulating an arrangement of big gaudy paper zinnias, having previously put together a nosegay of pansies interspersed with baby's-breath: the former in a glass bowl, the latter in a swell-bellied vase of green ceramic.

"Georgie, may I go to the bathroom?" It was big, goodnatured Gordie, who did everything well. His flower arrangement, a bowl of roses, was almost as good as one of Hayworth's, and Cornell had seen the instructor approve it somewhat jealously.

"Oh, gee," Cornell answered. "Do I have the authority?"

"Hughie Hayworth told me to ask you," Gordie said, smiling with his big square white teeth. "You don't know your own power."

Cornell shrugged boyishly. "It's all so new. Well, then, sure you can, if it's up to me."

As Gordie went out, some of the other fellows looked pettishly at him. Cornell must never forget masculine envy. He went to Hayworth and asked if he could make an announcement.

Hughie gestured fussily with his shears. "I'm just a paid employe here. You're the officer."

This statement amazed Cornell, but he replied smoothly:

"There is such a thing as courtesy, my dear. It's your class."

Hayworth, dried-up little man in his blue smock over a shapeless dress, was touched. "They must have slipped up when they made you barracks leader. You're actually a very nice person."

Of course Cornell enjoyed the compliment, but he had been given another worry. Did the authorities expect him to perform his office in a brutal manner? Was he being too easy on the men?

He made his announcement: "Permission will be granted to use the lavatory, but no more than two boys may leave the room at the same time." That seemed reasonable: there were but four booths in the facility, the door to which was just down the hall between theirs and another classroom with which they must share it. By Cornell's considerate arrangement the other class would have two booths available at all times.

Several men raised their hands. With index finger Cornell chose the closest and also the most pathetic-looking, a tall young man with a face empurpled by acne.

Hardly had the boy gone than he was back, and Gordie returned shortly thereafter.

"What a hassle," Gordie told Cornell. "That place is filled with kids from the embroidery class. They all crowded in at once, and there are only four potties and two washstands and one big mirror."

How unfair. Cornell went to the acned boy and said: "You didn't get to go at all?" The lad nodded unhappily. Cornell patted his hand and addressed the class.

"We're getting a raw deal, boys, and I'm going to straighten it out." He squared his shoulders, touched his bonnet of office, and marched into the hall.

There were a dozen or so men in single file outside the lavatory door. He pushed past the head of the line and swung the door open. All the booths were shut, and at least four boys were using washstands and mirror. One blond was elaborately working on his eyes.

"You," said Cornell, with waggling finger. "You just put away that eyeliner and come out of there. And you others"—he raised his voice so as to be heard in the closed booths—"you finish up your business as quickly as possible and leave." One toilet flushed immediately.

He stepped into the hallway.

"Are you boys under any kind of supervision?"

From behind him he heard a familiar voice.

"What's going on here?"

He turned very slowly. First he must maintain his authority. The second requirement was that he identify the voice and be prepared to deal with the person from whom it came. The pitch was a unique compromise of tenor and contralto, rather synthetic if you thought about it—and he never had thought about that particular matter during the days in jail.

He was all the way around by now, and just as he remembered the voice, he saw in a Sperm Service uniform dress like his own, and a similar yellow cloche, his erstwhile cellmate, Harriet.

"Who the hell are you to push my men around?" she asked.

Cornell's panic was manifested in an awful scowl. Recapitulating the incident later on, he believed this must have been the case: he did not know it at the time. To himself he seemed frozen. Yet he had a surrealistic memory that he had advanced upon her, as if rolled along on wheels pushed from behind, and that Harriet had retreated.

Less aggressively she said: "This is *my* group." Her voice now went into definite soprano. "I'm in charge here!"

He continued dumbly to advance, his hand coming up, as if mechanically operated, to do something: perhaps rub his mouth, his nose, his new nose. New nose. *She did not recognize him.*

"Don't get tough with me," she said fearfully.

He lowered his harmless hand. His power to direct himself began to return from the tips of his extremities.

He said: "Don't be foolish. Nobody's fighting you."

Immediately she became more cocky. "Lucky for you."

Her men tittered. This did not shame or even annoy Cornell. Now that his fright had eased, he had begun to develop a strange feeling of intimacy for this little undercover girl. They shared a piece of common history; he knew it, and she did not. Were she to find it out, he was in danger. Meanwhile he enjoyed the first advantage he had ever had over a woman.

At the same time he marveled at her mobility: from the Men's

House of Detention to the Sperm Service, still in the same basic pose.

He drew her aside and spoke in an undertone.

"We shouldn't quarrel in front of the men," he said. "It doesn't look good. I gather you are barracks leader of this group." He told her his boys should have a fair chance at the bathroom.

"Fair?" she asked. "My group got here first."

"You know how men are," Cornell said cleverly.

She narrowed her bright blue eyes and screwed up the little nose.

"What do you mean?"

"They like discipline. What bothers them is not abuse, but being ignored."

The statement took her by surprise. "Oh, yeah?"

"So," said Cornell, "I'm going to bring my boys out here, and *you* can tell them they have to wait."

She thought about that briefly. Then: "You're a smartass, aren't you?" She searched his face. "I know you." His heart faltered, but she relieved him immediately. "I know your kind. Give you a bonnet and you begin to identify with the staff. I'm not interested in power plays."

He continued to be strengthened by her failure to recognize him. He merely grinned now.

She stamped her foot. "All right, if it will make you happy, we'll divvy up the johns: two for your group and two for mine." Embarrassed by this submission, she turned away.

He decided to introduce himself, but to say "Georgie" was pushing it to the extreme. Surely that name, common as it was among the male population, would have special meaning for her. Then too, since assuming the B.L. bonnet, Cornell had been thinking it would make sense to separate himself in still another way from the men under him. They were all called by normal male diminutives. As their superior, wearing the yellow cloche, he should be addressed otherwise. "Leader," of course, was too pretentious.

"Name's Alcorn," he said to Harriet. "My friends call me Al."

She went on the offensive again. "That's a girl's name."

"When it stands for Alice. But it doesn't here."

They stared levelly at each other for a long moment.

Then Harriet smiled. She could not be called precisely handsome, but there was suddenly something about her face that seemed endearing—*seemed,* he firmly told himself; he could no longer afford the old habit of making favorable judgments on the basis of transitory expressions.

"You've got the answer to everything, haven't you?" she asked, saucily but not nastily.

"Just trying to get by," said Cornell. "This is a tough world."

"For men."

He would not be sucked into that trap, if such it was. He was a veteran of Harriet's tricks.

"For human beings," he said. "I think self-pity is a waste of time. Anyway, I don't have too much to complain about." He was in perfect control of this exchange, taking every initiative, and turning her thrusts back at her. Now he peered boldly and asked: "Do you?"

"I thought it was so urgent for your men to get to the toilets," said she. "And here you stand talking pseudophilosophy."

She marched to her line of waiting boys.

I expect that woman will be the last thing civilized by man.

GEORGE MEREDITH, 1859

9

As HE RETURNED to his class Cornell experienced a delayed negative reaction to the encounter with Harriet. What was she doing there? Instead of the stupid little one-upping exercise, he should have tried to probe her for information. He too was now a secret agent. And he did not even know which name she was currently using.

He took immediate measures to establish his own change of diminutive. Lining up his men in twos for the march to the bathroom, he announced that he was henceforth to be addressed as "Al." Eyebrows went up, and Jackie whined: "*Why*, Georgie, for heaven's sake?"

"No talking in ranks," said Cornell. His voice was somewhat harsher than he had intended, but perhaps that was to the good. He had permitted too much familiarity in the past.

A surprise awaited him as he led them into the corridor: Harriet and all her boys had vanished. The lavatory was empty. That was spite for you! Losing the contest, she had either taken her boys to another toilet somewhere, or— He halted his group, went along the corridor to the next classroom and peeped through the window in its door. There she sat, reading a newspaper, and her men were back with their embroidery hoops. Poor things, victims of her wounded ego. That was more the kind of thing you'd expect from a man—unless it was part of her act to be virilely bitchy. As it had somehow become his to be effeminately authoritative though just.

He returned to the file waiting at the toilet door.

"First two go in," he ordered. "The rest of you may converse, but in low voices that won't disturb the nearby class."

Immediately they began to chatter, and of course in a moment the volume rose too high, and he had to impose silence.

Lunchtime followed the flower-arranging class, and as Cornell led his boys to the dining hall, he saw what looked like Harriet's group some distance ahead, though since most of its members were taller than she, he spotted the yellow cloche only intermittently. And it could have been another group altogether. The camp was a great big one, and there were dozens of barracks—he caught himself by the elbow of the mind: what a silly thought, with a typical masculine lack of precision. *Great big, dozens:* to think in terms of that kind was the internal equivalent of the empty chatter to which too many men were given; it could be said that most boys didn't think at all. No wonder that women claimed authority.

"Georgie," said a voice at his elbow.

It was Jackie. "Georgie, do you really want to be called Al?"

"I want you to do what I tell you to," Cornell snapped. "And when we're marching somewhere, I want you to stay in ranks."

Two tears appeared in Jackie's eyes, but didn't fall, just hung there, quivering, on his sticky mascara.

Cornell saw his men seated, then with the new assurance of his office, boldly left the dining hall. He had no intention of eating another of those enormous meals. The mess officer, a robust, red-faced woman, nodded at him as he left. It was nice to be included in the sorority of power. He went across a patch of scruffy lawn to the recreation building, which was off limits this time of day to ordinary conscripts. Two other barracks leaders were sitting in the lounge, which was comfortable enough but a far cry from the one shown in the movie entitled *Introducing the Sperm Service.*

En route to the telephone booths at the rear of the central

hallway, Cornell saw a candy machine, placed a zinc dollar in the slot, punched a button, and received from the hopper a bar of what appeared to be chocolate, but proved rather to be, when bitten, a tasteless, brittle compound—identified on the wrapper, which he looked at only now, as Hi-Protein Energizer.

He spat it into a refuse container, found another zinc in his shoulder bag, and used the third phone booth after trying in vain the first two dead instruments. There was a weird whistle on the line, but he got through.

It was extraordinary that one could call the headquarters of a revolutionary underground organization, and perhaps as odd that, having so done, one must wait for a response through many rings. Could they have been raided? It suddenly occurred to Cornell that in such a case his troubles would be over—or at any rate, different.

But Frankie answered at last.

"Bon Ton Boutique."

"The assistant credit manager, please," said Cornell.

"Speaking."

"I bought a pair of patent-leather shoes last week, and they are cracking and peeling."

"I'm sorry, sir."

This exchange was to identify Cornell, "Patent Leather" being his code name. The disintegration of his mythical shoes referred to his having run into trouble.

"Of course, we'll make that good," said Frankie. "Either through replacement or refund. But you should talk to the manager of the shoe department. Let me switch you over."

The booth was nice and clean, in this all-male facility, with no phone numbers or filthy epithets scribbled on its walls. Booths to which women had habitual access were invariably defaced. Cornell wondered why females tended to be dirty. He remembered that when he was a child little girls were always saying "peepee" and "doodoo." And once two of them locked him in a school closet and wouldn't let him out until he pulled up his dress and took down his panties. And then they laughed, pointing at the thing that dangled between his legs. And then the teacher caught them—Mr. Roberts, gray hair piled high with the eternal pencil stuck in it, and his sneezy odor of dusting powder—and blamed Georgie: "You led them on." Which wasn't true! Just because he had winked and stuck out his tongue!

Stanley came on the wire.

"Shoes."

"Patent leath—"

"I've been told of your complaint," Stanley said impatiently.

"Maybe I'm exaggerating," said Cornell, a bit guiltily. "Maybe I can do something here at home, treat them with Vaseline, or something." He was trying to think up a way to tell Stanley about Harriet, using the awkward code. It was standard revolutionary operating procedure to consider every telephone as bugged by the female authorities. He had been supplied with a number of prearranged messages, covering, it seemed, almost any contingency but this.

"I can't get down to the store myself, but my *girl friend* might bring them in so you can take a look."

"Any way you want to do it." Stanley was being no help. He sounded as if he might hang up at any moment.

"She works at the Men's House of Detention, which is near the store."

"Uh-huh." There was no evidence of understanding in Stanley's voice.

"Actually, she's joining the Army soon. She's going to be a *staffer in a sperm camp.*"

"Sounds like a fine young woman. We'll take care of the matter, sir. Thank you for giving us the business." Stanley hung up.

What was that supposed to mean? Also, Cornell couldn't imagine any wiretapper's *not* being suspicious of such a preposterous conversation.

Well, he had done his duty. Harriet did not really worry him. The chances were that he would encounter her rarely. Their classes might be adjacent only once per week in this large camp. The mimeographed sheet given him by Sergeant Peters applied only to his group, but in some central office there must be a master schedule for all the barracks. As a precaution against surprise, he might just go there and copy down all the other places and times, if any, that he and Harriet would coincide.

Funny thing was, he resisted thinking about *why* Harriet was there at all. Looking at it objectively, he would have thought that was the important issue. Undoubtedly she was on some sinister mission. But what could he do about it, in any case? There was no way he could warn others without exposing himself. The obvious worry was whether she was on his own trail, had been assigned here to frustrate his mission. If so, she was doing a terrible job; couldn't recognize him when she fell over him. In their competitions he always won. The other thing that occurred to him was how strange a career she had. It might be exciting, but it was fundamentally bleak, negative. He could understand what would send a woman into the open police force or even the Army. The imposing of order by violence seemed a natural feminine need. But the sneakiness of spying, the living of a lie, the practice of incessant deceit—there must be something wrong with her, some real warp of soul.

He left the phone booth and went into the lounge, saying "Hi" to the two barracks leaders on the couch. They too were passing up the noon meal. When men got authority, they made the most of it.

The larger, fair-complexioned one immediately returned the greeting. The other, a sallow-faced brunet, lowered his pale-green eyelids once and raised them. Finally he uttered a sullen "Hello."

"Say," said Cornell, taking the duty sheet from his bag—he detested carrying that feminine clipboard of Peters' and had detached the document—"do you boys know where they make these up?"

The brunet was scanning his attire in a critical manner, even though they all wore the same uniform. Cornell wondered whether his pantyhose were wrinkled at the ankle—then remembered he wasn't wearing any. Stupid that another man's stare could automatically produce self-doubt.

The larger B.L. said phlegmatically: "Darned if I know. Or care."

But the brunet raised his eyes from Cornell's flat bosom and said: "Headquarters, the planning section." He smiled. He was a decent person after all. "Come here." He led Cornell to the window, pushed the dotted-swiss curtain out of the way, and pointed. "See the big building across there? Between the camp theater and the water tower?"

"Thank you very much," said Cornell. He told himself he must stop making these snap judgments about people. His first impressions were usually wrong. They were the product of insecurity. Which was absolutely irrational in this instance. He had as much authority, the same rank, as these two men. Their acceptance or rejection of him should be a matter of indifference. It was a new and peculiarly gratifying thought, even though it might be interpreted, technically, as unmasculine. But you couldn't let narrow sexual interpretations rule your life. As did the men in the Movement; as did Harriet. It was hard enough merely to be human, just to survive.

Cornell checked the time on a wall clock in the lobby. He still had a quarter hour before he must return and collect his men. From the dining hall he would take them to the barracks for their nap. Interpretive dancing was next, at three P.M.

He decided to go over and at least reconnoiter the headquarters building. On the way there he passed a post exchange and hesitated for a moment. He could have used a vial of *My Sin*. No scents were issued, but it was permissible to wear one's own.

Now that, after the weeks with the Movement, he was again dressed as a man, he missed the cloud of fragrance in which he had once moved. But duty called, choosing that moment to suggest that he might well discover, at headquarters, some information far more important than the whereabouts of Harriet at any given moment. When was the first semen collection scheduled?

Headquarters was the usual one-story building of raw wood, and because it was occupied exclusively by women, no effort had been made to soften the harshness of practicality. No flowerbeds outside and scarcely any grass. The entrance hall was decorated only with a directory board: the titles of offices and accompanying arrows: to the right for the Planning Section. None of the listings seemed to refer to semen collection.

Cornell went along the right-hand corridor, passing doors lettered with designations such as Adjutant, Judge Advocate, and the like, and at the very end reached the one he sought. He passed no one en route. It was lunchtime for the staff as well. He pushed open the planning-section door and entered a room of which one entire wall was an enormous comprehensive duty chart. The vertical columns indicated days of the week; the horizontal boxes, the hours of the day. The designations for the various barracks groups and their scheduled activities were printed on movable cards, which adhered to the chart, as Cornell discovered by peeling one back, by reason of three dots of self-stickum on the reverse. He stuck it back.

He traced the line of his interest and found, next to the card listing his own group (B-3—Flower Arranging, Bldg. 6, Rm. 11) that which was obviously Harriet's (K-1—Embroidery, same bldg., Rm. 12). He fetched out the mimeo'd schedule and laboriously went through the whole week, comparing it with the big board. There was not another juncture, in all seven days, at which their groups would be neighbors. And Barracks K-1 was presumably halfway across camp from his B-3.

That was that. He snapped his bag shut, and then looked for

evidence of the semen-collection times. The big board had told him nothing. Along the opposite wall was a bank of filing cabinets. Every drawer he opened was filled with old mimeographed schedules of years past. Time was growing short now, and he was nervous. He caught his pinkie when closing a drawer. Sucking it, he left the room. Collections simply went unlisted, unless under some code name he could not detect.

At last he met someone, a young lieutenant carrying a briefcase. They passed in the entrance hall. Cornell modestly lowered his eyes. He wondered whether she turned to look at his legs.

Cornell had taken his boys back to the barracks after lunch, and now they were napping. Most of them, anyway, but not he and not Farley, across the aisle. He and Farley were staring at each other from their respective cots, where each lay supine, head just high enough on the pillow to see the other. This went on for a long time, but, because of the distance and the comfortable situation, it was not, at least to Cornell, the defiant, exhausting kind of contest it would have been at close quarters.

Indeed, Cornell did not feel it was a contest at all. He had Farley's number, and he was considering a bold stroke. At last he smiled, and Farley answered in kind, though not with good humor. Their neighbors were fast asleep. Jackie, on Cornell's right, was snoring softly.

Cornell nodded in the direction of the washroom, rose, and went there quickly, quietly, in stocking feet. He sensed, rather than heard, that Farley followed. Having gone along to the last basin, the cement chilling his soles, he turned and saw the man, who, more self-protective than he, was wearing velvet slippers.

Cornell opened a faucet and gained the obscuring sound of running water. The room and the booths were empty. They would have a moment's edge on anyone entering from the dormitory.

Farley proceeded to run a faucet of his own. And again he

proved more practical than Cornell. He had brought along a towel.

"Farley," said Cornell, "I'll come right out with it. Why are you sleeping with Sergeant Peters?"

"Georgie," Farley replied instantly without a hint of embarrassment, "why have you changed your name to Al?"

Cornell was taken aback. He had lost the initiative on which he had counted.

"I asked first."

"Like you," said Farley, "I feather my own nest. A boy has to look out for himself in this world." He had dropped the plug in his basin and it was filling rapidly. "Unlike you, I don't have access to the captain."

Cornell gasped. "You don't think I—"

Farley closed his tap with a decisive twist.

"Come on, *Al,* at our age we can't claim to be virgins any more."

"Look, Farley, I thought I explained in our little talk the other day. I accepted the B.L. bonnet for two good reasons. One, it was offered to me. And I assure you, whether you believe it or not, I did nothing whatever to get it. The captain didn't touch me or try to. Second, it seemed to me that in a position with a little authority I might make it easier on the rest of the boys. And I think I have done that—like getting that toilet hassle worked out this morning."

Farley wore a derisive expression.

Cornell said indignantly: "You don't know what I went through for that!"

"You're quite the hero."

"You're being bitchy."

"Up yours."

Cornell felt like slapping his face. Instead, he breathed deeply and touched his fingers to Farley's forearm.

"We're being silly, do you know that?" He drew his hand

back and put it on his bosom. "I'm as bad as you. We should be friends and work together instead of competing. I agree with you that a boy has to look out for himself, but that concept should be widened to include other men as well. We all must look out for each other."

Farley flipped his thumb contemptuously at the door. "I should be concerned for those slobs?"

"They *are* our Brothers," said Cornell, parroting the Movement line. "We're all in the same boat. We're being used shamefully, Farley. We're prisoners here. Worst of all, we're treated like children. As if we were schoolboys again, with embroidery and flower arranging."

Farley closed his eyes, lowered his face into the basinful of water, and brought it out into the waiting towel. He gently blotted his eyes, then looked in the mirror to see whether the liner had run. It had, slightly. "You never find one that's really waterproof," he said.

"We're denied all pride, Farley." Cornell stamped his stockinged foot. It did not produce the dramatic sound that he had wished, and besides it hurt his sole. "We men are in a lifelong prison, really. We're *used* from the time we're born. When do *we* get to be the users? I ask you."

Farley said: "You're exaggerating. I agree that maybe things aren't always what they should be."

"What kind of job did you have?"

"I'm a beautician," said Farley.

"In a shop owned by a woman, right?"

"I don't see anything weird about that."

"Why don't *we* ever own businesses?"

"Because we're men. That just isn't the kind of thing we do." Farley's face was close to the mirror. He was concerned about his eyes. "We're not soldiers, either. Do you think we ought to be? And kill people?"

Cornell was beginning to regret having chosen Farley to

politicize. The Movement's arguments simply did not appeal to such a person. Cornell could understand that because he was himself much the same kind of boy—in a general way. Of course he would not have gone to bed with Sergeant Peters. He was also impressed by the fact that Farley had a real profession. He was not a whiner, a loser, who, because he never got anywhere personally, wanted to change the social order. Among the Brothers there were a few men like Jerry, nurse and self-trained surgeon, but even Jerry seemed motivated largely by spite. He had to prove he could do whatever a woman could.

Cornell smiled. "Well, personally I've never really been very political. I think men who are tend to be on the faggy side."

"That's something else I don't really understand," Farley admitted. "Exactly what a fag is."

"A homosexual."

"Oh, I know that, but I don't know what homosexuals are supposed to actually *do*. I mean, you hear the word all the time. But what does it mean except 'effeminate'?"

Cornell was wryly amused at this ignorance, given Farley's looseness of morals; but Farley was normal enough.

Farley added: "I mean, I've heard the word all my life, and yet I never met a man who tried to feel me or anything."

Cornell had to confess that neither had he. He was beginning to hit it off now with Farley.

Farley said: "Was this all you wanted to talk about, Georgie?"

"*Al.* Please. I'll explain some other time." He touched Farley's shoulder. "I didn't mean to criticize you earlier. Your private life is your own business."

They returned to the dormitory, where Cornell lay down again and Farley redid his eyes. In a little while Sergeant Peters came out of her room and cried: "Everybody up!"

She formed them into a double file, with Barracks Leader Cornell getting only the privilege of walking directly behind her in the front rank. Peters marched them to a nearby building which

Cornell had assumed was another barracks, but which proved to be a sort of laboratory full of machines attended by women in white uniforms. The men were ordered to pull up their skirts, pull down their panties, and sit upon the stool before each machine. The attendants then fastened to each male member a flexible metallic pipe terminating in a soft plastic tube which adjusted snugly to that which it gripped, and expanded when required. The power was turned on, and the thing began to surge and vibrate in a hideous way.

The yellow bonnet was inefficacious here. Cornell sat before the milking machine just like any ordinary conscript. He withheld as long as he could but inevitably gave way to nature at last. However, unlike many of the others, he did not howl or sob. When it was over, his jaws, from the clenching, ached more than his groin. His soul was limp with shame. On the stool to his left, Jackie had fainted. Farley sat to his right, quietly weeping.

Cornell was allowed to resume his authority at this point. Sergeant Peters slapped his back and said: "Take over, Alcorn. That's all for this afternoon. March 'em to the barracks. I got a date with a beer at the PX." She waved him farewell with her soggy cigar.

The history of mankind is a history of repeated injuries and usurpations on the part of man toward woman, having in direct object the establishment of a tyranny over her.

MANIFESTO, WOMEN'S RIGHTS CONVENTION,
Seneca Falls, 1848

10

"WHAT GETS ME," said Cornell, "is why *we* feel the guilt and shame. *They* do that to us, and yet it is we who suffer self-hatred."

Jackie said: "It's the same thing when a woman rapes a man. *He* feels guilty, and has this suspicion that maybe somehow, subconsciously, he provoked it."

Cornell was addressing the conscripts, who sat or lay in various attitudes on their cots. The incredibly degrading experience they had all undergone an hour before had evoked something new from his soul. It was inexcusable that the Movement indoctrination had not prepared him for impromptu semen-milkings. The masturbation scheme could not possibly have been carried out. Unless of course the men continually manipulated themselves to the point of swooning, so as never to be in condition to furnish the official supply. Even so, would not those terrible machines, which had some automatic cut-off that was triggered only by the end of the flow, keep pumping?

All at once, Cornell understood: the semen-strike was *intended* to provoke a ferocious reaction from the authorities. Cornell and his boys would be emasculated, and the Movement would then have an issue on which to capitalize in their propaganda. Oh, he had been so naive! He hadn't even asked Stanley what he should do *after* the strike. And no wonder Stanley had sounded so impatient on the phone. What difference did it make to his scheme that Harriet had turned up? In fact—and this was really an awful thought—was it merely coincidental that Harriet had appeared in camp at this time?

To his boys Cornell said: "They can do what they want to us, and we must accept it. That's what it amounts to. Because they are *women*. But it's strange, isn't it?, when you think that men amount to more than half of the existing population. About fifty-two or -three percent, I believe. So we're in the majority. And we're also individually a lot bigger, on the average."

"But we're not intellectually inclined," Jackie whined.

"Aren't we? Or is it just because we've been told that all our lives?"

A heavyset conscript whose name Cornell could not recall scowled with thick black eyebrows beneath forehead curls of platinum bleach.

Cornell nodded at him. "Do you disagree?"

"I wouldn't state an opinion," said the man. "I don't like to get involved in anything controversial."

"Did you like what they just did to us?"

"Well, it's why we're here, isn't it?" said the man. "It's our duty."

The word reminded Cornell to look at young Howie, the patriot. Howie's unhappy eyes were fixed on the floor. Gordie, though, big, blond, and robust, returned his gaze with candor.

"I guess we're just stuck for six months," he said. "It's not your fault, Al. I don't think any of us blame you. You're in the same boat with the rest of us when it comes to the milking session."

Cornell was somewhat irritated to have his remarks interpreted so personally. But what could you expect from your fellow men?

Gordie went on. "I mean, it was different than what they showed in the film the other day, but *everything* usually *is* different than what's promised. Did you ever take one of those Catskill vacations? The hotel room never looks anything like the picture in the brochure, and there are so many other unattached boys there that you spend all week dancing with each other—or squabbling over the few girls." He moued. "Once was enough for me."

Jackie flipped his head vainly. "Oh, I always get dates up there."

Someone on the other side of the barracks said, in a stage whisper, "I wonder how?"

"I heard that," said Jackie, staring daggers.

Snickers were heard.

"All right," Cornell said. "Let's not have that sort of stuff. You are demonstrating why we're in this position. Women like or at least tolerate one another and can work together for a cause that will benefit their sex in general. But what matters too often to us is some damned little petty spite." For emphasis he adjusted his barracks-leader's cloche, his elbows thrusting out. "What difference does it make *what* Jackie does to get a date?"

Jackie squealed, and Cornell turned to him. "And as for you, why should you give a hoot about some bitchy innuendo? The success you have in the Catskills should armor you against that. Among women, libertines are admired. They boast of their conquests. To be a Doña Juana is the next best thing to making money."

Jackie cried: "I'm no whore!" He put his face in his hands and wept. Cornell understood that he was not getting very far.

Howie was looking at him gravely.

"Did you want to say something, Howie?"

The boy asked quietly: "You don't admire loose men, do you, Al?"

Helpful Gordie offered an explanation: "I think what Al means is that there's a double standard, and you can't apply the same values to men as to women—"

"I can speak for myself!"

"Sorry," said Gordie. "I was only—"

Cornell lost his temper then. "Oh, shit! You are an impossible bunch!"

The vile language had its effect. Howie's peach complexion turned strawberry. The men were thrown into stunned silence.

Cornell looked at inanimate things like ceiling and floor as he proceeded to voice his chagrin, which was even more passionate than he himself had anticipated.

"You deserve to be clamped in those machines! You are a wretched, miserable, passive, negative sex. You are good for nothing but the menial, debased role that women have cast you in. You—"

"*You?* Are you excluding yourself, uh, Al?"

It was Farley who had spoken. He wore a mean, cynical expression. Cornell realized he had always hated Farley from the first, as, somehow, his only true rival, and he wondered at that: rival for what? And why? He was prettier than Farley and much more moral—or should he say moralistic? To question yourself was to admit weakness. He *was* weak, but to admit weakness was a kind of strength. Why a *kind?* Why was he invariably so tentative? So apologetic even to himself?

"You're right, Farley!" he said vigorously. "I don't mean *you.* I mean *us.* We're in this together, all of us. And not just here, in the Sperm Service, but in society at large."

"I don't understand that statement," Farley said, his legs crossed high, at the thighs, and his wrists clasped just under his small breasts, defining them as cones.

"Why do we let them get away with it?" asked Cornell. "What would happen if we refused to go to the next milking session?"

There were sounds of consternation. Cornell did not look at Howie.

Someone said: "We'd be castrated."

"Would we? You hear that threat all the time, but have you ever actually known anyone to whom it was done?"

Howie asked quietly: "Al, *who* are you?"

"I'm a man, Howie. I'm a man who is trying to understand what it means to be a man—or what it ought to mean."

"Al, you seem to be talking treason." Howie leaned forward,

his young face earnestly disconsolate. "Do you know what you're saying? I don't want to be unfair."

Gordie rose from his bunk, came to where Cornell stood, and embraced him lightly about the waist. "Don't worry so much, dear. We'll survive our sperm term, as thousands have before us. The first time is a shock, but we'll get used to it in no time. And it *is* our duty, as Greggie said." He nodded at the thick-eyebrowed platinum blond. "It makes the world go round. Without us there'd be no future people."

Cornell felt suffocated. He loosened himself from Gordie's thick forearm. He looked around at the faces of his men. They were watching him with what he interpreted as compassionate wonderment.

Gordie said: "Anatomy is destiny, Al. I guess all of us would rather have been born women."

Cornell cried: "But we *weren't*, were we? And this is the only life we have!"

"Please," said Gordie, seizing him again, this time not so gently as before. "Please, Al, you'll get into trouble. Suppose some passing officer hears you talking that way?"

"I hope she does," Cornell cried. He wrenched himself away from Gordie, and ran to the screen door. He hurled it open and shouted: "Rotten women!"

When Gordie grabbed him from behind, he rammed both elbows back, freed himself, and turned to meet the assault of not only Gordie, but Greggie, several others, and even Jackie.

He was subdued by his fellow men and carried into the lavatory and held under a cold shower.

"I'm all right now," he said five or six times before they let him out. He was still wearing the cloche, which now drooped with water. He went dripping into the dormitory and took out his spare uniform dress. Luckily he had not been wearing his shoes. The others followed him and stood around behind. He did not look at them. He had contempt for them all. But neither was he proud of himself. He should have seen it was hopeless to try to rouse them. He should not have lost control. He would do better next time. He didn't know quite what he would do, but he would do better. And it would be by, with, and for himself alone: not, certainly, for the Movement, and not, indeed, for the wretched male sex, whom he believed women were quite right to despise.

When he was fully dressed, except for the yellow cloche, which lay dripping where he had hurled it, he felt a touch at his shoulder. It was Farley, who had not been one of his subduers. He could imagine Farley's having lain sardonically on the bunk while the spectacle was in progress. But Farley had a point; Farley was always for himself alone.

"Georgie," said Farley. He took Cornell by the elbow, as Cornell had taken him for that heart-to-heart talk. But this was different. Cornell shook his hand off with a bird-wing movement.

"Don't touch me," he said, and turned away, seeking other eyes. But no one would look at him except Gordie, who had lately been his principal restrainer. Gordie raised his husky shoulders and let them fall; his broad pink face was expressionless. Jackie was seated again, working at his cuticles with an orange stick. Howie's back was towards Cornell and quivering slightly. Was he crying?

Cornell finally stared at Farley.

Farley shook his head. "You're sick, Georgie. You've got everything turned around. Marching us back and forth, calling yourself 'Al.' And now you go berserk. I should have seen it coming from your remarks in the bathroom. For a while I thought you were some kind of radical rabble-rouser, talking about the exploitation of men. But then you said you weren't interested in politics, and now you run amuck for no reason at all. What if some officer had heard you? What would happen to *us*?

"You need treatment, Georgie, professional treatment. Let's go to sick call."

"Who are *you?*" Cornell screamed. "When did you get so stinking big?"

Farley slipped an arm around his waist.

Gordie, as usual the diplomat, said: "It wasn't Farley's idea personally, Georgie. We all got together and decided. And we elected Farley because you and he are friends. So don't resent him. It isn't an easy job, by any means."

Jackie raised his face at that and said spitefully: "Georgie didn't break down when he and *I* were best friends."

"And I haven't broken down now, you shits!" Cornell screamed. He ripped himself away from Farley, then seized Farley and threw him onto the seated Jackie. Jackie fell back and Farley tumbled to the floor. Gordie advanced, and Cornell kicked him in the testicles. Gordie instantly lost his high color, clutched his stomach, and without a sound collapsed onto Farley, whom his big body covered entirely.

Without these leaders, the other men fell back and continued to give ground in an expanding semicircle as Cornell moved into the aisle.

"Georgie."

He turned and saw young Howie, who had climbed over a cot to reach him. Howie wore a sorrowful expression, but somehow Cornell was not offended by it as he had been by the fake sympathy of Farley and Gordie, which was really cynicism in the service of bitter envy.

"Howie," Cornell said, "you understand, don't you? You know I'm not nuts." He gestured. "Look at them, the disgusting little slaves. That's all they're good for—to be milked. Well, not me! I'm busting out of here, and I can do it. I've done it before. No woman can stop me!"

Howie's hand came out, and Cornell reached to shake it, but

missed because it moved too rapidly, changing into a fist which struck him on the point of the jaw, causing him to smell a sulfurous odor and to lose consciousness.

When Cornell awakened, he was dressed in a frilly pink nightgown through the neckline of which was threaded a satin ribbon. He lay in bed, alone in a small room with walls of raw plywood. A doll in a gaudy evening gown sat on one corner of a vanity table, the top of which was otherwise furnished with cosmetic bottles, boxes, and jars. A skirted stool stood in front of the vanity. There was a bedside table with a pink-shaded lamp, which provided the only light in this windowless enclosure. An air-conditioner, set into the wall, hummed quietly.

After a moment Cornell swung out of bed and went to the doll. He picked it up, and it spoke in a tinny voice.

"Hi! I'm Larry. What's your name? Won't you be my friend?"

With his free hand Cornell felt his jaw, which ached from Howie's punch. He had a feeling that had happened a long time before. He turned the doll over, raised its stiff satin dress, lowered its pantyhose and lace bikini, and found the button between Larry's buttocks, looking like the stub of a dildo which had been broken off there. He pressed the button, then let it out, and the doll repeated its salutation. He looked around front and saw that Larry was indeed represented as anatomically male. Its little plastic pudenda looked both pathetic and ridiculous. When Larry was horizontal, his eyes were closed. Cornell erected him, and one blue eye clicked open. The other was stuck. Cornell pried it open with a fingernail, and then suddenly was murderously sick of Larry, picked him up by the heels and was about to knock his head off, when the door opened.

"Go ahead, Georgie." It was a plump young officer. She had dark hair and could not have been more than twenty-five. Her collar showed a first-lieutenant's silver bar and the golden medical emblem. The summer uniform of tan shirt and trousers was a tight fit on her chubby body.

"Go ahead," she repeated. "Bust it." Her round pink cheeks and tiny teeth were smiling."

Cornell carefully lowered the doll to the vanity table, back on its button. He picked up a comb and, looking in the oval mirror, began to work on his rumpled hair.

"I'm Lieutenant Aster, or if you like, Doctor. You might prefer to call me Doctor: the decision is up to you."

Cornell winced as the comb caught in a tangle.

"You probably wonder where you are, if you have just woken up. You were brought to the camp hospital yesterday. While you were under sedation we had an interesting talk. Then you were brought to this private room, which is still in the hospital but isolated from the wards."

Cornell's face was smooth. Someone had shaved him. He pulled the front of the nightgown away and looked down. His chest, between the scars of his vanished breasts, was smooth as well. His fingertips went under his arms, then swooped down to rub his calves: both areas had been shaved. He took the pink stool from the slot in the vanity table, sat down and, ignoring the lieutenant's reflection, went back to work on his hair with a rat-tailed brush he had discovered among the cosmetic accessories provided.

The lieutenant stood behind him. "Believe me, Georgie, I know quite a bit about you: wishes, dreams, hopes, fantasies. But my diagnosis is encouraging. It is my belief that you are emotionally disturbed, surely, but not crazy." She hooked her thumbs in her woven belt and was probably leering into the mirror, but he avoided her eyes.

"Now, I'm new around here, and you are kind of a test case for me. What happens to *you* will largely determine what happens to *my* career." She touched his shoulders lightly with her two hands. "There's a new generation in psychiatry, Georgie, and I belong to it. For example, we believe that anal therapy is ineffectual in many cases and perhaps in some even deleterious, and only as a last resort would we recommend castration. I'm not criticizing the older practitioners, mind you. They were the pioneers, coming upon a frontier by covered wagon, as it were, to build log cabins. But time moves on and new building materials have been discovered, new techniques of construction."

Bending, she put her head close to his and spoke confidentially. She smelled of a familiar women's lotion, Saddle Leather, bringing Cornell an oddly unpleasant memory of a certain former girl friend who had reeked of it.

She said in his ear: "I had to fight quite a battle to get you, Georgie. Everybody else around here is Old Guard. If it were up to them, you'd get the dildo, and if that didn't work, the knife. So I'm asking for your cooperation." She straightened up and resumed her normal tone.

Cornell kept brushing.

"Femininity," said the lieutenant, "is fundamentally a psychic and not a physical quality, though it takes its origins from biological and anatomical reality. Now, we in the new psychiatry believe that all human beings, of whichever sex, understand this, to put it in layman's terms, in their heart of hearts, guts, soul, or whatever you want to call what *we* call the Center of Basic Awareness. The old school also believes in a kind of CBA, but locates it differently for each sex—in women, in the brain; in men, the gonads. Hence the typical psychiatric surgery: frontal lobotomy for a female, castration for a male."

Cornell had never heard of a woman who went literally mad, though he had known a great many he would have called eccentric—in fact, they all were—and he did not understand the word "lobotomy." Nor was he interested in the lieutenant's monologue. If he had told all under the influence of the drug, his situation was hopeless, and she was toying with him sadistically. The solace lay in cosmetic particulars. He brushed his hair so hard that tears came to his eyes, but they were superficial water: physical, not emotional.

"We," the lieutenant went on, "do not locate the CBA in any precise organ. It is contributed to by every cell of a living person." She patted Cornell's shoulder cap again. "Emasculation may make a man socially tractable, but except with the really dangerous sex criminal, we think society loses more than it gains thereby. Thereafter he is useful only for heavy labor. He is no longer a man but a thing. We think men have their place in the world as men. The human race could not get along without them." The lieutenant chortled. "At least not until one sex able to reproduce itself is invented."

Cornell looked at the brush. The bristles were clogged with hair. He bent across and explored his temples with a forefinger. The hair was definitely receding. And his recent ordeal had accentuated his crow's-feet.

"Emotions emanate from the CBA, and that's where the trouble starts. They start out fine and true and healthy, and somehow become warped while en route, so that when they reach the outside world of reality they are perverse, crippled and crippling. The answer is not to try to eliminate the CBA by locating it in a particular organ which is then excised. The CBA is not a thing in itself; it is rather a process."

The lieutenant cleared her throat. "This is a very complex subject, Georgie, and I'm sure your little head is spinning right now. Come over here, please." She took his hand and led him to the bed. "Sit down, dear." She drew up the stool for herself.

"I have got permission to work with you in a program based on this new approach. There is opposition to it, as I indicated, and such cooperation as I receive from my superiors is rather grudging, I'm afraid. I can survive that because my conviction is firm. But what I can't go on *without* is your cooperation, dear Georgie."

She took his hand again and sought his eyes. She was so young that there were those satiny patches across her tear sacs.

For lunch Cornell was served a cheeseburger, french fries, and a chocolate milk shake. The tray was delivered by Lieutenant Aster. He had seen no one else for two days, and the door to the room was locked from the outside. When he washed or used the john, the lieutenant blindfolded him and led him to a lavatory consisting of a stall shower, basin, and toilet. She waited outside the door until he finished, and blindfolded him again for the return trip.

Now she handed him the catsup bottle. Cornell upended it, and naturally nothing came out until he shook it vigorously; next his plate was swimming in gore. He screwed up his nose and chased it with squirming lips.

"Oh, that's good," said the lieutenant, "that expression. You're recapturing something authentic there. I'll bet you did that when the teacher announced a test, or when something really ooky was served in the cafeteria, like baked halibut."

Cornell rather liked her by now, but he also had a contrary urge to resist her smugness. "That's the same face I make to this day if the coffee is too hot or something is sour."

"Good!" She was undiscourageable. "There you have another link to a normal childhood. It's a childish expression, Georgie, male-childish. A girl's facial reaction by age seventeen is usually significantly different, showing not so much disgust as sullenness. An adolescent girl has the scent of her power and responsibility to come. She is growing impatient. A boy on the other hand is reluctant to mature and clings to the mannerisms of infancy. He will find them useful all his life."

Cornell sighed and salted the catsup on his cheeseburger.

"I don't get very hungry just staying in this room and listening to records, you know."

"I realize that, Georgie. It's the best we can do at the moment in the way of a controlled environment."

She was sitting on the stool as usual, Cornell was on the edge of the bed, the tray in his lap. He must be careful not to slop catsup on his tartan midiskirt. He wore white ankle-socks and penny loafers, a simple white blouse, a gold locket on a long chain, and a bouffant wig. This outfit was an approximation of that which he had worn as an actual teenager, except that the current wig was platinum-blond, whereas in his real adolescence he had teased and sprayed his own auburn hair, which was too short now for such treatment. The wig was the only one Lieutenant Aster could provide. As she had frequent occasions to say, her resources were limited.

"Under optimum conditions," she went on now, "you would be with other patients undergoing the same therapy, but they would have to be at the same stage. Really, they should be at the same ages as you are at present, both in reality and in the therapeutic reprise."

The latter term was psychiatrist's jargon, often abbreviated to "TR." The TR was supposed to get you back to your CBA, as Cornell understood it. The lieutenant's theory, that of the new school of psychiatry to which she belonged, was that emotional illnesses were not born but made somewhere along the line. She used the image of a highway, with toll stations representing the various stages of life: Young Manhood, Adolescence, Pubescence, Boyhood, Infancy.

She intended to take Cornell back to the stage at which he had gone wrong, taken an exit, as it were, instead of continuing along the main route. She was extremely earnest and really rather sweet, but ironically enough Cornell had had more respect for his old therapist, the brutal Dr. Prine. Not that he yearned for anal treatment, but at least it seemed more *serious* than this playacting. Both methods of course had the same aim: to reconcile him to being a slave.

"How's the shake?" the lieutenant asked brightly.

It was extra-thick, a semisolid sludge. He pushed the straw aside and spooned a taste.

"Authentic?" she asked.

He did not like to disappoint her, but she was, presumably, seeking the truth.

"It's actually a *malted*, Lieutenant. What I always drank was a milk shake, and never so thick."

She snapped her fingers in chagrin. "Georgie, I goofed. I'm sorry. I gave you the wrong one. Here, you've barely touched it." She seized the cardboard cylinder and left the room.

Cornell took a bite of tepid cheeseburger and spongy roll and soon spat it into his paper napkin. It was absolutely beyond his powers to eat one greasy, red french fry. He cleared a space on the vanity table and deposited the tray there.

He squatted on the floor next to the portable record player the lieutenant had brought him the day before, along with a wire rack of some 45's that had been current a decade and a half earlier: "Chewing Along," by a group called the Chiclets; Millicent Duff, singing "Butterscotch Hop"; etc. As a teenager he had really preferred semiclassical, rendered by big orchestras with swelling strings, like Thelma Verner's "Rocky Mountain Rhapsody."

He found and plucked out "Jumpin' " by Mae MacMurray. *That* he recalled only too well. One boy used to play it incessantly, at a volume that made it impossible to sit in the high-school rec room and read the fashion magazines. Cornell and he had once had a hair-pulling contest over this matter, and naturally it was Georgie who ended up on the headmistress's carpet.

He had just snapped the record in two when Lieutenant Aster returned.

"Here you go," she said with her customary enthusiasm, handing him a container. To take it, he had to rid himself of the fragments of record, and she saw them.

"Oh, too bad! Which one is it? I'll see if I can get another. Though it won't be easy. I had to look all over the junk shops for those. Have you noticed how the popular tastes of boys change drastically every few years?"

He stuck the pieces into the rack. She was not interested in the breakage except as a pretext for making another presumably therapeutic comment. The lieutenant was obsessed with her project—as Stanley and the men of the Movement had been with theirs; and Harriet with hers. Cornell never had a *personal* association with anyone. Everyone he encountered was a monomaniac of some sort, working compulsively to affect someone else: to alter their personality, change their mind, catch them out, set them straight. Everybody else always *knew better* about sex, society, history, you name it—but always in a general way, with absolutely no acknowledgment of one single, particular, individual human being: by which he meant himself.

The lieutenant persisted. "Last year's songs, like last year's clothes, are beyond the pale this year. But let enough time go by, and nostalgia sets in. When your generation of boys reaches its middle thirties, these tunes will be reissued. And if any of the original records are left, they will command high prices as collectors' items."

Cornell took the milk shake from her. "Sorry you had to make another trip to the PX," he said. "I wonder if it was worth it."

She shook her neat, dark head. "There couldn't be anything more important than this, Georgie. If we succeed, think of the advance we will have made not just for you, but for all the thousands of sick boys. And never doubt we are progressing. This is only the second day, and already you have recaptured a particular taste that was peculiar to your teen-aged personality."

She lowered her bottom to the bed. Cornell was still sitting on the floor, his legs drawn in under the tartan skirt, the opening of which was secured by an oversized, ornamental safety pin. He had never owned a garment of this exact design, but other contemporaries had. For classes of course they had worn uniforms: navy-blue skirts and jackets with white blouses. One was proud to get into high school and out of the gray uniform of the lower grades, with its wide-brimmed flat-crowned hat and Mary Jane shoes. After classes ended at 4:00 you could wear your own clothes, purchased from your allowance. Cornell had had a lovely sweater in avocado nylon. That was before the fashion of wearing prominent breasts.

He now decided to confess that he had broken the record.

"Splendid, Georgie! You see, it's really working. You are returning little by little to the emotions of that time. Now can you remember, recover, your reason for the anger against that boy, Was it because he monopolized the phonograph? Or was it that you disliked the record itself?"

"Neither. It was simply because of the noise. I liked to look at magazines. There was no other place you were allowed to— you couldn't take them to the dorm. The noise—he played it too loud—and also the repetition of the same song over and over and over."

The lieutenant's fat, fresh face looked even younger when she frowned.

"Hmm, repetition. Now, that may be significant. Each sex has a different response to ritual—note that I am extending the concept of repetition. In women—"

There she went again. Cornell grasped the straw and was about to put it into his mouth when he noticed that the end was slightly crimped, the opening not a perfect circle. He squeezed it into shape: it was also damp. There was a high-fluid line inside the container; an inch or so of milk shake was missing. Someone else had begun to drink it!

In quick disgust he lowered the cylinder so abruptly that some of the liquid slopped out onto the hem of his skirt.

The lieutenant was as quick to notice.

"Another memory!" she cried.

"No," Cornell said petulantly, "an observation. Someone else has been at this shake. It is a used drink!" He turned his sulky face away. "And the burger is cold, and I don't think this treatment is going to work." He seized a record from the rack and put it on the turntable of the little red-plastic phonograph. He worked switches and knobs, but the wretched thing wouldn't work.

"Swing the arm all the way to the right until you hear the click, then allow it to swing back on its own."

"I don't want to listen to that stupid music anyway." He rose swiftly and walked across the small room and stood in a corner.

"Georgie," the lieutenant said softly, reasonably. "I am sorry. I've done a bad job. Will you forgive me?"

She was the first woman he had ever heard admit a mistake. There wasn't anything anyway to look at in his corner but the joint of the plywood panels. What a funny room it was, with walls of new wood and a floor of concrete. Sometimes he heard the distant sound of vehicles. Were it not for the electric clock on the bedside table, he would not have known the time of day —not that he looked at it often, not that he did anything much when the lieutenant was gone but sleep. It occurred to him that perhaps she sprinkled sleeping powders on his food, or mixed them with the salt. He had become a total vegetable. Perhaps he should assert himself.

He turned around, flipping his hands. "Forget about it."

Lieutenant Aster went to the rack of records, knelt, and began to pluck through the discs. She made a selection and put it on the turntable. A foggy, whiny but hard voice began to sing of "love, when push comes to shove, hard fist in a soft glove . . ."

"Do you remember this one?"

"Sarah Heathfield, 'Boxing Glove Love,' " Cornell said, with a shiver. It had been a big hit during his senior year. By request, the orchestra had played it repeatedly at that prom to which he had been taken by Judith, with whom he had afterwards had that hideous experience he had told Charlie about—the near rape—which reminiscence had led to their quarrel, the subsequent arrest, his flight from jail to the Movement, the assignment to the Sperm Service, this treatment.

Lieutenant Aster got to her feet and came to him.

"May I have this dance?"

She held out her hands. Cornell backed away.

"I was never much of a dancer."

"I can't believe that. All young boys love to dance. They even dance with each other."

"I was never much good," said Cornell. "I was different in that way." In fact he had loved to dance and seldom lacked a partner at the hops.

She seized him gently but surely, raising his left hand with her right, her other at his waist.

"Come on now, Georgie. Give in to the music."

He refused to move. She exerted force, still smiling.

"No," said Cornell. "You can't make me."

"Aha, we've touched a nerve! Is it the song specifically, or dancing in general that bothers you? Are you an awkward boy?"

"Lieutenant, I don't want to be defiant, believe me, but I can't stand always being just an object for somebody else to move around."

"I understand," Aster said. "Now let's dance."

She again sought to move him. He held her off and attempted to explain further.

"Look, I'm just a man, and according to you I am sick besides, but I don't *feel* ill. Does that mean I'm sicker than ever? I've always heard that if you're just neurotic you know it, whereas a maniac doesn't know she's insane."

"All I know," said the lieutenant, "is I'm crazy about you, Georgie. You're the prettiest boy in school."

She eluded his defenses and, slipping both arms around his waist, pulled him against her soft belly and began to vibrate. He got a hand over each of her shoulder caps and pushed, an action which moved her trunk away but brought her lower portion even closer, her thighs squashed against his. He had a loathsome urge to slump so that their groins would be level, but checked it and stood straight and rigid.

Suddenly one of her hands left his waist, went into his crotch, and squeezed his testicles—not hard enough to hurt, but enough to break his resistance.

His arms rose, he breathed out, and she whirled him around. He was dancing, or at any rate in motion, stepping on her feet and his own, skirt flying out behind.

Women are only children of a larger growth.

LORD CHESTERFIELD, 1748

11

LIEUTENANT ASTER MAINTAINED a strong lead. Cornell was help-less, a captive of the rhythm. And as usual it was a nonsensical situation. His head was now bent into the hollow of her neck: were he straight he would be looking down on her scalp. Never-theless he began to dance seriously; dancing was the only thing for which he had ever been praised—the only talent or craft, that is: he had frequently been called pretty, but that was a gift of fate, not an accomplishment.

He was actually disappointed for a moment when the record ended and he opened his eyes. But seeing the silver bar on her collar—it was a wonder he had not cut his nose on it—he was back in sullen reality.

"Sorry, Georgie." She let him go. "I hope I didn't hurt you. It was necessary to break that rigid seizure. Let me ask you this: when you danced with other boys, who led?"

"I don't remember."

"Of course you do. There is something about dancing that threatens you, isn't there?" She took his hand and squeezed it with about the same amount of force she had applied to his crotch: not so much a punishment as a reminder. But his gonads were defenseless, while his hand was virtually invulnerable to her small fingers.

"If the other boy was bigger than I, he led. If smaller, I did."

"Is that the usual practice with boys?" the lieutenant asked, releasing him. "I really don't know."

He frowned. "I think so. I never thought about it." He looked down at her. "It makes sense, though, doesn't it?"

"Does it?"

"Of course."

"Why?"

"Well, it doesn't make sense that the smaller one pushes the big one around."

"Push? You see it as aggression?"

"I wouldn't say that."

"But you did say 'push.' " She grinned. "Dancing is supposed to be pleasure, is it not?"

"But it involves two persons," said Cornell. "That means someone has to lead. Otherwise you'd bump into each other."

"O.K., then tell me this: what happens when both persons are more or less of an equal size?"

Cornell shrugged. "If another guy really wants to lead, I'd let him. I certainly wouldn't struggle over it. As you say, dancing is supposed to be fun. Anyway, I forget whom I'm dancing with. I shut my eyes." He deliberated for a moment. "Not everything is a matter of domination."

"If you really understood that, Georgie, you wouldn't be here. Intellectual opinions are another thing than emotional convictions. But we're making progress." She went again to the record rack. "How about something fast? The kind of thing you dance to without holding your partner. Wasn't that in fashion in your day?"

He was reminded of her youth. She was smaller, softer, and younger than he: yet she was the doctor and he the patient.

She held up a disc. "How about 'Rattrap'? Do you recall it? Is it fast?" She looked again at the label. "By Ruthless Ruth and the Rowdies."

"Well, now I *am* telling the truth," said Cornell. "I really didn't like that kind of dancing."

"So, even though you forget your partner, you want to be held. That's significant." She smiled up at him.

"Whatever you say, Lieutenant." He sighed and sat down on the stool. Larry, the doll, stared glassily at him.

Lieutenant Aster put the record away and sat down on the bed. "All right," she said. "We won't bother with that, then. We'll work on the slow songs. There's something there that hasn't quite emerged. Why, if you loved to dance and were very good at it, did you resist when I went to take you in my arms? And explain that strange remark about being an object, please."

"I've changed since those days." Cornell touched one of Larry's little silver slippers. "I used to play with dolls, too, at one time."

"You've got older."

"I guess."

"That happens to every boy. You can't change that, but you *can* change your attitude towards it."

"Why isn't growing old the horror to women that it is to men?"

The lieutenant congratulated him. "Excellent question, Georgie! Do you remember our conversation about relative sizes?"

"I don't remember any *conversation*," said Cornell. "I remember *your* theory."

She looked as though she wanted to frown but suppressed the urge in favor of her good-humored optimism, if that is what it could be called. Perhaps he was only imagining this conflict. But perhaps her good humor was another face of tyranny. However benevolent she seemed, she *had* deliberately hurt him in his most sensitive place.

She said brightly: "Oh, we agreed, don't you recall, that anatomical matters were superficial."

"Yet you were able to get me in motion just now by hurting my testicles! Nature has cursed men with those awful, dangling, grotesque things. *You* don't have to worry about anything like that. You are smaller and weaker, but you don't have those stupid, useless, ugly, and vulnerable organs hanging outside your body. If you had squeezed harder just now, I'd be curled up on the floor in agony."

Cornell seized Larry, raised the skirt and pulled down the wispy underwear. Larry gave his automatic greeting.

"Look at this ridiculous thing!" Cornell violently spread Larry's cold pink legs and jabbed at the tiny pudenda.

"*This*, and this alone, is why men are basically inferior! All that talk about spiritual and moral differences! Women would be just like men if they had a penis and balls. Why don't men play football? Because they might get hit there. And the same goes for boxing and wrestling. Women might be smaller, but they are invulnerable. It's nature's cruel joke to make men the larger and stronger sex and then give them this, which nullifies everything else."

Cornell passionately ripped most of the clothing from Larry and waved the nude doll at the lieutenant. A shred of pantyhose hung from Larry's one leg.

"You don't know what it is to have this between your legs! It hangs there all your life. It bangs against your thighs when you run. It gets sweaty and itchy in hot weather. You bump into desk-corners and hurt yourself. Certain kinds of underpants give you a rash. Sometimes you sit down in a certain way or cross your legs and you squeeze it painfully. If anything goes wrong with your bladder, the doctor runs a tube up through the little hole in the end."

He pointed at Larry's organ, but the plastic molding had not been so precise: the doll's phallus was not equipped with a terminal aperture. "A *huge* tube, thick as a pencil. And to take a semen specimen, the doctor goes in through your rectum and massages the prostate gland, and you ejaculate out front: you can't help it. Not to mention the milking process here: another thing you can't help. Men were constructed to be penetrated and manipulated!

"You might say this nasty thing can be controlled by anyone but its owner. A part of your own body that you can't manage! Can you imagine that? I can lift my arm when I want to, wiggle my fingers, kick my feet, wrinkle my nose." He had dropped Larry to demonstrate these movements. "I can't move my ears, but neither do they do anything on their own. A penis gets hard and stands up of its own volition—or at the bidding of someone or something outside. When you're riding on a bus, for example. Or when you wake up in the morning and have to urinate. And there are other times."

Cornell stopped here. He felt hot subcutaneous blood all over his body. He picked Larry up again.

The doll said: "Hi, I'm Larry—"

Cornell thrust it onto the vanity. "Why don't little girls play with dolls? Why do boys need little models, dummies, of themselves, to dress and rock to sleep, and why do they always like small, soft pets, puppies, hamsters, baby chicks?" He slapped Larry's bare crotch. "Because they have this filthy thing—and it's obscene even in its basic functions: urine and semen use the same passage. And it makes them feel totally helpless, and they need to have something living—or that pretends to live, like a doll, talks, opens its eyes—that they can control, or pretend to; that needs them, or pretends to, because nothing and no one really is controlled by or needs a man."

Cornell could feel his mouth grinning in a ghastly, cruel way. "If you think of it, a penis is a sort of doll." He seized Larry's miniature member and pantomimed erecting it—which couldn't really be done owing to the stiffness of the plastic and indeed the modest size of the shaft. In falsetto, Cornell said: " 'Hi, I'm Petey. Won't you be my friend?' "

Then in an access of fury, he found a manicure scissors and attacked Larry's pudenda, hacking away, trying to sever them. But the material was adamantine in this immovable part of the doll, and the scissors were dull. He produced only a few scratches and little curly hairlike wisps of pink plastic.

Lieutenant Aster spoke at last. He had forgotten she was there. She said quietly: "Do it to your own."

He dropped the scissors and began to cover Larry's nudity with the torn doll's clothes.

The lieutenant said: "If you hate it so much, why then when you were under the drug did you talk only of your fear of losing it?"

He was thirsty all at once. He picked up the milk shake and took the used straw in his lips.

"Georgie, life is not always easy for women either. Does it surprise you to hear that? And I don't mean simply the ulcers and high blood pressure which are traditional in businesswomen, and the greater incidence of heart attacks, the higher female death rate, etcetera. Those are after all the maladies of winners, the price that must be paid for success."

The shake was lukewarm by now, and Cornell was incapable of compassion for women.

"There are others, however, many more than you would suppose, who cannot cope. They find it difficult to live as women— just as many males find it difficult to live as men. Emotionally disturbed males have more options. They wear women's attire, smoke pipes and cigars, attend boxing matches and football games and identify with the athletes, and so on: in other words, pretend they are women.

"Not so with psychoneurotic females. They seldom put on dresses, crochet, play with dolls, etcetera. No, no. Instead they try more and more strenuously to prove their femininity. If young enough they join the army and volunteer for combat. They go hunting on one of the big-game preserves. They practice karate and other martial arts. Or perhaps they simply get into street and barroom fights. They become auto racers, or merely drive theirs cars in a homicidal manner.

"Sooner or later, if they aren't killed in their violent professions or sports, they will blow out their brains. Many so-called hunting accidents are really intentional suicides."

The lieutenant paused. Cornell sucked in more of the tepid

milk shake. He had known the occasional girl of this absolute type, but actually all women had something of that character. They might be the creative sex, but they were also the destroyers. It was up to men to preserve and maintain—and be bored. Suicide was at least interesting. But you had to have the female tools to commit it: with his manicure scissors he couldn't even sever a doll's pecker.

"These of course are the spectacular types," said the lieutenant. "At least they go out with a bang, some like the war heroes, in a blaze of glory. Others are not so glamorous. They are modest, mousy persons basically, but somewhere in their souls is a strain that yearns for the kind of assertion that is not possible without the accompanying courage. They are quite as suicidal in the long run. They continue to live, but in pain, without satisfaction, without hope."

"Yes," said Cornell. "Yes." But as the lieutenant proceeded, he realized she was still talking of the other sex.

"This kind of woman seldom understands her problem until it is too late for help. She grows more and more confused, more and more bitter. She does a bad job at her work, and she knows it; and while superficially she blames others, in her unconscious she is gradually being consumed by self-contempt. She is fortunate if she breaks down in some manner that is visible to her colleagues."

"Like me," said Cornell.

Lieutenant Aster's eyes rounded in assent. "Precisely, Georgie. Now, it is the conviction of my school that, contrary to the old psychiatry, the problems of women and men are interrelated. The old way was to treat disturbed women with lectures of the stiff-upper-lip sort and a vigorous regimen of calisthenics and cold showers."

The lieutenant rubbed her smooth chin. "I've decided to take you into my confidence. I'm doing this because after only two days the results have far surpassed my expectations. The way you lost yourself in that dance, the passionate concentration, was remarkable. Followed by that extraordinary outburst, from the heart, concerning the love-hate relationship you have with your genitals. You may not yet be conscious of the gain, Georgie, but I *am*, and I assure you it is remarkable.

She leaned forward, a hand on each kneecap. Her trousers had ridden up, and white flesh showed between her olive-drab anklets and the cuffs. Years of wearing trousers wore all the hair off a woman's shins. A girl friend of Cornell's had once demonstrated that odd effect.

"I was permitted to have this room built in a storage area of the camp hospital. It is isolated and near the ambulance garage. As I mentioned, the powers that be were none too keen about the experiment in the first place. I bought the plywood for the partitions and the furniture from my own pocket and paid the camp carpenters, who worked here in their off-duty hours."

She slapped her blunt knees and rose. "Well, Georgie, I must be going. I have other obligations, much as I'd like to give all my time to you. I must put in a shift on the neuropsychiatric ward, where the approach is orthodox. If you'd like to go to the lavatory now . . . ? I won't be back for a few hours."

Cornell found the blindfold and handed it to her.

She shook her head. "No need for that any more. Distraction is no longer a menace."

She opened the door. Outside was a large, warehouse-like space, lighted here and there with bare bulbs and furnished with stacks of cartons and medical equipment, sun lamps, treatment tables, and those hatrack-shaped things with bottles hanging on them, which Cornell recognized from TV medical shows as being for blood transfusions.

He hesitated at the door. "Why, then," he asked, "do I have to be locked up at all? I'm not going to run away. I've got no place to go, I assure you."

Lieutenant Aster drew him away from the door and closed it.

She sighed. "It's always hard to decide how much to tell a patient. There are sometimes unfortunate consequences: rivalries, for example. On the other hand, sometimes rivalry, envy, are beneficial. A healthy contest might develop between patients. They compete in a positive way, each determined to make more progress than the next."

Cornell said: "You've got more of these special rooms, and patients?"

"Just one."

"You don't want me to communicate with him?"

"Her," said the lieutenant. "And not even by accident, on the way to the lavatory. At least not at this time. She hasn't yet made your progress, Georgie, and a confrontation might be unfortunate for both of you. Perhaps later on it might be possible to bring you together."

She looked at the floor. "But I'm thinking about it." She raised her eyes and clapped the small of his back. "But not yet."

"I know who she is," said Cornell.

Lieutenant Aster hunched her shoulders and opened the door. "Now, that's quite enough to digest for the moment. Perhaps I've already told you more than you should know at this point."

"It's a woman named Harriet, isn't it?"

The lieutenant made her familiar smile. "That I can certainly answer: no. Don't speculate any more, Georgie. Concentrate on your own situation while you're alone. Play the records, dance by yourself, dig into your memories, especially those that are sensitive, even painful."

She led him out and along a corridor made by the cartons. It went directly to the washroom. Neither en route nor on the return did he see another door behind which his female counterpart might be confined.

Cornell was peering into the mirror. He wore the dark lipstick of his teen years, spots of bright rouge on his cheeks, false eyelashes but no shadow or liner. He picked up a large jar of cleansing cream and thought about throwing it at the clown-face he saw. But he put it down. These impotent gestures of rage were self-degrading. To break material objects, to scream and cry, to lose control—were these the proper work of a man? Instead of hurling the jar at his image, he unscrewed the top, dipped two fingers inside, and brought a supply of cream to his face. He would remove the makeup and thereafter adorn himself no more.

Of course, if somebody squeezed your testicles, you had to dance; if you were attached to a semen-milking machine, you must ejaculate. There were many situations in life in which you obviously lacked power and must acquiesce. But recognizing necessity did not mean you had the concomitant obligation to despise yourself.

Once that was established, you could go on to the next discovery. His face was soon clean. He peeled off the false eyelashes and dropped them into the greasy Kleenexes in the flowered wastecan. The bouffant wig was next to join the rubbish. His own hair was matted in some places, standing up in others. He grimaced at it and otherwise let it alone. He was about to screw the top back onto the jar of cream when he observed that the tin disk was large enough, if bent to conform, to protect the testicles against assault.

He searched awhile for a tool before it occurred to him to take the lid in his two strong hands and bend it with the counterforce of the thumbs. He lifted his skirt and pulled down his panties. It took some more bending and shaping until the lid fitted. The guard covered only the scrotum. When the panties were drawn up, the snug crotchpiece curved the penis around the protector. After an uncomfortable moment the cold metal began to warm, but it still was not pleasant, and walking was awkward. No doubt he would be chafed if he wore it habitually.

He had a better idea. He took another pair of briefs from his lingerie drawer, removed the ones he had on, and putting one pair inside the other, inserted the ball-protector between the double crotch so formed. More shaping was needed, for now it would guard the entire complex of genitalia. Finally, he took a needle and thread he had found in a search of the vanity drawers and stitched the crotches together around the edges of the cup.

He stepped into this garment and tested its efficacy by banging his knuckles against the armor: *tok, tok.* He walked up and down. He was certainly conscious of the device but not physically inhibited by it. With a lovely feeling of invulnerability, he kept grabbing hard objects from the vanity and knocking himself harmlessly in the groin. Hairbrush: *tok-tok.* Hand-lotion bottle: *tok-tok-tok.*

He was now an inventor. Georgie's Ironpants. To be sure, what he wore was but a crude prototype. The production model would be a single pair of briefs, doubled only in the crotchpiece to make a little pocket for the protective cup, which could be removed for laundering the garment. The cup should be rimmed with rubber padding. No doubt a better shape might be molded with the proper tools, the whole thing made neater, more comfortable and convenient.

It was an amusing daydream anyway. He had no clue as to how one went into the manufacture of underwear. And for all he knew, it was illegal for a man to protect his genitals in this fashion. It should be, if women had any sense. He would settle for his own new sense of security and the gratification that came from having identified a problem and conceived a solution in his mind and executed it with his hands.

He swirled the kilt-skirt around his hips and fastened the big ornamental safety pin, concealing his invention. He could hardly wait until Lieutenant Aster again asked him to dance.

The lieutenant returned at six o'clock, carrying the tray. This time the meal was a large pizza and a bottle of Pepsi. She displayed no reaction to his lack of makeup and wig.

Cornell lay supine on the bed, legs extended and wide apart, letting his hidden invention breathe, as it were.

Aster put the tray on the vanity. "This typical teen-age glop will evoke more useful reactions than if we tried to duplicate the stuff you were served at regular meals in the high-school dining room. You would probably pick at dinner, and then afterwards go down to the pizza joint and gorge."

Cornell played along. "They called it 'supper,' and it was served at five-thirty. Afterwards you could go out, but you had to be back at seven and do your homework in the study hall. At nine you could go to the rec room. By ten you had to be in the dorm, in bed. Saturday nights they had dances, and girls would come over from one of their schools.

"There were never enough of them, because for them it was voluntary, and lots of girls didn't like to dance. They could go bowling or to the movies, and girls fourteen and older could go to a bar and drink beer. When they were sixteen they could drink whiskey, cocktails, anything. They could save up their stipends and buy cars. After three-fifteen during the week they could go anywhere and do anything they wanted as long as they were back by nine o'clock next morning, and they were off from Friday afternoon till Monday."

"Uh-huh," said Aster, to whom this would not be news. "You resented that."

"I don't think I did in those days. It was just the way things were." He swung himself off the bed and bent over the record player. Already waiting on the turntable was "Boxing Glove Love." He had no trouble now with the switching mechanism. Sarah Heathfield began to belt out the sadistic lyrics. He remembered the album cover: Heathfield in prizefighter's trunks and jersey, high-laced shoes, and of course the enormous padded gloves. She held her fists at the ready and wore a menacing look under her pompadour.

He straightened up and stood with his back to Aster, waiting for her to take the bait.

But she said: "Turn the volume down, would you? Let it play as a background while you reminisce."

He walked deliberately away, defying her request. Obliviously she went to the record player and diminished the sound until the song was only a series of remote thuds of drum and bass and distant bestial howls from Heathfield.

"When did you begin to date?"

"Whenever I was asked," Cornell said in a snotty way. But again the lieutenant proved a cool, or perhaps merely insensitive, customer.

"Naturally," said she, taking a long, limp triangle of pizza from the tray. "Here."

"*You* eat it."

She calmly put it back and wiped her hands on a paper napkin.

"What kind of girls asked you out?"

"Pretty sad ones."

"Sad?"

"That was the slang of that day. It meant, well, unattractive, jerky, creepy. The opposite of keen or neat. Ones with skin problems or bad breath. Or awful bores with slicked-down· hair and tight suits, who thought they were clever, cracking jokes everybody had heard on TV. Once a football player dated me. Talk about your pizza! She ate a whole one herself, drank two giant malteds, and fell asleep afterwards in the booth."

"How about sex?" asked Aster. "Did you have any sexual experiences at that age?"

"You'd sometimes get groped," said Cornell, biting his lip. "In a car at the drive-in movie. But often they wouldn't even try for a goodnight kiss."

"Did you want to have sex?"

Cornell stared at her. "Never."

"Another sore spot," the lieutenant said in triumph.

"Yeah, that's right! That's all it is, soreness, pain. It's hateful and stupid."

"Stupid?" She seemed genuinely puzzled.

"What's the point?" asked Cornell. "I mean for a man? A girl can boast of her conquests. She proves her femininity. But what does a man gain from it except a bad reputation?"

"Uh-huh." Aster moved her round chin up and down.

"You never participated in a relationship that made you feel emotionally intimate with your partner? That you were helping each other to fully realize yourselves?"

"I don't know what that means," Cornell said. "For me, sex has been merely a stick up my rectum, and I will kill the next woman who tries it. *I will put my penis into her vagina and kill her.*"

This was a genuine outburst, unplanned.

"Georgie," said the lieutenant, and walked to him and claimed his hands. "Now, you sit right down." She pulled him to a seat on the bed. "You're never going to rape anyone. You're a normal, gentle man who got sidetracked." She retained one of his hands and put her other arm about his waist. It was too short to reach his far hip: nature had not constructed her for this. A man could better hold a woman, owing to his longer arms. His larger hands were made to clasp and not be clasped.

Aster squeezed him affectionately, or tried to with her ineffectual appendages.

"Georgie, you can't kill a woman by inserting a penis into her vagina. That's an old superstition. Emotionally it would be a perverse act, of course, and socially it would be destructive. It would certainly indicate a hostility to women that would suggest latent homosexual tendencies—but not homicidal ones."

She squeezed him again. Cornell felt as if he were being suffocated—not physically, of which feat she would be incapable, but morally.

"Men who *talk* about committing violence seldom *do* it. Believe me, you're absolutely harmless."

He freed himself and jumped up.

"How old are you, Lieutenant?"

"Nineteen."

"Nineteen. When did you get your M.D.?"

"This June." She was frowning sympathetically. "Why do you ask?"

Cornell ticked off some fingers. "You must have started when you were twelve."

"Thirteen, the usual age, in high-school premed. Then the normal two years of med school. In the latter I specialized in psychiatry."

"I'll soon be thirty."

She shook her head. "Georgie, you and your fantasies! You're twenty-five. I have your records. I never thought I'd hear a man lie about his age to make himself *older.*"

"I'm a revolutionary," said Cornell. "I was sent here by an underground male-liberation movement."

"You're being silly now," she said.

He shouted: "Everybody knows that putting a penis into a woman will kill her."

"Grow up, Georgie. Children used to be told that to discourage them from perverse experiments."

"If that's true, then what's wrong with it?"

"It's unnatural, obviously. Anatomically, it could result in a disease called pregnancy. Pregnancy might kill a woman, if that's what you mean. But not the mere insertion of the male organ."

"It is true that in ages past women bore children in their own bodies?"

"They also burned people at the stake for saying the earth was round, Georgie. It took human beings a long time to understand a lot of things. For centuries they reproduced like animals. Imagine creating new life through illness, distortion of the body, and pain! And society had no control over the population. There were often too many people for the food supply. Most unfortunate of all was that in the final stages of the disease, a woman was incapacitated, unable to practice her profession. Suppose a president were to give birth at a time of national crisis, a general in time of war."

Cornell shook his head violently.

"There's something wrong there somewhere."

"There *was* something wrong," said Aster. "Many people could not realize their potential."

"People? You mean women."

She rose, hitching up her trousers and tucking in the shirt where it bagged.

"Know how I got in this mess in the first place?" Cornell asked. "I put on women's clothes and was arrested."

"Now there," said the lieutenant, "is the kind of social control that I find misguided. I can't see the community is threatened by such a mild form of deviation. In fact, transvestism might work as a safety valve that releases, in a harmless way, certain pressures that if blocked might eventually lead to serious criminal behavior."

She rubbed her nose with a thumb. "I can't see that repression yields positive results. I'm not alone, Georgie. There's a whole new generation of women coming along who believe in persuasion, tolerance, patience, understanding: qualities that have traditionally been called masculine, but wrongly in our view. Not evil, but wrong. There is no intrinsic reason why women cannot be as sympathetic as men. It is not necessary to be brutal to be feminine."

She fished a rumpled handkerchief from her back pocket and blew her nose.

Cornell went to the phonograph and started up "Boxing Glove Love."

"You want to dance, Lieutenant?"

"Not now, Georgie. I have to look in on my other patient." She patted his extended hand. "You're coming along very nicely. Your defenses are falling away. These passionate outbursts are all to the good. The first step in dealing with a fantasy is to verbalize it."

He moved in on her, seized her wrist, and lifted her hand.

"Now, now," she said calmly, "no false aggression." She stood stock-still. He pulled her against his armored groin, his hand sliding onto her round, fat, firm buttock. "Aha," she said, still dispassionate, "I can feel something naughty." She pushed away with a sudden effort and brought her knee forcefully into Cornell's crotch.

The protective device did not work as well as he had anticipated. The blow pushed the cup against his penis, his phallus pressed against his testicles, and the latter were squashed against his thighs. It was hardly better than no guard at all. He clutched himself and bent over.

She said: "You're being silly, Georgie. When I come in with breakfast, I'd like to see you back in your makeup and wig. Good night, dear." She left the room.

For women have sat indoors all these mil-lions of years, so that by this time the very walls are permeated by their creative force, which has, indeed, so overcharged the ca-pacity of bricks and mortar that it must needs harness itself to pens and brushes and business and politics.

Virginia Woolf, 1928

12

CORNELL WAS AWAKENED by the sound of the key in the lock. He was lying, nude below the waist, on his opened skirt; during the writhings of sleep, caused by a dream he could not remember, the waistband closure had burst.

He covered his bare groin with both hands as Aster entered with the breakfast tray, the cup of cocoa and sweet roll. She placed it on the vanity and turned to him. He felt that a guilty effort to close the skirt would be inept and undignified: he had had enough of that sort of thing.

She smiled sympathetically. "Good morning, Georgie. Go right ahead with what you're doing. As it happens, I got to thinking last night that perhaps we hadn't gone back far enough in your therapeutic reprise: perhaps the late teen years were too recent, and we should try early pubescence. Instinctively you had already arrived at that conclusion on your own, taken off your makeup and wig, and now I find you playing with yourself. Excellent!"

Cornell stared at her. "I'm not masturbating."

"Then what *are* you doing?"

"I'm protecting myself."

Her smile turned derisive.

"Nobody wants to steal that little thing of yours, believe me." Now she was candidly sneering. "What would she do with it?"

Cornell leaped up, seized her, and hurled her onto the bed. He ripped at her uniform, but the fabric was too strong for him, and he had to denude her by less passionate means, unbuttoning, unbuckling, and opening the zipper in the standard way. For women's clothes were rape-resistant, unlike the attire of men.

He had stripped her to T-shirt and jockey shorts when it came to his notice for the first time that she was not resisting, indeed had not moved of her own will since being hurled to the bed, had been lifted and shoved like a dummy filled with sand. She was unconscious. She had banged her skull on the bedstead.

He put his ear to the low bulge of her left bosom. Her heart was ticking stanchly away. He rolled up the T-shirt, exposing the broad flat band of canvaslike fabric which depressed her bosoms. He raised the heavy, warm, unconscious trunk and undid the chest-band fasteners in back: they were of the same sort as those on a man's bra, though of a thicker gauge of wire. He peeled off the band.

The size of her naked breasts amazed him. Cornell had never seen any except in pornographic pictures of the sort owned by Charlie. Hers were much larger than his synthetic ones had been, though not as well shaped. In fact, hers had no shape at all, being neither spheres nor cones, but big soft blobs of flesh which flowed into her armpits when she lay flat. However, when he elevated her back, they developed the form of canteloupes carried in a string bag, and sagged almost to her waist.

He took one gently into his palm: so warm, so soft and yet massive, substantial, actual. The lieutenant murmured, and through her living flesh he felt the sound.

He looked up. Her mouth was trembling slightly, though not with what seemed discomfort or disgust. He lowered his head and took her nipple in his lips, like a baby with the feeding tube. He had no conscious memory of his own time as an infant, but at one point during his years with Dr. Prine she had suggested he had some sort of fixation on his birth facility, No. 1182, in Jersey City, and as a therapeutic measure on the following Sunday he had gone over there and taken the guided tour.

From a glass-enclosed balcony he and the other visitors, all male, looked down on the ranks of stainless-steel incubating tanks being tended by white-uniformed attendants. Of course he had no way of recognizing which of the capsules had borne him, if indeed it was still in service after all these years.

A high spot of the tour had been the actual delivery of a baby. A technician checked the dials, threw a lever, opened a glass porthole of the type found on front-loading washers, and slid out a tray containing a newborn child. Then she snipped off the plastic umbilicus that attached it to the tray, knotted the end on the child's belly, held the infant by the ankles, and spanked it into life.

They could hear nothing on their enclosed balcony, but the little upside-down face was contorted as if it were crying. The baby was male. The genitals at birth were already very large relative to the size of the body.

Next they were conducted to a gallery overlooking one of the nurseries, where each rank of infants was separated from the next by a long horizontal cylinder from which feeding hoses ran to the cribs. There he saw babies sucking as he was now.

The tour ended with a visit to the enormous computer that named the new human beings as fast as they were born. It was linked electronically to the master system in Washington, D.C., and could issue every second a first-and-last-name combination which would not duplicate that of any other person born at that facility for a ten-year period. Thus there might now be a Georgie Cornell who was either nineteen or thirty-nine but not another who was twenty-nine in the Mideastern area of the country. That is, if the computer was working properly. One of the technicians ran off a demonstration name for the tour group: the little tag that emerged from the slot read: *Jhon Simth*.

Cornell encircled the breast with his two hands and pushed and worked and kneaded. The nipple grew until it seemed to fill his throat. His eyes were tightly shut, and he made sounds of the sort that issued from the newborn piglets he had once seen, on a school trip years before to the Children's Zoo: they sucked the dugs of an enormous sow. Not too long previously, they had come out of her belly. She was a huge, bristly, snouted thing, with tiny eyes. She was their "mother." And they were drinking literal "mother's milk." The children of course snickered, and one naughty boy whispered that word to Cornell, who, not then knowing it was obscene, repeated it to the teacher, who subsequently, back in class, made him write fifty times on the blackboard: "I have a foul mouth."

The lieutenant's teat was dry. Cornell gave it up at last, took his mouth and hands away, and raised his head. Aster now was looking at him: her eyes were open, anyway, but she seemed to be in a coma.

He was not ashamed, even though he had stripped her to her shorts and himself below the waist, baring her breasts and his penis, because there could be no connection between those mutually exclusive organs, and it had never been his intention to kill her, and he had at no time so much as touched her genital region, and for a moment he was actually thinking that maybe he could get out of it somehow, dress her again, and resume the therapy as if nothing had happened. Because he was really at heart a good boy, and he had had a lot of troubles, and he wasn't criminal or crazy, and his phallus was limp, and she had always been understanding and generous.

But the blow on the head, or his piggishness at her paps, or both, had worked some awful change on her. She did not respond with voice or even a focus of eye. He had heard that people could be made idiotic by skull damage. He *knew* that women were killed by complete rape, and suspected they could be driven mad by an attempt—regardless of the lieutenant's newfangled theories: indeed, look where they had got her, stripped, helpless, supine, non compos mentis.

He climbed into her trousers, which were so tight in the waist that he could not close the fastener, but ran the zipper up as far as he could and hid the opening with the belt buckle. The legs were too short, the hips and seat too ample, but he was covered. Owing to the stoutness of her trunk, the shirt could be managed, though the cuffs came scarcely below mid-forearm. He rolled up the sleeves, and tried to remember how to knot the necktie. He was wearing no underwear. He retained the teenager anklets and penny loafers. He combed his hair female-style, with a part, and was ready to leave.

But what if Aster were suffering some damage which, if treated promptly, was reparable? Left alone and unreported, in this isolated place, she might remain interminably in a vegetable state. He went to her. She was still gazing at nothing. He sat on the edge of the bed, lifted her neck, and explored her scalp. It was wrong that she should have suffered for her liberalism. Never had he raised a hand against tyrannical Dr. Prine. He felt terribly tender towards poor Aster, lying there with bared breasts and in her jockey shorts, and he rubbed her neat pate. She wore a modified crewcut, but her hair was too silken to stand up. With his little finger he traced the convolutions of her delicately modeled ear, penetrating the shell-pink aperture. . . .

Aster jerked her head away and next her trunk, reared up on the far elbow, and said, in an objective kind of voice: "I guess it didn't work. I bit off more than I could chew."

Her melon breasts had dropped into their alternative position, the left one hanging very near his forearm. ·

"How do they get so big when they are bound all your life?" There was a certain resentment in his question.

She got off the bed and stood on the far side, hands on hips, without shame, in all her rounded softness.

She said levelly: "Now, Georgie, you stand up and take off my clothes."

"I guess if they weren't bound they would grow even bigger."

She lifted one hand and twitched the index finger.

"Come on."

He cleared his head of the distracting wonderment and asked: "Are you O.K.?"

She continued to twitch her finger.

"I didn't intend to hurt you. I don't think I did, anyway." He frowned. "Or maybe I did. Anyway, I *hope* I didn't. I mean both: I hope I didn't want to hurt you, and I hope I didn't hurt you." Was he talking gibberish?

"I'm giving you a direct order," said Aster. She had definitely changed.

He looked at her awhile. "If you're O.K., then it doesn't matter what I meant, I guess."

She straightened her finger and pointed it at him like a weapon. "Let me tell you this, Georgie. Only I stand between you and emasculation. I've had enough of your nonsense. Now you drop those trousers and bend over." She seized the rat-tailed hairbrush from the vanity table and held it by the bristle-end.

Cornell stared at the long, tapered handle. He shook his head, saying ironically, without fear: "I thought you belonged to the new school."

He had struck home. She colored and turned the brush around. "I'm just going to spank your fanny. You've been a bad boy."

But she had lost it by now and soon threw the brush down. "Just give me back my uniform, please. It doesn't fit you anyway. We'll forget what happened. This type of therapy is still in the formative stages. Obviously there are many bugs to iron out. That doesn't mean it won't work. We simply have to try harder. We must put accidents of this sort to a positive use."

"You're scared," he said, "and you're talking shit." The ugly word seemed appropriate to his attire. "I stripped these clothes off you and I'm keeping them—unless you're big enough to take them back. It's as simple as that. If you're cold, put on the stuff I took off. I'm keeping the uniform, not because I prefer female clothes, which I've only worn when in some kind of crisis, but because I'm going to get out of here—out of this cell, out of the hospital, out of the camp."

He raised a fist. "Don't try to stop me. If you are thinking of kicking or grabbing my balls, just remember your breasts are vulnerable too, and besides, they're naked."

She crossed her arms on her bosom.

"Where will you go, Georgie? You're only running away from yourself."

"I'm going to get away from women."

"Where would that be? We are everywhere." She made a mocking mouth. "There are supposed to be a few savage tribes, in remote spots like the South American jungles and New Guinea, where men are dominant, but women are still *there*."

"I don't want to be a boss," Cornell shouted. "Can't you understand? I just don't want to be bossed. Is that crazy?"

"It's unrealistic. The human condition is such that, of two sexes, one will dominate. Men held power for centuries—"

"That's true?" shouted Cornell.

"—and lost it," Aster said.

"That's not the history I was taught in school."

"Naturally not. You don't dare tell that to children. They would be confused about authority. They wouldn't know what to believe."

"But I haven't heard it since growing up, except from perverts and revolutionaries."

"Well," Aster said, still hugging herself, "it's simpler just to let it go unsaid. What harm does it do? And even many adult males might get the wrong idea if they knew. History is the bunk anyway. Life is lived *now*."

He asked: "You weren't unconscious at any time, there on the bed, were you? But you didn't resist, either. Why?"

"I was trying to understand."

"Did you feel anything when I was sucking your breasts?"

She nodded vigorously. "You know I'm sincerely interested in curing you, Georgie. I'm paying most of the expenses out of my own pocket. But the whole experiment will go out the window if you run away. I'll be seriously embarrassed."

"I don't mean that," said Cornell. "I mean, did you feel anything *personal*?"

"Of course, I just told you."

"That's professional!"

He opened the door.

"Georgie!" cried Aster.

He left the room. It seemed to him that, all in all, she was worse off than he. He had never before thought that of a woman. But with power came a terrible responsibility: you had either to wield it or relinquish it.

Before him was the aisle which led through the cartons and dead-ended at the lavatory. He went left, along a wall of white-washed cinder block, at length found a door, opened it, and looked into a garage containing several ambulances painted in olive-drab with big white crosses. A mechanic in grease-spotted coveralls was leaning on the hood of the nearest vehicle. She started when she saw him, threw down her cigarette, and ground it to fragments with the sole of her Army boot.

"Sorry, ma'am." She backed away obsequiously and disappeared around a stack of thick-treaded tires above which was posted a large no-smoking sign. She had taken him for an officer —in a uniform which pinched in some places and bagged in others, and showed an inch of skin between the trouser cuffs and the tops of his bobby socks. But the insignia of a first lieutenant in the Medical Corps were pinned to the collar.

He went between the ambulances and out the wide entrance onto the parking lot of blacktop, from which point he could see part of the hospital complex, with its one-story wards connected by covered ramps. He had no geographical sense of which section of camp he was in. It was terribly hot there on the asphalt under the ferocious, dirty yellow sky of—September? When typing Ida's correspondence in the old days he could seldom remember the date from one letter to the next, having to consult his desk calendar each time. Now he had even lost the seasons. If it was September, he would be thirty next month.

Away in the distance he could see groups of conscripts being marched hither and yon. He had no idea which direction one would choose to reach an exit gate. He had grown to the age of thirty not only without acquiring any skill: he lacked the precision of mind from which a skill could be developed. He was at the edge of a big, hot, empty parking area; over there were some buildings and beyond them some people. The heat was dampening his armpits, which were unprotected in this female shirt without perspiration shields, and the trousers were stifling his lower body.

He had been standing there helplessly for some time when an olive-drab staff car came around the corner of the hospital and pulled up on the asphalt. The driver, an enlisted woman, got out and opened the door for the passenger in the rear.

Cornell turned and walked quickly into the garage, but before he could reach a place of concealment he heard a shout.

"Ma'am! Lieutenant! Will you come here, please? The general wants a word with you."

He could do nothing but return. When he reached the car, the driver, a corporal, still holding open the rear door, said: "General Cox is inspecting the hospital. She would like a tour of the garage."

A tall, robust, leathery-skinned woman emerged from the car. She was in her late fifties and wore a beautifully tailored uniform of lightweight cloth, mirror-polished shoes, and a cap with a shiny bill and gold braid.

"You are the garage officer," said she, giving him a withering once over. "And you are a disgrace, girl. Where's your cap? And look at that mess you call a uniform." When her inspection reached his feet, she exploded: *"Sweat socks and loafers?* What the hell goes on around here? I just found a secret room with a half-naked officer in it, stretched out on the bed, crying her eyes out. It was obvious from the furnishings that she had been keeping a man there."

Cornell rubbed his nose.

"And you slob you, what's your name?"

"Hind," answered Cornell in a slurred way and in a higher octave than his normal voice.

"Hind what?"

"Hind, Ida."

The general stuck her face into Cornell's and cried: "Hind, *ma'am!"*

"Yes, ma'am."

"I'll tell you this, Hind: you're going on report. Now escort me through this garage of yours. From here it looks like the camp dump."

Cornell led the general into the mouth of the garage.

"Here are our ambulances, General. And there's a stack of tires. Now, over there you see one of those gadgets that lift a car up high so you can get in under it and oil the wheels. And that, I think—the upright thing near the far corner—is a gas pump, or else it's to put air in the tires with."

The general wiped her face with one hand while fisting the other.

"Hind, are you that weakminded or are you pulling some sort of shit on me?"

Before Cornell could respond, a door in the rear opened and in came the mechanic he had encountered earlier. She was smoking again. She saw them and ran out.

"One of your women, Hind?" cried the general, growing apoplectic. "Smoking around gas and oil?"

"Oh, no, ma'am. That's strictly forbidden." Cornell pointed to the sign.

"Hind," said the general, "I should say you have a very feeble hold on your grade as of this moment." She kicked a greasy rag into a standing pool of oil. "How often do you wash these ambulances?"

"Every once in a while," Cornell answered. He looked around and saw a hose hanging from an overhead tank. There was a pistol-shaped nozzle on the end of it, which he seized and brandished. "We have the latest in car-washing equipment."

"That's a grease gun, you fucking idiot!" The general threw her head back and roared: "Put yourself under arrest!"

"Yes, ma'am." Cornell's intention was to let the gun swing away, but his finger caught in the mechanism and in trying to free it he pressed the trigger and squirted grease on the general's shirtfront. Purely an accident, but while the general looked incredulously down at the green-black mess, Cornell deliberately shot more grease into her eyes.

He ran to the storeroom door, opened it, and dashed inside. To go straight ahead would be to reach the room where he had left poor Aster. Back in the garage, the general was going vocally berserk. He should have given her a mouthful of grease as well.

He turned left, wending through the crates in the dim light from the occasional overhead bulb. Somewhere must be a door that led to a ramp connecting this wing with the rest of the hospital. He followed the wall, with detours here and there because of the stacked cartons and in one place a wheeled stretcher, at last gained a door, tried it, and found it locked.

He went on several steps, stopped decisively, and returned. He was large enough to break it down, the way even small policewomen did it on TV crime shows. He was about to hurl himself against it, shoulder foremost, when he decided instead to kick it in. He first raised, then, getting a still better idea, lowered, his foot. He searched through the pockets of the lieutenant's trousers and found a ring of keys.

A nearby ceiling light enabled him to be precise. He looked

at the name on the lock, "Yale," and then sorted through the keys to find which if any bore a similar designation. There had been a time when Cornell would have stupidly, malely, applied each key to the hole without predetermining its appropriateness. He found three Yales, tried them, and the second worked.

He swung back the door—and saw not an exit but a room of the size of that in which he had lately been confined. The rumpled bed was heaped with a tartan blanket. Miniature portraits of baseball players were stapled to the wall above. A football and a plastic tommygun lay on top of a chest of drawers, and the floor was littered with various souvenirs of female childhood: Indian headdress of plastic feathers, toy cars, rubber hunting knife, and two holstered six-guns on a cartridge belt.

Looking alternatively at the cowboy pistols and the machine gun, Cornell decided to arm himself. If he were stopped when leaving the camp, he would show his toy weapon. He seized the tommygun and pressed the trigger: *click-clack.*

He heard a whimpering noise from the bed. Something was in it, something too small to make a large enough lump for him to have noticed hitherto. Something with the blanket pulled over its head.

He was startled and frightened and might have run out had he not been holding the tommygun, which of course was only a toy, but it was something to clutch. He went to the bed and with the black muzzle lifted the edge of the blanket.

Her eyes were pinched shut and her mouth was grimacing and her fingers were in her ears and her legs were thrashing, but it was Harriet all right, and she was having a tantrum.

A woman is to be from her house three times:
When she is christened, married, and buried.

THOMAS FULLER, 1732

13

CORNELL THREW THE GUN ASIDE and with his hands pulled the blanket to the foot of the bed. Harriet wore a yellow jersey with a big number 18 stenciled on the chest. Below the waist her outfit consisted of short pants in navy blue, striped anklets, and dirty sneakers. She was dressed as a girl of eleven or twelve.

Harriet *was* the other, the female, patient. Aster had lied to him. He hated to be lied to! Then and there he might have stamped his foot—but, instead, oddly enough, he considered an alternative. Was her name really Harriet? The only one she had given him in jail was Harry. He had always used to jump to conclusions; perhaps he had changed.

He touched her shoulder. She squeezed her eyelids together even more dramatically and further knotted her face, to the degree that her little nose almost disappeared. He looked at the slight swellings on the bosom of the jersey. Were her breasts also larger than one thought? His hand traveled down and felt the taut band that stretched beneath the figure 18.

Instantly her eyes and mouth opened, she seized his fingers and sank her teeth in his thumb. He grasped her short blonde hair and pulled until her eyes were mostly white. She let him go, and he returned the favor.

He shook his hand, loose-fingered, then put it in his mouth. She rolled over, plunged to the floor, and pulled something from under the bed. It was a girl's toolkit. She took out a half-size hammer and shook it at him.

Cornell threw up his hands. "Come on," he said. "Cut the

clowning. The experiments are finished, and poor Aster will probably be court-martialed. Let's get out of here before they come looking for us."

"The doctor sent you, didn't she? It's a trick. She's trying to make me into a girl, but she can't. I'm a man, and I can prove it."

"All right," he said. "Have it your way. But I'm getting out."

He stopped on the threshold. He had a certain feeling that she would change her tune.

She cried: "Wait a minute. I won't go dressed like this." She went to the chest of drawers and began to take out various items of male attire: skirt, frilly blouse, wispy underwear, high-heeled shoes, and even an old-fashioned garter belt. She had zipped down the fly of the shorts and was about to drop them when Cornell understood.

"No," he shouted. "Listen to me. We're going to steal an ambulance and get out of here, but I can't drive." He went to her. "You've got to do the driving." He put his hands at her slender waist, feeling with the lower fingers the sudden swell of her hips.

She twisted around and moved away.

"Don't touch me!" she said. Then: "I still don't trust you, but anything is better than pretending to be a ten-year-old. That Aster is the crazy one. I don't care what happens to her. She deserves anything she gets."

"We can't let the gate guard see a man at the wheel."

"A little girl is not much better."

It was true. His plan had been too facile.

"Let's see. You and I could switch shirts. Only the upper part of your body will be seen through the ambulance window, and that would look legitimate, a woman driving. I think that jersey would stretch enough so I could wear it and pose as the little girl."

She frowned. "Officers don't drive ambulances."

"What designates an officer?" Cornell asked. "Just these collar pins. We'll take them off." He stripped to the waist and, after unpinning the insignia, handed her the shirt and tie. She peered at the scars from his breast-removal, then turned her back and pulled the jersey over her head. Behind the rear closure of the breastband, her spine was deeply grooved. He would have liked to run his finger through that warm slot.

Harriet, if that was her name, tucked the shirttails into her shorts and turned around.

"That's not a bad outfit," he said. "Sort of like a girl scout. Kind of cute."

She scowled. "Don't make fun of me. It's not my idea."

"You want to get out of here, don't you?"

"It's the only reason I'm going through with this."

She gathered together the male clothing she had found in the dresser. "I'm taking this along, and as soon as we're outside the camp, I'm putting it on."

"I won't try to stop you," Cornell assured her. "It's certainly more comfortable below the waist. You don't have to worry about modesty when wearing trousers, but that's all you can say for them. They chafe."

"Just a minute." She was very rational again. "You don't think you can get away with posing as a little girl on a field trip?"

"You're right," he said. "The only thing that would make sense would be for me to put on the blouse and skirt, and you to get into these trousers, making a complete uniform. Then anybody seeing us would take you for a soldier and me for a sperm-term conscript who was being taken out of camp for some reason."

She started to object, but he raised a hand. "I've got it. On the way to the garage there's a wheeled stretcher. I'll get on it and you push me to the ambulance. I'll be a patient, see, who has to be taken to a civilian hospital in Newark or some place for treatment for some condition that they don't have the facilities for here. Something like radium treatment, you know."

He ran the zipper halfway down while facing her, and he was naked beneath the fly.

"Do you mind turning around?" he asked.

"You're the one who's undressing. *You* turn." She defiantly brought her eyes up to his.

"All right," said he, and dropped the trousers to his shoes. "You asked for it."

She continued to stare at his face. He stepped out of the pants, stooped, and brought them up from the floor.

"O.K., let's have that male stuff."

She looked at his chest and shoulders. "You're too big. You'll burst the seams or stretch things out of shape." She held the bundle behind her back.

"Come on."

"No," she said. "No. I don't want my outfit ruined."

"All I want to do is get out of here," said Cornell. "It's nothing personal."

There was a folded blanket at the foot of the bed. He wrapped himself in it, put his socks and loafers on, got the men's clothes from the floor and brought them to her.

"I've got a better idea," he said. "While I'm on the stretcher I won't need to wear anything but a blanket. I guess you're right: this stuff wouldn't fit me anyway."

Holding his blanket together, Cornell went into the storeroom and fetched the wheeled litter. The whole business about clothing was arbitrary and probably nonsensical. The olive-drab blanket was the most comfortable attire he had ever worn. The wool was slightly scratchy, but that effect could be alleviated by loosening the wrap so that it touched fewer areas of the body. It could be arranged to hang mostly from the shoulders; underneath, the naked body moved freely.

When he had brought the stretcher up to the door of her room, the girl wore the trousers. The uniform was a little too big in every dimension, but still fitted her better than it had him.

He climbed onto the stretcher and arranged the blanket over his body, tucking up his feet so the loafers could not be seen. The girl grasped the vehicle and wheeled it rapidly through the storeroom.

"Stop here," he said when they had reached the door to the garage.

"Now what?"

"Listen," said he. "We have to cooperate for a while yet. Can't we at least be friendly enemies?" He tried to smile.

"If you give me some respect."

"I don't want your damned clothes," said Cornell, himself offended again. "You can stick them— No, I don't mean that. What I mean is, let's try to avoid this petty bickering. Now please open that door and push me into the garage, right up to the back door of one of the ambulances."

"What happens if someone tries to stop us?"

Cornell suddenly remembered the general. He got off the stretcher with his blanket, opened the door, and peeped out. The general was gone. The mechanic was back and doing something under the raised hood of the nearest vehicle.

Cornell closed the door. "There's an enlisted woman out there. You can bluff her."

"Suppose you tell me how."

He suppressed the urge to say something rude again—"You've been a woman all your life" or "What about all the viciousness you showed at the Men's House of Detention, and then your aggressiveness about who used the toilet," etc.—because that would only have led to more wrangling, and all he wanted at the moment was to get out of a place where female domination was at its extreme—in view of which need, why should he complain that she deferred to him at a juncture at which a decision must be made and forceful measures taken?

"Here's how."

He flung the door open and cried: "Hey, you!"

The startled mechanic dropped her wrench clatteringly into the engine, straightened up, and froze without turning.

"Over here. Give us a hand!" Cornell let the door swing to, quickly climbed on the stretcher, and covered himself.

The girl asked: "Who's that?"

"A mechanic, I told you. You're in an officer's uniform."

"Without the insignia. You took it off, stupid!"

He checked himself. "It doesn't matter. She won't notice. She's so dumb she smokes around gasoline."

After they had waited for a time and nobody appeared, he said: "Go see what became of that jerk."

"Why don't you?"

"Because she may be on her way and I'm supposed to be the patient and I'm naked."

She grudgingly looked out. "There's nobody there." She wheeled him onto the floor of the garage. He peeped over the edge of the blanket. The mechanic had run off as usual.

"She was working on this one," he said, pointing at the nearest ambulance. "Try the next."

But the girl wheeled him instead towards the third vehicle. She was naturally contrary. He looked forward to their quick separation when they got out of camp.

She pushed the stretcher to the right side of the ambulance, left it there, and walked towards the hood.

"I think it loads from the rear," he said.

"Let's see whether I can get it started, first."

"Good thinking," said Cornell, and since nobody else was in view, he got up and off and immediately stepped into a pool of oil. He went to a clean patch of concrete and rubbed the soles of his loafers.

She sat in the driver's seat now, and in a moment the engine started. Then came a hideous grinding of gears, and the vehicle began slowly to back out of the garage.

Cornell supported himself with a hand on the stretcher while he stood on one foot and looked at the other to see whether it was clean of oil. When he saw what she was doing, he rushed the litter to the rear of the moving ambulance and shoved it at an angle against the loading doors and the folded-up cast-iron entry step that formed a kind of bumper. The stretcher keeled over with a crash that went directly into a screech as the heavy vehicle crushed the tubular frame.

The ambulance stopped rolling. Cornell ran to the driver's door.

"You were trying to run out on me!"

"I was not!" She pointed at him. "Get hold of yourself. I've never driven one of these. It's got all kinds of gears. I was just trying to find reverse."

"I don't believe you."

"Well," she said, "you have to. You need me. And besides, you're naked."

He looked down, covering himself with cupped hands. He went back to fetch the fallen blanket. He had just pulled the wrecked stretcher aside when, out on the blacktop apron, the general's car came into view. There seemed to be several people inside. Cornell snatched up the blanket, opened the rear doors of the ambulance, and climbed in. He had expected to find something to lie on, but the interior was bare metal.

He called up to the front: "Get the hell out of here."

She backed onto the blacktop at the same sluggish speed she had used when he thought she was dumping him. He heard shouts from outside, and next the crash as she struck what was surely the general's car. Cornell was thrown against the rear doors.

"Damn you," he shouted.

She screamed: "I can't get this into first."

He crawled up front and looked out the right window. The general had not been killed: she stood there roaring and purple-faced in her grease-stained shirt. Alongside her were the camp commandant who had addressed the conscripts on their first day in camp and another officer.

The general recognized Cornell.

"You!"

He turned and looked down at the knobbed lever which the girl was trying to move with her small fist. He covered her hand and shoved.

"Let me get the clutch all the way in." She tromped on a pedal. He applied force. The lever moved forward and the vehicle followed suit. She shouted: "Let my hand go. You're crushing it!"

He gave her a dirty look but said nothing. Instead he sat up and looked out again. Now the officers were running to the front of the ambulance.

"Step on it!"

She did, and barely missed hitting the general.

She shouted: "Now pull it straight back!"

"What?"

"The gearshift!"

Ah, the lever again. It moved quite easily now; she could have done it herself. Their speed increased just as the third officer, whom Cornell did not recognize, leaped onto his side of the ambulance, hooking an arm into the window frame.

"You're under arrest!" she cried.

Cornell kneeled on the seat, put his hand in her face, and shoved. She disappeared. The girl now moved the lever on her own, and they began to roll quite rapidly across the blacktop.

"Who was that?" she asked.

"I don't know," said Cornell. "She had little crossed pistols on her collar."

"Then she's military police."

She made a final shift and pressed her right foot down; they accelerated off the asphalt onto the camp road, which fortunately was straight on, for at that speed they could not have turned: Cornell knew that much about driving.

"Take it easy," he warned, "or we won't live to get out." The air was whipping his face.

She suddenly applied the brakes. He would have gone through the windshield had he not caught himself against the dashboard.

When she had corrected the subsequent skid and they were at rest, she said: "O.K., you take the wheel."

"Don't be so sensitive. I wasn't criticizing you."

But after they were underway again, as fast as ever, he could not help thinking: *You wouldn't even have got it in gear without me. You wouldn't have had the idea in the first place. You were lying there helplessly, dressed as a child.*

However, there was no doubt that they had a better chance to get out of camp together than he would have had alone.

"Do you know where this road goes?" he asked.

"No. We'll have to keep our eyes open."

They were approaching a barracks area. She hunched over the wheel, squinting, grim-mouthed, her short hair disordered by the wind.

"Watch out," he cried. "That column of men is going to cross the street." He closed his eyes and braced himself. She accelerated further. When he next peeped out they were gaining a crossroads, with an Army truck approaching from the left and a speeding jeep from the right.

"You can't make it!"

She cried: "An ambulance has the right of way." Her knuckles were white against the wheel.

He closed his eyes and, with two fingers, his ears as well. She made it, somehow. At length he unmasked his senses and saw a gate ahead, with a flanking sentry box.

"Got your story straight?"

"Screw that," she said. "I'm blasting through."

As they shot past the little kiosk, Cornell got a glimpse of the guard inside: she seemed asleep. He had always thought of soldiers as the very models of discipline, efficiency, and order.

The girl slowed down and turned onto the public highway.

"Well," she said, slowing more, "where do you want off?"

He stared at a landscape of weeds and deteriorating billboards. "I'm not yet used to the idea I'm out." He stuck his head through the window and looked back at the camp. There was something scary about being free—whatever "free" was.

"You're really a good driver," he said, coming back in.

She grimaced. "How about Newark?"

He rubbed his eyes. He felt faint.

She glanced at him. "You O.K.?"

The question touched him. "Sure, I'll be all right. Newark will be fine."

They had traveled only a few hundred yards when she pulled off the highway, continued across the shoulder, and drove onto a patch of mud behind a billboard.

She climbed over her seat and into the back of the ambulance, carrying her bundle of men's clothes.

When Cornell saw her begin to undress, he asked: "Shouldn't we get farther away from camp?"

"I'm not going another inch until I'm properly dressed." She was already shouldering out of the lieutenant's shirt. Embarrassed, Cornell looked away. He wondered again about the mystique of clothing. Both men and women had legs which could either be encased separately in trousers or swathed generally in a skirt. Men did have those exterior genitals which were perhaps more accessible, more vulnerable, when covered with an open-ended sack, but there were cultures in which females, even soldiers, wore kilts, like Scotchwomen, or miniskirts of many pleats, like the Greeks: both races in fact being noted for their ferocity in battle. And in certain Oriental countries men wore pants.

The girl flung the shirt up to the cab. Cornell was none too eager to get back into its confines from his carefree nudity. In another moment the trousers arrived by air, landing across the gearshift which without his strength at a crucial moment she could not have moved. By chance the garment fell so that the knobbed lever protruded phallicly between the division of the pants legs.

From the rear he heard the whisper of soft fabrics. Would she actually put on that lacy white garterbelt? Cornell hadn't worn one for years, pantyhose being so convenient and a good deal more comfortable: nothing was worse than to sit on a garter clip. Comfort and convenience seemed to have become his ruling criteria as to attire. The blanket served both. Truly he was growing old.

He swiveled the rear-vision mirror around to examine his face, which without makeup was as naked as his body. Physically he was at the moment a kind of blank tablet on which anything might be inscribed. He could for example let his hair grow on his lips and chin, and chest, underarms, and legs as well—but only if he lived in utter isolation from the rest of society. His eyes as usual looked smaller in the absence of liner, and shallower without shadow. His hair was definitely receding at the temples.

He looked past the reflection of his left ear, wholly exposed by the feminine shortness of hair, and saw the girl's peachlike backside underneath a virtually transparent film of underpants. The cleft was practically as clear as if she were nude. How gross, obscene, shameless. It was the kind of thing that a burlesque dancer might wear while wiggling his bum at the dirty old women sitting below the runway.

She hooked the garterbelt at the small of her back. Her waist was so small he could almost have encompassed it with his two hands; just below began that extraordinary slope to the terminal globes of her bottom.

She sat on the floor and began to pull on a dark stocking. The light that came through the two little back windows was not so good as that from the windshield, and she revolved on her seat to face forward, to fasten the unfamiliar front clip of the garter-belt. Oblivious to all else, biting her pink mouth, rumpled blonde head lowered, one thigh stretched out, the other knee in the air—

There was a double thickness of fabric in the plump vee of the crotch, but double spiderweb, and in her contortions the narrow strap became a ribbon and then a string and finally a thread which disappeared within a silken furrow of flesh.

Cornell scraped his teeth across his lower lip, forced his eyes from the mirror, and cocooned himself tightly in the blanket, shuddering with revulsion and something worse. Eventually she finished and climbed into the driver's seat with a show of garters and hosiery.

She wore a Kelly-green nylon blouse with a panel of ruffles. It was much too large for her. A chocolate-brown maxiskirt, split to the knee. Textured stockings in navy blue, and enormous black patent-leather sling shoes with three-inch heels.

Mary! What an outfit. Above it, her unkempt blonde head and those small features, so incongruous on one dressed as a male. Despite the attire, she didn't seem masculine at all. Cornell in his various female outfits had looked much more like a woman than she resembled a man.

She started the engine and probed, with her preposterous shoe, for what he remembered as the clutch. The spike-heeled shoe, which was outlandishly too big, fell off her foot, which was scarcely larger than Cornell's hand. He realized only now that he had seen her vulva when she was putting on the stockings. It seemed to be a continuation of the division between the buttocks. How neat and efficient, how unlike a man's pendulous growth. So up inside it, theoretically, was a complete Birth Facility. Hard to believe, looking at the small abdomen. As a schoolboy he had heard horror stories of perverted, criminal women who produced babies from their own bodies by some process that sounded like defecation, but in those days he had always been appalled by anything creepy, weird. He had first learned of menstruation when he lived with Pauline Witkovsky, the painter, who was wont to clog the commode with stained Kotexes, and it was he who had to work the plumber's suction cup.

He remembered another odd thing: that somehow he had felt guilty because she bled. That made no sense at all. He had never seen a woman's bare groin; when they had you, they naturally stayed dressed, strapping the dildo over their trousers.

The girl fetched her shoe from the floor.

"Look around," she said, "and see if you can find some paper to stuff in the toe."

"That's big enough to fit me," said Cornell.

"It was the smallest I could find."

"You stole this stuff from a sperm conscript," he said.

"See if you can find some paper, will you?"

"You were supposed to be a man who was drafted like me. What about the civilian clothes you came in?"

"They weren't in good taste. I threw them away."

Cornell's eyebrows rose.

"Don't you think this is a nice outfit?" she asked.

"Swell." He studied her for a while, and then he finally picked up the shirt and trousers that lay between them.

"I don't know who you really are," he said, "or even what you're pretending to be any more. But I'll tell you something, I don't think you are crazy. And I also don't think that *you* think you're a man."

"Georgie Cornell," said she, in the most matter-of-fact voice, "don't look a gift horse in the mouth."

"What did you call me?"

"It's the name you used in jail."

"Jail?"

"The Men's House of Detention, my dear cellmate." She said these things in a self-satisfied rhythm punctuated by insolent stresses. He had an impulse to slap her face.

"You think you're smart, don't you?" Here she had known his identity all along, but his immediate feeling was one of competitiveness rather than fear.

That was stupid. After what he had gone through in the past few months, he should be capable of something better. He forced himself to grin.

"Well, I guess you're right. You *are* smart." He felt better for having said that, because it was the truth. "I thought the nose job made me look different."

"It does." His praise had taken the edge off her. She looked aside in a certain delicacy. "Actually, I probably wouldn't have recognized you."

"Was it my voice, when we had that run-in over which group used the john?"

She peered earnestly at him. "Georgie, the Movement was using you as a dupe."

"I figured that out for myself after a while. . . . I guess you know the whole thing, the masturbation scheme? It couldn't possibly have worked. . . . Stanley tipped you off about me, didn't he?"

"Stanley? I didn't know his name."

"Now it seems I have betrayed *him*," Cornell said stoically. "Oddly enough, that doesn't please me—even if he does deserve it."

"The name is probably false," she said, sitting there behind the wheel in her oversized male clothing. "Is he the leader?"

"I can't tell you anything else," said Cornell. "Even if they did set me up as they did. I don't intentionally sell out anybody. That would make me their sort, you see—people who manipulate others, and for what? They want to liberate men, but *I'm* a man, and they would have got me castrated. I may be dumb, but I'm smart enough to understand that."

She said hastily: "You're not dumb, Georgie! You're the only prisoner to have escaped from the Men's House of Detention in ten years."

Strange praise from her.

He shrugged. "That took no great intelligence and not even a large amount of courage. Despite the brutality of the jailers, the place was barely guarded. The woman on the front door was asleep—like the sentry back there at the camp gate." He looked out the window at the rear of the billboard. "Speaking of which, we're only a hundred yards or so from the camp. Is this the place to sit and talk? Won't they be searching for us? Any pursuers who looked closely could see our wheels from the road. There's a space under the billboard."

She was smiling. "There you are: you're pretty shrewd."

"Yeah," he said in chagrin, "so clever I forgot for a moment that you are one of *them*. What's your game?" Suddenly he turned hostile and shook his fist. "Get this thing going if you don't want your face smashed in."

She threw back that small, fragile face and laughed, a movement which caused her trunk to arch and the front of the loose blouse to show the projection of her breasts, which she had freed, when donning the male clothing, from the constraining band. They were small, but conical and definite.

Nevertheless he shook his fist again and said: "I'm warning you." He had a great fear of being conned.

"Georgie," said she, "will you please get me some paper to stuff in my shoe?"

He looked at the threatening hand: he had forgotten he was still holding her sling pump.

She said: "You had your chance to beat me up that time we fought in jail, and you didn't use it. Even though I deserved a beating for what I did to you. You exerted just enough force to subdue me. I was impressed by that. You know, I used to wrestle in college. I had never before been overpowered without being hurt."

He found a big, almost clean handkerchief in the back pocket of the lieutenant's trousers, easily tore it in two, and stuffed a half into the toe of each shoe.

"Try this. If you're going to keep dressing like that, remember a hanky is better than newspaper, because it doesn't rustle. Just plain Kleenex is good, too, but you need quite a bit because it compacts."

She put on the shoes and stamped her feet. "Feels O.K."

"It occurs to me to ask where'd you get the men's clothes you wore when disguised as an inmate in jail and a sperm conscript? You're awfully small, and yet they seemed to fit."

"The FBI had a wardrobe department."

Cornell pursed his lips, but like most men he couldn't whistle. "You're FBI?"

"Sexual sedition is a federal crime."

"You're an FBI woman and you were assigned to *me?* Good heavens, I was just an insignificant little secretary. I really did get into all this by accident."

With her shoe firmly seated, she depressed the clutch and put the gearshift into reverse.

"Don't worry," she said. "That's all over for me. I really am defecting."

When she had backed out to the road, she had the old trouble with the shift lever. Once again he had to assist her to get it into first.

Our women's movement resembles strongly the gigantic religious and intellectual movement which for centuries convulsed the life of Europe, and had, as its ultimate outcome, the final emancipation of the human intellect and the freedom of the human spirit.

OLIVE SCHREINER, 1911

14

THEY WERE APPARENTLY on some sort of back road, the main purpose of which was to furnish access to the camp. No other vehicles appeared while they were on this stretch. They were not pursued. This failure was not one of which Cornell could complain, but it amazed him, and he mentioned it to the girl.

"That's the Army for you," she said. "They're probably making a half-assed search for us in camp. They probably think we're drunk and joyriding around. It wouldn't occur to them that we were going over the hill."

She had her foot all the way down again, and they were speeding past the billboards, which were now separated from the road by a drainage ditch full of litter.

"They're a bunch of idiots in the Army," she said. "Believe me, I know. I've worked with Army Intelligence on espionage cases. Once their agents arrested some of *us* as spies."

The wind was whipping his face, and Cornell instinctively began to roll up the window so his hair would not be disordered. Then he remembered he really had no coiffure to be ruined.

Up ahead a big motorway appeared and soon they reached its feeder road. The girl turned onto it so swiftly that he felt the wheels on his side leave the ground. But he had anticipated this and clamped his fingers under the seat, and then braced himself for the inevitable braking. After a scream of tires, a skid, and a correction, they eventually stopped with the nose of the ambulance within a foot of the motorway on which the vehicles were motionless and bumper-to-bumper. A young woman in the sedan they would have struck shook her fist and raved inaudibly behind closed windows.

The girl with Cornell made a vulgar motion with her vertical middle finger.

"I don't know why women get so ferocious when they're behind the wheel," Cornell said. "I used to have a very calm and gentle girl friend who would become insanely mad at other drivers. Once she climbed out of the car in the middle of some intersection and got into a fistfight. Imagine that. Because somebody cut her off or something."

"Have you had many girl friends?" She looked straight ahead.

"Not many regular ones," Cornell said. The question made him a bit shy. He looked into the lap of his blanket. "Like the one I'm talking about. I had maybe three dates. After that she stopped calling." He cleared his throat. "The story of my life." The girl was staring through the windshield. "How about you? Have you had many boys?"

She continued to study the hood. "I've dated a few." She blinked. "But I've never *had* one." She turned and looked him in the eye. "So you can put your clothes on now."

Cornell could feel his blush go all the way down under the blanket.

"How dare you make such an innuendo!"

"Well, why are you still naked?"

"I'm not." He grasped his blanket. What hurt was that just as he thought they had established a genuine rapport she pulled this dirty trick. Indignantly he flipped his face in the other direction, but no sooner had he done so than he suddenly understood that she was paying him back spitefully for his undiplomatic remark about drivers.

It wasn't easy, but he managed to turn back and say, reasonably, while still blushing, or perhaps blushing again and more furiously from this effort: "Believe me, I wasn't trying to lure you or anything. I simply forgot, because this blanket is so comfortable."

Now it was she who seemed embarrassed, whether by his display of self-control or by a sudden realization on her part that she had been needlessly mean. She did not apologize in so many words. Instead she quickly directed an abstract wrath at the traffic.

"Look at that," she said, pounding the steering wheel. "We'll be here for hours!"

Still he made no move to put on the lieutenant's uniform, which was lying across his lap. Matters of attire seemed so trivial in view of their odd partnership, an association so complex as to have restrained him thus far from asking the obvious questions. But having deflected her thrust, he found the energy to begin.

"Have you been following me ever since I broke out of jail?"

She grimaced. "Does it matter?"

"I guess not." He reached over and touched the nearer of the two hands which still gripped the wheel tenaciously though the vehicle was at rest.

She pulled away. "Don't do that!"

He frowned. "What's wrong with you? I'm just trying to be nice. But you make it terribly difficult."

"Just keep your paws to yourself, that's all. I don't like to be touched."

He looked back at the road and saw the line begin to move. The car they had almost hit was stalled in place, leaving just enough room to get by. The girl deftly inserted the ambulance onto the motorway.

The traffic, though solid, was moving at a reasonable speed, a speed preferable to Cornell over the rate at which she would have been driving had the lanes been empty.

When Cornell awakened, his calves were tucked under him, the side of his head was against the seat-back, and he was looking at the girl's thighs. The split skirt had parted and he could see one of those stockings all the way to the garter clip: in some ways a more grotesque image than had been her naked leg. Say what you would, styles of clothing had a reference to modes of existence: in his brief association with her, she had been many different persons rather than the same one dressed in various costumes—but that was a silly reflection. He looked at her face. Extraordinary: she now wore lipstick and eye make-up.

"When'd you do that?" he asked, straightening up. Her eyes looked sore or burnt. A very sloppy job. And that purple shadow!

She opened her smeared scarlet mouth and he saw red on her teeth.

"What?"

"The makeup."

"Oh. When we got stuck for a while. You dozed off."

"Where'd you get it?"

She lifted a beige purse from the floor. "It was in this." A beige bag, with black shoes, green blouse, brown skirt, navy stockings.

He realized that they were not moving and looked out to see why. They were no longer on the motorway, but in an urban situation, at an intersection controlled by a traffic light from which the green lens was missing along with half of the red. On the left side was a junkyard full of rusted car bodies; to the right, the crumbling shells of abandoned multiple dwellings, the occasional wino or junkie slumped in a doorway.

"Where are we?"

"Newark," she said. "Where do you want out?"

An evil-looking character had heaved itself up from a pile of refuse at the curb and was approaching the ambulance, wearing rags, grinning with purple teeth.

"Get going!" Cornell cried. He couldn't find how to lock the door.

"It's a red light."

"No cars are coming! Will you *go?*"

But she made no move, and there was that loathsome face against the window. Cornell shrank over against the girl. The bum gestured, and shouted: "Gimme, gimme, gimme!"

The girl leaned around Cornell, ran down the window, and said flatly, "Fuck off." The bum dropped her hands and quietly lurched away to lie down in the rubbish.

"I don't get it," the girl said to Cornell after the light had changed and they were in motion again. "You handled that MP officer. But then you're frightened of some sick old wino."

"I don't know," he answered. "I have my ups and downs. But I couldn't bear to put my hands on something so dirty."

"Neither could I. I didn't have to, did I?"

Cornell made a thoughtful mouth.

"See," she said, "authority doesn't have to be physical. In fact, when you have to go that far you're usually in trouble."

"That's a woman talking, an FBI woman besides. I'm a secretary by profession. Nobody ever does anything because I tell them to. The only times I ever got anywhere were when I used force, and if I did, it was because I was already in trouble. Like in jail."

She winced, and he added: "If you'll pardon my saying so."

She said quickly: "You were right in that case."

"I don't get *you* at all," he confessed, as if the lack were his, but he was shaken not so much by the bum, nor even by his craven reaction, which was perfectly normal in a man; nor for that matter by her statement about authority, which she was certainly equipped to give—no, what moved him strangely was her persistent approval of his role in overpowering her. He might himself enjoy that memory, but why should she?

He saw that the area through which they drove was degenerating further, if that were possible. Now instead of collapsing buildings they passed mountains of sheer rubble.

The girl again asked where he wanted to get off.

"Mary!" said Cornell.

She shrugged. "It'll get better when we're out of the business district."

"Where are *you* going?"

"I don't know." She leaned forward and squinted at the dashboard dials. "Not far, I guess. We're almost out of fuel."

"I'll look for a filling station," said Cornell, peering strenuously ahead, to prove he was of some use.

"How will we manage that?"

"Well," said he, "I never would have thought two people who looked like us could get this far in an Army ambulance, but not even on that crowded motorway did anybody pay the slightest attention. So I doubt some gas-station girl in this godforsaken place—"

"I'm referring to money," she broke in. "Do you have any?"

He searched the pockets of the lieutenant's pants, finding nothing but the keys. "Hey, what about that purse of yours?"

"I left the change thing behind when I stole it."

"That was clever."

"It would have been really stealing to take that."

Cornell stared at her and shook his head. Then he thought of something. "Listen, when you were posing as a sperm candidate, a barracks leader in fact, you had a bag of your own, and a man's uniform. So why now when you're running away are you dressed in that outlandish outfit?" He pursed his lips. "See what I mean? Since your FBI service seems to have consisted of your posing as a man, and presumably it drove you crazy from what I gather, then how come you aren't running away to become a normal woman?"

"Outlandish. Is that what you think of me?"

He was not deterred. "Yes. You're in the worst of taste, if you want to know."

"Oh, fuck you!" She swung into the curb and braked. "Get out."

He opened the door and stepped gravely out into the litter, careful to hold his blanket so it would not trail. She threw the chino shirt and pants at him, slammed the door, and drove away. He surveyed his situation, amid the piles of broken bricks and fragments of concrete with rusted rods protruding from them. Not a person in sight—fortunately, given the sort of person who might be found there. But he wondered where the rubbish came from, if no people were extant. Apparently the sanitation trucks came from the outlying residential areas to dump their filth in downtown Newark.

Beneath the blanket he struggled into the shirt and trousers. He heard the noise of an engine and saw the ambulance backing down the street. When it reached him, the girl leaned across, opened the door, and said tartly: "Now that you're dressed, come on."

"No," said he, turned and started to trek away.

She shouted: "I can't leave you here! I'd never forgive myself." He kept going. "Please, Georgie! I apologize!"

He was stopped by the novelty of it, or so he told himself. He slogged slowly back, head down, and climbed in. Then he glared at her, but she was smiling. Finally he could not help smiling too.

"Give me that purse," he said. As expected, there was a supply of Kleenex within. He removed a tissue and, boldly grasping her chin, wiped away most of the pigment on her lips. He held her face away for inspection. "This lipstick's too red for your complexion and features." Her chin felt so small in his hand. She seemed to have diminished in size since their first meeting in jail.

"You know," he said, "I can't help thinking that you were a strange choice for the assignments given you by the FBI. I've never seen anybody who looks less like a man. I'd think they would use some big, husky woman."

"I fooled *you*," she said. "For a while, anyway." She blinked the heavily mascaraed lashes. "It's like what I was saying about authority before. You don't have to be physically big and strong. It's your belief in yourself that other people see."

"Now, about those eyes," said Cornell. He reluctantly let her chin go at last and searched the bag on the off chance he might find some cleansing cream. There was none. A boy did not expect to have to redo his eyes completely while out somewhere; the usual boy, that is, though Cornell had known vain types who went everywhere with valise-sized cosmetic kits.

He wound a Kleenex around his index finger and did what he could with the worst failure of her eyeliner, then took the tiny brush from the tube and touched up here and there.

"I guess you're right," he said, going back to her theory. "In jail you weren't wearing any makeup at all, and yet I assumed you were a man. And you didn't wear any as barracks leader either. But then of course I knew who you were." He got out the mascara kit and did what he could with the little brush on her clogged, sticky lashes. "When did you recognize me?"

"As soon as I saw you in the classroom corridor." She was completely submissive as he worked on her. "You see, once again it was because of a conviction, an expectation. I knew you were in camp, and the informant had also said you had had a nose job. I also remembered your general build and the way you moved. Taking off the breasts didn't change that. Then of course when you spoke. . . ."

"There," said Cornell, putting away the eye stuff and taking the mirror from its pouch in the lining of the bag. "Take a peek. I'm not going to try to do anything with the shadow: I'd only make it worse. If you want to stop at a drugstore, I'll help you choose the right things. I like the Revlon line myself. And you'll need perfume or cologne anyway, and nail polish—"

"And Tampax," she said bluntly, in one of her brusque changes of tone, slammed in the gear, and accelerated down the street. After a block or so, she said: "Why are you encouraging me?"

A good question. Perhaps it was because Cornell, who had forsaken cosmetics for himself, was nostalgic for them. His answer was, however, "I don't see that it hurts anybody. You know, that arrest for transvestism, which I really was not guilty of, in the sense of perversion, opened my eyes. It ruined my life, but maybe something good has come of it. My life wasn't that much to begin with, and I learned—well, what can I call it? Not tolerance exactly." He raised his eyebrows. "Not tolerance at all! More likely bigotry. You know how ordeals are always supposed to make you a nicer person in the end, more forgiving, patient, understanding, kind, and generous? Well, I'm less of those now than I was when I used to foul up Ida's correspondence, get runs in my pantyhose, and spend evenings home alone with a Chinese TV dinner, head in curlers, undies soaking in the washbasin."

"Hey," said the girl, "maybe we'll find a gas station soon." They had come into a warehouse area. Some signs of life at last: trucks being unloaded by portly male figures in coveralls, various women standing about talking or sitting on platforms eating sandwiches from metal lunchboxes.

"Look at those eunuchs," said Cornell. "That's what I've got to look forward to if I'm caught."

Without turning her head, the girl said: "Georgie, do you want to stick with me for a while? We've got a better chance together."

"You're not just saying that?"

She nodded silently.

"I don't want anybody to feel responsible for me," he said.

She swallowed. "It's me. I don't know if I could make it alone."

"You?" But he sensed her embarrassment, and quickly said: "It's O.K. with me."

It soon turned out that he had misinterpreted her admission. He thought she meant she was scared to defect from the FBI, to continue to dress as a man, whatever her motives, which he still did not understand, for so doing: they were her own, whatever they were, and he could not claim a right to his freedom while denying it to another, even a woman.

But what she proceeded to say was not germane to this argument.

"There it is, a Citgo station." She pointed through the windshield. "Three blocks up the street. We're going to hold it up."

Cornell turned the mirror, which she had not taken, on himself and watched his ghastly smile.

"Well," she went on, "what choice do we have? No gas and no money."

He returned the mirror to the purse.

"Look," she said, "you don't have to do anything unless the attendant jumps me. Even then, I can probably take her alone. I had judo and karate training at the FBI Academy. But some of these girls keep a pistol near the cash register. If she goes for it, grab her. That's all you have to do."

Cornell prissily closed the catch on the bag. "Uh-huh," he muttered, matching two thuds in the series issuing from his heart. His voice sounded as if it came through a sack: "What are you going to use for a weapon?"

"One of these tubes, lipstick or eyeliner, inside my pocket. She'll think it's a gun barrel."

She had slowed down while sketching this insane plan. Still they approached the station too rapidly for Cornell's comfort. He was considering a desperate lunge for the brake.

"Only," he said breathlessly, "you don't have any pockets. You're wearing a skirt."

"Right! *You're* in the pants. *You* do it."

"Oh, come on," said Cornell, taking great gasps that would have made his quondam breasts leap.

They were only a block away now. She reached over, patted his thigh, and suddenly kicked the gas pedal. Before his terror crested, she had wheeled into the station, passed the pumps, and made a tire-shrieking stop at the door of the office.

This did not seem to startle or even interest the attendant who sat inside at a desk, reading a comic book. Cornell could see her quite clearly through the glass wall.

"Get going!" The girl pushed him violently. He fell against the ambulance door, caught himself on the handle and so depressed it. The door opened and had he not got a foot under him and a hand extended, he would have met the concrete with his behind. As it was, he probably sprained both ankle and wrist. He struggled up, the bad foot threatening to give way and the hand benumbed.

In a moral state like sleepwalking, he limped through the open door of the office and faced the comic book, which was *Wonderwoman.*

He waited an eternity without acknowledgment from the attendant. He stared through the glass at the girl, who was gesticulating madly in the cab of the ambulance.

Dully, he said: "Your money or your life."

The attendant lowered the comic book and said in an even duller voice than his: "Standard or high test and how many?" She was about twenty, low-foreheaded and acne-cheeked.

Cornell had forgotten to pretend there was a gun in his pocket. He began to tremble.

"You don't understand," he said nevertheless. "This is a holdup."

The attendant remained motionless, impassive, the comic book flat on the desk. Cornell touched his thigh with his left hand, the right still feeling numb. "Don't make me use this," he said. By accident he had patted his penis, which had lodged there in the disorder of the fall. He made his ghastly grin again.

The pimpled attendant was trying to say something. Cornell leaned helpfully over the desk in an effort to hear.

The frightened youth pushed her chair back. "Don't kill me," she said. "Take it all."

She pointed at a cash register on top of a showcase full of canned oil arranged in a pyramid. Cornell went there and pried at the drawer. "Press the No Change button," said the youth. He did so. The drawer shot out, making a bell ring and hitting him in the belt buckle.

He claimed the bills from all three slots, and took the zinc dollars too. He was wondering about the lesser change when he heard the ambulance horn.

"Thank you," he told the attendant, and ran to the door, where he stopped long enough to say: "I wouldn't really have killed you!"

The girl was behind the wheel, but a hose from the gas pump was attached to the filler pipe of the ambulance and the pump was whirring away.

The girl pointed down the street to something he could not see from his angle. "Cops!" she shouted. "Let's go," and started off as he climbed in. He heard the gas hose tear away and then a sharper noise as they roared off the apron. Looking back, he saw the attendant shooting at them with a pistol. A police car came slowly up the street and stopped abruptly when its occupants saw the attendant. Both cops got out and began to fire at *her*. At this point the girl negotiated the corner in a sweeping turn that took them over the curb and across a portion of sidewalk before she could straighten the vehicle.

After they had bumped down into the street again, she asked: "How much did you get?"

Cornell stared at the money still clutched in his hands. He had probably dropped some of the zinc dollars. He counted the bills. "Forty-seven dollars in paper. . . . And six zincs."

"You're kidding."

"That's it."

"Enough for two hamburgers."

"With coffee," said Cornell. He had become strangely calm since climbing into the ambulance, perhaps owing to the total unreality of the experience. It was impossible to believe he had robbed a gas station.

"No wonder she didn't resist," said the girl. "You sure you got everything in the register?"

"I cleaned it out."

She peered at the fuel indicator. "Good thing I thought about the gas. About half a tank. Next time we get filled up first, *then* hit the register."

"Next time?" He instantly felt awful again.

"We'd better pick a station in a more prosperous area. Forty-seven dollars!"

"Plus six zincs."

"Damn!" She hit the wheel. But after a moment she said: "You did a good job, Georgie. I knew you had it in you."

His ankle and wrist were sore again. He had forgotten them during the action.

"I don't know what I would have done if she had pulled out that pistol while I was in there."

"Kick it out of her hand," said the girl. "Karate-chop her arm."

Cornell closed his eyes and breathed deeply.

"Where are we heading? New York?" He looked out. Once or twice a year the smog was slight enough between Manhattan and Jersey so that you could see one from the other. It was too much to expect this would be one of those days. "We can reach Manhattan on the gas we have now, can't we? So why rob more stations?"

"We can't go to New York," she said firmly. "That's definite.

Eventually, even the Army will get around to putting out an alert, and some time or another even a stupid New York cop might spot one of us, even if we maintained our disguises. You don't look like a real girl, and I don't look like a man."

This puzzled Cornell, though it was true enough.

"Then what was all that stuff about you wanting to be a man?"

She was driving intently. "What stuff?"

Cornell was annoyed. "Why," he said, "that act back at the hospital, and then the desperation about getting into those clothes as soon as we left camp. And before that Lieutenant Aster told me you had sex-identification problems. And what about in jail and as a barracks leader? You must have thought you looked like a man then!"

She murmured, not in the least disturbed, "Mmm."

"*Mmm?* I think you owe me an explanation."

"Well, what about you?" He saw now that she *had* been pricked and that behind her apparent calm she had prepared a counterattack. "You were all aggressive and effective at the hospital. You took charge. But as soon as we got into the ambulance you acted like a basket case, huddled there naked in your blanket, whimpering and sniveling."

"I was *not* whimpering and sniveling."

"You were too."

"I was—" He halted. This was degrading. He cleared his throat and said: "Well, I'm not in the blanket now. As to the ambulance, I don't know how to drive. That puts me in a weak situation. I can go only so far when I lack knowledge of how to do something. The girl friend who was supposedly teaching me to drive sneered at every little mistake I made and kept joking about men drivers. That attitude may be why men *are* often none too effective behind the wheel—and at a lot of other things as well."

Now she surprised him again by nodding in agreement. "Maybe it is. And maybe always expecting a woman to perform perfectly in any assignment, or if she meets with a reverse to accept it like a female, with a stiff upper lip, never surrendering to pressure, never betraying her emotions—maybe that's wrong too."

"I never thought of that," said Cornell. "I always assumed women had things pretty much their own way."

She laughed bitterly. "You know that treatment of Aster's? I *hated* to play with guns when I was a child. I made the mistake of telling her that, and how they made me be a cowboy and forced me to play cops 'n' robbers, and how I'd get hysterical and vomit. She said that's why we should try to recapitulate that time of life and brought me that toy tommygun. And I was terrible at sports and I hated them. So she brings the football and baseball bat and hockey stick!"

"Careful," said Cornell, pointing to an acute fork into which the street divided. She chose the right leg and darted into it. They were now getting towards the suburbs, passing five-story apartment houses separated one from the next by concrete yards full of clotheslines, the kind of places where male commuters lived. One of the boys at Huff House lived in Jersey and swore by it, despite the two-and-a-half hour trip he had to make to reach Manhattan each day: said it was worth it to breathe fresh air in the evening. It was true that the atmosphere here had just a tinge of yellow, nowhere near the bright lemon hue of the New York sky, which often indeed deepened into dark mustard.

Cornell got some relief from observing the area. He was rather embarrassed by the girl's confession, though he had solicited it. "Gee," he said, "I haven't worn a gas mask in—" How many days was it since he had come to camp? Not even a week?

Or was he jealous of her emotional problem, having a massive one of his own? If so, then he was weaker than she.

"Yes," he said, "that therapeutic reprise didn't work with me, either. But I don't think it disturbed me as much as yours did you. She never really drew blood with me. I was mainly bored as a teenager." Which of course was not true. He had been utterly miserable since the beginning of pubescence, getting a beard, pubic and armpit hair, and an odor to his sweat. "But I always liked the dolls they made us play with as little kids, though I could seldom get the one with the prettiest dress."

"I stole a doll for my very own once," the girl said slyly. "But they took it away from me."

"I remember some girl doing that!" Cornell said eagerly. "Which elementary facility were you in?"

"AC-2967, in Boston."

"Couldn't have been you then. I was in New York. But of course you're a lot younger than me anyway."

"I'm twenty-two," she said. "You can't be over twenty-five."

He murmured. But then this other self (whether a better one or worse had yet to be proved) again made its assertion. He stared bravely at her. "I'll be thirty next month, to tell the truth."

She frowned. "How can that be?"

He explained.

"Well," she said, "you don't look it."

He thanked her ritually, but was more interested in another matter than in the compliment. "I thought you would have known that, being FBI."

"I don't know anything about you, Georgie, except you got away from me in jail." She steered around a pothole in the street. "The liaison between the Bureau and the New York Police Department is very poor. I was on assignment in the Men's House of Detention without the knowledge of the police. It's our practice to let them in on a case only at the arrest, otherwise they would blow the whole operation, either because of ineptness or corruption. Most of them are on the take from criminal elements. For example, that men's-lib movement. The police have known for years about the subway tunnel."

"They have?"

She removed a hand from the wheel and rubbed two fingers

together. "The payoff. We've known about it too, but have failed to act for different reasons. To arrest those Movement clowns would be to give them undeserved publicity. As they are, they're completely ineffectual. This sperm-camp action, the jerking-off stunt you were supposed to incite, is the only new idea they've had in years. You saw how hopeless that was. Otherwise it's endless so-called revolutionary manifestoes, which they can't get any boy to read, let alone believe."

"You could hardly have been waiting in jail for me," said Cornell. "It was totally accidental that I was there at all." She looked a lot better since he had toned down her makeup; he was even getting used to the clashing colors of her outfit.

"It was a crappy assignment," she went on. "With no particular aim, just to sniff out whatever sedition might exist. We had anonymous reports from time to time that the prisoners were talking revolution. And of course, if they were it might be serious, unlike that subway Movement, prisoners being supposedly hardened, ruthless criminals, not a bunch of prating buffoons with mimeograph machines."

"I saw some of them," said Cornell. "I tried to get them to break out with me."

"Then you know." She smirked. "Alongside of them, even that ridiculous Movement looks dangerous. The ones who have enough spirit left to get off their bunks sell their tails to the guards for extra food." The corners of her mouth drooped. "Lousy assignment. I got it because I screwed up every other one I was ever given."

"Really?"

"And in that case you knocked me down and tied me up. You, a little secretary, arrested for the first time in your life."

Cornell felt compassion for her. "I'm little only in a figurative sense. Actually I'm a head taller than you. But up to that fight, you did a terrific job. You don't look basically anything like a man, and yet you fooled me for a whole day, wasn't it?"

"I've always been a flop as a federal agent," she said. "In two years I haven't made one arrest. I had a bank robber cornered once, but just as I was about to take her, I got menstrual cramps, and she knocked me out. Lucky I wasn't killed."

"Maybe you're too hard on yourself," said Cornell. "After all, you're still young and able to profit from your mistakes."

She shook her head. "It's all over now. See, after you overpowered me, I was taken out of the field and put on a desk. When the tip came in that you had turned up in the camp, another agent got the assignment to go after you. But she's a friend of mine, and I talked her into letting me take it. Now she'll be in the soup too."

"Gee," Cornell said. "Who'd think they'd go to such trouble to catch a first-offender transvestite?"

"You crossed a state line," said the girl. Then she gave him a sensitive glance. "Also, to save face I told them you were a dangerous saboteur."

To alleviate her embarrassment he looked out his window. Now they were traveling past private houses, the kind owned by minor executives, who often kept men in them. The slang term for this male role was "mattress." Cornell of course had been Pauline Witkovsky's mattress years before, but at least she was a creative artist and not some commuting business-bore with narrow-brimmed felt hat and attaché case. He saw two of these boys on the sidewalk now: both wore curlers, and one pushed a shopping cart full of supermarket bags. The plight of the kept man was often the subject of magazine articles: empty days spent alone in front of the TV or gossipy card parties with their neighbors. A lot of them reportedly lived on tranquilizers, and many had a drinking problem.

At one house a dopey-looking, frizzy blond in a flowered housecoat was only now, almost noon, fetching in the newspaper and milk from the front step.

Cornell asked: "Where do you live?"

"The Zoo."

"That's that new section of the Central Park Towers, isn't it? It looks pretty posh, from the outside anyway."

"It's expensive, if that's what you mean. But half the time we don't have hot water, and the day I moved in, I opened a window and it fell down to the street—the whole sash."

"That's the kind of thing I thought happened only in men's apartment buildings."

"It's not only men who have troubles," she said. "You really ought to try to understand that, Georgie, and not be just another male injustice-collector. Most men will refuse to accept responsibility when it's offered, and then they whine about the dirty deals they get."

"*I* never did. I might have been miserable, but I never blamed it on women. At least not until I got arrested. And you must admit that *was* a dirty deal."

"Know what you should have done? Kicked the shit out of the cop who tried to arrest you. She would never have reported it."

"There were two of them!" Cornell wailed. "And they carry guns, don't they?"

"I bet they didn't pull them on you."

Cornell sulked. "You're really being unfair. I'm not a born lawbreaker. I was paralyzed with fright when they showed their badges. For that matter, I was also shaking with fear back there at the gas station. If I had known the attendant had a pistol, I would have fainted."

"You'll have to get over that sort of weakness," said she. "From now on, we can only survive as outlaws, you and I."

Cornell deliberated for a while. At last he said: "Listen, you can square yourself with the FBI by bringing me in. You ought to do that. You've got a fine profession and you shouldn't throw it away. It was my fault you were humiliated and demoted in the first place, and I'd like to make it up to you. What happens to me doesn't matter. I might be happier as a eunuch after all." He forced a smile. "At least then I can't be milked!"

"You'd do that for *me?*"

"Who said it's for you?" He turned his head. "It's pure and simple selfishness. The first time in my life I've had real power— the power to decide something on my own that will seriously affect both my own existence and someone else's. Now that I think about it, that's even worth dying for."

"How about making a decision worth living for?" she asked angrily. "Can you get that through your stupid male head?"

It was a funny question. Two funny questions in fact.

He said mockingly: "At least I see I won't have to endure your maudlin gratitude."

She shouted: "Know why I came to camp after you? Revenge! What do you think of that?"

"Come on, let's go to the FBI office."

She spoke into her lap. "When I found you, I didn't want to hurt you."

"That's nice," Cornell said lamely.

"I really did crack up, and turned myself in to the nut ward."

Cornell sympathetically patted her thigh.

"Stop that!" she screamed. Then, paradoxically, she said: "I want you to stay with me."

"Then don't be so nasty!" He drew back against his door.

"I don't like being touched."

"I was just trying to be nice."

Her face was distorted. "I know."

"I didn't mean to take liberties," said he. "I really have a high opinion of you. But you're not easy to figure out." He paused. "I'd like to stay with you too, but I don't want to quarrel."

"Are you just saying that?"

"No," Cornell said, "I'm quite serious. I don't want to be bossed around any more."

"I mean, that you want to be with me?"

"Oh, sure. But I can't stand constant friction. Constructive criticism is O.K."

She developed a smug expression, turned, and drove away from the curb. Cornell had the definite feeling that she might not keep the bargain. The funny thing was that nevertheless he seemed to have the edge on her: it was *she* who had asked *him* to stay.

I suffer not a woman to teach, nor to usurp authority over the man, but to be in silence.

THE BIBLE, I Timothy 2:12

Men have authority over women because Allah has made the one superior to the other, and because they spend their wealth to maintain them. Good women are obedient. . . . As for those from whom you fear disobedience, admonish them and send them to beds apart and beat them.

THE KORAN, Chap. 4

Before her marriage a woman was under the authority of her parents or, should they have died, of her nearest relations. As a wife she lived in subjection to her husband, and as a widow is subservient to her son or, if she has more than one, to the eldest.

CONFUCIUS

15

As THEY DROVE ON, the suburbs became more gracious, the lawns larger, the houses more prosperous, and the "mattresses," when seen, younger, and no longer on the sidewalks but lounging in bikinis alongside private swimming pools. Also there was some traffic here, as there had not been in the more modest areas. Many of these boys had their own cars, usually of the sports type, gifts of their doting "sugar-mommas." Old Eloise Huff lived in a similar community, up in Westchester. Years before she had kept Stanley in this luxury; then, when he aged, she had made him office janitor. Now he led a male-lib movement which the FBI could not take seriously.

A gorgeous redhead shot by them in a pea-green open Jaguar, roared up a long driveway, and skidded to a stop before a colonial doorway. He flounced out and entered the house. He could not have been more than eighteen. His off-white ensemble was stunning.

A silver-gray Rolls Royce, of the kind Cornell's analyst owned and parked in the continuous line of luxury cars outside the building she shared with other doctors, turned into the street and drove ahead of them.

Cornell stared. He thought he recognized the back-of-head, as well.

"Hey. I think that's my shrink up there: Dr. Prine." The silver car made a left turn, and he saw a profile that convinced him. "Sure, that's her! She must live over here now. Follow that car."

The girl frowned, but she performed as asked, entering the

nicest street yet: it even had trees along its curbs and enormous green lawns under revolving sprinklers.

"This is what my money went for," Cornell said, gesturing with his thumb. "That mean old quack." He clapped his hands. "There's our chance! Her briefcase is always stuffed with the cash she doesn't declare on her income tax. Force her to the curb!"

The girl gave him a quick look of astonishment, but then she gunned the ambulance into the left lane and drew abreast of the Rolls. Cornell looked out his window, preparing to signal Prine to pull over. A middle-aged woman was at the wheel of the luxury car, but when she turned her head, he saw it was not Dr. Prine.

"Damn," he said. "It's not her. Keep going."

"The hell I will. It's a good idea." She began to close the gap between the cars. When the other woman saw the brutal olive-drab fender nearing the impeccable gloss of hers, she slowed abruptly.

The girl parked the ambulance at an angle, just beyond the hood of the Rolls. Cornell was unhappy again, but he did not wait to get pushed into the street.

He leaped out, dashed to the car, and spoke harshly at the driver's closed window.

"This is a holdup."

She had Prine's iron-gray hair, but her nose was bulbous and webbed with broken veins.

He tried the door. It was locked. He rapped on the window; the woman gave him an indignant stare.

"All right!" He turned and shouted at the girl: "Pull back and ram her."

The woman opened the door. "What do you want of me?" She was frightened now, and that pleased Cornell. He leered at her.

"Get out, and don't try anything if you don't want to get hurt."

She swung her polished oxfords to the street. She was heavy-set and tall for a woman. Her voice quavering slightly, she said: "I don't carry very much money."

Cornell's hand was extended and twitching. "Let's count it."

She brought a lizardskin wallet from the inner breast pocket of her suit. He snatched it. It was stuffed with bills of large denomination, and in another compartment were a half-dozen credit cards.

"Get back in."

She had begun to do so when Cornell touched her shoulder. "Get out."

Her mouth was out of order. "I thought you wouldn't hurt me."

"That's right," said Cornell. "We're just taking the car." He gestured to the girl.

"We're taking this Rolls," he told her when she reached them.

She smiled in admiration. "When you get going, you really get going."

The woman took courage to say: "You won't get away with this. Do you know who I am? Senator Maybelle Heppletree. The FBI will track you down like the animals you are. I'm a United States senator."

The girl made a horselaugh. She told Cornell to get back of the wheel. "With this car, all you have to do is steer."

The senator said: "You must be crazy, both of you."

"What about her clothes?" Cornell asked. Thrilled and frightened by the girl's suggestion that he drive, he was postponing the moment. The senator wore a summer-weight suit in banker's gray with a lighter gray pinstripe, white shirt, and blue polka-dotted tie. She was as stout as Lieutenant Aster and significantly taller.

"They'd be a better fit than what you're wearing," said the girl.

He opened the rear door and pointed within. "Get in, Senator, and slip out of your clothes."

She began to bluster. Cornell said: "Unless you want me to bust your false teeth." He did not of course mean that. She was in her late fifties and a dignified public figure. He had some vague memory of seeing her on TV as he had dialed past the news shows, or passing her picture in the paper while en route to the dress ads.

The threat was effective. She put a trembling hand to her mouth, spat her teeth into it, and climbed meekly into the back of the Rolls.

Cornell realized he was pulling off another caper without even pretending to be armed. Neither the gas-station attendant nor the senator had made any resistance whatever.

He asked the girl: "Are you serious about me driving?"

"Oh, you must." She put her fingers on the back of his hand. He liked that gesture, but then resented it in view of her aversion to *his* touch. However, it was stupid to keep score as to who got away with what. No doubt there were peculiarities of his that she had had to put up with already, with more to come.

He looked into the car and saw Senator Heppletree in a one-piece suit of that summer underwear called BVD's. She was still holding her teeth, and the lower part of her face looked like an empty Gladstone bag. He suddenly understood it was not right to humiliate her further. She had after all been elected to the Senate by a plurality of her fellow women.

"Please put those back in," he said. "And give me the clothes. It's nothing personal."

Carrying her suit, he went to the ambulance, in the rear of which he made still another change of attire. The new outfit was a better fit than the uniform had been. The waistband of the trousers could be closed; and if the legs were still short, the senator's high-rise socks of dark lisle concealed his shins. The shoes, though, were hopelessly small, and he retained his penny loafers. He carried the tie in his hand.

He returned to the Rolls with the chino pants and shirt and gave them to the senator, advising her to put them on. She needed no urging. She definitely was thicker than the young lieutenant had been, and could not get the fly zipper past the midpoint of her belly. But she was covered.

"Now," he said, "if you can drive an ambulance, that one's yours."

She climbed out. "You're mad dogs," she said, her fat chin quivering in rage, rather than fear, now that she realized he would not hurt her. "I'll have you tracked to the ends of the earth if necessary."

The girl had got into the front seat of the car. Now she slid across and pushed a manila envelope out the door. "Look what I found in the glove compartment."

Cornell opened it and came upon several Polaroid snapshots of a young man in black underwear and knee-high red boots belaboring the senator's naked behind with a whip.

Cornell blushed furiously.

The girl said: "She's being blackmailed. A routine case."

He couldn't bear to look at the senator for a while. When he did, he saw her running heavily towards the ambulance.

"What luck," said the girl as he got in behind the wheel. She took the envelope from him.

"Throw those filthy things away," he said. "Now let me see if I remember anything about driving."

"I'm keeping them. She won't cause trouble for us now. It would mean the end of her career if these pictures got out."

Cornell snatched the envelope and opened the door, but it was too late. The senator had got the ambulance going and was already speeding around the corner.

"I was going to give them back," he told the girl. "I feel rotten about taking that kind of advantage. I'll steal money, clothes, and car, but that is really rotten."

"Why?" Her face was ingenuous. "That dirty old perv."

Cornell moistened his lips. "You might say the same thing about us."

"Us?" she asked. "What's wrong with us?"

"We're *perfectly* normal." But the irony was lost on her. "Would you mind?" he asked, and gave her the polka-dot tie. She flipped it around her neck, made a knot, slipped it over her head, and returned it to Cornell, who put it on. He had been treating the thick wallet as though it were a clutch-purse. The girl picked it up and handed it to him. "Put this in the inside breast pocket of your jacket."

For all his changes of costume, this was the first woman's suit he had ever worn. There was something in every pocket: hand-kerchief, pen, address book, change, little knife-and-nailfile com-bination, keys.

"How do I turn the motor on?"

"It's already running. See?" She stabbed her foot across onto the accelerator and pushed: he heard the subdued roar of the engine. "Now you put it in 'Drive' and just steer."

Pulling away from the curb was as smooth as running velvet ribbon through your hand. As they neared the corner, she said: "The only other pedal down there is the brake." He looked for it, but felt his steering waver, and anxiously raised his eyes. A de-livery truck was speeding towards the intersection from the right.

"I can't stop!"

"Take your foot off the gas." Then she put her shoe across his loafer and depressed the brake. The truck, coming from the left, turned the corner in its own lane. It would not have hit him anyway.

"I'm sorry I panicked," he said. "Maybe you should take over."

"You can do it," she told him, as she had previously assured him she had known he could rob a gas station. "Anyhow, it looks better, the way we're dressed." She snorted. "People will think we're some rich bitch and her mattress." The idea seemed to please her.

Cornell said: "I can't get over how we escaped notice in that ambulance."

"Nobody looks to see who's driving an ugly thing like that. A chimp could be behind the wheel."

While the car was at rest, Cornell checked out the positions of the gas pedal and brake and satisfied himself that henceforth his foot could find them without the help of his eyes.

He had been driving for several hours, and he was not certain where he was. Meandering through the New Jersey suburbs, he had come upon a traffic-clogged motorway presumably leading to New York and of course rejected that; kept going and found nearby an older, deserted, secondary sort of road, took it, took others of the kind when they intersected the one on which he was traveling and his taste was for a change, but kept rolling. Within an hour it seemed that he had been driving all his life. A serenity came over him. The powerful, beautiful, comfortable car, which responded immediately, precisely, to the touch, yet remained virtually silent, was an instrument of his will.

Eventually he was far enough from the New York area to find an empty superhighway. He swung onto it and pressed his foot down. Within a few moments of surging acceleration the speedometer needle reached 100. He maintained this speed for an hour and a half before seeing another vehicle. Then a car with a flashing red light appeared in the rear-vision mirror. Finally Cornell realized he was being pursued by a police car. There was still some unused power in the Rolls, which he could bring into play merely by pushing down his shoe. He pressed the pedal to the floor. Within a few miles, he lost his competitor altogether.

He made a cackle of triumph. "How about that?" But she was

asleep. At more than a hundred miles an hour, while being chased by a cop! With a man at the wheel. He had never before been the recipient of that sort of confidence.

He saw no other cars. The landscape at length became green and rolling, with a horizon of purple hills. Insofar as, obsessed with the driving, he noticed it, he thought it very nice. In a distant meadow he noticed some black-and-white horses: no, cows. Cornell was familiar with few of the particulars of nature. He had lived all his life in a forest of people—or really, of women.

The appearance of the only gas station he had seen since the one he robbed caused him to look at the gas gauge. Feeling the physical and spiritual disappointment of deceleration, he glided in the entry lane and came to rest at one of the clusters of pumps. The place, though well kept, had a deserted look. Apparently nobody much drove anywhere these days except around New York and the few other large cities whose traffic problems were always being shown on TV.

A neat-looking attendant appeared. She wore a spotless tan uniform and saluted Cornell with a finger to her cap. He push-buttoned the electric window down, and was met by a terrible blast of heat. He had forgotten the car was air-conditioned.

"Yes, ma'am. How many?"

Cornell was pleased by the authority with which he said, as if it were routine: "Fill 'er up." He raised the window again, and turned and saw the girl's eyes come open.

"You want to use the restroom?"

She sat up and looked out. "Where are we?"

Cornell shrugged. "Darned if I know."

She was somewhat testy after her snooze. "Don't you think we should find out?" She climbed out into the heat. Cornell watched her go towards the station. He was in some suspense as she clearly headed for the outside door marked "Women." He scrambled out and called: "Wait a minute."

She had her hand on the doorknob of the women's room. He reached her, and saying "Excuse me," gently pushed her aside and entered the female john.

Later, while paying the attendant from the senator's wallet, he asked: "Where is everybody? I haven't seen a car all day."

"Over in Boston," said the young woman. "Nothing much but military traffic here." She narrowed her eyes and assumed an inside-dopester tone. "They built this highway for the invasion of Canada, you know." She jerked her shoulder at the Rolls. "Nice machine. What'd it set you back?"

She was beginning to assume a too-familiar style for a person of her rank. Did she suspect?

Cornell said haughtily: "If you have to ask, you can't afford one."

The girl returned then, still somewhat out of sorts. As he pulled onto the superhighway, she asked: "Did you find out where we are?"

"Massachusetts."

"I'm hungry!" she said petulantly.

The speedometer was soon at 100 again. How marvelous it was to drive, to feel that smooth force under you.

"I don't know if there are any restaurants around here," he said. "But whoever keeps those cows has to buy food someplace. We'll take the next exit and look for a little town with a grocery." He glanced at her sulky face. "O.K.?"

She shrugged and crossed her legs, the split skirt opening up. He remembered that when she was dressing he had seen no hair on her legs, or perhaps it was too pale to be conspicuous. He felt his own chin and its slight stubble. What would happen if he did not shave again? How long would the facial hair grow? All at once his sanguine mood changed. "Look, my offer still stands. We could turn back and go to the FBI office in Boston—"

"I don't want to hear that."

"We've driven for hours with no destination. Where are we

going? What will we do? We can't keep driving forever."

She was silent.

"It's all been romantic and adventurous so far, but what about tomorrow and the day after? And where are we going to spend the night?"

She said: "It took all these years for you to get some nerve. Don't lose it now."

"Easy for you to say. You lost *yours* at the sperm camp."

"That's a rotten thing to mention."

His reply was lofty: "I'm sorry, but it's true. What's a woman without her work?"

"Why, why," she sputtered, "you shit, you! My work was apprehending *you*."

Cornell didn't like what he was doing, or at least he told himself that, with certain guilty, delicious reservations, but he did not want to be eternally responsible for her unwomanning: as, in an access of clairvoyance, he realized she would try to make him if she gave up her career.

"Let's not get personal," he said. "Basic principles are involved."

"Go to hell."

He put his chin in the air and made no reply. He had done his duty, whether she thanked him for it or not.

Twenty minutes later they cruised into the main street of a little town, passed what looked like a former movie theater, the marquee blank, the interior now a washer-dryer salesroom; a bar with blacked-out windows; a police station with accompanying volunteer fire-department garage; and finally saw a sizable supermarket. He pulled into the vacant parking lot behind it.

He asked the girl what she wanted to eat.

She was waspish. "Steak and baked potato."

"All right, all right. You were whining about being hungry. What do you want to eat?"

"Anything you want."

"Oh, for Mary's sake." He climbed out and entered the store by the rear door. He used to go out with a girl with the same exasperating trait: *What are you in the mood for tonight? . . . Anything you want. . . . You name it. . . . Really, anything's O.K. with me.* Sometimes this would go on for a quarter of an hour. He had preferred women who picked a place and took him there without comment, and once inside the restaurant imposed their tastes on him: he had always liked any dish that was recommended confidently. It occurred to him that the situation was reversed now.

He marched to the meat section and seized a package of liverwurst. The place was vast, brightly lighted, and unoccupied except by one person way up at the checkout counter. Cornell found a tier of breads and chose a loaf of sliced rye. A quart of milk and two oranges completed his list. He carried the provender to the checkout.

The clerk was a big, dull-eyed eunuch in a dirty green skirt and pale blue smock. He wore a pathetic pair of cheap mother-of-pearl earrings. He index-fingered Cornell's purchases, listlessly rang them up, and sacked them as if in a dream. Cornell gave him thirty dollars from the senator's wallet.

"Big store," said Cornell, "for a little town. I guess the farmers come from miles around."

"From miles around," repeated the eunuch, counting on his fingers, and then returning the change. He droned, as if by rote: "Come back soon."

This encounter depressed Cornell further, but when he got to the car the girl was in a good mood.

"What's for supper?" She grabbed the bag and found the meat package. "Oh, *no!* Not liverwurst!" She threw it on the top of the dashboard. "I hate liverwurst."

He angrily produced the wallet. "I specifically asked you what you wanted and you refused to say. So go in and get what you like." He handed her a fifty-dollar bill.

She spurned it with outthrust lower lip and seized an orange. He made himself a sandwich and chewed in silence: the bread was dry as a shingle and the liverwurst was tasteless. He opened the spout of the milk carton and drank awkwardly from it.

"Look," he said, "we have to think seriously about tonight. It's almost six o'clock. There'll still be a couple of hours of daylight, but what then? Should we look for a motel? I don't know if we can find one out here in this godforsaken part of the world."

She had peeled her orange and was eating a segment.

"We could sleep in the car."

"I never thought of that."

"Sure," she said, sucking noisily at the pulp, "no problem. As long as it runs, this can be our home. In fact, it can even stop running. We could park it in the woods somewhere and live there."

"You're kidding," said Cornell.

She raised her eyebrows and popped another wedge of fruit into her mouth.

Cornell said: "Isn't it crazy? I don't even know your real name. I thought of you for a long time as 'Harriet,' because in jail you called yourself 'Harry.' "

She kept chewing, making liquid sounds.

After a few moments he said: "Well?"

She swallowed. "What does it matter?"

"I've got to call you something, don't I?"

"How about 'You'?" She blinked, exposing those purple lids.

"You know *my* name."

"I mean, you can call *me* 'You.' Names are a lot of crap anyway. They come out of a computer at the birth facility. They're not really personal."

"Well, what is, if it comes to that?" He found her peculiarities very tiresome. He sighed and said: "How can I call you 'You'? It's confusing and stupid, if you ask me."

She peered at him. "Now that you can drive, you don't need

me at all. It wouldn't take much for you to beat me up, I'll bet, throw me out of the car, and drive away alone."

Cornell lost the control he had been so careful to retain. "You really take advantage of a person!" He was close to tears. "You don't know how to be a friend. You are unfair and nasty and horrible and—"

She grinned triumphantly: "See!"

"Oh, shut up!"

"Go on," she said. "Hit me."

He drew himself against his door. "I wouldn't touch you with a ten-foot pole." He started the car. He had to back up to get out of the parking slot, and he had never done that before. Now his faculties were corrupted by indignation.

At last he shouted: "Dammit, tell me how to get this thing out of here!"

"I'm not speaking to you," she said. "You owe me an apology."

He would sooner have bitten off his tongue. He took his hands from the steering wheel and crossed his arms on his breasts— or where they once had been: it still felt funny not to feel them in this attitude.

She sat there eating the remainder of her orange. He seized the other one, peeled it, and threw the refuse out the window. Her peelings, he noticed, were overflowing the ashtray onto the carpet. He mimicked her piggish sounds with his own orange, slurping loudly and smacking his lips.

Finally she said, looking straight ahead: "You are the most childish person I have ever known."

He replied frostily: "Aster didn't take *me* back to age of ten and give me toys to play with."

"You are really malicious."

That remark hit home. He stopped eating the orange and threw the rest out the window.

"Please," he said, "tell me how to put this in reverse."

"Why don't you try 'R'?"

He blushed. How blind could you get from anger?

He drove in stoic silence for a time and then, unexpectedly encountering another large motorway, took it, traveling with the sun on the back window, in the direction marked "Boston."

The girl made no protest—not that one would have done her any good. He intended to realize the plan she had rejected: go straight to the FBI office, surrender himself, and clear her name. It was the only answer. Having a conviction, a destination, he felt whole, as he had not since—that evening on which he had unsuspectingly started for Charlie's? No, since birth he had lived a pointless life; and from the time of his arrest on, it had been a burlesque and he a sexless monstrosity without an identifiable self.

Castration held no terror for him: in the moral sense he had always been a eunuch. Ironically, until now. He would lose his manhood through an assertion of his virility.

Virility? His progression of thought, so straight and clear and true, was suddenly tortuous, befouled, corrupt. What was masculine about self-assertion? He floundered for a while in the swamp of his emotions—though driving steadily—but firm ground was reached at last. He was not a pervert. He was *sacrificing* himself: there was absolutely nothing more masculine than that.

At peace, he proceeded to become one with the fluid motion, the hum of the wheels, the rushing ribbon of road.

Within an hour, he passed, at a hundred miles an hour, not one but five exits leading to metropolitan Boston, and followed the motorway on its swing towards the north.

Furthermore, he did this with only the faintest glimmer of reflection, and no shame whatever. It was as if by the very making of the resolve he had satisfied it. At bottom, he was still a normal man.

Be ready, when the hour comes, to show that women are human and have the pride and dignity of human beings. Through such resistance our cause will triumph.

CHRISTABEL PANKHURST, 1911

16

THEY HAD TRAVELED the entire length of the Maine Turnpike and were now on a narrow asphalt road to both margins of which grew an unbroken wall of big Christmas trees, and it was dark and they had no place to stay the night.

In addition to which the fuel gauge told a bleak story. He passed it on to the girl, who an hour or so back, when it became clear that they were leaving civilization, had got over her sulk and was by now almost jolly.

"Well," she said, "it looks as if we've done it."

He, on the other hand, had got more and more sardonic.

"We sure have. No gas, food, or shelter." And it was cold outside. A long time earlier she had shut off the air conditioner, and about ten miles back she had switched the heater on.

She stretched her short legs and wriggled smugly.

"Listen," said he, "I'm not kidding. See for yourself. We're out of fuel. And look at that forest. What do we do when the car stops?"

"I told you ages ago: sleep in it."

He rolled his eyes.

"Plenty of room. You can have the rear. It's beautiful, padded leather." She turned around, kneeled on the seat, and began to poke at something on its back. "Hey, you know what? There's a bar here, a little built-in bar, and it's full of bottles." He heard a *clink*. "Isn't that terrific?"

"What's terrific about it? Are they full of gas?"

She was leaning so far over that her behind was almost across the top of the seat. He had a strong urge to slap it.

Her fishing produced a bottle. "It wouldn't matter if you ran off the road here." She sounded drunk already. He had known girls like that, whom the very prospect of drinking made irresponsible. With a few actual glasses under their belts, they were capable of becoming downright disorderly.

"Put that away," he said firmly. But she went on, trying to unscrew the top. He was driving slowly now because of the darkness. The very brilliance of the headlights tended somehow to falsify surfaces and distances and give the effect of traveling through a tunnel.

She had finally got the bottle open, and he heard a gurgle and smelled the unpleasant odor of strong drink.

"I told you to put it away!"

She said: "Since when are you the boss?"

The word gave him pause. He had said repeatedly that what he wanted to escape from was authority in itself, no matter who the master and who the underling.

"I'm not," he hastened to say. "It's for your own good. You haven't eaten anything but an orange all day."

" 'Swhy I need this," said she, already slurring her speech and waving the bottle inordinately. It was just as he feared: she was one of those. She upended the bottle again. The whiskey smell was awful in the closed car. Cornell feared he might get woozy from the fumes. He opened the window. The air was quite cold and had a marked scent of its own, which, after several deep, breaths, he decided was rather the absence of an odor. For the first time in his life he was smelling unadulterated air. He had read this about Maine, a strange state where hardly anybody lived. What a place to choose for escape: they might never be caught, but how could you survive without other people to sell you liverwurst, TV dinners, and Kleenex?

The girl leaned against him. "C'mon, take a blast." She shoved the bottle in front of his eyes. He dodged it, and almost ran off the road.

"*Please* put that away," he said, trying to be nice.

Her answer was surly: "Make me."

He replied pleasantly: "You know I could."

"You could shit too." She took another swallow.

"You're beginning to get on my nerves," he said.

"You bore my ass off," said she.

"Now, listen! That's enough of the foul language. You're disgustingly drunk already." Diplomatically he added: "A fine girl like you."

Glug-glug. "What's fine about me? I'm a flop, Cornell."

"So am I. That doesn't have anything to do with being fine."

"I don't think you're fine. I think you're an asshole. I want you to take a drink!" She shoved the bottle at him again. "I *order* you to take a drink, you man you."

Cornell accepted it by the neck and threw it out the window.

She studied him for a while in the light from the dashboard, and then said, slowly, thickly: "Somewhere you got the erroneous idea I'm afraid of you."

He continued to drive, but ever more slowly owing to his worry about the fuel.

She said: "I'm going to have to cut you down to size, Cornell. No man is gonna push me around." She climbed onto her knees on the seat, and faced him.

He shrugged. "Let's talk about that later." From the corner of his eye, he saw her cock a fist and begin a swing at his head. While maintaining control of the wheel with his left hand, he raised his right shoulder to take the blow. It was sharper than he expected, given her condition.

"Are you crazy?" he shouted. "I'm driving."

"C'mon," she said. "Fight like a woman." She threw another punch at him. It glanced off his shoulder cap and struck the base of his head, not hurting him really but shaking his skull in an ignobling way. He slammed on the brakes, and she fell hard against the dashboard. He pulled her up, none too gently, but then, she being limp, was anxious: "Are you hurt?"

His arms were under her slender shoulders. In a moment he became aware that his hands had of their own volition descended to enclose her breasts. The oddest sensation in the world. He had been wont, before the dressing-table mirror, to cup his own bosoms, when he had had them, to try out alternative profiles with a new brassière in mind. The current experience was similar but different. He had never touched a woman's breasts before fondling and sucking Lieutenant Aster's. These were smaller, firmer, and warmer, even through the blouse.

The girl had not answered his question. However, she was breathing regularly: in fact, a bit faster than that. He should probably search her head for cuts or bumps, but he could not move his hands—hers were covering them.

Her phobia against being touched had apparently been diluted by the alcohol—as in fact had Cornell's own inhibitions against wearing women's clothes, that night so long ago at Charlie's, and look where that had led.

He was suddenly desperate to get free, and tore his hands from under hers. She groaned, became conscious at once, lurched away, opening the door. She stumbled out into the night, and he heard her throw up. He waited considerately until the sounds ended, and then was sliding across to aid her when she returned. He gave her the handful of Kleenexes.

After using them, she said: "I didn't eat anything all day."

"I know."

"I never could hold my liquor."

"Neither can I," he said.

She was shivering. "It's freezing out there."

Cornell closed his window and turned the heater to maximum. She said: "And these clothes are so thin."

He got out of the senator's jacket and draped it around her. He began to drive again.

"Look," she said. "There's a clearing!"

So there was. The trees swung away from the shoulder, leaving a semicircular patch of low bushes and weeds several car-widths wide. He drove in, with a noise of crushing vegetation, and some small furry thing went bounding through the headlight beams and plunged into the forest.

"Did you see that?" he cried.

"What?"

"Some awful animal. I just hope it's not a rat."

"This far from a city?"

"Are there wild rats?"

"I don't know," she said. "But I'd think this big car would scare them."

He switched off the ignition. "Well, this is it for tonight, I guess. I think I'll just leave the lights on."

"You'll run down the battery."

"Hey, the heater's stopped."

"Of course. It's electric."

"No light and no heater all night?"

She shook her head. "We don't have any choice." She was showing no effects from her recent performance. Cornell found himself wondering, strangely, whether it had been all it seemed. She had got drunk in a second, and sobered almost as quickly. For a moment he was afraid of her. Perhaps she intended to violate him in some fashion while he slept.

But this wilderness was obviously genuine, and she was stuck in it as hopelessly as he. Anyway, now that the engine was off, he was suddenly too exhausted for apprehension and opened the door and started to climb out, regardless of the animal.

"Did you say I could have the back?" he asked when he had already claimed it, tucking his legs in and lying on his side.

She looked over the seat. "Sweet dreams."

"Same to you."

She stayed there for a while, silhouetted against the light from the dashboard. "Are you warm enough?"

"Yes, thanks." He closed his eyes. "You keep the jacket."

When he looked again she had disappeared, and in a moment the dashboard lights went out. He turned onto his back and immediately felt constricted in those clothes. He opened the collar of the shirt and loosened the tie. The trousers were also uncomfortable, cutting into his crotch. He considered slipping them off in the dark, but he might not awaken until after she did next morning, and he wore no underwear.

A brighter morning light than he had ever seen woke him up. He looked through the window at the brilliant, moist greenery of the world outside. For a moment he thought of himself as alone in a new, fresh existence, but then he remembered the girl and looked for her over the seat.

His jacket was there, but she was gone. He left the car. There she came, emerging from the forest. She held her skirt well above the calves to avoid the clutching underbrush, and was barefoot.

"How'd you sleep?" he asked.

"Great. And you? Were you cold?"

"I guess I was too tired to know."

She had reached the car and put a hand on the fender to support herself, lifting a foot and exploring its undersurface. "I'm not used to this." She plucked at something. "Thorn." She put her foot down and tested it. Her bright hair was irradiated by the sun. She looked so fresh though having spent the night in a car. He realized that the remains of the makeup, including the purple eyeshadow, were gone. So were the navy-blue textured stockings.

"Did you wash your face somehow?"

"There's a brook back there. It's ice-cold, though, I'm warning you. But you feel great when you're out."

"Were you *in?* I mean, a real bath?"

"I went for broke."

"Mary." Cornell was impressed.

She pointed. "See that fuzzy tree? Well, you go back that way, between that tree and the big boulder, and before very long you'll hear the sound of the water."

He supposed he would have to meet the challenge, but there was little in the world that Cornell loathed more than cold water. He daintily picked his way through the woods. Most of the trees were fuzzy, and there was more than one boulder. He could always claim he couldn't find the brook.

But in all honesty, you couldn't miss it once you got back in there a way. The gurgling could not be ignored. It was very pretty, like a painting on a calendar. He sat down on a rock and watched the stream run enthusiastically wherever it was going.

At last he knelt, scooped up a double handful of the icy liquid, paralyzing his fingers, and stunned his face in it. *Wow.* He sputtered and blew. After a deep breath, he wet a finger and rubbed his teeth.

On the way back he peed in a bush. He might have done the other had he something with which to wipe, but he was probably constipated anyway owing to yesterday's diet. Zipping up, he thought he saw a snake nearby and caught some hair in the fastener, but the serpent was just a stick on which the sun, filtering through the foliage, had made a moving pattern.

Back in the clearing he told the girl, who sat in the sun on the fender of the Rolls, "You're right. It was certainly, invigorating. Now how about breakfast? The rest of the bread and liverwurst is in the glove compartment." He raised his shoulders. "I know you don't like liverwurst, but that's all there is."

"Then it'll have to do." She had mellowed, perhaps because of the sun. She put her arms behind her and leaned back, her nipples marking the blouse front.

He made two sandwiches. She ate hers without complaint. He had not been hungry until he bit into his, and then instantly became ravenous and even finished the crusts, something he seldom did in civilization.

The girl's eyes were closed and the sun was brilliant on her fair face. She had pulled the long skirt above her knees. He now saw that her legs were not completely hairless, but showed a fine golden down.

"What do you think?" he asked. "Do we start driving again and look for gas as long as the car keeps going?"

"It might stop in a worse place," she said. "And then where would we be?"

"What about food?"

"I saw some berries back in the woods." She opened her eyes slowly and looked at him with a hint of derision. "And also what I suspect you called a rat. It was a rabbit."

"I know what a rabbit looks like. It's got big ears." He squinted. "But what were you suggesting, anyway?"

"We kill it and eat it."

"Oh, come on." He rolled his eyes.

"Would you rather starve?"

"What about those berries? I don't care that much for meat anyway."

She shook her head. "How do we know they aren't poisonous? Anyway, you'd have to eat gallons of those little things to fill your belly."

"Sorry I brought up the matter," he said. "You were so happy there in the sun. Go back and sit there again. I'll try and think of something. It's my responsibility."

"Why?"

"Men are traditionally responsible for food, aren't they? I was once a pretty good cook." Suddenly he felt the perverse urge to confess he had been Pauline Witkovsky's mattress as a young man, but in resisting it, he went too far. "And I hijacked the car and drove all the way up here and got you into this."

Her hitherto friendly expression chilled. "You make it sound as if I'm so much baggage."

He had offended her again. She tossed her head and climbed onto the fender. Before he had decided what to do, she cocked an ear.

"Hear that?"

"What?"

"It's a car."

He heard nothing, then the drone of a distant insect.

"Get your ass out on the road," she cried.

"Don't give me orders!"

She cried out in desperation. Actually, it did sound like a car now, and very close. In fact, before he got halfway to the road, the vehicle went by.

It was a battered green pickup truck, driven by someone with a profile of hatbrim, long nose, short pipe, and pointed chin. She looked straight ahead and did not seem to see them or the Rolls Royce.

Cornell ran onto the road to chase the truck. It was a futile act, but served to postpone the moment when he would have to face the girl. When he reached the asphalt, the truck had disappeared. The reason was that scarcely fifty yards beyond the clearing the road descended a hill, which he had not seen in last night's darkness.

He ran to the beginning of the slope and looked down. At the bottom, less than a quarter mile away, the woods gave way to a village. He watched the truck enter it, then trudged back to the clearing.

After accepting the girl's glare, he jerked his thumb at the Rolls. "Come on. I'm not going to starve here. Let's take our chances on the road."

Sullenly she climbed down and got in. He pulled onto the asphalt, drove fifty yards to the declivity, and began to roll down.

The village consisted of little more than everything they needed: a general store with a gas pump in front of it. The pickup truck was being refueled by its driver, the crusty-looking old character Cornell had seen speed past him. Apparently she was the storekeeper. He left the Rolls and walked all the way up to her before she saw him. She must have had a sort of tunnel vision.

But then she smiled briefly and said, in an unusual accent: "Maanin'," which he was pleased to identify as "Good morning" and responded to in kind. She kept the gas hose in the filler hole and sucked away at the black pipe that fortunately was not lit.

"You sell food as well as gas?"

She took the pipe out of her mouth and pointed at the store. "I don't, but she does."

"Excuse me," said Cornell. "I thought you were the proprietor."

"Nawp." She put the pipe between her ill-fitting false teeth. "I'm the game warden."

He started towards the store, then turned and went back to the car. "You come along this time," he told the girl. "I don't want to hear again that you don't like what I bought to eat."

At the entrance she stepped in front of him, opened the screen door, and held it for his passage. She had very nice manners when she wanted to show them.

He had never seen such an establishment as this store, with its huge wheel of cheese, rackful of axes, bins of dried beans, coils of rope, whole hams, and a full-sized canoe, all cheek by jowl. Behind the counter was a wide but not really fat woman, her cheeks naturally as red as if she had used men's rouge. The sleeves of her plaid shirt were rolled up to her meaty biceps, and on the right one she had a tattoo: "U.S. Marines," on an elaborate scroll.

"Maanin'," said she.

Cornell answered, and the girl nodded. She then began to point: "One of those hams and an axe and ten pounds of those beans and a sack of flour and—" The woman seized a pencil and started scrawling the list on the end of a mounted roll of wrapping paper. Cornell was astounded.

"Twenty feet of rope, a dozen cans of condensed milk, a sack of sugar, a side of bacon—"

Cornell had never heard the like. He walked away from her obsessive litany, finding himself at a rack of cellophane bags of potato chips and Fritos. He loved the latter and had not eaten any since he went to the sperm camp. He unclipped a small bag and took it to the counter.

The girl was saying: "And a jackknife, a shovel, a skillet, some pots and pans—" She saw Cornell's bag of Fritos, and said: "Put that back."

The big woman raised her eyebrows. Cornell realized instantly how it looked—the girl had forgotten she was dressed as a man and he as a woman—and not wanting to complicate matters further, he responded: "No, dear, I know you love them, and you should get some reward for memorizing that grocery list."

He smiled brilliantly at the storekeeper, who asked: "Whereabouts is your camp? Loon Lake?"

He was stopped momentarily by the implications of the question. So that was what the girl planned: camping out. He looked at her, but she had gone to the far wall and was examining the lanterns that hung there.

"Actually," he told the storekeeper, "we just came up from New York. We haven't found a camping place yet."

"Loon Lake is your best bet. It's a real nice place." She threw up a big arm. "You go right out of town heading east. Twenty-eight and three-tenths miles, there's a dirt road to the left. It's an old logging road, is what it is. About seven miles in, there's the lake. Full of bass and a lot of dead wood there for fires. I'd get me a saw, though, to cut it with. That axe will raise a few blisters if you ain't used to handling one. And what about clothes?" She pointed. "My dry goods department's in the back. That real nice suit of yours won't do for campin'."

"True," said Cornell.

"Work shirts and jeans. Also stuff for your boy friend." She jerked her chin at the girl. "That finery's for town. Pretty little thing, ain't he?"

The girl came back with a lantern. She had heard the comment, and Cornell was happy to note a change in her style.

"We'll need this, too, don't you think?" she asked.

The order when completed filled the trunk of the Rolls and the back seat as well. Finally the big woman filled the gas tank. Attached to the pump she found a note.

"Huh," said she, sticking it in a rear pocket of her corduroys. "That Mabel. She's our game warden. You'd think she'd come in for a few words when she gasses up. Not her. She writes how many gallons on an I.O.U. and drives off."

"Are there many people up here?" Cornell asked.

"Not many. There's a lumber camp fifty-two miles to the northwest. They drive in a truckload of them lumberjacks every Saturday night. They're eunuchs, you know, except for the forewomen. It's a big treat for 'em to come in here. I got a lunch counter in back and a jukebox. They have their hamburgers and listen to the jukebox and think they're having a big time. Pathetic. Still, I'm glad to see them. I'm glad to see anybody by the end of a week. Most of the few women who live around here are peculiar, like old Mabel."

The gas pump's whirring stopped with a *clunk*. The woman read the amount on its face, got out a bill for the food and gear, computed with the pencil stub from behind her ear, and said: "All told, $3,382.76."

Cornell paid with four greenbacks from the senator's stuffed wallet. The girl spoke up when the storekeeper was fishing for the change in her pockets.

"Prices are as high up here as in New York."

"Higher, I would expect. Except for the gas, which Shell comes by with once a month, I truck in the rest of my merchandise from Boston twice a year. Used to go to Bangor years ago, but there's nothin' left there now. Everybody's in Boston, like I guess everybody down south's in New York."

"How do you make a living?" Cornell asked.

"Them lumberjacks and a few old farts like Mabel. The occasional campers like yourself." She gave Cornell his change and wished them good camping. The screen door slammed behind her wide, corduroyed rump.

The dirt road to Loon Lake was deeply rutted and full of boulders. Cornell winced with each bang against the undercarriage of the lovely Rolls; it was as if he was being struck in his own lower belly.

"This is awful," he said. "We're being torn apart." He drove as slowly as he could and performed a virtuoso job of steering, trying to avoid the worst hazards.

"If we can just get there," said the girl, "we're O.K."

She had made the same remark several times, and finally it got to him, even in the midst of his task. He wrenched the wheel one way to avoid a particularly brutal-looking rock, and then the other way to evade a cavernous rut, and said: "You mean we're going to stay here forever?"

"Nothing is forever."

He shook his head. "You're nuts."

"Well, why did you take this road? And why do you keep driving? Do you have an alternative?"

"No. That doesn't mean it's any the less nuts, though."

"It might be fun."

"Oh, sure."

After another hour or so they had covered the seven miles and there was the lake.

The girl clapped her hands. "Just look at that." It really was nice: an expanse of royal-blue water, the surrounding greenery, the golden sunlight, white puffs of cloud.

"Mmm," murmured Cornell. The road continued, very likely circling the lake, but he doubted if the surface would improve. "Should we stop here?"

"Keep going until we see a good spot for the tent. Someplace with a slight grade, for drainage. Near enough to the shore so we don't have to carry water too far, but not too close, in case there's a storm."

He commented on her expertise.

"FBI Academy," she said. "Wilderness survival course. Never tell when that might come in handy, they always said. And here it is."

They had crawled and bumped halfway around the lake before she approved a campsite. It was on a modest knoll, perhaps eight feet above the shore. Running down to the rocky beach was a natural drainage channel, which also served as a path to the water, a function the girl demonstrated by running down it and stubbing her bare toe on a stone. She sat down and cursed vilely.

"Will you put on those sneakers?" asked Cornell.

He carried the folded tent from car to knoll, then looked down at the beach. She was skipping flat stones across the surface of the lake, having a simpleminded good time while he worked. The funny thing was that he did not resent this. There was something so innocent in her pleasure. Besides, he was built to carry loads.

After a moment, as if she felt his eyes, she turned her head. "Isn't this fabulous?" A flurry of wind blew her hair across her forehead. "Why don't you stop working and come down and throw stones?"

"I'd better get the tent up if I can figure it out. Suppose it rains?"

"Look at that sky. Don't be silly."

He carefully went down the path and joined her. He looked all around the shoreline.

"We're really alone here. I can't see another tent or car or person."

"Here," said she, "you hold it like this." She showed him the flat stone between her thumb and forefinger. "Then you snap your wrist when you let it go." She threw one that jumped three times off the water before it plunked and sank.

It took him a while to get the hang of it. By the time they had gone up to erect the tent, following the instructional pamphlet provided, the sky had clouded over. While Cornell was pounding in the third tent peg with the back of the axehead, the rain started.

Among the things they had forgotten to buy was rain gear of any type.

A perfect Woman, nobly planned,
To warn, to comfort, and command.

WILLIAM WORDSWORTH, 1807

17

CORNELL SAT THERE on the air mattress, a knee on either side of his face, and stared at the water falling outside the tent door. The girl was in a similar situation on the other mattress. Neither had had the opportunity to change her, or his, impractical attire for the workclothes, and both were soaked.

There had been complications with the tent, and a pool of water lay between the mattresses, another just inside the entrance. Water fell in droplets from one point in the sloping roof, on Cornell's side, where the canvas had somehow got pinched. He had made it worse by rubbing the spot with his finger.

He said now, with a gesture of chagrin: "We should have sat out the shower in the car. How dumb can you get?"

"Well, we didn't," she answered acerbly, but then turned philosophical. "We can't think of everything."

He rose wetly and went the two steps to the open entrance, his head lower than his shoulders, the highest point of the roof being about five feet off the ground, and looked down at the Rolls Royce glistening the rain. A gust of wind gave him a faceful of water. The manufacturers had failed to include the tent door of which the instruction pamphlet spoke so confidently.

He fingered the drops off his eyelashes and suggested: "Why don't we get into those dry workclothes and stay in the car till it stops?" He looked the other way, out at the lake, which the rain had made a blue blur. Then, because she had not responded, he turned to her, supporting himself, in his bent stance, on the front tentpole. "Isn't that the answer?"

But she gave another one. "You go. I'm sticking it out." Her hair was plastered to her head, which seemed thereby even smaller. His own coiffure must be in a similar state: he didn't dare touch it. Her thin, drenched blouse was probably pasted to her chest, but her drawn-up knees concealed her breasts, and the long skirt swathed her legs. Anyway, the light was dim over there in the corner. The whole place was gloomy and sopping.

He asked: "Why should we make ourselves as miserable as possible? I thought it was your idea, yesterday, to *live* in the car."

"That would be a cop-out." She dug her heels into the wet grit of the floor—there wasn't much earth on their rocky knoll and therefore, at least, very little mud—and pushed herself back, unfolding and stretching full length on the air mattress. He saw her obscurely and foreshortened, with prominent, dirty soles.

He asked: "You see this as some kind of challenge?"

She spoke to the sagging roof. "It's just that, you know, if you're going to do something, then you have to go and do it."

His neck had begun to ache. He bent his legs so he could straighten his head, and took some of the weight off his hand by putting it on the pole.

"I just wish I knew what we were doing. I keep coming back to that. It's really got crazier and crazier, if you look at it. Here we are, two wet transvestites in the wilderness. What can we look forward to? When our food supply runs out, do we go back to that store and buy more? When the money's gone, do we commit more robberies? If we stay here, how will we survive the winter? If we move on, where will we go? Do we intend to keep pretending to be the opposite sexes forever?"

She ignored the moral issues. "We can catch fish and kill rabbits and squirrels."

Cornell's calves were beginning to feel the strain from his crouch, but he had no taste to go back and sit, still less lie down, on that clammy rubber mattress. "Some outdoor type of girl took me fishing a couple of times. She put the worms on the hook—but *hunting—!*" He grimaced. "Shooting those soft little things, with their bright eyes."

"You know how rabbits reproduce?" she asked, still horizontal. "The male fucks the female."

Cornell was offended. "Must you use that kind of language?"

She proceeded as if she had not heard him. "But fish don't fuck. They have their own kind of birth facilities. The female deposits the eggs in the water somewhere and leaves. The male comes along later and fertilizes them."

Cornell said, a bit crossly: "How do you know so much about that?"

She sat up suddenly and cried: "You know why even a lot of women who have no objection to fishing disapprove of hunting?" She didn't wait for Cornell's response, which anyway would not have been forthcoming if she had tarried all night. She clapped her hands together. "It's because fish don't fuck, and warm-blooded animals do."

"I'm glad you figured that out." He slid down the pole and sat in the puddle of water. His legs were sore, and his fanny was wet already, and there was apparently nothing he could do about her language.

"We don't like to kill animals," she said, "because they remind us of ourselves." This statement seemed to Cornell to negate the previous one she had made with so much vigor. "But!" She pointed rhetorically. "We don't fuck."

"Listen," said Cornell, feeling again the call of self-respect. "I've had about enough of this."

"I mean really. Buggering is called that, but it's fake, it's an imitation, and you know of what?"

Cornell put up his hand. "Don't say it again, please."

As if that made any difference to this foul-mouthed woman. "Fucking! A dildo is an imitation penis. Now, doesn't it strike you as strange that the dominant sex would by nature have recessed genitals and that the recessive sex would have an organ that looks like a weapon?"

Cornell lost his concern about terms. "It's really a lot more vulnerable, though." His favorite argument. "You may not realize that. That's why we're weak though larger. I just recently figured that out. It's nature, and you have to accept it. I mean, we're not to blame."

"What does that mean, 'blame'?"

He peered at her. "What a crooked thing humanity has made of what is so straight with animals. Is that what you're saying?"

She surprised him by answering: "I don't know."

"That makes two of us." He sat there in the pool of water.

"I'm pursuing a train of thought," she said.

He said: "I've done a lot of that myself since escaping from jail. It usually ends by making my head spin. I don't know if I'm very bright."

She pulled her legs up again and clasped the wet skirt to her shins. "Suppose everything you've been told all your life is a lot of shit."

He shook his head. "And maybe it isn't. Animals don't build bridges or fly airplanes. And what do they do when it rains?"

"What are we doing?"

"You've got a point." He started to pull himself up on the tentpole. It came away from the roof, and the forward half of the tent collapsed on him.

He astounded himself by not panicking amidst the wet canvas and darkness. He crawled about patiently putting things in order. While he did this, the rain stopped, and immediately he smelled the bouquet of wet greenery. The girl was laughing inside the tent.

He secured the pole, laughing back at her, and went outside to watch the sunshine emerge from the clouds and gradually claim the lake and then their knoll.

The girl came out, plucking the damp blouse away from her breasts and shaking it. "Look at you," she said.

His tie was askew and in his exertions he had lost a shirt button and the cuffs were filthy. The whole outfit felt unbearably nasty. He took off jacket, tie, and shirt, and rolled them into a bundle. The sun was warm on his breast scars.

He tensed the muscles in his chest, something he hadn't had nerve to do since the operation. When he had tits, this would make them rise slightly. He lifted his arms and made a pair of biceps.

She said: "Stop bragging."

He went down to the car and unlocked the trunk. He rooted through the packages, boxes, and bags until he came upon the new clothing: for her, a wraparound skirt of denim, a black-and-white checked blouse of gingham—cut like a woman's shirt—blue canvas sneakers, and white cotton schoolboy underpants. There were jeans for him and a blue chambray shirt. He changed in the back seat of the Rolls. When he emerged she wore the new outfit.

He saw the axe and seized it. "We should start a fire and dry these clothes in a hurry. I'll go chop some wood." He went to the nearest Christmas tree and was starting to swing when she cried: "Hold it!"

"What's wrong now?"

"The tree is green. The wood wouldn't burn." She pointed. "The third one over, with the broken-off trunk and most of the bark gone? It's dead."

"It's certainly big," said Cornell. The jagged fragment of trunk was as tall as he, and about a foot in diameter. He wondered how a tree could get broken off in the middle of deserted woods. The rest of it, about fifteen feet, lay on the forest floor nearby, decorated with moss and screened by ferns. The breakage wasn't new.

He stepped to the standing portion and raised his axe.

"Don't cross your hands that way," the girl said. "You'll break

your wrist. Right hand above the left, like a baseball bat. Here."
She took the axe, and saying, "Stand back," swung the blade
against the tree. A little chip flew off. She did it again, with no
more of a result. At this rate it would take all day to get a fire
of confetti.

"I get the idea," he said diplomatically, taking the axe.

"O.K. I'll get some kindling." She tramped off into the woods.
He had to get used to seeing her in this latest ensemble, which
as always was too large.

His own chopping at first achieved little more than hers, but
gradually he learned the technique, the rhythm, and finally he
was able to put his foot against the enormous messy wound he
had hacked out; he pushed, and over went the hunk of wood.
Now he must chop it into several short logs. He was breathless
and his new shirt was soaked with perspiration. He sniffed his
armpits. He had applied no deodorant since leaving the sperm
camp. Clasping the axe handle again, he was conscious of an unpleasant warmth in his palms, followed soon by outright pain.
He dropped the axe and saw that his hands were bleeding.

Holding them out, he looked around for the girl. She was not
to be seen. He went to the lake, knelt as close as he could without
getting water in his shoes, and washed his poor palms. He got
the senator's white shirt from the ball of damp clothing and,
wincing, tore it in fragments and wrapped them around his
hands.

The girl appeared with an armload of twigs. She saw the
bandages and dropped her burden.

"What happened?"

"I'm not used to this," he said. "I'm an office worker."

She unpeeled the wrappings, which were already bloodied
inside.

"You poor thing." She pulled him by the elbow. "Come on."
In the trunk, amidst their purchases, she found a first-aid kit.

He recoiled. "No iodine!"

She examined a tube. "Unguentine. This should do it." She squirted ointment on his palms.

He held out his greasy hands. "A lot of use I am."

"You've learned a lesson," she said. "We have to take care of ourselves. We should have bought gloves."

He sat on the front seat of the car, in the open doorway, and rested from the ordeal. She retrieved her kindling and carried it to the knoll. Then she gathered a number of large stones, each of which looked too heavy for her, and carried them one by one up in front of the tent and arranged them in a circle.

"Good thing," she said, coming down, "that the storekeeper advised us to get a saw." She found it in the back seat. It had a light metal frame in the shape of a bracket; across the fourth side ran a slender, toothed blade. She wrapped the handle in what was left of the shirt, went to the tree felled by Cornell, and began to saw it into pieces.

After dinner they lay on the air mattresses, long since dried by an afternoon of sun, and watched the lake gradually fade away in the falling light. As it turned out, the rest of the morning and most of the afternoon had been needed to assemble the materials for, and to start, the fire. Despite the FBI's wilderness-survival course, the girl was none too effective at the task, and Cornell of course was totally inexperienced in the area, as in most others, and invalided now to boot.

And once the fire had been got seriously under way, as opposed to the many false starts which consumed several loads of kindling without igniting the logs, the drying rack she had painstakingly constructed from branches erected between boulders collapsed, dropping their city clothes into the fire, somehow burning them hopelessly even though the garments had been sopping to the touch.

And they learned while preparing the meal, which started out to be lunch, that it took hours to bring water to boil over a campfire, and almost as long to heat a slice of ham in a skillet, though the grease in the pan would soon burst into flame. So it was twilight before they ate their burned meat, half-raw potatoes, and cold peas from the second can she tried, the first having blown up when heated in the embers.

But she stayed in an astoundingly good mood throughout, saying at every disaster, "We've got a lot to learn," or "Back to the old drawing board," an expression which made Cornell grit his teeth. He was not nearly so philosophical. It hurt his hands to cut the ham and spear morsels of hard potato, and gathering peas on the flat camp fork was a nightmare.

The girl had made the meal as well. He lowered the tin cup filled with tepid, acrid coffee and said: "I'm totally dependent on you."

She gazed at the lake, which had gone almost black now from the insufficiency of light. "Either one of us might get incapacitated for a while, so the other has to do the work. I'll be only too happy to let you do the chores when you're better." She turned to him. "How are the paws?"

He put down his cup and carefully uncrooked the finger that had been through its handle. "Better, thanks. It was a shock to see them bleed." He flexed his hands, feeling really more stiffness of skin than pain now. "Blood always does that to me. I almost faint if I cut myself shaving."

"Women bleed every month for more than half their life." She smiled weirdly. "And it's absurd, you see. It's useless."

He remembered that while posing as "Harry" in jail she had delivered a diatribe against menstruation. He had then thought it odd that a man would care.

She added: "The only time it's supposed to stop is during pregnancy."

He stared at her. "You could say that about digestion. It stops when you have stomach cancer."

"But digestion *does* something."

He took another sip of coffee. "How about the appendix? I mean, sometimes nature can goof."

This was the time of evening at which every moment was discernibly darker than the last. You could watch sky and woods and water merging into a single night before your eyes.

"Do you know that in all of nature only female human beings, apes, and a few monkeys menstruate?"

"No, I didn't," said Cornell. "I have never done research into the matter." He hoped he didn't sound bitchy. But it seemed to him a waste of time to worry about what couldn't be changed.

Now he could see her mainly by the glow of the fire behind them, which, though it had gone mostly to embers, was brought to flame by random gusts of wind, a wind which had also begun to chill him. He buttoned the collar of the chambray shirt. On the storekeeper's advice they had also bought woolen shirts, thick and loose as jackets. In a moment he would fetch them from the car, as well as the lantern and the sleeping bags.

"Are you cold?" he asked.

She extended her legs from the mattress and shook her body from the waist. "No."

He rose. "I better get the rest of our stuff before it's too dark to see." He went down to the car, stumbling sometimes en route. The trunk had an automatic light in it, and he soon found what was needed.

But though they had bought the lantern and a gallon can of kerosene, and filling the former from the latter was simple enough, he did not understand how to light the wick. He kept striking kitchen matches against the box and dropping them down the glass chimney, but they invariably went out.

He would not call her to help with that. He had botched the woodcutting and since been useless. He knew usefulness mattered to her above all things because of the complaint about menstruation: there was no utility in it.

He lifted the can and poured kerosene down the chimney.

Next time the match took hold—so violently he dropped the lantern into the trunk. It broke and the fire spilled from it and ran across the piled sleeping bags, and somehow the kerosene can had gone over on its side as well and the entire trunk was immediately ablaze with a yellow, smoking fire, driving him away with its heat.

From the knoll he heard the girl shout: "The lake!"

Yes, water was the answer. "Bring a pot," he yelled, dashing to the shore. She came down her path and met him there. She carried nothing. There was lots of light now.

He was incredulous. "How will we carry the water?"

She screamed into his face: "Get in the lake! The gas tank will go up."

They ran through the shallows. Within thirty feet the stony bottom dropped off abruptly, and they both went under for a moment. During this second the car exploded. As Cornell came up, the fiery fragments were moving through the air, some in his direction. He reached over and pushed the girl's head under and followed her.

On his reappearance, he felt the heat on his face. There was fire in the tops of trees as well as in the underbrush, and up on the knoll the tent was ablaze.

For an instant he could not find the girl, then discovered he was still holding her under. He let her rise. She spluttered and gasped and clutched him around the neck. It took him a while to understand she was choking him. He broke her hold and pushed her to where the shelf began, forced her to lie supine in the shallow water, with just her nose out. Meanwhile, kneeling there himself, half exposed, he felt as though he were being sunburned. The whole world seemed to be on fire just beyond the rocky beach, and the heat was intense off shore.

He ducked his face occasionally, but whenever he did so, loosing the pressure on the girl's trunk, she tried to struggle up.

At last he had no choice but to punch her in the jaw. She fell back into his left hand.

She came to later, but finding herself securely held in shallow water, she did not return to panic. He rolled her over then, and with their elbows on the bottom and their legs floating, with frequent duckings to keep their faces and shoulders wet against the heat, they watched the total consumption of their worldly goods.

At last the conflagration settled down, what was left of the car burning less ardently. The remains of the tent, which had been quickly consumed, smoked in growing obscurity. The treetop blazes had mostly gone out, and the brush fire had retreated into the woods, where it seemed to be guttering. Cornell remembered with gratitude the morning rain that had soaked them and left the forest damp.

Neither had spoken since her accurate prediction that the gas tank would explode. He had no gauge to measure how long ago that had been.

Finally he said: "I really did it that time."

She splashed her legs. "You saved my life. I never learned to swim."

With the dwindling of the fire, it was getting dark again. The crescent moon had come out when it wasn't needed, and now was gone.

He said: "I would have been blown up without your warning." He got his feet under him and rose from the water. "I think it's O.K. to go in now." He put his hands out for her.

He stayed where he was for a moment, surveying the shore and saying: "Wow." They started to wade in. He said: "We've got nothing left."

"We're not dead."

"No thanks to me."

She stopped two paces from land, the water not quite covering their toes, and told him firmly: "All right, it was your fault. Because of you we are up shit creek without a paddle. So you owe me something, and here's what I want: your promise you will never mention it again. You did it, and it was outrageous and inexcusable. And I will only forgive you if you forget it."

She marched onto shore, a stanch little dripping figure in what was left of the several firelights. He ran to catch up, his sneakers squishing. She stopped some distance from the blackened and torn car, which still emitted quite a bit of heat and also an odd stench.

"What I regret most is that all the liquor's gone." She turned on her bare heel and climbed to the knoll, Cornell following. A gust of wind caused the ashes of the tent to glow.

"Hey!" She crouched and looked alongside the campfire which had been so hard to light. It seemed to be out now. "The skillet's all right and the pans." They had stacked them with the cutlery and metal plates and cups, to be washed next morning.

She stood up exultantly. "We're still in business." She strode further and yelled again. "One mattress is still O.K."

Cornell squished there. The other mattress had sustained a great burn in the middle, probably from one of the flying fragments of car, and was largely blackened and totally shriveled. But the one from which she was now brushing dead ashes seemed sound.

She sat down on it. He joined her, beginning definitely to feel chilly now.

"All right," she said, "let's see where we are. Tomorrow we'll search the ashes for the axehead. If the fire hasn't destroyed its temper, we can make a new handle from a branch." She patted her pocket. "I still have the jackknife." She socked her hands together. "I left the saw over there after cutting those logs. It will be O.K."

Cornell shivered and crossed his arms. "Aren't you cold?" he asked.

"We'll look in the wreckage of the Rolls for fragments of metal that can be used as arrowheads to kill animals. We can make a bow from an elastic branch and your shoelaces." She had never worn her own sneakers; they had been in the car, along with the senator's jacket containing the senator's wallet.

As if he weren't sufficiently wet, he was struck by a drop of water. "Oh, no!" he wailed. "It's starting to rain."

"That can't hurt us."

With the water falling on him, it occurred to Cornell that there was something awful about how she coped so lustily whenever he was at a loss, whereas he could perform effectively only when she was in trouble, as during the near-drowning. It seemed on the one hand to be a kind of competition, and on the other, a reciprocal arrangement, an alternation of assertions and recessions.

Despite the rain, she was still thinking positively. "With axe and saw, we can build a shelter, even a real cabin in time. We don't need nails. We can notch the logs together."

"Wouldn't it be better if I just hiked back to that store? That woman seemed a pretty good sort. Maybe she'd give us credit."

"I wouldn't ask that cunt for anything," the girl said emphatically. "I know women. I've been one all my life. She wouldn't give you the sweat from her crotch. Besides, how would it look if after arriving in a Rolls Royce, you had to come back on your knees asking for charity?"

"Is this the time to be proud?" Cornell asked.

She was glaring at him, insofar as he could tell in the dark. "We've got our chance now to prove what we can do on our own. We don't need any of *them*."

Cornell was strangely stung by this remark, although it was general and not personal. "Why are *you* so bitter?" he asked jealously, bitterly. "You've always been a woman. You've had all the privileges, all the power. *You're* one of *them*."

She was silent for a moment. Then: "I asked you to forget about your mistake."

"How can I?" he shouted. "The reason I dropped that lantern was because all my life I've been told I couldn't understand hardware. I couldn't figure out how to light that rotten thing!"

"You drove beautifully."

"You said that car could drive itself. After a whole day behind the wheel, *you* had to tell me how to back it up. *You* sawed the wood and made the meal and told me to get in the lake when the fire started."

He paused. The rain was pouring down his body and he was going mad with shame. He came out with it in a rush: "I need you, and I hate you because I need you."

She said, in a taunting, infuriating tone in view of his desperate confession—for she was not generous at all, she was the same old oppressor: "And what are you going to do about it?"

He reached blindly through the falling water, twisted her around, got two hands on her blouse and tore it apart. He expected resistance then, and raised a fist to knock her teeth out, but she was instead doing something with her shoulders, perhaps readying a dirty judo trick to catch his hand and break the wrist —he would not wait for it, but sank his hands into the waistband of the skirt and ripped it away, and then tore at those schoolboy panties.

Meanwhile she had encircled his neck, trying to strangle him again as when drowning, but he had no urge to preserve himself now; let her choke away, he would kill her first, and his hands went to find that vital place wherein he would do murder.

It was soft and moist and quick, yet did not retreat but rather came to him like an urgent mouth. He reclaimed his fingers before they were ingested, went to his own core, and found it already denuded and occupied by both hands. If she could not strangle him she would emasculate him, excise him at the root: the realization of the old nightmare, perhaps even a relief.

He did not fight, for there was no pain but rather the burgeoning of force, status, ambition, the perverse values which he honored in his delirium. He was drawn forward and he was met, and briefly obstructed, then something parted like a veil; she cried out, and he was swallowed alive by that which he would kill.

He worked with his whole person to resolve that paradox. She was in combat now, at the eleventh hour, writhing, battering against him, as if she, with that small body, could dislodge his mass. Her fingernails were incising his back, her heels hammering his legs. He was immune to, amused by, these pathetic gestures. His power was ever rising, he was adamant, invulnerable, brutal, and masterful beyond any dream. The moment arrived at which, with one supreme thrust, he demolished her and reigned as absolute tyrant of the world.

And then, all at once, he lost it all. In killing her he had destroyed himself as well. He fell back onto the stony ground and sobbed into the water falling from the sky.

"Our other crimes were nothing compared to this," she said, just below his chin. He realized that she had crawled on top of him, her head on his chest.

"You're not dead?" He stroked her narrow back, which was slick with water. "Did I hurt you?"

"Of course!" She nodded vigorously, even with enthusiasm, banging her chin on his breastbone: *that* hurt.

"Wasn't that *it?*"

She hugged him and wriggled. "That was it." She squeezed him and added: "So far as I know."

"I guess it doesn't kill a woman, then."

"I guess not."

"At least not right away," said Cornell. Her body was deflecting most of the rain from his. He ran his fingers along the wet trough of her spine. "But what about if you contract pregnancy?"

"Do what the rabbits do, I guess."

She wasn't disturbed in the slightest. He remembered now how nothing worried her: she was ready to build a cabin with a broken axe and kill animals with a homemade bow.

She said: "That's a lie that childbearing will kill you. It doesn't kill a rabbit. And there's a tribe of Indians in South America who do it all the time."

"Oh yeah?"

"I read about them in *National Geographic*."

"That's fantastic," said Cornell. He thought it was unfair of him to get all the advantage and wanted to roll over to protect her from the rain, except he would be too heavy.

"Anyway, I don't think it happens every time you do it."

"What?"

"That you get pregnant. I mean, at least they tell you that when you're a woman, so you won't get too scared if you're raped."

Cornell's hands had slid onto the halves of her wonderful behind. "I guess that's what I did," he said. "Raped you."

She put her hands on his chest and pushed up. "Like hell you did."

He was relieved. "That takes a load off my conscience."

She lowered herself and snuggled in. "You have a tendency both to blame yourself for disasters and boast about accomplishments that you are not wholly responsible for."

He shrugged with her on him. His chest was strong enough for that. He decided not to argue. She really had a more attractive image of him than he had ever been able to conjure up.

As if to prove this theory, she said: "But there's nothing that you can't do. Once you were shown how to light a lantern, you could do it every time. And you can build a cabin too, and kill animals."

"Me?"

She said irritably: "How in hell am I going to do it if I give birth?"

"Maybe that won't happen from doing it once. You said that yourself."

"Then we'll keep doing it."

"You're nuts." But he had another response between his legs. She tried to stay on top. "You're too damned heavy!"

But he easily rolled her over.

"It's time I caught the rain," he said. And he inserted himself this time. If he was going to be builder and killer, he could be boss once in a while.

Also, he was the one with the protuberant organ.

Woman was God's *second* mistake.

FRIEDRICH NIETZSCHE, 1895